THE STOIC

BOOKS BY
Theodore Dreiser

The Stoic
An American Tragedy
The "Genius"
The Financier
The Titan
Sister Carrie
Jennie Gerhardt

ABOUT THEODORE DREISER
My Life with Dreiser by Helen Dreiser

The Stoic

THEODORE DREISER

Cleveland and New York

THE WORLD PUBLISHING COMPANY

Published by arrangement with Doubleday and Company, Inc.

Copyright 1947 by Helen Dreiser

Manufactured in the United States of America

THE STOIC

THE STOIC

Chapter I   THERE were two most disturbing problems confronting Frank Cowperwood at the time of his Chicago defeat, when, so reducingly and after so long a struggle, he lost his fight for a fifty-year franchise renewal.

First, there was his age. He was nearing sixty, and while seemingly as vigorous as ever, it would be no easy matter, he felt, with younger and equally resourceful financiers on the scene, to pile up the great fortune which assuredly would have been his if his franchise had been extended. That fortune would have been all of $50,000,000.

Secondly, and of even greater importance, in his realistic judgment, was the fact that by this time he had still not achieved social connections of any value; in other words, social prestige. Of course, his youthful incarceration in the penitentiary in Philadelphia had not helped matters, and then, too, his natural varietism, plus his unfortunate marriage to Aileen, who had been no real social help, and his own determined and almost savage individualism, had alienated many who otherwise might have been friendly to him.

For Cowperwood was not one to make friends of those less forceful, subtle, or efficient than himself. It smacked too much of meaningless self-depreciation and was, at best, in his opinion, a waste of time. On the other hand, he found, the strong and cunning or genuinely significant were not always easy to acquire as friends. Particularly here in Chicago, where he had fought so many of them for position and power, they had chosen to combine against him, not because he represented morals or methods different from any they were willing to practice or accept in others, but rather because he, a total stranger, had ventured on financial preserves presumably their own and had risen to greater wealth and power, and in less time, than they had. Moreover, he had attracted the wives and daughters of some of the very men who were most jealous of him financially, and so they had set out to ostracize him socially and had well-nigh succeeded in doing so.

So far as sex was concerned, he had always desired individual freedom and proceeded ruthlessly to achieve it. At the same time, he had always held the thought that somewhere he might well meet a woman so superior that in spite of himself he might be held, not to absolute faithfulness—he was never willing to count upon that in regard to himself—but rather to a genuine union of understanding and affection. For eight years now he had felt that he had really found that ideal individual in the girl, Berenice Fleming. Obviously, she was not overawed by his personality or his fame, nor at all impressed by his usual arts. And because of that, as well as the deep aesthetic and sensual spell she cast over him, there had arisen in him a conviction that she, with her youth, beauty, mental awareness, and certainty as to her own personal value, could contrive and maintain the natural social background for his force and wealth, assuming, of course, that he were ever free to marry her.

Unfortunately, for all his determination in connection with Aileen,* he had not been able to divest himself of her. For one thing, she was determined not to give him up. And to have added a contest for freedom to his difficult railway fight in Chicago would have been too much of a burden. Moreover, in Berenice's attitude, he saw no trace of the necessary acceptance. Her eyes appeared to be set toward men not only younger than himself but with conventional social advantages which his personal record made it impossible for him to offer her. This had given him his first real taste of romantic defeat, and he had sat alone in his rooms for hours at a time convinced that he was hopelessly beaten in his battle for greater fortune and for the love of Berenice.

And then suddenly she had come to him and announced a most amazing and unexpected surrender, so that he experienced a sense of rejuvenation which almost at once definitely restored his old constructive mood. At last, he felt, he had the love of a woman who could truly support him in his quest for power, fame, prestige.

On the other hand, as frank and direct as had been her explanation of why she had come—"I thought you really might need me

*See *The Titan*, Chapter 57.

now . . . I have made up my mind"—still, there was on her part a certain hurt attitude in regard to life and society which moved her to seek reparation in some form for the cruelties she felt had been imposed on her in her early youth. What she was really thinking, and what Cowperwood, because of his delight at her sudden surrender did not comprehend, was: You are a social outcast, and so am I. The world has sought to frustrate you. In my own case, it has attempted to exclude me from the sphere to which, temperamentally and in every other way, I feel I belong. You are resentful, and so am I. Therefore, a partnership: one of beauty and strength and intelligence and courage on both sides, but without domination by either of us. For without fair play between us, there is no possibility of this unsanctioned union enduring. This was the essence of her motive in coming to him at this time.

And yet Cowperwood, aware as he was of her force and subtlety, was not so fully aware of her chain of thought in this direction. He would not have said, for instance, looking upon her on that wintry night of her arrival (perfect and flowery out of an icy wind), that she was as carefully and determinedly aligned mentally. It was a little too much to expect of one so youthful, smiling, gay and altogether exquisite in every feminine sense. And yet she was. She stood daringly, and yet secretly somewhat nervously, before him. There was no trace of malice in regard to him; rather love, if a desire to be with him and of him for the remainder of his days on these conditions might be called love. Through him and with him she would walk to such victory as might be possible, the two of them wholeheartedly and sympathetically co-operating.

And so, on that first night, Cowperwood turned to her and said: "But Bevy, I'm really curious as to this sudden decision of yours. To think you should come to me now just when I have met my second really important setback."

Her still blue eyes enveloped him as might a warming cloak or a dissolving ether.

"Well, I've been thinking and reading about you for years, you know. Only last Sunday, in New York, I read two whole pages about you in the *Sun*. They made me understand you a little better, I think."

"The newspapers! Did they, really?"

"Yes, and no. Not what they said about you critically, but the

facts, if they are facts, that they pieced together. You never cared for
your first wife, did you?"

"Well, I thought I did, at first. But, of course, I was very young
when I married her."

"And the present Mrs. Cowperwood?"

"Oh, Aileen, yes. I cared for her very much at one time," he confessed. "She did a great deal for me once, and I am not ungrateful,
Bevy. Besides, she was very attractive, very, to me at that time. But I
was still young, and not as exacting mentally as I am now. The fault
is not Aileen's. It was a mistake due to inexperience."

"You make me feel better when you talk that way," she said.
"You're not as ruthless as you're said to be. Just the same, I am many
years younger than Aileen, and I have the feeling that without my
looks my mind might not be very important to you."

Cowperwood smiled. "Quite true. I have no excuses to offer for
the way I am," he said. "Intelligently or unintelligently, I try to
follow the line of self-interest, because, as I see it, there is no other
guide. Maybe I am wrong, but I think most of us do that. It may be
that there are other interests that come before those of the individual,
but in favoring himself, he appears, as a rule, to favor others."

"I agree, somehow, with your point of view," commented Berenice.

"The one thing I am trying to make clear to you," went on Cowperwood, smiling affectionately at her, "is that I am not seeking to
belittle or underestimate any hurt I may have inflicted. Pain seems to
go with life and change. I just want to state my case as I see it, so
that you may understand me."

"Thanks," and Berenice laughed lightly, "but you needn't feel you
are on the witness stand."

"Well, almost. But please let me explain a little about Aileen. Her
nature is one of love and emotion, but her intellect is not, and never
was, sufficient for my needs. I understand her thoroughly, and I am
grateful for all she did for me in Philadelphia. She stood by me, to
her own social detriment. Because of that I have stood by her, even
though I cannot possibly love her as I once did. She has my name,
my residence. She feels she should have both." He paused, a little
dubious as to what Berenice would say. "You understand, of
course?" he asked.

"Yes, yes," exclaimed Berenice, "of course, I understand. And, please, I do not want to disturb her in any way. I did not come to you with that in view."

"You're very generous, Bevy, but unfair to yourself," said Cowperwood. "But I want you to know how much you mean to my entire future. You may not understand, but I acknowledge it here and now. I have not followed you for eight years for nothing. It means that I care, and care deeply."

"I know," she said, softly, not a little impressed by this declaration.

"For all of eight years," he continued, "I have had an ideal. That ideal is you."

He paused, wishing to embrace her, but feeling for the moment that he should not. Then, reaching into a waistcoat pocket, he took from it a thin gold locket, the size of a silver dollar, which he opened and handed to her. One interior face of it was lined with a photograph of Berenice as a girl of twelve, thin, delicate, supercilious, self-contained, distant, as she was to this hour.

She looked at it and recognized it as a photograph that had been taken when she and her mother were still in Louisville, her mother a woman of social position and means. How different the situation now, and how much she had suffered because of that change! She gazed at it, recalling pleasant memories.

"Where did you get this?" she asked at last.

"I took it from your mother's bureau in Louisville, the first time I saw it. It was not in this case, though; I have added that."

He closed it affectionately and returned it to his pocket. "It has been close to me ever since," he said.

Berenice smiled. "I hope, unseen. But I am such a child there."

"Just the same, an ideal to me. And more so now than ever. I have known many women, of course. I have dealt with them according to my light and urge at the time. But apart from all that, I have always had a certain conception of what I really desired. I have always dreamed of a strong, sensitive, poetic girl like yourself. Think what you will about me, but judge me now by what I do, not by what I say. You said you came because you thought I needed you. I do."

She laid her hand on his arm. "I have decided," she said, calmly. "The best I can do with my life is to help you. But we . . . I . . . neither of us can do just as we please. You know that."

"Perfectly. I want you to be happy with me, and I want to be happy with you. And, of course, I can't be if you are going to worry over anything. Here in Chicago, particularly at this time, I have to be most careful, and so do you. And that's why you're going back to your hotel very shortly. But tomorrow is another day, and at about eleven, I hope you will telephone me. Then perhaps we can talk this over. But wait a moment." He took her arm and directed her into his bedroom. Closing the door, he walked briskly to a handsome wrought-iron chest of considerable size which stood in a corner of the room. Unlocking it, he lifted from it three trays containing a collection of ancient Greek and Phoenician rings. After setting them in order before her, he said:

"With which of these would you like me to pledge you?"

Indulgently, and a little indifferently, as was her way—always the one to be pleaded with, not the one to plead—Berenice studied and toyed with the rings, occasionally exclaiming over one that interested her. At last, she said:

"Circe might have chosen this twisted silver snake. And Helen, this green bronze circlet of flowers, perhaps. I think Aphrodite might have liked this curled arm and hand encircling the stone. But I will not chose for beauty alone. For myself, I will take this tarnished silver band. It has strength as well as beauty."

"Always the unexpected, the original!" exclaimed Cowperwood. "Bevy, you are incomparable!" He kissed her tenderly as he placed the ring on her finger.

Chapter 2

THE essential thing which Berenice achieved for Cowperwood in coming to him at the time of his defeat was to renew his faith in the unexpected and, better yet, in his own luck. For hers was an individuality, as he saw it, self-seeking, poised, ironic, but less brutal and more poetic than his own. Where he desired money in order to release its essential content, power, to be used by him as he pleased, Berenice appeared to demand the privilege of expressing her decidedly varied temperament in ways which would make for beauty and so satisfy her essentially aesthetic ideals. She desired not so much to express herself in a given form of art as to live so that her life as well as her personality should be in itself an art form. She had more than once thought, if only she had great wealth, very great power, how creatively she would use it. She would never waste it on great houses and lands and show, but rather surround herself with an atmosphere which should be exquisite and, of course, inspirational.

Yet of that she had never spoken. Rather, it was implicit in her nature, which Cowperwood by no means always clearly interpreted. He realized that she was delicate, sensitive, evasive, elusive, mysterious. And, for these reasons, he was never tired of contemplating her, any more than he was of contemplating nature itself: the new day, the strange wind, the changing scene. What would the morrow be like? What would Berenice be like when next he saw her? He could not tell. And Berenice, conscious of this strangeness in herself, could not enlighten him or any other. She was as she was. Let Cowperwood, or any, take her so.

In addition to all this, she was, he saw, an aristocrat. In her quiet and self-confident way, she commanded respect and attention from all who came in contact with her. They could not evade it. And Cowperwood, recognizing this superior phase of her as the one thing he had always, if almost subconsciously, admired and desired in a woman, was deeply gratified as well as impressed. She was young, beautiful, wise, poised—a lady. He had sensed it even in the photograph of the twelve-year-old girl in Louisville eight years before.

But now that Berenice had come to him at last, there was one thing that was troubling him. That was his enthusiastic and, at the moment, quite sincere suggestion of absolute and single devotion to her. Did he really mean that? After his first marriage, particularly after the experience of children and the quite sober and humdrum nature of his domestic life, he had fully realized that the ordinary tenets of love and marriage were not for him. This was proved by his intrigue with the young and beautiful Aileen, whose sacrifice and devotion he subsequently rewarded by marrying her. Yet that was as much an act of equity as of affection. And subsequent to that, he considered himself wholly liberated, sensually as well as emotionally.

He had no desire to attempt, much less achieve, a sense of permanency. Nonetheless, he had for eight years been pursuing Berenice. And now he was wondering how he should present himself honestly to her. She was, as he knew, so extremely intelligent and intuitive.

Lies sufficient to placate, if not really deceive, the average woman, would not advantage him much with her.

And worse, at this time, in Dresden, Germany, there was a certain Arlette Wayne. Only a year ago he had entered on the affair with her. Arlette, previously immured in a small town in Iowa and anxious to extricate herself from a fate which threatened to smother her talent, had written Cowperwood, enclosing a picture of her siren self. But not receiving a reply, she had proceeded to borrow money and appear before him in person in his Chicago office. Where the picture had failed, the personality of Arlette had succeeded, for she was not only daring and self-confident, but possessed of a temperament with which Cowperwood was really in sympathy. Besides, her object was not purely mercenary. She was genuinely interested in music, and she had a voice. Of that he became convinced, and he desired to help her. She had also brought with her convincing evidence of her background: a picture of the little house in which she and her widowed mother, a local saleswoman, were living, and a quite moving story of her mother's struggles to maintain them and further her ambition.

Naturally, the few hundred dollars which her aspirations required were as nothing to Cowperwood. Ambition in any form appealed to him, and now, moved by the girl herself, he proceeded to plan her future. For the time being, she was to have the best training Chicago could offer. Later, should she really prove worth while, he would send her abroad. However, so as not to commit or entangle himself in any way, he had specifically arranged a budget on which she was to live, and that budget was still in force. He had also advised her to bring her mother to Chicago to live with her. She therefore rented a small house, sent for her mother, and established herself, and in due course Cowperwood became a frequent visitor.

Yet because of her intellect and the sincerity of her ambition, their relationship had been based on mutual appreciation as well as affection. She had not been moved by any desire to compromise him in any way, and it had been only shortly before Berenice's arrival in Chicago that he had persuaded Arlette to go to Dresden, for he had realized that he might not be a personal part of Chicago much longer. And had it not been for Berenice, he would have presently visited Arlette in Germany.

But now, as he compared her to Berenice, he felt no sensual pull in her direction, for in that way, as in all others, Berenice promised to absorb him completely. However, still interested in Arlette as an artistic temperament, and concerned to see her succeed, he intended continuing to aid her. Only, as he now felt, it might be best to drop her from his life completely. It would mean little to him. She had had her day. Best start on a new footing entirely. If Berenice was going to demand absolute romantic faithfulness on pain of separation, then he would do the best he could to conform to her desires. She was surely worthy of really important sacrifices on his part. And in that frame of mind, he was more inclined to dream and promise than at any time since his youth.

Chapter 3

THE following morning, a little after ten o'clock, Berenice telephoned Cowperwood and they agreed to meet at his club for a talk.

As she entered by a private stairway to his apartment, she found him waiting to greet her. There were flowers in the living room and bedroom. But still so dubious was he as to the reality of this conquest that, as she came leisurely up the steps, looking at him and smiling, he scanned her face anxiously for any suggestion of change. But as she crossed the threshold and allowed him to seize her and hold her close, he felt reassured.

"So you came!" he said, gaily and warmly, at the same time pausing to survey her.

"Did you think I wouldn't?" she asked, laughing at the expression on his face.

"Well, how was I to be sure?" he queried. "You never did anything I wanted you to do before."

"True, but you know why. This is different." She yielded her lips to his.

"If you only knew the effect your coming has had on me," he went on, excitedly. "I haven't slept a wink all night. And I feel as though I'd never need to sleep again. . . . Pearly teeth . . . Slate blue eyes . . . rosy mouth . . ." he went on admiringly. And he kissed her eyes. "And this sunray hair." He fingered it admiringly.

"The baby has a new toy!"

He was thrilled by her comprehending, yet sympathetic, smile, and bent and picked her up.

"Frank! Please! My hair . . . you'll get me all mussed up!"

She protested laughingly as he carried her to the adjoining bedroom, which seemed to flicker with flame from the fireplace, and, because he insisted, she allowed him to undress her, amused at his impatience.

It was late in the afternoon before he was satisfied to "be sane and talk," as she put it. They sat by a tea table before the fire. She insisted that she was anxious to remain in Chicago, so as to be with him as much and as long as possible, but they must arrange things so as not to attract attention. As to this, he agreed. His notoriety was then at its terrific peak, and, in consequence, particularly because Aileen was known to be living in New York, his appearance with anyone as attractive as herself would be the signal for a flood of comment. They would have to avoid being seen together.

For now, he added, this matter of franchise extension, or, rather, as it stood now, no franchise, did not mean a cessation of work any more than it meant that he was to lose his street railway properties. These had been built up over a period of years, and shares in them sold to thousands of investors, and they could not be taken from him or his investors without due process of law.

"What really has to be done, Bevy," he said to her intimately, "is to find a financier, or a group of them, or a corporation, to take over these properties at a value that is fair to all. And that, of course, can't be brought about in a minute. It may take years. As a matter of fact, I know that unless I step forward and personally request it as a favor to me, nobody is likely to come in here and offer to do anything. They know how difficult it is to manage street railways profitably. And then there are the courts, which will have to pass on all this, even if these enemies of mine, or any outside concerns, are willing to try and run these roads."

He was sitting beside her, talking to her as though she were one of his fellow-investors or financial equals. And while she was not greatly interested in the practical details of his world of finance, she could sense how intense was his intellectual and practical interest in these things.

 "Well, I know one thing," she interpolated at this point, "and that is, you will never really be beaten. You are too wise and too clever."

"Maybe," he said, pleased by her tribute. "Anyhow, all that takes time. It may be years before these roads are taken off my hands. At the same time, a long delay of that kind might cripple me, in a way. Supposing I should want to do anything else; I should feel handicapped because of the responsibility here." And for a moment, his large gray eyes stared into space.

"What I would prefer to do," he mused, "now that I have you, would be to loaf and travel with you, for a time, anyhow. I've worked hard enough. You mean more than money to me, infinitely more. It's odd, but I feel all at once as though I've worked too hard all my life." He smiled and fondled her.

And Berenice, hearing him say these things, was suffused with pride and power, as well as real tenderness.

"That's perfectly true, dear. You've been like some big engine or machine that's tearing full speed somewhere, but doesn't know exactly where." She toyed with his hair and smoothed his cheek as she talked. "I've been thinking of your life, and all you've accomplished up to now. I think you should go abroad for a while, and look at things in Europe. I don't see what else you could do here, unless you want to make more money, and Chicago certainly isn't a very interesting place. I think it's terrible."

"Well, I wouldn't say that, exactly," returned Cowperwood, defensive for Chicago. "It has its good points. I came here originally to make money, and certainly I have no complaint to make on that score."

"Oh, I know that," said Berenice, amused at his loyalty despite the bitterness and worry that his career here had involved. "But, Frank . . ." and here she paused, weighing her words most carefully, "you know, I think you're so much bigger than that. I have always thought so. Don't you think you ought to take a rest, look about and see the world, apart from business? You might find something you could do, some big public project that would bring you praise and fame, rather than money. There might be something you could undertake in England or France. I'd love to live in France with you. Why not go over there and give them something new? What about the traffic situation in London? Something like that! Anyway, leave America."

He smiled at her approvingly.

"Well, Bevy," he said, "it does seem a little unnatural to be in-

dulging in a practical conversation like this with a pair of beautiful
blue eyes and a sunburst of hair opposite me. But all that you say
has the ring of wisdom. By the middle of next month, perhaps
sooner, we *are* going abroad, you and I. And then I think I can
find something to please you, for it hasn't been more than a year
since I was approached concerning a proposed tube system for
London. At that time I was so busy here I didn't have time for
anything else. But now . . ." and he patted her hand.

Berenice smiled a satisfied smile.

It was dusk before she departed, discreet and reserved and smiling
as she entered the carriage that Cowperwood had called.

A few moments later, it was a gay and much more vital Cowperwood who stepped forth, thinking how, the next day, he would
arrange first with his lawyer for a conference with the mayor and
certain city officials to determine on ways and means of divesting
himself of his various and immense holdings. And after that . . .
after that . . . well, there was Berenice, the one great dream of his
life really come true. What of defeat? There was no defeat! It was
love that made life, certainly not wealth alone.

Chapter 4

THE proposition to which Cowperwood
referred as having come from an Eng-
lish source some twelve months before had been brought to him
by two adventuring Englishmen, Messrs. Philip Henshaw and
Montague Greaves, who carried letters from several well-known
bankers and brokers of London and New York, establishing them
as contractors who had already built railroads, street railways, and
manufacturing plants in England and elsewhere.

Some time before, in connection with the Traffic Electrical Company (an English company organized for the purpose of promoting
railway enterprises), they personally had invested ten thousand
pounds in a scheme to promote and construct an underground
railway, to run from Charing Cross Station, the center of London,
to Hampstead, four or five miles away and a growing residential
district. It was a *sine qua non* of the scheme that the line in prospect
was to afford direct means of communication between Charing
Cross Station (the terminal of the Southeastern Railway which

fed the south and southeast coasts of England and was one of the main arteries of travel to and from the Continent) and Euston Station, the terminal of the London and Northwestern Railway, serving the northwest and connecting with Scotland.

As they explained it to Cowperwood, the Traffic Electrical Company had a paid-up capital of £30,000. It had succeeded in getting through both houses of Parliament an "act" permitting them to build, operate, and own this particular tube or line; but in bringing this about, contrary to the general idea held by the English public in regard to its Parliament, a considerable sum of money had to be expended—not directly to any one group, but, as Messrs. Greaves and Henshaw hinted, and as Cowperwood, of all people, was fully capable of understanding, one must resort to many ways and means of currying favor with those who were in a better position to influence the minds of a committee than outsiders coming directly with a request for a valuable public privilege, especially when, as in England, it was granted in perpetuity. To that end, recourse had been had to a firm of solicitors: Rider, Bullock, Johnson & Chance, as clever, socially reputable, and technically well-informed a combination of legal talent as the great Empire's capital could boast. This distinguished firm had innumerable connections with individual shareholders and chairmen of various enterprises. In fact, this firm had found persons whose influence had not only persuaded the committee of Parliament to grant the act for the Charing Cross and Hampstead, but also, once the act was in hand and the original thirty thousand pounds nearly gone, suggested Greaves and Henshaw, who, for a two-year option for the construction of the tubes, had, about a year before, paid down £10,000.

The provisions of the act were nominally stiff enough. It had required the Traffic Electrical Company to deposit exactly sixty thousand pounds in consols as security that the proposed work would be performed in accordance with provisions requiring partial or final completion of construction on or before certain dates. But, as these two promoters had explained to Cowperwood, a bank or financing group, for the usual brokerage rates, would be willing to maintain the required amount of consols in any designated depository, and the Parliamentary committee, again rightly approached, would doubtless extend the time limit for completion.

Nevertheless, after a year and a half of work on their part, although £40,000 had been paid in, and the £60,000 in consols deposited, still the money to build the tube (estimated at £1,600,000) had not been found. This sprang from the fact that although there was one quite modern tube already in fairly successful operation—the City and South London—there was nothing to show English capital that a new, and particularly a longer and so more expensive, tube would pay. The only other lines in operation were two semi-undergrounds or steam railways running through open cuts and tunnels—the District Railway, about five and one-half miles, and the Metropolitan Railway, not more than two miles, both by agreement having running power over each other's rails. But the motive power being steam, the tunnels and cuts were dirty and often smoke-filled, and neither paid very well. And without any precedent to show how a line costing millions of pounds to build could be made to pay, English capital was not interested. Hence a search for money in other parts of the world, which had ended with the journey of Messrs. Henshaw and Greaves—via Berlin, Paris, Vienna, and New York—to see Cowperwood.

Cowperwood, as he had explained to Berenice, had been so completely occupied with his Chicago troubles at the time that he had listened only casually to all that Messrs. Henshaw and Greaves had said. Now, however, since he had lost his franchise fight, and more particularly since Berenice had suggested his leaving America, he recalled their scheme. To be sure, it had appeared to be sinking under a load of expenditures such as no businessman of his experience would consider taking over; yet it might be well to look into this London tube situation with a view to doing something on a grand scale, and perhaps, in this instance, free from such trickery as he had been compelled to practice here in Chicago, and also without any undue profit-taking. He was already a multimillionaire, so why should he continue this money-grubbing to the day of his death?

Besides, his past being what it was, and his present activities so grossly and savagely distorted by the press and his enemies, how wonderful it would be to win an honest acclaim, particularly in London, where supposedly quite impeccable commercial standards prevailed. It would achieve for him a social standing such as he never could hope to reach in America.

The vision thrilled him. And it had come to him through Berenice, this chit of a girl. For it was her natural gift of knowing and understanding that had enabled her to sense this opportunity. It was amazing to think that all of this, this London idea, everything that could possibly derive from his association with her in the future, had sprung from that purely sporting venture of some nine years before, when, in company with Colonel Nathaniel Gilles, of Kentucky, he had gone to the home of the then *déclassée* Hattie Starr, mother of Berenice. Who was it said that good could not come out of evil?

Chapter 5   IN THE meantime, Berenice, now that the first excitement of her union with Cowperwood had worn off, took time to consider and weigh the stumbling blocks and dangers that beset her. Fully aware of these when she had finally decided to go to Cowperwood, nevertheless she now felt that she must face them squarely and unflinchingly, and without loss of any more time.

First, there was Aileen, a jealous, emotional wife, who would certainly use any means at her disposal to destroy her if ever she felt that Cowperwood loved her. Next, the newspapers. They would certainly publicize her connection with him, if they were seen together in any conspicuous way. And then there was her mother, to whom she would have to explain this latest move of hers; and her brother Rolfe, for whom she now hoped to secure some means of livelihood through Cowperwood.

All these things meant that she would have to be consistently and firmly cautious, wily, diplomatic, courageous, and willing to make certain sacrifices and compromises.

At the same time, Cowperwood was thinking much along the same lines. Since Berenice was to be the principal force in his life from now on, he was extremely conscious of her welfare and her prospective movements in connection with himself. Also, the London idea was growing in his mind. Accordingly, on the following day when they met, he began at once discussing seriously all phases of their problems.

"You know, Bevy," he said, "I have been thinking of your London idea, and it appeals to me very much; it has interesting possibilities."

And from there on he recounted just what he had in mind, and gave her a history of the two men who had called on him.

"The thing for me to do now," he continued, after his explanation, "is to send someone to London to see whether that offer they made us still holds good. If it does, it may open the door to what you are thinking of." He smiled affectionately on Berenice as the author of all this. "On the other hand, the thing that stands in our way, as I see it now, is the matter of publicity and what Aileen is likely to do. She is very romantic and emotional; she functions through her emotions rather than through her mind. I have tried for years to make her understand how it is with me, how a man may change without really wanting to. But she cannot see that. She thinks people change deliberately." He paused and smiled. "She's the kind of woman who is naturally and entirely faithful in her heart, a one-man woman."

"And you resent that?" inquired Berenice.

"On the contrary, I think it beautiful. The only trouble is that up to now I haven't been that way."

"And will not be, I'm thinking," Berenice twitted him.

"Silence!" he pleaded. "No arguments! Let me finish, dear. She cannot see why, because I loved her so much at one time, I should not continue to do so. In fact, her sorrow has now turned into something like hatred, I'm afraid, or she tries to make herself think that it has. The worst part of it is that it's all tied up with her pride in being my wife. She wanted to shine socially, and I wished her to at first because I had the notion that it would be best for both of us. But I soon learned that Aileen was not clever enough. I gave up the idea of trying in Chicago. New York, I thought, was much more important, the real city for a man of wealth. And so I decided to try there. I was beginning to think I might not always want to live with Aileen, but, if you will believe it, that was after I saw your picture in Louisville—the one I have in my pocket. It was only after that that I decided to build the house in New York, and make it into an art gallery as well as a residence. And then, eventually, if you ever became interested in me . . ."

"And so the great house that I am never to occupy was built for me," mused Berenice. "How strange!"

"Life is like that," said Cowperwood. "But we can be happy."

"I know that," she said. "I was merely thinking of the strangeness of it. And I wouldn't disturb Aileen for anything!"

"You are both liberal and wise, I know. You will perhaps manage things better than I could."

"I believe I can manage," returned Berenice calmly.

"But besides Aileen, there are the newspapers. They follow me everywhere. And once they hear of this London idea, assuming that I undertake it, there'll be fireworks! And if ever your name becomes connected with mine, you'll be pursued as a chicken is by hawks. One solution might be for me to adopt you, or maybe carry this idea of my being your guardian on into England. That would give me the right to be with you and to pretend to be looking after your property. What do you think?"

"Well, yes," she said, slowly. "I can't see any other way. But that London matter will have to be thought out very carefully. And I am not thinking of myself alone."

"I'm sure of it," replied Cowperwood, "but with a little luck, we should get by. One of the things we must do is to avoid being seen together too much, I suppose. But first of all, we must think of a way to distract the attention of Aileen. For, of course, she knows all about you. Because of my contact with you and your mother in New York, she has suspected for a long time that there was an intrigue between us. I was never in a position to tell you that; you didn't seem to like me well enough."

"Didn't really *know* you well enough," corrected Berenice. "You were too much of an enigma."

"And now . . . ?"

"Just as much so as ever, I fear."

"I doubt that. In regard to Aileen, though, I have no solution. She is so suspicious. As long as I am here in this country, and appear in New York occasionally, she doesn't seem to mind. But if I left, and appeared to be settling in London, and the newspapers discussed it . . ." he paused, meditating.

"You're afraid she will talk, or follow you and make a scene—something of that sort?"

"It's hard to say what she might or might not do. With a little diversion of some sort, she might not do anything. On the other hand, and particularly since she's taken to drinking in the last few years, she might do anything. Several years ago, in one of her brooding fits, and when she was drinking, she tried to kill herself." (Berenice frowned.) "I prevented that by breaking in and talking rather forcibly to her." He described the scene, but did not picture himself as uncompromising as he had been.

Berenice listened, convinced at last of Aileen's undying love, and feeling that now she was adding one more thorn to her inescapable crown. Only, as she reasoned, nothing that she could do would change Cowperwood. As for herself, and her desire for some sort of revenge on society . . . well, she cared for him, too. She really did. He was like a strong drug. His mental as well as his physical charm was enormous, really irresistible. The important thing was to achieve this constructive relationship without doing any additional harm to Aileen.

She paused, thinking, and then said: "It is a real problem, isn't it? But we have a little time to consider it. Let it go for a day or two. She is certainly on my mind, all of the time . . ." She looked at Cowperwood, wide-eyed, thoughtfully and affectionately, a faint and yet cheering smile playing about her mouth. "Together we'll manage, I know."

She rose from her chair by the fire, walked over to sit on his lap, began to rumple his hair.

"All problems are not financial, are they?" she said, quizzically, touching his forehead with her lips.

"They certainly are not," he replied lightly, cheered by her affectionate sympathy and encouragement.

And then, for diversion, he suggested that since there had been a heavy snowfall the previous day, a sleigh ride would be a delightful way to end the day. He knew of a charming inn on the North Shore, where they might have dinner beside the lake under a winter moon.

Returning late that night, Berenice sat alone in her room before the fire, thinking and planning. She had already telegraphed her mother to come to Chicago at once. She would have her go to a certain North Side hotel and register for both of them. With her mother there, she could outline the course which she and Cowperwood had in mind.

What troubled her most, however, was Aileen, alone in that great house in New York, with youth, if not beauty, gone forever, and recently, as Berenice had noticed, suffering the handicap of too much flesh, which apparently she had not troubled to overcome. Her clothes, too, ran more to richness and show than to real taste.

Years, physical appearance, and lack of a gifted mentality: all of them made it impossible for Aileen to contend against one like Berenice. But never, as she told herself, would she be cruel, however vengeful Aileen might be. Rather, she proposed to be as generous as possible, and also she would not countenance the least cruelty or even thoughtlessness on Cowperwood's part, if she could detect it in time. Actually, she felt sorry for Aileen, very sorry, realizing how she must be feeling in her torn and discarded heart, for already, as young as she was, she herself had suffered, and her mother also. Their wounds were still all too fresh.

Hence, the thing to do, as she now decided, was to play as subdued and inconspicuous a role as possible in Cowperwood's life, going about with him, true enough, since that was his greatest desire and need, but without being identified too clearly. If only there were some way of diverting Aileen's mind from her present ills, and so keep her from hating Cowperwood, and, once she knew all, Berenice herself.

At first she thought of religion, or rather, wondered if there were not a priest or minister whose religious counsel might be of benefit to Aileen. There were always such well-disposed, if politic, souls, who for a bequest, or the hope of it, at her death, might gladly minister to her. Back in New York, as she recalled, was such a person: the Reverend Willis Steele, Rector of St. Swithin's of the Episcopal Diocese of New York. She had occasionally visited his church, more to dream over the simple architecture and agreeable service than to plead with God. The Reverend Willis was middle-aged, airy, bland, attractive, but without much money, although possessed of a high degree of social polish. She recalled him as once having approached her, but further thought of him only caused her to smile, and she dismissed the idea. But surely Aileen needed to be looked after by someone.

Suddenly she bethought herself at this point of one of those affable social ne'er-do-wells so common in New York society, who, for enough cash or entertainment, might be relied upon to create a fairly gay, if not exactly conventional, social scene about Aileen, and thus divert her, for the time being, anyhow. But how to go about reaching and influencing such a person to that end?

Berenice decided that this idea was really too shrewd and too cunning to come from her as a suggestion to Cowperwood. She did feel, however, that it was too valuable to be neglected. Her mother, perhaps, might throw out the hint to him. Once the bare thought of it was flicked before him, he could be counted on to react in a practical manner.

Chapter 6

HENRY de Sota Sippens was the man whom Cowperwood thought of at once to send to London to spy out the physical aspects and financial possibilities of the London underground system.

Years before, he had discovered Sippens, who had been invaluable in the negotiations to secure the contract for Chicago gas. And with the money made from that venture, Cowperwood had invaded the Chicago street railway field, and had included Sippens, because, as he had learned, the man had a genuine talent for spying out and aiding in the development of any public utility or service. He was inclined to be nervous and irritable, easily set jangling, therefore not aways diplomatic; but on the other hand, he was wholly loyal, though possessed of an uncompromising midwestern "Americanism" which often proved as irritating as it was valuable.

In the opinion of Sippens, at the present moment, Cowperwood had received an almost fatal body blow in the defeat in connection with his local franchises. He could not see how the man could ever restore himself with the local financiers who had invested with him and were now likely to lose some of their money. Since the night of the defeat, Sippens had been nervous about meeting him again. What was he to say? How sympathize with a man who up to a week ago had been one of the world's seemingly unconquerable financial giants?

Yet now, only the third day after that defeat, there came to Sippens a telegram from one of Cowperwood's secretaries requesting him to call on his former employer. Meeting him and finding him cheerful, sparkling, vibrating with good humor, Sippens could scarcely believe his eyes.

"Well, how's the Chief? I'm glad to see you looking so well."

"I never felt better, De Sota. And how are you? Ready for any fate?"

"Well, you ought to know, Chief. I've been standing by. It's whatever you say with me."

"I know that, De Sota," replied Cowperwood, smiling. For in truth, because of his compensating success with Berenice, he was feeling that the greatest pages of his life's history were about to be opened and written upon, and he felt not only hopeful but kindly toward all. "I have something I want you to undertake for me. I sent for you, De Sota, because I need reliability and secrecy, and I know you're the man!"

And for the moment his lips stiffened, and his eyes took on that hard, fixed, metallic, inscrutable luster which those who mistrusted and feared him hated. Sippens threw out his chest and chin and stood at attention. He was a little man, not more than five feet four, but heightened by high-heeled shoes and a top hat that he never doffed to anyone but Cowperwood. He wore a long double-breasted and skirted coat, which he thought gave him height and dignity.

"Thanks, Chief," he said, "you know I'd go to hell for you any time." His lips almost trembled, so wrought-up was he, not only by Cowperwood's combined faith and flattery but by all that he had been compelled to endure during the past few months as well as throughout the years of their association.

"But it's nothing like going through hell this time, De Sota," said Cowperwood, relaxing and smiling. "We've just done that here in Chicago, and we won't have to do it again. And I'm going to show you why. What I want to talk to you about now, De Sota, is London and its underground system, and the possibility of my doing something over there."

And here he paused and motioned blandly and easily to Sippens to take the chair closest to him, while Sippens, thoroughly aroused by the bare possibilities of something so different and interesting, fairly gasped.

"London! You don't say, Chief. Great! I knew you'd do something, Chief! I knew it! Oh, I can't tell you how this makes me feel, Chief!" As he spoke, his face brightened as with a light turned on within, and his fingers twitched. He half rose and then sat down again, a sure sign of excitement within him. He pulled at his fierce and rather top-heavy mustache, while he contemplated Cowperwood with brooding and wholly reassured admiration.

"Thanks, De Sota," commented Cowperwood at this point. "I thought it might interest you."

"Interest me, Chief!" returned Sippens, excitedly. "Why, Chief, you're one of the wonders of the world! Why, here you are, scarcely through with these Chicago bastards and you're ready to tackle a thing like this! It's marvelous! I always knew no one could put you down, but after this last thing, I confess I was prepared to see you sag a little. But not you, Chief! It just isn't in you to wilt. You're too big, that's all. I'd break under a thing like that myself. I know I would. I'd quit, I admit it. But not you! Well, all I want to know is what you want me to do, Chief, and I'll do it! And no one will know a thing, if that's what you want, Chief."

"Well, that's one of the things, De Sota," said Cowperwood. "Secrecy and that good hard-boiled traction sense of yours! It'll come in handy in connection with this idea of mine, if I go through with it. And neither one of us is going to be any the worse off for it, either."

"Don't mention it, Chief, don't mention it," went on De Sota, tense almost to the breaking point. "I've had enough out of you if I never get another cent between now and the time we pass out. Just you tell me what you want and I'll do it to the best of my ability, or I'll come back and tell you that I can't do it."

"You never told me that yet, De Sota, and I don't believe you ever will. But here it is, in a nutshell. About a year ago, when we were all busy with this extension business here, there were two Englishmen here from London, representing a London syndicate of some kind. I'll give you the details later, but this is a rough idea . . ."

And he outlined all that Greaves and Henshaw had said to him, concluding with the thought which was in his own mind at the time.

"It's all too top-heavy with money already expended, as you see, De Sota. Nearly $500,000 and nothing to show for it except that act or franchise for a line four or five miles long. And that has to be connected in some way by track rights over these two other systems before it can really come to anything. They admitted that themselves. But what I'm interested in now, De Sota, is to find out not only all about this whole London underground system as it stands now, but the possibility of a much bigger system, if such a thing is possible. You know what I mean, of course—with lines that would pay, say, if pushed into territories not yet reached by any other. You understand?"

"Perfectly, Chief!"

"Besides that," he went on, "I want maps of the general layout and character of the city, its traction lines, surface or underground, where they start from and where they end, together with the geological formation, if we can find that out. Also the neighborhoods or districts they reach, the sort of people living in them now or who are likely to live there. You understand?"

"Perfectly, Chief, perfectly!"

"Then, too, I want to know all about the franchises covering those lines as they exist now—those acts, I believe they call them—their duration, the length of the lines, who owns them, their biggest stockholders, how they're operated, how much their shares pay—everything, in fact, that you can find out without attracting too much attention to yourself, and certainly no attention to me. You understand that, of course, and why?"

"Perfectly, Chief, perfectly!"

"Then, De Sota, I'd like to know all about wages, as well as opertional costs, in connection with the existing lines."

"Right, Chief," echoed Sippens, already in his own mind planning his work.

"Then there's the matter of digging and equipment costs, the losses and new costs in connection with changing lines which are now in existence from steam—which is what I understand they use over there—to electricity, the new third-rail idea they're talking about using in New York in that new subway. You know, the English do differently and feel differently about these things, and I want all you can tell me about that. Lastly, maybe you can find out something about the land values that are likely to be made by what we do, and whether it might be worth while to buy in advance in any direction, as we have done here in Lakeview and other places. You remember?"

"Certainly, Chief, certainly," replied Sippens. "I understand everything, and I'll get you everything you want, and maybe more. Why, this thing's wonderful! And I can't tell you how proud and happy I am that you've called on me to do it. When do you suppose you'll be wanting me to go?"

"At once," replied Cowperwood; "that is, just as soon as you can arrange your affairs in connection with your present work out there in the suburbs." He was referring to his rural Union Traction system, of which Sippens was then president. "Better have Kitteredge take over, and you give it out that you're going to take the winter off somewhere: England, or the Continent. If you can keep any mention of your presence out of the papers, so much the better. If you can't, make it look as though you were interested in anything but traction. And if you hear of any railroad men over there who appear to be alive and who would be good to take over along with such lines as they are connected with, let me know of them. For, of course, this is going to have to be an English, not an American, enterprise from start to finish, De Sota, if we take it over. You know that. These English don't like Americans, and I don't want any anti-American war."

"Right, Chief, I understand. All I ask, though, is that if I can be useful to you anywhere over there afterward, I hope you'll keep me in mind. I've worked with you so long, Chief, and so close, it would be hard on me if after all this time . . ." he paused and stared at Cowperwood almost pleadingly, and Cowperwood returned his look blandly but at the same time inscrutably.

"That's right, that's right, De Sota. I know, and I understand. When the time comes, I'll do whatever I can. I won't forget you."

Chapter 7

HAVING instructed Sippens as to his duties and also ascertained that insofar as Chicago was concerned he would have to go east to consult with certain financiers if he were to extract any immediate sums from his holdings, Cowperwood's mind naturally reverted to Berenice and the matter of traveling and living in such a way as to attract as little attention as possible.

Of course it was all so much clearer in his own mind than in that of Berenice—the long chain of facts and associations connecting him with Aileen and with no one else so intimately. It was something which Berenice could not fully realize, particularly because of his ardent pursuit of her. But he himself was compelled to doubt the wisdom of any action in regard to Aileen other than something decidedly diplomatic and placative. It would be too great a risk, particularly if London were invaded, and so soon after this hue and cry in connection with his corporations and his social methods in Chicago. He had been accused of bribery and anti-social methods in general. And now to provoke public complaints as well as possibly some form of public action on the part of Aileen—tips to the newspapers about his relationship with Berenice—that would never do.

And then there was another problem, quite capable of causing trouble between himself and Berenice. And that was his relationship with other women. Several of these affairs were by no means closed. Arlette Wayne was temporarily disposed of, and there were others which had no more than a casual life, but there was still Caroline Hand, the wife of Hosmer Hand, wealthy Chicago investor in railways and packing houses. Caroline had been a mere girl-wife when Cowperwood first met her. She had since been divorced by Hand because of him, but with a handsome settlement. And she was still devoted to Cowperwood. He had given her a house in Chicago, and throughout the Chicago fight he had spent quite a lot of time in her company, for he had become convinced that Berenice would never come to him.

And now Caroline was thinking of going to New York in order to be near him when he finally decided to leave Chicago. She was a clever woman, not jealous—or openly so, at least—beautiful, though a bit unconventional in her style of dress, and witty to a degree which invariably succeeded in diverting him. She was now thirty, but looked twenty-five, and retained to the full the spirit of twenty. Up to the very hour of Berenice's arrival, and since—although Berenice did not know of this—Caroline Hand kept open house for Cowperwood, inviting whomsoever he wished to receive there. It was her establishment on the North Side to which the Chicago newspapers had referred in their bitterest attacks on him. She always protested that when he no longer cared for her, he should say so and she would not seek to hold him.

Considering the case of Caroline, he pondered over the idea of taking her at her word, explaining as she had suggested, and then departing. Nevertheless, much as he cared for Berenice, that seemed a little unnecessary. He might be able to explain to both of them. At any rate, nothing should be allowed to mar his relationship with Berenice, to whom he promised to be as faithful as it was possible for him to be.

But his mind returned continually to the problem presented by

Aileen. He could not avoid recalling the various happenings that had drawn them together. That first intense and dramatic fever that had bound her to him in Philadelphia, and which had contributed to, if it had not wholly brought about, his first financial ruin! The gay, unreasoning, emotional Aileen of those days, giving all of herself so feverishly and expecting in return that perfect security which love, in all its destructive history, had never yielded to anyone! And even now, after all these years, after what liaisons in his life and hers, she had not changed, she still loved him.

"You know, dear," he said to Berenice, "I feel really sorry for Aileen. There she is, in that big house in New York, without any connections that are worth while, sought after by a lot of bounders who do nothing but persuade her to drink and carouse and then try to get money from her to pay the bills. I know that from the servants, who are still loyal to me."

"It certainly is pathetic," commented Berenice, "but understandable, too."

"I don't want to be hard on her," continued Cowperwood. "As a matter of fact, I take all the blame. What I'd like to do would be to find some attractive fellow in New York society, or on the edge of it, who, for a given sum of money, would undertake the job of socially managing and entertaining her. I don't mean that too literally, of course." And here he smiled ruefully at Berenice.

But she pretended to take no notice of it, unless a blank and brief stare, coupled with faint twitchings at the corners of her mouth, could be construed to convey the sense of satisfaction with which she received the news that he was so much in accord with her own idea.

"I'm sure I don't know," she said, cautiously. "Maybe there are such people."

"There must be scores of them," said Cowperwood, practically. "Of course, he'd have to be an American. Aileen doesn't like foreigners, male foreigners, I mean. But one thing is sure, this problem should be settled soon if we're going to have any peace and be able to move about freely."

"I think I know of a man who might do," interjected Berenice, thoughtfully. "His name is Bruce Tollifer. Of the Virginia and South Carolina Tollifers. Perhaps you know him."

"No. Is he anything like the type I have in mind?"

"Well, he's young, and very good-looking, if that's what you mean," went on Berenice. "I don't know him personally. The only time I ever saw him was at the Dania Moores, in New Jersey, at the tennis matches. Edgar Boncille was telling me that day what a sponger the fellow was, and how he made his living out of rich women, Mrs. Dania Moore, for one." Here she laughed, and added: "I think Edgar was a little afraid I might become interested in him, and I did like his looks." She smiled elusively, as though she knew scarcely anything about this person.

"Sounds interesting," said Cowperwood. "No doubt, he's pretty well known around New York."

"Yes. I remember Edgar said he played around Wall Street. Wasn't really in it; just pretense for the sake of impressing people."

"Indeed!" said Cowperwood, looking quite pleased. "Well, I dare say I'd have no trouble locating him, although there are plenty of his type. I've met quite a few in my time."

"It's a little shameful, I feel," mused Berenice. "I wish we needn't talk of it. And I think you should make sure that Aileen doesn't get into any trouble through anyone you decide to use in this way."

"I mean only the best for her in every sense, Bevy. You must know that. I simply would like to find someone who could do some of the things for her that neither she nor I, singly or together, could achieve." And here he paused and gazed speculatively at Berenice, and she a little darkly and ruefully at him. "I want someone who can be of service to her in the way of entertainment, and I am willing to pay for it, and pay well."

"Well, we'll see," said Berenice, and then, as if wishing to change an unpleasant subject: "I'm expecting Mother around one o'clock tomorrow. I have arranged for rooms at the Brandingham. But now I want to ask you about Rolfe."

"What about him?"

"Oh, he's so impractical. He's never had any training. I wish I could find something for him to do."

"Well, don't worry about it. I'll have one of my men here take care of him. He can come out here as secretary to one of them. I'll have Kitteredge write him."

Berenice looked at him, not a little affected by the ease with which he solved everything, and by his generosity to her.

"I want you to know that I'm not ungrateful, Frank. You're so good to me."

Chapter 8

At the very time Berenice was speaking of him, Bruce Tollifer, the handsome ne'er-do-well was resting his considerably abused body, as well as his varied and colorful mind, in one of the lesser bedrooms of Mrs. Selma Hall's rooming house on East Fifty-third Street, a once semi-fashionable but now rather *déclassé* New York "brownstone front" neighborhood. In his mouth was a sickly taste, the aftermath of late hours the night before; but at his elbow, just the same, on a rather time-eaten taboret, were a bottle of whiskey, a siphon of seltzer, and cigarettes. And lying at his side, in the folding wall-bed, was a decidedly attractive young actress, whose salary, room, and other possessions he shared.

Both were half-dozing at a little before eleven in the morning. But a few moments later Rosalie Harrigan opened her eyes, and surveying the none too attractive room, with its wallpaper once cream-colored but now a faded brown, its low, triple-mirrored dressing table, and chest of drawers, decided that she must get up and remove the unsightly array of clothing strewn around the room. There was also an improvised kitchen and bathroom, and just to the right of the taboret was a writing table upon which Rosalie served such meals as were eaten in the apartment.

Even *en déshabillé,* Rosalie was an enticing creature. Curly, tousled black hair, a small white face, with small, searching black eyes, red lips, a slightly turned-up nose, a figure gracefully and sensually rounded, all combined to hold, for a time, anyhow, the rakish, restless, handsome Tollifer. She was also thinking that she would mix a drink for Tollifer and hand him a cigarette. Then, if he were interested, she would make some coffee and boil a couple of eggs. Or if he chose not to stir or pay any attention to her, she would dress and leave for rehearsal, which was called for twelve o'clock, and then return to his side to await his eventual wakefulness. For Rosalie was in love.

Essentially a squire of dames, Tollifer was never more than lukewarm in return for all such favors. For why should he be? A Tollifer, of the Virginia and South Carolina Tollifers! He was entitled to go with the best people anywhere! The one trouble was that except for Rosalie or any girl of her type, he was usually without a dime, and worse, drunk and in debt. Nevertheless and notwithstanding, he was a magnet where women were concerned. However, after some twenty-odd years of trifling, he had failed to make an important social connection with any of them, and so was now inclined to be brief, sarcastic, and dictatorial with anyone he might choose to favor.

Tollifer was of a good southern family, one that had once been wealthy and socially prominent. In Charleston, at that very time, was still standing an old and charming residence in which was housed what was left of a branch of the family that had endured since before the Civil War. In their possession were thousands of dollars' worth of Confederate bonds made worthless by the outcome of that conflict. And in the Army at this time was a brother, Captain Wexford Tollifer, no less, who considered Bruce a waster and a social loafer.

And in San Antonio, Texas, was another brother, a successful rancher, who had gone west, married, had children, and settled down, and now looked on Bruce's ambitions in connection with New York society as the limit of folly. For if he were ever going to do anything—bag an heiress, for instance—why hadn't he done so years before? True, his name had been in the papers from time to time, and once it had been rumored that he was about to marry a wealthy New York debutante. But that was ten years before, when he was twenty-eight, and nothing had come of it. Neither of his brothers nor any other relative had by now the least faith in him. He was through. Most of his one-time friends in New York society were inclined to agree. He was too much a victim of his desires. He had too little respect for his social worth or position. And so they had long since reached the point where they would lend him nothing more.

Yet there were still others, men and women, old and young, who, on meeting him occasionally when he was sober and perfectly groomed, could not help regretting that he had not married a fortune and so restored himself to the groups which he could so well adorn. His warm southern accent, when he chose to employ it, was so delightful, and his smile so winsome.

The present affair with Rosalie Harrigan was but eight weeks old, yet bidding fair not to endure much longer. She was merely a chorus girl, earning thirty-five dollars a week. She was gay and sweet and affectionate, but, as he felt, not forceful enough to get anywhere. It was her body, her lust, and her love that held him for the time being.

And now, on this particular morning, Rosalie surveyed his ruffled black hair and his finely modeled mouth and chin with a delight that was wholly pathetic, since it was tinged by the all too desperate fear that he would be taken from her by another. It might be, as she well knew, that he would awaken with growls and savage oaths and orders. Just the same, she wished that she might remain with him for hours, if only to touch his hair.

On the other hand, the mind of Tollifer, half in dreams and half in wakefulness, was contemplating the ills with which his daily life was streaked. For at present, other than the money he took from Rosalie, he had nothing. And now his interest in her was already dulled. If only he could find a woman of wealth, with whom he might splurge financially, even marry, and so show a lot of these local upstarts who now looked down on him what it meant to be a Tollifer, and a rich Tollifer!

Soon after he had come to New York, he had attempted to elope with a lovesick heiress, but her parents had spirited her abroad. And he found himself denounced in the public press as a fortune-hunter, one who should and would be guarded against by all respectable families of wealth who wished their daughters to marry happily and well. And that failure, or mistake, along with drink, lust, gambling, had closed to him for all of these years the doors he wished to enter.

On fully awakening this morning, and while dressing, he began growling at Rosalie about a party of the night before into which she had inveigled him, and at which he had become intoxicated and belittled and ridiculed those around him until they were heartily glad to be rid of him.

"Such people! Such bounders!" he cried. "Why didn't you tell me those newspapermen were going to be there? Actors are bad enough, God knows, but those newspaper snoops, and those publicity hounds who came with your actress friends! Bah!"

"But I didn't know they were coming, Bruce," pleaded Rosalie, who, pale and picturesque, was doing her best to toast a slice of bread over a gas jet. "I thought it was just for the stars of the show."

"Stars! You call those people stars! If they're stars, then I'm a whole sidereal system!" (A comparison entirely lost on Rosalie, who had no notion of what he was talking about.) "Those bums! You wouldn't know a star from an oil lamp!"

Then he yawned, wondering how long before he would find nerve enough to brace up and quit this. How low was he going to fall? Sharing with girls who earned no more than enough for themselves, and then drinking and gambling with men with whom he couldn't share and share alike!

"God, I can't stand this!" he cried. "I'll have to quit. I just can't hang around here any longer. It's too damned degrading!"

He walked the length of the room and back again, his hands thrust angrily into his pockets, while Rosalie stood silently near him. Fear would not permit her to speak.

"Well, do you hear me?" he demanded. "Are you going to stand there like a dummy? Oh, you women! You either fight like cats, or lie down and say nothing! God, if I could find one woman, just one, with a little sense in her nut, I'd . . . I'd . . ."

Rosalie looked up at him, her mouth twisted into a tortured smile. "Well, what would you do?" she said, quietly.

"I'd hang on to her! I might even love her! But, my God, what's the use? Here I am, fiddling around in this hole, and accomplishing what? I belong to another world, and I'm going to get back into it! You and I are going to have to separate. It can't be otherwise. I can't go on like this a day longer!"

And so saying he went to the closet, and taking out his hat and overcoat, moved toward the door. Rosalie, however, edged in before him, throwing her arms around him and pressing her face to his. She was weeping.

"Oh, Bruce, oh, please! What have I done? Don't you love me any more? Isn't it enough that I'll do anything you want? I don't ask anything of you, do I? Please, Bruce, you won't leave me, will you, Bruce?"

But Tollifer, pushing her aside, broke away.

"Don't, Rosalie, don't," he went on. "I won't stand for it! You can't hold me this way. I'm getting out because I have to!"

He opened the door, but as he moved, Rosalie threw herself between him and the stairs.

"Oh, Bruce," she cried, "for God's sake, you can't go! Listen, you can't leave me this way! I'll do anything, anything at all, I tell you! Oh, Bruce, I'll get more money, I'll get a better job. I know I can. We can move to another apartment. I'll fix it all. Bruce, please sit down, and don't carry on this way. I'll kill myself if you leave me!"

But Tollifer was adamant by this time. "Oh, cut that, Rosie! Don't be a damn fool! I know you're not going to kill yourself, and you know it, too. Brace up! Just be calm, and I'll see you tonight or tomorrow, maybe, but I've got to make a new deal, that's all there is to it. Do you get that?"

Rosalie weakened under his gaze. She realized now that the inevitable was not to be avoided. She knew she could not hold him if he wished to go.

"Oh, Bruce," she pleaded once more, pressing close to him. "I won't let you go! I won't! I won't! You can't go this way!"

"Can't I?" he demanded. "Well, just watch me!" And he pulled her away from the door and went out, hurrying down the stairs. Rosalie, breathless and filled with terror, stood staring as the house door slammed, then turned wearily and re-entered the room, closing the door and leaning against it.

It was nearly time to go to rehearsal, but she shuddered as she thought of it. She didn't care now. There was nothing . . . unless, maybe, he would come back . . . he would have to come back for his clothes . . .

Chapter 9

THE thought which Tollifer was cherishing at this time was that he might get a job in a brokerage house or trust company dealing with the affairs, or, more particularly, the fortunes, of widows or daughters of men of wealth. His difficulty, however, was that he had passed out of the group of society handy men that flourished not only on the fringe, but in the very heart, of New York society of that day. Such men were not only useful, but at times absolutely essential, to those with money but no background who sought to enter society, as well as to passé debutantes who, because of encroaching years, wished to maintain a conspicuous place.

The qualifications were considerable, including the best American descent, appearance, social flair, and a sophisticated interest in yachting, racing, polo, tennis, riding, driving—especially the four-in-hand coach—the opera, the theater, the sporting ring. These men followed the wealthy to Paris, Biarritz, Monte Carlo, Nice, Switzerland, Newport, Palm Beach; the duck blinds of the south and the country clubs everywhere. In New York their principal haunts were the smart restaurants, the "Diamond Horseshoe" of the opera, and the theaters. It was necessary that they dress well and appropriately for any occasion; be of service and skill in obtaining the best seats for a horse show, a tennis match, a football game, or the current popular play. It helped if they were able to take a hand at cards and explain the finer points of the game, or, on occasion, give advice or make suggestions as to clothes, jewels, or the decoration of a room. But, above all, they must see that the names of their patrons appeared with comparative frequency in *Town Topics* or the newspaper society columns.

To work at this sort of thing continuously, however, meant that in some not too discreditable way, the handy man must be rewarded for the efforts, and sometimes sacrifices, he had to make, particularly the sacrifice of the zest and thrill which otherwise would come to him through his companionship with youth and beauty. For principally his attentions must be devoted to the middle-aged, those like Aileen, who feared the dreadful hour of social or emotional boredom.

Well, Tollifer had been through all that, years of it, and at about thirty-one or -two, had begun to tire of it. And, from sheer boredom and sometimes sickness of heart over the whole thing, he would disappear, to drink and amuse himself with a beauty of the stage world who had fire and love and devotion to offer him. Just the same, at this time he was once more entertaining the thought of visiting such restaurants, bars, hotels, and other places as were frequented by the people who could do him the most good. He was going to brace up, stay sober, get a little money from somewhere—from Rosalie, maybe—and with it make such a sartorial and financial display as would cause him to be looked upon again as a possibility in the social sense.

And then . . . well, watch him this time!

Chapter 10

In New York at this time was Aileen racking her wearied and disillusioned wits as to how to make a life for herself. Although by now the Cowperwood mansion, as it was called, was one of the most ornate and beautiful houses in New York, still, for Aileen, it was but a hollow shell, an emotional as well as a social grave.

As she saw it now, she had greatly wronged Cowperwood's first wife and their children. She did not know then what his wife would have to suffer. But she knew all its bitterness now. In spite of her sacrificial love, having given up home, friends, society, reputation, for Cowperwood, she was now in the depths of despair. Other women, ruthless, cruel, had attached themselves to him, not for love, but for his wealth and fame. He took them because of their youth and charm—which were in no way superior to her own of but a few years before. But she would never let him go! Never! Never should one of these women call herself Mrs. Frank Algernon Cowperwood! She had sealed that tie with a true love and a true marriage, and never should that be taken from her! He would not dare assail her in any open or legal way. The world, as well as she herself, knew too much, or she would see that it did, if ever he sought to displace her. She had never forgotten his open declaration of love for the young and beautiful Berenice Fleming. Where was she now? Possibly with him. But she could never have him legally. Never!

And yet, how lonely she was! This great house, these rooms with their floors of marble, their carved doors and ceilings, their painted and decorated walls! The servants, who might be spies, for all she knew! And so little to do, so few people to see, so few who wanted to see her! The occupants of those great houses that lined the Avenue not deigning to notice either herself or Cowperwood, for all of their wealth!

There were a few seeking admirers whom she tolerated, and one or two relatives, among them her two brothers, who lived in Philadelphia. They were wealthy and socially significant themselves, but because they were religious and conservative and their wives and children did not approve of her, she saw little of them. They came occasionally for lunch or dinner, or to stay the night when they were in New York, but always without their families. And it would be a long time before she would see them again. She knew how it was, and they did, too.

But as for life other than this, there was no one who meant anything to her. Actors and society wastrels, who occasionally sought her company, mainly to borrow money, yet really interested only in their younger friends. How could she, after Cowperwood, imagine herself the beloved of one of these petty pleasure-seekers. Desire, yes! But only after dreary and lagging hours of loneliness and torturing thoughts, turning to anyone, so long as there was physical attraction, a patter of words, and liquor! Oh, life, loneliness, age, its futility, and the flight of all that had been worth while!

What a mockery, this great house, with its galleries of paintings and sculpture and tapestries! For Cowperwood, her husband, so rarely came. And when he did come, always so cautious, though pretending affection before the servants. And they naturally subservient to him as her superior, as in truth he was because of his power to dispose of everything that was here maintained by him. And if she chose to scoff or rebel, how suave and winsome he could be, taking her hand or touching her arm gently, and saying: "But, Aileen, you must remember! You are and always will be Mrs. Frank Cowperwood, and as such you must do your part!"

And if for the moment she raged or wept, eyes filling and lips trembling, or hurried from his presence in a storm of emotion, he would follow her, and after a long argument or subtle appeal bring her to his point of view. Or failing that, he might send her flowers or suggest that after dinner they go together to the opera—a concession which almost invariably betrayed her vain and weak soul. For to appear with him in public: did not that, in part at least, prove that she was still his wife, the chatelaine of his home?

Chapter II   DE SOTA SIPPENS, departing for London with such assistants as he needed, took a house in Knightsbridge when he arrived there, and proceeded to gather all the data he felt Cowperwood would require.

One of the things that struck him at once was the fact that in connection with the two oldest undergrounds—the Metropolitan

Railway and the District Railway, or Inner Circle, as it was called —there was a downtown loop, similar to that which had made the Cowperwood system of Chicago so useful to himself and so irritating and expensive to his rivals. These two London lines, the first of the world's undergrounds, both badly built and operated by steam, actually enclosed and reached all of the principal downtown points, and so served as a key to the entire underground situation. Paralleling each other at a distance of about a mile, and joining at the ends in order to afford mutual running rights, they covered everything from Kensington and the Paddington Station on the west to Aldgate in the Bank of England district on the east. In fact, everything of any importance—the main streets, the theater district, the financial district, the shopping district, the great hotels, the railway stations, the houses of Parliament—was in this area.

Sippens was quick to learn that these lines, due to their poor equipment and management, were paying little more than their expenses. But they *could* be made profitable, for there was as yet, apart from buses, no other such convenient route to these districts.

Moreover, there was not only considerable public dissatisfaction with the old-fashioned steam service on these lines, but a distinct desire on the part of a younger financial element now entering the underground field to see them electrified and brought up to date. Among this element, and one of the principal minority shareholders in the District Railway, was Lord Stane, of whom Cowperwood had spoken. He was also one of the most prominent figures in the London social world.

This picture of the situation, written at great length by Sippens, was sufficient to stir Cowperwood. The central loop idea, if seized upon now, and bolstered with franchises or acts for extensions into the outlying areas, would give him exactly the type of control which he needed to make him the head and center of any future development.

And yet, unless he chose to dig into his own pockets, where was he to get the cash for all this? Probably a $100,000,000 eventually! He was at the moment dubious of inspiring a financial following which would furnish the capital, particuarly since no one of the present London tubes appeared to be more than paying expenses. Certainly, this venture was a daring thing to consider at this time, and would have to be preceded and accompanied by an extremely subtle barrage of propaganda which would paint him in the best possible light.

He thought over all of the important American financial leaders, and their institutions and banks, principally in the east, to whom, by reason of past dealings, he could now appeal. It should be made plain that he desired the credit rather than any exorbitant financial profit. For Berenice was right: this last and greatest of his financial adventures, if it came to pass, should be on a higher level than any of his previous enterprises, and so atone for all sins coupled with his customary jugglery.

In his heart, of course, he was by no means prepared to give over entirely his old tricks in connection with organizing and managing a traction development. Rather, since his schemes were not as well-known in England as in his own country, he was more than ever bent upon organizing a company for this and a company for that, one for each branch or existing system that was to be added or done over, the watered stocks of which would be sold to a gullible public. That was the way of such things. The public could always be hood-winked into buying anything that was made to look sufficiently promising. It depended on the strength, respectability and stability that might be given to it by the proper associations. Having decided all this in his own mind, he at once cabled Sippens his thanks and instructions to remain in London pending further word.

In the meantime, Berenice's mother had arrived in Chicago and established a temporary ménage, and both Berenice and Cowperwood, in their different ways, made clear to her what had happened and how from now on they were all to be joined in this new and possibly troublesome relationship. Although at first, and in the presence of Berenice, Mrs. Carter did indulge in some tears—based principally on self-criticism of her past, which, as she truly enough insisted, was the real cause of her daughter's present course—nevertheless she was by no means so reduced as her quite unstable conscience at times made her believe. For, after all, she reflected, Cowperwood was a great man, and, as he himself now stated to her, Berenice would not only inherit a goodly portion of his estate, but if Aileen died, or granted him a divorce, he would most certainly marry her. For the present, he, of course, was to continue as before: as Mrs. Carter's friend and the guardian of her daughter. Whatever happened, and whatever the rumors from time to time, this explanation was to be maintained. And to that end, their public contacts were to be as few and as conventional as possible. What he and Berenice might privately devise for themselves was their own affair, but they would never travel on the same boat or train, nor stop at the same hotel anywhere.

As to London, Cowperwood fancied there might be considerable social life for all of them there, particularly since, if all went well, he expected to ally himself with the higher financial circles and possibly to use his connection with Berenice and her mother as a means of inducing a meeting of forces and friends most favorable to him at their home, since he was looking to Mrs. Carter to maintain such an establishment as would seem natural and proper for a widow and her daughter who were wealthy and of good repute.

Berenice, of course, since originally this was her idea, was enthusiastic. And Mrs. Carter, as she listened to Cowperwood, regardless of her conception of him as ruthless and almost cruelly uncompromising where his personal comforts were concerned, was almost persuaded that all was for the best. Berenice had presented her own case in the most practical manner:

"I really care for Frank, Mother," she had said to her, "and I want to be with him as much as possible. He never tried to force me, you know; it was I who went to him, and it was I who suggested this. You know, it hasn't seemed right to me for a long time, ever since I knew that the money we have been living on wasn't yours but his, to take all and give nothing. And yet, I've been just as much of a coward as you have been, too selfish and thin-skinned to face life without anything, as would have been the case if he had left us."

"Oh, I know you're right, Bevy," said her mother, almost pleadingly. "Please don't reproach me. I suffer so much as it is. Please don't. It's your future that I've always been thinking of."

"Please, Mother, please," begged Berenice, softening toward her, for, after all, she loved her mother, foolish and errant as she had been. True, in her school days she had been inclined to belittle her mother's taste, knowledge, and judgment. But now that she knew all, she had come to look on her mother in a different light, if by no means exempting her wholly, still forgiving and sympathizing with her in her present state. She made no more belittling or condescending remarks, but on the contrary gave her only kindness and understanding, as if she were trying to make up to her for the human ills that had befallen her.

And so now she added, softly and soothingly: "You remember, Mother, I found out quickly enough, when I tried for myself to see what I could do, that I hadn't been brought up in a way that prepared me for any of the conditions I would have to face. I had been guarded and petted too much. And I'm not blaming you, or Frank, either. But there's no future for me in a social way, not in this country. The best I can do, I'm sure, is to join my life with Frank's, for he's the one person who can really help me."

Mrs. Carter nodded in agreement and smiled wistfully. She knew that she must do whatever Berenice wished. She had no life of her own, no way of living outside of dependence on Cowperwood and her daughter.

Chapter 12 AND it was following this general understanding that Cowperwood, Berenice, and her mother left for New York, the women going first and Cowperwood following later. His purpose was to investigate the American investment situation and also to find some international brokerage house through which he might have the original proposition in regard to the Charing Cross line redirected to him for his consideration; that is, without his appearing to be interested.

Of course, there were his own New York and London brokers, Jarkins, Kloorfain & Randolph, but in such a portentous business as this he did not wholly trust them. Jarkins, the principal figure in the American branch of the concern, though cunning and in some ways useful, was still too self-interested and also at times talked too much. Yet to go to a strange brokerage firm would be no better. It might even be worse. He finally decided to have someone whom he could trust suggest to Jarkins that it might be wise for Greaves and Henshaw to approach him again.

In this connection, he recalled that one of the letters of introduction presented to him by Greaves and Henshaw on their first call was from a certain Raphael Cole, a retired New York banker of considerable wealth, who some years before had tried to interest him in New York transit. Though Cowperwood had been too engrossed at the time with his Chicago affairs to consider Cole's proposition, the conversation had resulted in a friendship, and later Cole had invested in some of Cowperwood's Chicago properties.

His present idea in regard to Cole was not only to prime him for a possible investment in this London venture but to get him to suggest, through Jarkins, that Greaves and Henshaw approach him again. He decided to invite Cole to dinner at his Fifth Avenue home, with Aileen as hostess. Thus he would begin the placation of Aileen and at the same time give Cole the impression that he was a contented husband, for Cole led a more or less conventional life. And this London plan would certainly require some such conventional background in order to forestall public criticism. In fact, Berenice had said to him, just before leaving for New York: "Now, remember, Frank, the more attention you show Aileen publicly, the better it will be for all of us." And with that she had given him a still, blue look, which in force and suggestiveness seemed to embody all the subtlety of the ages.

And in consequence, en route to New York, thinking over the wisdom of Berenice's words, he wired Aileen of his coming. And, incidentally, too, he now planned to get in touch with a certain Edward Bingham, a bond salesman of the social type who came to see him quite frequently, and who would probably be able to supply information in regard to this man Tollifer.

And it was with this full program that he telephoned Berenice at the Park Avenue home which he had recently given her. After arranging for a meeting with her later in the day, he telephoned Cole. He also learned, after calling his office in the Netherlands Hotel, that among other messages there happened to be one from Bingham asking when it would be agreeable for Cowperwood to see him. Finally, he proceeded to his home, a man very different in mood from the one Aileen had seen some months before.

In fact, seeing him enter her bedroom this morning, she sensed at once that something agreeable was afoot, since his look and his stride so indicated.

"Well, how are you, my dear," he began at once, in the genial manner he had not seen fit to display before her for a long time. "I suppose you got my telegram."

"Yes," returned Aileen, calmly and a little dubiously. At the same time, she watched him interestedly, since in her feeling for him there was affection as well as resentment.

"Ah, reading a detective story!" he said, observing the book on her bedside table and at the same time contrasting in his mind her mental resources with those of Berenice.

"Yes," she replied, crossly. "What would you have me read—the Bible, or one of your monthly balance sheets, or your art catalogues?"

She was sad and hurt because of the fact that throughout his Chicago troubles he had neglected to write to her.

"The truth is, my dear," he went on, placatingly and graciously, "I've been intending to write you, but I've been rushed to death. I really have. Besides, I knew you were probably reading the papers. It's been in all of them. But I did get your wire, and it was nice of you, very! I thought I answered it. I should have, I know." He referred to an encouraging telegram Aileen had sent him just after his much publicized defeat in the Chicago City Council.

"Oh, all right!" snapped Aileen, who at eleven o'clock in the morning was still idling over her dressing. "I'll assume that you did. What else?"

He noticed her snowy, flouncy, white dressing gown, the kind she always favored, since it tended to show off her red hair, which at one time he had so greatly admired. He also noticed that her face was heavily powdered. The necessity for it weighed on his mind, as it was probably weighing on hers. Time! Time! Time! Always the erosive process at work! She was getting older, older, older. And she could do nothing except bleed at the heart, for well she knew how much he disliked signs of age in a woman, although he never mentioned it and appeared even to ignore it.

He felt not a little sorry for her, and therefore inclined to be amiable. In fact, looking at her and thinking of Berenice's broad-minded view in regard to her, he saw no reason why this seeming reconciliation between them should not be stretched to include a trip abroad for Aileen. It need not necessarily be in his immediate company, but rather around the same time, in order to give the impression that all was well in regard to his married life. She might even go on the same boat, if it could be arranged for this Tollifer, or someone else, to take her off his hands. For it would be well that the person chosen to interest himself in her should pursue her abroad as well as here, since she must be kept out of the path of Berenice and himself.

"Doing anything tonight?" he asked, ingratiatingly.

"No, nothing special," she replied, coldly, since his look, friendly as it was, seemed to imply that he wanted something of her, though what it was she could not guess. "Are you expecting to stay here for a while?"

"Yes, for some little time. At least, I shall be in and out of here. I have some plans which may take me abroad for a few weeks, and I want to talk to you about that." He paused here, a little uncertain as to how to proceed. It was all very difficult, very complicated. "And I'd like you to do a little entertaining for me while I'm here. Do you mind?"

"No," she said, briefly, sensing his aloofness. She felt that his thoughts were not with her, even now after their long separation. All at once she was too tired and too discouraged to argue with him.

"You wouldn't care to go to the opera tonight, would you?" he then asked her.

"Why, yes, if you really want to go." After all, it was a comfort to have him, even for a little while.

"Certainly, I do," he replied, "and I want you to go with me. After all, you're my wife, and mistress here, and regardless of how you feel about me, it's necessary for us to keep up a favorable public appearance. It can't do either of us any harm, and it may help us both. The fact is, Aileen," he continued, confidentially, "now that I've had all this trouble in Chicago, I find it necessary to do one of two things: either drop all business activities in this country and retire—and I don't feel much in the mood for that—or find something different to tackle somewhere else. I don't want to die of dry rot, exactly," he concluded.

"Oh, you! 'Dry rot'!" interpolated Aileen, looking at him amusedly. "As though dry rot would ever overtake you! More likely you would overtake dry rot and chase it out!"

This caused Cowperwood to smile.

"At any rate," he went on, "the only two things I've heard of so far that might interest me are a proposed subway scheme in Paris —which doesn't appeal to me very much—and . . ." here he paused and meditated, the while Aileen studied him, wondering if this were true . . . "or something in London; I think I'd like to look over the underground situation there."

At these words, and for some reason which she could not have explained—telepathy, psychic osmosis—Aileen brightened and seemed to envision something interesting.

"Really!" she said. "That sounds rather promising. But if you do go into something else, I hope you fix it this time so that there will be no possibility of trouble afterwards. You seem almost to create trouble wherever you go, or it creates itself for you."

"Well, I've been thinking," went on Cowperwood, ignoring her last comments, "that if nothing else turned up, I might try to do something in London, although I hear that the English are very unfriendly to American enterprise in any form. If that's the case, I wouldn't have a chance to break in there, particularly after my Chicago trouble."

"Oh, Chicago!" exclaimed Aileen, at once defensive and loyal. "I wouldn't worry about Chicago. Everyone with any brains knows what a pack of jealous jackals they are! I think London would be a wonderful place for you to start in again. You certainly ought to know how to fix things so as to avoid all the franchise trouble you appear to be having in Chicago. I've always felt, Frank," she ventured here, and this on the strength of the years she had spent with him, and without any particular hope of ingratiating herself, "you're too indifferent to the opinion of others. Other people—I don't care who they are—just don't seem to exist for you. That's why you stir up all these fights, and you always will, unless you bother to be a little more considerate of other people. Of course, I don't know what you have in mind, but I'm sure that if today you wanted to start out and be the least bit nice to people, why, with your ideas and your way of getting around people when you want to, there'd be no stopping you, that's all," and with that she paused, waiting to see if he would make any comment.

"Thanks," he said, "you may be right, at that. I don't know. At any rate, I'm thinking seriously of this London matter."

Sensing the certainty of action in some direction on his part, she went on: "Of course, as for us, I know you don't care for me any more, and never will. I can see that now. But at the same time, I feel that I've been an influence in your life, and if for nothing more than that—all I went through with you in Philadelphia and Chicago—I shouldn't be kicked off like an old shoe. It isn't right. And it can't bring you any good in the long run. I've always felt, and still feel, that you might at least keep up a public pretense as far as I'm concerned; show me at least a little attention and not leave me to sit here alone week after week and month after month, without one word, one letter, anything . . ."

And here once more, as so many times in the past, he saw her throat tighten and her eyes mist with tears. And she turned away, as if unable to say more. At the same time, as he saw, here was exactly the compromise of which he had been thinking ever since Berenice had arrived in Chicago. Plainly, Aileen was ready for it, though to what extent he could not guess as yet.

"The thing I have to do," he said, "is to find something else and find the cash for it. In the meantime, I want to keep this residence here and make it appear that everything is going on as before. It will make a good impression. There was a time, you know, when I wanted a divorce, but if you can bring yourself to let bygones be bygones and go on with an outward relationship, without quarreling with me over my private life, why, I think we might work out something. In fact, I'm sure we can. I'm not as young as I used to be, and while I reserve the right to regulate my private life to suit my personal needs, I see no reason why we shouldn't go on as we have been, and even make things look better than they do now. Do you agree with that or not?"

And since Aileen had no other desire than to remain his wife, and also, despite his ill-treatment of her, wanted to see him succeed in anything he undertook, she now replied:

"Well, what else is there for me to do? You hold all the cards in your hands. What have I, really? Exactly what?"

And here it was that Cowperwood suggested that in case he found it necessary to go away and Aileen felt it would look better if she accompanied him, he would have no objection to that, or even to press notices indicating a marital harmony between them, so long as she did not insist on any routine form of contact which might embarrass him in his personal life.

"Well, if you want it that way," she said as to this. "It is certainly no less than I have now," but at the same time thinking that there might be another woman behind all this—probably that girl, Berenice Fleming. If such were the case, there would be no compromise on her part. For as to Berenice, never, never, would she allow him to humiliate her with any public relations with that vain and selfish upstart! Never, never, never!

And so, interestingly enough, while Cowperwood was thinking that he had made considerable progress, rather quickly, in the direction of his present dreams, Aileen was thinking that she had made at least some little gain; and that the more public attention she caused Cowperwood to pay her, at whatever cost to her private feeling, the stronger would be the evidence of her holding him, and the greater her public if not private triumph.

Chapter 13

THE matter of interesting Cole in having Greaves and Henshaw reapproach him was accomplished by Cowperwood in but a few moments out of an evening of dining and drinking. Indeed, Cole expressed the thought that in London Cowperwood might find a better field for his powers than Chicago had ever offered him, in which case he would be glad to hear further in regard to any investment plans which might be devised.

Equally satisfactory was the talk with Edward Bingham, from whom Cowperwood drew out some interesting information regarding Bruce Tollifer. According to Bingham, Tollifer, at present, was in a sorry state. Although at one time a person of excellent social connections, and having some money, today he was without either. Still handsome, he looked dissipated, shabby. Until recently he had been associating with gamblers and other persons of questionable reputation; most of those who had formerly known and liked him had apparently stricken him from their lists.

On the other hand, as Bingham felt called upon to admit, within the past month Tollifer had been exhibiting attempts at rehabilitation. For he was now living alone at a modest so-called bachelor's club, the Alcove, in Fifty-third Street, and was seen occasionally dining in the best restaurants. He believed that Tollifer was seeking to do one of two things: either to ingratiate himself with a wealthy woman who would be glad to pay him for such services as he could perform for her, or get himself a job in a brokerage firm where his one-time social connections might be considered worth a salary. This critical conclusion on the part of Bingham caused Cowperwood to smile, since it was exactly in this state that he had hoped to find Tollifer.

He thanked Bingham, and after he left telephoned Tollifer at the Alcove. That gentleman, at the moment, was lying down, half-dressed, rather dismally awaiting the arrival of five o'clock, at which time he intended to venture forth on one of his "cruises," as he called them—those searchings in clubs, restaurants, theaters, bars, in order to exchange such casual greetings as might reopen old or create new friendships. It was three o'clock now, and a windy February day, when he came down into the main corridor to answer Cowperwood's call, a half-smoked cigarette in his fingers, his hair ruffled, and his lounging slippers a little the worse for wear.

At the announcement: "This is Frank A. Cowperwood speaking," Tollifer stiffened and pulled himself together, for that name had been a front page headline for months.

"Oh, yes, Mr. Cowperwood, what can I do for you?" and Tollifer's voice was a blend of extreme awareness, civility, and willingness to accommodate himself to whatever might be asked of him.

"I have in mind a certain matter which I think might interest you, Mr. Tollifer. If you care to call at my office in the Netherlands at ten-thirty tomorrow morning, I'll be glad to see you. May I expect you at that time?"

The voice, as Tollifer did not fail to note, was not exactly that of a superior addressing an inferior, yet it was authoritative and commanding. Tollifer, for all his social estimate of himself, was intensely curious and not a little thrilled.

"Certainly, Mr. Cowperwood, I'll be there," he replied immediately.

What could it mean? It might be a stock- or bond-selling proposition. If so, he would be delighted to take on such a job. Sitting in his room meditating on this unexpected call, he began to recall things he had read in regard to the Cowperwoods. There was that business of their trying to break into New York society, and the rumors of certain discomfitures and snubs in connection therewith. But then he returned to the idea of a job, and what that might mean in the way of social contacts, and he felt strangely cheered. He began to examine his face and figure, as well as the clothes in his closet. He must get a shave and a shampoo, and have his clothes well brushed and pressed. He would not go out this night, but rest and so refresh himself for the morrow.

And on the following morning he was at Cowperwood's office,

more repressed and pliable than he had been for a long time. For this, somehow, seemed to bode a new start in life. At least, so he hoped as he entered and saw the great man sitting behind a large rosewood desk which occupied the center of the room. But at once he felt reduced and a little uncertain of himself, for the man before him, although far from lacking in courtesy and a certain atmosphere of cordial understanding, was still so aloof and remote. Certainly, he decided, he might be described as handsome, forceful, and dominant. Those large, magnetic, and wholly unrevealing blue eyes, and those strong, graceful hands resting so lightly on the desk before him, the little finger of the right hand wearing a plain gold ring.

This ring, years before, Aileen had given him in his prison cell in Philadelphia, when he was at the lowest dip of his ever since ascending arc, as a token of her undying love, and he had never removed it. And here he was now, about to arrange with a somewhat *déclassé* social dandy to undertake a form of diversion which would preoccupy her in order that he might enjoy himself blissfully and peacefully with another woman. Really nothing short of a form of moral degradation! He fully realized that. But what else was he to do? What he was now planning must be as it was because it sprang out of conditions which life itself, operating through him and others, had created and shaped, and in any event not to be changed now. It was too late. He must work out matters bravely, defiantly, ruthlessly, so as to overawe people into accepting his methods and needs as inevitable. And so now, looking at Tollifer calmly and rather coldly, and motioning him to a chair, he began:

"Mr. Tollifer, do sit down. I telephoned you yesterday because there is something I want to have done which requires a man of considerable tact and social experience. I will explain it more fully a little later. I may say that I did not call you before having made some investigation of your personal history and affairs, but without intending you any harm, I assure you. In fact, quite the contrary. I may be of some service to you, if you can be so to me." And here he smiled a bright smile, to which Tollifer responded in a somewhat dubious but still genial fashion.

"I hope you didn't find so much against me as to make this conversation useless," he said, ruefully. "I haven't been living a strictly conventional life, I will admit. I wasn't born for that type of thing, I'm afraid."

"Very likely not," said Cowperwood, quite pleasantly and consolingly. "But before we discuss that, I want you to be quite frank and tell me all about yourself. The matter I have in mind requires that I know all about you."

He gazed encouragingly at Tollifer, and he, in turn, noting this, told in abbreviated form, and yet quite honestly, the entire story of his life, from his boyhood up. Whereupon Cowperwood, not a little entertained by this, decided that the fellow was a better sort than he had hoped for, less calculating—frank and random and pleasure-loving rather than sly and self-seeking. And, in consequence, he decided that he might speak to him more clearly and fully than at first he had intended.

"Financially, you are on the rocks, then?"

"Well, more or less so," returned Tollifer, with a wry smile. "I think I've never been off the rocks, really."

"Well, they're usually crowded, I believe. But tell me, aren't you, just at this time, trying to pull yourself together, and, if possible, reconnect yourself with the set to which you used to belong?"

He noticed an unmistakable shadow of distaste flicker cloudlike across Tollifer's face as he answered: "Well, yes, I am," and again that ironic, almost hopeless, yet intriguing, smile.

"And how do you find the fight going?"

"Situated as I am just now, not so good. My experience has been in a world that requires considerably more money than I have. I've been hoping to connect myself with some bank or brokerage house that has a pull with the sort of people I know here in New York, because then I might make some money for myself, as well as the bank, and also get in touch again with people who could really be of use to me . . ."

"I see," said Cowperwood. "But the fact that you have allowed your social connections to lapse makes it, I take it, a little difficult. Do you really think that with such a job as you speak of you can win back to what you want?"

"I can't say because I don't know," Tollifer replied. "I hope so."

A slightly disconcerting note of disbelief, or at least doubt, in Cowperwood's tone just then had caused Tollifer to feel much less hopeful than only a moment before he had felt. At any rate, he went on bravely enough:

"I'm not so old, and certainly not any more dissipated than a lot of fellows who have been out and gotten back. The only trouble with me is that I don't have enough money. If I'd ever had that, I'd never have drifted out. It was lack of money, and nothing else. But I don't feel that I'm wholly through by any means, even now. I haven't stopped trying, and there's always another day."

"I like that spirit," commented Cowperwood, "and I hope you're right. At any rate, it should not prove difficult to get you a place in a brokerage house."

Tollifer stirred eagerly and hopefully. "I wish I thought so," he said, earnestly, and almost sadly. "It certainly would be a start toward something for me."

Cowperwood smiled.

"Well, then," he went on, "I think it might be arranged for you without any trouble. But only on one condition, and that is that you keep yourself free from any entanglements of any kind for the present. I say that because there is a social matter in which I am interested and which I may want you to undertake for me. It involves no compromise of your present bachelor's freedom, but it may mean that for a time at least you will have to show particular attention to just one person, doing about the same sort of thing you were telling me of a while ago: paying attention to a rather charming woman a little older than yourself."

As Cowperwood said this, Tollifer felt that there must be, perhaps, a wealthy, elderly woman of Cowperwood's acquaintance on whom he had financial designs and that he was to be the cat's-paw.

"Certainly," he said, "if it is anything I feel I can do for you, Mr. Cowperwood."

At this point Cowperwood leaned back easily in his chair, and, putting the fingers of his hands together, regarded Tollifer with a cold and calculating gaze.

"The woman I refer to is my wife, Mr. Tollifer," he announced sharply and brazenly. "For years now, Mrs. Cowperwood and I have been—I will not say on bad terms, for that is not true—but more or less estranged."

At this point Tollifer nodded as though he understood fully, but Cowperwood continued hastily:

"I do not mean that we are permanently so. Or that I wish to obtain any legal evidence of any kind against her. I do not. Her life is her own to live as freely as she chooses, yet within limits, of course. I would not tolerate any public scandal, and I would not allow anyone to intrigue her into scandal of any kind."

"I can understand that," commented Tollifer, who by now was beginning to sense demarcations which would need to be fully grasped and carefully observed if he were to have the opportunity of profiting by the proposal.

"Not quite yet, I believe," retorted Cowperwood, a little coldly, "but I shall make myself perfectly clear. Mrs. Cowperwood was a very beautiful girl, one of the most beautiful I have ever seen. She is still very attractive, although she is middle-aged. And she could make herself much more attractive if she were not so despondent and inclined to be morbid. It is because of our break—and for that I accept all the responsibility and charge her with nothing—you understand that fully, I hope . . ."

"I do," said Tollifer, interested and respectful.

"Mrs. Cowperwood has been allowing herself to slip—physically as well as socially—a course which may have justification to her mind, but none in reality. That is, she is still too young and has too much to live for, whatever she may think."

"I can understand her feeling, though," again interrupted Tollifer, with a trace of philosophic defiance which Cowperwood liked. It indicated sympathy and understanding.

"Very likely," said Cowperwood, dryly and rather pointedly. "The task I am offering you, and for which I will, of course, provide the means, is that of intervening in some way—ostensibly without my knowledge and, of course, without her knowing anything about this conversation of ours—to make her life more interesting and colorful than it is now. She is alone too much. She sees too few people, and those not of the right sort. My purpose in calling you here is to see whether—the necessary money provided for you, of course, and no conduct in any way open to question indulged in—you cannot find ways of broadening her interests, surround her with a type of person more in keeping with her means and her mentality. I may say here, I am not seeking any contact with society, either for her or myself. But there are intermediate worlds with which I think she might be brought in touch, to her advantage, as well as, in a way, to my own. If you understand what I mean, perhaps you can make some suggestions."

Whereupon Tollifer proceeded to outline as exactly as he could the possibilities of a life for Aileen such as Cowperwood had indicated. Cowperwood listened and seemed pleased with Tollifer's grasp of the situation.

"There is one thing more, Mr. Tollifer," he continued. "I want you to understand that your services in connection with the brokerage house which I will select will be directed by me personally. I hope we understand each other as to that," and he rose from his chair, indicating that the interview was at an end.

"Yes, Mr. Cowperwood," said Tollifer, rising and smiling.

"All right. Now I may not be able to see you very soon again, but you will not be left without instructions. I will see that a drawing account is arranged for you. That is all, I believe. Good morning!"

And this salutation, accompanied by a resumption of aloof dignity, was sufficient once more to impress Tollifer with a sharp sense of the vast gulf that still lay between himself and this man.

Chapter 14 THE effect on Tollifer of this amazing interview was extremely exhilarating. Leaving Cowperwood's office, he walked north along Fifth Avenue, in order to gaze at the beautiful Cowperwood mansion. After examining the impressive Italian palace lines and decorations, he turned, and with a sense of adventure, hailed a hansom cab for a ride to Delmonico's, at Fifth Avenue and Twenty-seventh Street. This region was alive at the luncheon hour with the most pretentious and ambitious of the New York social world and stars of the theatrical, artistic, and legal world, coming to see and be seen. Before he left the restaurant, he had spoken with at least six of the better known patrons, and because of his exuberant and authoritative manner, had registered himself sharply on the minds of many others.

In the meantime, Cowperwood had instructed the Central Trust Company, of which he was a director and stockholder, to notify a certain Bruce Tollifer, then resident at the Alcove, on Fifty-third Street near Park Avenue, that his services in connection with its special account department were to be considered, and that if he would call at once he would receive instructions. The execution of this arrangement, which took place on the same day, with an advance

of one month's salary at $200 a week, so thrilled Tollifer that he felt
as though he were walking on air. At once he made it his business to
inquire, as casually as possible, concerning the New York history of
the Cowperwoods, not only among newspapermen but the various
know-it-alls of the bohemian bars and restaurants of the city: the
Gilsey House, the Martinique, the Marlborough, and the Metropolitan at Broadway and Forty-second Street, the mecca for sports and
rounders of the day.

And discovering that Aileen had been seen with this and that
actor, and at certain restaurants, or races, or other public events, with
various personalities, he decided to get himself somehow included in
those gatherings where she was certain to be. A proper formal introduction, of course, would be the best possible entrance for him.

And now Cowperwood, having moved in this matter of a social
chaperonage for Aileen, was free to devote his attention to the business of arranging for the sale of at least a portion of his Chicago
holdings. At the same time, he was awaiting developments of negotiations by Cole with the representatives of the Charing Cross line.
His main object, at the present time, was to reduce them to such a
state that when he did see them they would be willing to make a
reasonable offer.

And so, upon the arrival of Jarkins, with news that Greaves and
Henshaw were once more anxious to obtain an interview with him,
he affected no great interest. If they really had an advantageous offer
to make, and were not merely haggling as before, and if they would
appear within the next ten days . . .

Whereupon Jarkins immediately cabled his London partner, Kloorfain, emphasizing the necessity for prompt action. Within twenty-
four hours Messrs. Greaves and Henshaw were on a boat sailing for
New York. And for several days after their arrival they were closeted
with Jarkins and Randolph, going over the data which they would
present to Cowperwood. And after arranging for an interview, and
ignorant of the fact that Cowperwood himself was the instigator of
this meeting, they were finally brought into his presence by Jarkins
and Randolph, equally unenlightened as to their part in the matter.

True enough, as Cowperwood knew, Greaves and Henshaw were
men of great contracting and engineering import in England. They
were comparatively wealthy, as he had been informed by Sippens.
Also, in addition to their contract with the Traffic Electrical Com-

pany to build the tunnels and stations of the new underground, they had recently paid an additional £30,000 for a further option to take over the entire "act."

But plainly the Traffic Electrical Company was on the rocks. Consisting of Rider, Lord Stane, Johnson, and some of their friends, it had the advantage of considerable legal and financial knowledge, but none of these men had any real conception of how to finance or successfully operate such a road, and were in no position to finance it themselves. Stane had already invested heavily in the two central loop roads: the District and the Metropolitan, but had not made any money. Hence his desire to divest himself of the Charing Cross line and the offer of it to Greaves and Henshaw upon payment of £30,000 additional to the £10,000 previously paid by them to secure the right to construct it. Actually, since he now had this larger loop scheme in mind, Cowperwood was interested, because, as he saw it, it might either be operated separately, or, better yet, should he secure control of the District and the Metropolitan, be combined with those as an extension, a most excellent entering wedge for him.

Nonetheless, when Greaves and Henshaw, shouldered and bolstered by Jarkins and Randolph, entered his office, his manner was not overwhelmingly cordial. Greaves was a man of great height and bulk, of florid complexion, and a solid middle-class conviction of his own worth. Henshaw, though also tall, was thin and pale, with the air of a gentleman. Allowing them to spread out their maps and papers, and once more listening to the entire story as though he did not already know it, Cowperwood asked only a few questions.

"One thing, gentlemen," he announced, "assuming that I chance to be interested in this idea to the extent of looking into it further, how much time may I have for an investigation? I assume, of course, that what you really want to do is to sell the complete control of this project, together with your contract to construct the line. Am I right?"

At this both Greaves and Henshaw stiffened visibly, for it was not at all what they wished to do. What they really desired, as they now explained, was to sell for £30,000 a 50 per cent interest. The other 50 per cent, together with their contract for construction, was to remain in their hands. For this share, however, as they naïvely stated, they were willing to use their influence to help market the $8,000,000 worth of $100 shares which the Traffic Electrical Company had al-

ready printed but had never been able to sell, surrendering a portion
of their 50 per cent so to do. But, as they added, a man like Cowperwood could help finance and operate the road in such a way that it
would be sure to pay—a suggestion which caused Cowperwood to
smile, for it was not the building or operation of this line which was
so important, it was the control of the entire underground system
that was his dream.

"But I judge from our talk so far that you expect to make a reasonable profit out of constructing the road for the parent company, not
much less than 10 per cent, I take it," said Cowperwood.

"Well, yes, we expect to make the usual contractors' profit, but no
more," returned Greaves.

"That may be true," said Cowperwood, suavely, "but if I understand you correctly, you two gentlemen expect to make at least
$500,000 for yourselves out of the construction of this road, and en-
tirely apart from your return as partners in the company for which
you are doing the work."

"But for our 50 per cent we expect to bring in some English capital," explained Henshaw.

"How much English capital?" asked Cowperwood, warily, for he
was thinking that if he could secure 51 per cent of the road, it might
be worth considering.

But as to that, as he now discovered, they were a little vague. If he
came in and took over the load of consols and gave the actual construction an appearance of certainty, perhaps as much as 25 per cent
of the entire cost could be sold to the public.

"But would you *guarantee* to do that?" asked Cowperwood, rather
interested by the idea. "That is, would you make your share of the
company contingent upon your raising so much money before you
received your share?"

Well, no, they could not do that, exactly, but if they failed, they
might be willing to take something less than 50 per cent, say 30 or 35,
provided they were permitted to retain their contract to construct.

Cowperwood smiled again at this point.

"What interests me, gentlemen," he went on, "is that you who
appear to understand the engineering business thoroughly should
assume the business of financing to be less difficult. For it isn't, of
course. Just as you have had to study for years, and then by practical
work get to the place where your reputations would command such

contracts as I know you are accustomed to, so I, as a financier, have had to do exactly the same thing. And, of course, you cannot expect any man, however great his wealth, to step forward and agree to construct and operate a road as large as this out of his own pocket. He couldn't do it. It would be too great a risk. He would have to do what you are planning to do: get other people to invest. And he would not raise money for any enterprise without first a profit for himself, and, second, a profit for those whose money he was using. And in order to do that he must have much more than a 50 per cent interest in anything he undertakes."

Greaves and Henshaw were silent, and he went on talking.

"Now, you are not only asking me to raise the money, or most of it, while I make it possible for you to raise the rest, but to pay you to construct the line and then afterward operate it jointly with you. If that is what is really in your minds, of course we need not talk any further, for I am not interested. What I might do would be to take over your £30,000 option, provided it gave me full control of the road, and possibly leave you the £10,000 you have paid in and your contract to build, but not more than that. For in addition to all this, as I know, there are £60,000 of consols, carrying interest at 4 per cent, which have to be looked after."

Jarkins and Randolph were beginning to feel by now that they had in some way mishandled all of this. At the same time, Greaves and Henshaw, sensing that they had overreached themselves in a situation where they might have profited, gazed at each other dubiously.

"Very well," said Greaves, finally. "You are your own best judge, Mr. Cowperwood. But we want you to understand clearly that there isn't a sounder proposition in the world. London is the ideal field for undergrounds. It has no united system, and lines like this are absolutely necessary, and will come. The money will be found for them."

"Possibly," said Cowperwood, "but as for myself, if after again looking over the situation you still find yourselves unable to work out your plan and are willing to accept mine, you may say so in writing, and I will then consider it. However, if I decide to become interested, it would have to be with an option to close on my own terms. That, of course, would not mean that I would disturb you in the matter of your construction contract. That could stand, I think, provided your specifications were satisfactory."

He drummed on his desk with his fingers as if to indicate that the interview was over, and then paused to add that since there was no proposition before him now that he could consider, he would take it as a favor if no publicity of any kind resulted from what he had said. Then he signaled Jarkins to remain, and the moment the others had gone, turned to him and said:

"The trouble with you, Jarkins, is that you never completely grasp an opportunity even when it's in your hands. Look what's happened here today! You bring me two men, who, according to your story and theirs, control an important traction proposition in London, which, if rightly handled, might readily lead to much larger things for everyone concerned. Yet they come here with no conception of the way I do business. You know what that is: full control for myself. I doubt if even now they have any clear knowledge of my experience in this field and what I could do with such a project. They thought they could sell me a half-interest in something which they and their friends would control. I tell you, Jarkins," and here he glared with a finality which sent chills up and down the spine of Mr. Jarkins, "if you're to be of any service to me in this matter, I would advise you not to bother with this particular proposition but to look into the entire London underground situation and see what can be done with that. And furthermore, I want you to keep all of your private speculations in regard to me and my affairs to yourself. If you had gone to London before bringing these men to me, and ascertained all there was to know about them, you would not have wasted my time and theirs."

"Yes, sir," said Jarkins, who was fat and forty, a very model of sartorial excellence, and, at the moment, because of nervousness, wet with perspiration. He was a flabby, waxlike man, with black, acquisitive eyes, below which a small, pointed nose stuck out, and below that a soft, puffy mouth. He was forever dreaming of some speculative coup which would make him a multimillionaire, and a well-known figure at first nights at the theater, polo games, dog shows, and other society functions. In London he had as many friends as he had in New York.

In consequence, Cowperwood had the feeling that he might have some use for him, and yet, at the moment, he was not willing to do more than throw out vague hints, knowing that they would, in all probability, cause him to go tearing after Greaves and Henshaw to set himself right with them, and, who knows, he might even go over to London, where . . . well, what better press agent could he have than Mr. Jarkins?

Chapter 15 AND true enough, it was not many days after Greaves and Henshaw had departed for London that Jarkins also sailed, all aquiver with the expectation of becoming a part of an enormous adventure which might lead to those dreamed-of millions.

And while this preliminary move in connection with Greaves and Henshaw and their Charing Cross line appeared to have ended less definitely than Cowperwood had hoped, it made no change in his determination to proceed. For there was the information provided by Sippens, and because of that he was determined to get control of some underground line, if not the Charing Cross. And so there were not only consultations, but a number of dinners at his home, from which latter Aileen took the impression that her husband was at least a little interested in the old life which had made her early days in Chicago with him her most colorful and happy memory. She was beginning to wonder whether, by some strange turn of fate, the Chicago failure might not have sobered him, so that he had decided to accept, if not necessarily relish, the old-time outward relationship, which, little as it meant to him, could still be so comforting to her.

But the truth was that Cowperwood was becoming more and more intrigued by the temperament of Berenice. There was about her a certain playful and inventive whimsy, which, combined with her practical as well as poetic and rhapsodic moods, delighted him. In fact, he was never weary of studying her, and in the comparatively short period since she had arrived in Chicago, he had come to experience and relish the equivalent of a mental fever in regard to her.

One of Berenice's fancies, and one which had affected Cowperwood most profoundly, had occurred more recently in Chicago. One late afternoon they had driven out for dinner to the inn where they had dined a couple of evenings previously. But before entering, she had led him to the nearby woods, where in a snow-flecked patch of scrub oak and pine stood a snow figure in his own image, part caricature and part an arresting likeness. She had driven out alone early that very morning and shaped it. For the eyes she had used two bright gray-blue stones, and for the mouth and nose, small pine cones of different sizes. She had even brought out one of his hats and placed it jauntily atop the snowman's head, thus serving to emphasize the likeness. Suddenly confronted with this figure at dusk, a wintry wind whispering among the trees and the last rays of a blood-red sun spearing through, Cowperwood was startled.

"Why, Bevy! Of all the odd things to do! When did you do this, you pixie?" And he laughed at the touch of the comic, for she had placed one eye the least bit askew, and the nose was a little exaggerated.

"I did it this morning. I drove out here alone and made my lovely snowman!"

"It does look like me, by Jove!" he said, amazedly. "But, Bevy, how long did it take you to do it?"

"Oh, perhaps an hour," and she stepped back and eyed it appraisingly. Then, taking his cane from him, she placed it against one of the snowman's pockets, which were indicated by small stones. "Now, see how perfect you are! All snow and cones and stone buttons!" and she reached up and kissed the mouth.

"Bevy! If you're going to do that, come here!" and he seized her in his arms, feeling that there was something here that was eerie, elfin. "Berenice, dear, I swear you puzzle me. Have I a real flesh-and-blood girl, or a sprite, a witch?"

"Didn't you know?" and she turned and spread out her fingers at him. "I'm a witch, and I can turn you into snow and ice," and she came eerily toward him.

"Berenice, for heaven's sake! What nonsense! Sometimes I think you are the one who is bewitched. But you may witch me all you care to, only don't leave me," and he kissed her and held her tight in his arms.

But she drew away and turned back to the snowman. "There, now!" she exclaimed, "you've gone and spoiled it all. He's not real, after all, darling. And I made him so real. He was so big and cold, and needed me so much out here. And now I'll have to destroy him, my poor snowman, so that no one will have ever truly known him but me." And all of a sudden she dashed the figure apart with Cowperwood's cane. "See, I made you, and now I'm unmaking you!" And as she talked she powdered the snow through her gloved fingers, while he gazed at her wonderingly.

"Come, come, Bevy, sweet. What are you saying? And as for making and unmaking, do both, but don't leave me. You are taking me into strange places, new and strange moods, a wonder world of your own, and I am happy to go. Do you believe that?"

"Of course, dear, of course," she now replied as brightly and as differently as though no such scene as this had ever been. "It's meant to be so. It must be." And she slipped her arm under his. She appeared to have come out of some trance or illusion of her own, concerning which he would have liked to question her, but he felt that he should not. Yet, and more at this moment than ever before, there was that about her which thrilled him, as he realized that he could come and see and touch her, without let or hindrance, and that now, as never before, he was allowed to walk and talk and be with her. This was the substance quite, of all real earthly good and delight. Truly, he would never wish to part from her, for never before had he encountered anyone so varied, so different, so reasoning and practical and yet at the same time so unreal and whimsical as this. Histrionic, yes, and yet the most resourceful and colorful of all the women he had known!

And on the purely sensual side, there was something about her which from the beginning not only surprised but enticed him. She refused to permit herself either to be lost in or wholly ravished by the male. No mere commonplace fleshly instrument for the satisfaction of the lust of himself or any other was she. On the contrary, and always, however amorous or fevered she might be, still she was quite definitely conscious of her charms: the swirl of her red-gold hair about her face, the magnetism and implication of her inciting and compelling blue eyes, the sweetness of her mouth, with its enchanting and enigmatic smile.

Indeed, as he thought after the most shaking and reducing transports with her, hers was never a mere gross and savage lust, but a glorified and intense awareness and evaluation of her own beauty, enforcing its claims by the art of suggestion and thereby producing an effect that was different from any he had ever known. For it was not Berenice but himself who was most ravished mentally and sensually, indeed all but submerged in her own exotic consciousness of what this relationship implied.

Chapter 16

REALIZING that it would be necessary for him to co-operate with Tollifer, at least in some small way, in order to bring about effective results in regard to Aileen, Cowperwood decided that he would inform her of his planned trip to London in a few weeks' time, suggesting that if she chose to she might accompany him. And he would notify Tollifer to this effect, making plain to him that he would be expected to entertain her so that she would not be torturing herself with her husband's neglect as she had in the past. His mood at the time was one of the best. After the long period of tragic emotional cleavage between them, he felt that at last he was about to adjust matters in such a way as would ease her sufferings and bring about at least a semblance of peace.

At sight of him—ruddy, assured, genial, a gardenia in his lapel, grey hat, grey gloves, and swinging a cane—Aileen was compelled to restrain herself in order not to smile more pleasantly than she felt he deserved. At once he began to talk of his affairs. Had she noticed from the papers that one of his bitterest enemies in Chicago had recently died? Well, that was the end of that worry! What were they going to have for dinner? He would like Adrian to prepare some sole Marguéry, if it wasn't too late. By the way, he had been very busy; he had been to Boston and to Baltimore, and shortly he must go to Chicago. But this London matter . . . he had been looking into that, and probably, very shortly, he would be going over there. How would she like to go along? Of course, he would be very busy while there, but she could run over to Paris, or Biarritz, and he might meet her week ends.

Whereupon Aileen, taken aback by this new development, leaned forward in her chair, her eyes alight with pleasure. Then catching herself, remembering her true relationship to this husband of hers, she sank back again. There had been too many subterfuges on his part for her to be sure of anything. Nevertheless, she decided it was best to assume that this invitation meant a genuine desire for her company.

"Fine! Do you really want me?" she asked.

"Would I be asking you, dear, if I didn't? Of course, I want you.

This is a serious move for me. It may prove a success, and it may not. Anyway," and here he lied with his usual bland utilitarianism—a stab in the very vitals of love—"you were with me at the beginning of my other two adventures, and I think you should come in on this one, don't you?"

"Yes, Frank, I would like to be in on it, if you feel that way. It would be wonderful. I'll be ready whenever you decide to go. When do we sail—what boat?"

"I'll have Jamieson find out, and let you know," he said, referring to his personal secretary.

She walked to the door and rang for Carr to give him the order for dinner, her whole being suddenly revivified. A touch of the old life, this seemed, wherein she had been a part of both power and efficiency. She also ordered Carr to get out the luggage and report on its condition.

And then Cowperwood, expressing concern for the health of the tropical birds he had imported for his conservatory, suggested that they go and look at them. Aileen, now in a most cheerful mood, walked briskly beside him, watching him as he studied the two alert troupials from the Orinoco, and attempted by whistling to induce the male to utter his pellucid cry. Suddenly he turned to Aileen, and said:

"As you know, Aileen, I've always planned to make this house into a really fine museum. I keep buying these things, and eventually it should be one of the finest private collections. And I've been thinking a lot lately about how to arrange with you so that when I pass on, as I will, sooner or later, it will be kept, not so much as a memorial to me, but as a pleasure for people who care for things like this. I'm going to draw up a new will, and that's one of the things I want to consider."

Aileen was a little puzzled by all this. What did it mean?

"I'll soon be sixty," he went on, quietly, "and while I'm not thinking of dying just yet, I certainly feel that I ought to clear matters up. As three of my five executors, I've been intending to name Mr. Dolan, of Philadelphia, and Mr. Cole, as well as the Central Trust Company here. Both Dolan and Cole are men who understand the financial and executive side of things, and I'm sure they would carry out my wishes. But since I intend leaving you the use of this house for your lifetime, I've been thinking of joining you up with Dolan and Cole, so that you can either open the house to the public yourself or see that arrangements are made to do so. I want the house to be beautiful, and remain beautiful after I die."

Aileen was now even more thrilled. She could not imagine what had brought about this serious consideration of herself in connection with her husband's affairs, but she was flattered and gratified. It must be that he was beginning to take a more sobered view of life.

"You know, Frank," she said, trying not to be too emotional, "how I've always felt about everything in connection with you. I've never had any other real life, and never want to have any, apart from you, although you don't seem to feel that way any more. But as far as this house is concerned, if you leave it to me or make me one of your executors, you can rest assured that nothing will ever be changed by me. I never pretended to have the taste and knowledge that you have, but you know that your wishes will always be sacred to me."

While she talked, Cowperwood was poking his finger at a green and orange macaw, whose harsh voice, harmonizing with his brazen colors, seemed to mock at the solemnity of his mood. Yet he was touched by Aileen's words, and reached over and patted her on the shoulder.

"I know that, Aileen. I only wish the two of us could look at life from the same standpoint. But since we cannot, I want to make the best of all possible compromises, because I know that whatever has been or may be, you care for me and are likely to continue to do so. And whether you believe it or not, if I can make any return for that, I am only too anxious to do it. This matter of the house, and some other things I am going to talk to you about presently, are a part of it."

At the dinner table later, he told her of his idea of endowing a hospital with extensive research facilities, and spoke of other bequests. In this connection, he indicated how necessary it would be for him to make frequent returns to New York and to this house. And on such occasions he would prefer her to be there. Of course, there would be intermittent trips abroad for her, too.

And seeing her so happy and satisfied, he congratulated himself on the manner in which he had brought her around to his terms. If only they could continue that way, all would be well.

Chapter 17

IN LONDON at this time Jarkins was busily engaged in impressing his partner, Kloorfain, with the news that the great Cowperwood, he believed, was really interested in the London underground situation as a whole! He described Cowperwood's attitude and words, and at the same time he explained that they had made a mistake in not sensing that a man with such immense holdings would certainly not want to bother with one little underground system. How ridiculous for Greaves and Henshaw to think they could interest him in 50 per cent of their line! Why, there was no chance of him accepting any such terms. Nothing short of a full 51 per cent control for him! Did Kloorfain think that Greaves and Henshaw were ever likely to find the money for their line in England?

To which Kloorfain, a stout, oleaginous Dutchman, as shrewd in small practical ways as he was deficient in large financial vision or courage, replied:

"Not at all! Too many 'acts,' as it is. Too many companies fighting each other for single routes. No willingness on the part of any one company to join up with any other to give the public a through route at a reasonable fare. I've seen it myself, for I've been riding around London for years. Why, just think, there are these two central lines, the Metropolitan and the District, which together control a circle around the very business heart of London" . . . and he proceeded to point out some of the practical as well as financial errors made by these two lines, and their resulting difficulties. They had never been willing to merge and build feeder lines, not even to electrify and modernize those they had. They were still running steam engines through tunnels and open cuts. The only company which had shown any sense at all was the City and South London, which ran from the Monument to Clapham Common. It had an electric system which operated with a third rail, and it ran smoothly, was well lighted, and the only well-patronized road in the city. But even so, it was too short; its passengers had to transfer and pay an extra fare on the London loop. London certainly needed a man like Cowperwood or a group of English financiers who would get together and finance and enlarge the system.

As to proposed lines which Cowperwood might secure, well, there was the Baker Street and Waterloo, being promoted by a Londoner by the name of Abington Scarr. Scarr had had his act for the last sixteen months and done nothing. Then there was some talk of extensions being made by the District, but in both cases capital was wanting.

"In fact," concluded Kloorfain, "if Cowperwood really wants that Charing Cross, I don't think he'd have much trouble getting it. Traffic Electrical gave up trying to finance it over two years ago. Since then these two engineers have had it, but until this suggestion in regard to Cowperwood came up, I'm sure they never had a bid of any kind. Besides, they're not railroad men, and unless they find a man with as much money as Cowperwood has, I doubt if they'll ever be able to put it through."

"Well, then, there's no use worrying about them, is there?" commented Jarkins.

"I think not," reiterated Kloorfain. "But I think we ought to look up some of the people connected with the two old central loop lines, the District and the Metropolitan, or some of the bankers down in Threadneedle Street, and see what we can find out. You know Crawshaw, of Crawshaw and Vokes. They've been trying to find money for Greaves and Henshaw ever since they took over the option. Of course, they've failed, just as the Traffic Electrical crowd failed before them. They want too much."

"Traffic Electrical?" queried Jarkins. "That's the company that had this line originally. What sort of people are they?"

At once, and quite briskly, Kloorfain recalled a number of things in connection with them, not all that Sippens had discovered, but enough to interest both men. For now, emerging out of the pool of Kloorfain's memories came Stane, Rider, Bullock, and Johnson, but more particularly Johnson and Stane. They had been among the principal promoters of Charing Cross and Hampstead. Stane was of the nobility and a large stockholder in District as well as City and South London. Johnson was counsel for Stane, as well as for District and Metropolitan, and also a stockholder in both lines.

"Well, why not try and see this man Johnson?" queried Jarkins, all ears and attention because of his rift with Cowperwood. "He must be pretty well informed on all that's going on."

Kloorfain was standing at a window, looking down into the street.

"Capital!" he exclaimed, turning around to face Jarkins. "The very idea! Why not? Only . . ." And now he paused and looked dubiously at Jarkins. "Is this all quite ethical? As I understand it, we haven't the right to say we represent Cowperwood. From what you say he only agreed to hear Greaves and Henshaw in New York because we asked him to. He didn't appoint us to do any work in connection with them."

"Well, anyhow, I think it might be a good thing to sound out this fellow Johnson," returned Jarkins, "indicate to him that Cowperwood, or some American millionaire that we know, is interested in a plan to unite some of these lines, and then suggest that the Charing Cross line, if they could get it back, might be sold to him. In that case, as the agents bringing them together, we ought to come in for a pretty neat bonus, and we'd be entitled to it. Besides, if any shares can be picked up now or sold for them or Cowperwood, we might come in as purchasing or selling agents. Why not?"

"Not a bad idea," said Kloorfain, becoming more eager. "I'll see if I can get him on the telephone."

He lumbered into an inner office, and was about to make the call when he stopped and looked at Jarkins.

"The simplest way, I think, is to ask for a consultation in connection with a financial problem which is before us but which cannot be explained over the telephone. He'll think there's a fee in it for him, and we'll just let him think so until we explain what it is."

"Good!" said Jarkins. "Let's call him now."

So, after a very cautious explanation by Kloorfain to Johnson over the telephone, he turned and said: "He says he'll see us tomorrow at eleven o'clock."

"Capital!" exclaimed Jarkins. "I think we're on the right track now. Anyway, we're moving. And if he isn't interested himself, he may know someone who is."

"Quite right, quite right," repeated Kloorfain, who was mainly concerned at this time to see that due credit for his share of all this fell to him. "I'm glad I thought of him. This may turn out to be the biggest thing we've ever done."

"Quite right, quite right!" echoed Jarkins, who was elated enough, but not as elated as he would have been had the whole problem been worked out by himself. For Jarkins had always thought of himself as not only the brains but the dynamic force of this combination.

Chapter 18

THE offices of Rider, Bullock, Johnson & Chance, as well as that of Lord Stane, were in one of the dingiest sections of Storey Street, adjacent to the Inns of Court. In fact, the whole region, except for the Inns of Court, would be regarded by Americans as most inappropriate housing for distinguished legal talent. Small, remodeled three- and four-story residences or one-time lofts and stores now contained offices, libraries, consulting chambers, for as many as a dozen solicitors, their stenographers, clerks, errand boys, and other assistants.

Storey Street itself was so narrow as almost to forbid the companionable stroll of two pedestrians arm in arm. As for the roadway proper, it might admit the easy passage of two pushcarts, but by no means two vehicles of any greater size. Yet through this lane poured a veritable host of workers, including those who used it for a quick cut to the Strand and adjacent thoroughfares.

The firm of Rider, Bullock, Johnson & Chance occupied all of the four floors of 33 Storey Street, a building no more than twenty-three feet wide, though fifty feet deep. The ground floor, originally the reception and living room of the residence of a singularly retiring judge of a preceding generation, was now the general reception room and library. Lord Stane occupied a small office in the rear of the first floor; the second floor was given over to the three most important members of the firm: Rider, Johnson, and Bullock. Chance, along with the various assistants, occupied the third floor. Elverson Johnson's office, at the extreme rear of the second floor, looked down on a small court. Its cobbled paving had once been part of an ancient Roman courtyard, but its historic luster was dimmed by too great familiarity for those who were compelled to contemplate it day after day.

There was no elevator, or "lift," to use the English term. A fairly large air shaft extended from the middle of the second floor to the roof. The offices were also equipped with a rather antique form of air wheel, which was supposed to add to the oxygenization of the air within. In addition, each room contained a fireplace—in which soft coal was burned throughout the foggy, rainy days of winter—and this added immensely to the comfort as well as charm of these interiors. In each solicitor's room were spacious and well-made desks and chairs, and a white marble mantelpiece on which stood books or bits of statuary. The walls were hung with rather dusty engravings of bygone English legal lights or bits of British scenery.

Johnson, the authoritative and financially ambitious member of the firm was, in the main, a practical person, and followed, for the most part, an individual course that would be most advantageous to his personal plans. In one corner of his mind, however, was a complex which led him to speculate on the value of religion and even sympathize with the advancement of the nonconformist doctrines. He was given to meditating upon the hypocrisy and spiritual stagnation of the High Church party, and also upon the earthly as well as heavenly significance of such famous religionists as John Knox, William Penn, George Fox, and John Wesley. In his complicated and curious mental cosmos, he sheltered obviously rival and even antagonistic notions. He felt that there should be a ruling class which should advance and maintain itself by a desirable if not always justifiable cunning. Since in England this class was already buttressed by laws of property, inheritance, and primogeniture, it was important, correct, and all but unalterable. Hence the poor in mind as well as substance might best trust themselves to obedience, hard work, and a faith in a Heavenly Father who would, in the last analysis—perhaps—look after them. On the other hand, the immense gulf between not always witless poverty and unearned wealth seemed to him cruel and almost evil. This viewpoint supported his more urgent religious moods, which verged at times upon the sanctimonious.

Though he had come out of the lesser world of the socially weak and ineffective, he was ever aspiring to those upper walks where, if not he, then his children—two sons and one daughter—would be as secure as those whom he so greatly admired and criticized. In fact, he was aspiring to a title for himself: an unpretentious "Sir" to begin with, which later, if luck favored him, might be accentuated by further royal consideration. To win to that, as he well knew, he must not only secure more money than he now had, but also the favor of those who possessed money and title. In consequence, he intuitively attuned his actions to the ambitions and welfare of the members of that class.

He was small, pompous, wiry, authoritative. His father, a bibulous carpenter of Southwark, had wretchedly maintained a family of seven. Young Johnson was apprenticed to a baker, for whom he delivered bread. His diligence attracted the attention of a customer who was a printer, and by him he was taken on as a "devil" and encouraged to read and fix his mind on some practical line of work which would lift him out of the drab and miserable state in which he then moved. And Johnson was an eager pupil. Delivering printed matter to all manner of merchants and tradesmen, he finally came in contact with a young solicitor, Luther Fletcher by name, who, campaigning to represent one of the Southwark divisions in the London County Council, found in young Johnson, then not more than twenty years old, one who interested him as a legal possibility. His inquisitiveness and industry so fascinated Fletcher that he sent him to night school for the study of law.

From that point on, Johnson's affairs prospered. The firm to which he was ultimately articled was not long in being impressed with his intuitive legal sense, and he was soon undertaking most of the detail work of the phases of law in which this firm was interested: contracts, property rights, wills, and the organization of companies. At the age of twenty-two, he passed the necessary examinations and was admitted solicitor. At twenty-three he encountered Mr. Byron Chance, of Bullock & Chance, solicitors, who offered him a partnership in that firm.

Bullock, a man of standing with the barristers of the Inns of Court, had for a friend one Wellington Rider, a solicitor of even more influential connections than himself. Rider managed the affairs of a number of large estates, among them that of the Earl of Stane, as well as the legal business of the District Railway. Also becoming interested in Johnson, he was seriously moved to persuade him to leave Bullock and join up with him. However, both self-interest and friendship dictated that he seek some other way of obtaining Johnson's services. A talk with Bullock finally brought about the present legal union, which had now lasted for ten years.

With Rider came Gordon Roderick, Lord Stane, eldest son of the Earl of Stane. At that time Stane was fresh from Cambridge and, his father thought, properly equipped to succeed to the paternal dignities. Actually, however, because of certain quirks and idiosyncrasies of temperament, the young man was more concerned with the practical and decidedly unhistoric phases of the world about him. He had come into the world just when the luster and supremacy of mere title were not only being questioned but, in many instances, over-shadowed by financial genius. At Cambridge he was an interested student of economics, politics, sociology, and inclined to give ear to the socialists of the Fabian school, without by any means losing consciousness of his prospective inheritance. Encountering Rider, himself interested almost solely in the immense companies which he was constantly being called upon to represent, Stane was easily converted to Rider's view that the real lords of the future would be financiers. What the world needed was advanced material equipment, and the financier who devoted himself to supplying that need would be the greatest factor in society's progression.

It was with such thoughts in his mind that Stane pursued the study of English company law in the office of Rider, Bullock, Johnson & Chance. And one of his chief intimacies was with Elverson Johnson. In Johnson he saw a shrewd commoner with a determination to rise to high places, while in Stane, Johnson recognized an inheritor of social and financial privilege who yet chose to inform and bestir himself in practical pursuits.

Both Johnson and Stane had from the first recognized the enormous possibilities of the London underground traction field, and their interest was by no means confined to the formation of the Traffic Electrical Company, of which, in its origin, they formed the nucleus. When the City and South London, with its up-to-date construction, was first proposed, they and their friends put money into it, with the understanding that a combination of the two old lines then threading the heart of London—the Metropolitan and the District—was to be considered. Like Demosthenes addressing the Athenians, Johnson persisted in his belief that whoever could find the money to pick up enough of the ordinary stock of these two lines to provide a 51 per cent control, could calmly announce himself in charge and thereafter do as he pleased with them.

After his father's death, Stane and some of his friends, together with Johnson, sought to buy a control of the ordinary stock of the District, hoping in this way to gain control of both roads, but it had all proven too much for them. There was too much stock outstanding, and they could not get together enough money. Therefore, since the management was unprogressive and the stock did not pay well, they had resold a large part of what they had acquired.

And as for the still unconstructed Charing Cross line, to promote which they had formed the Traffic Electrical Company, they had never been able to raise enough money or resell enough of the printed shares to provide the £1,660,000 needed to build it. At last, through Greaves and Henshaw, they had been seeking to find a financier, or group of financiers, who would either take this Charing Cross line off their hands or unite with them in their dream to take over the Metropolitan and the District.

But so far, nothing had come of this. Johnson by this time was forty-seven and Lord Stane forty, and both had become a little weary and more than slightly dubious of this great task.

Chapter 19

INTO this situation, and into the office of Elverson Johnson, enter Mr. Jarkins and Mr. Kloorfain, desiring to confer with Mr. Johnson on a highly important matter. It related to the Messrs. Greaves and Henshaw, who had recently gone to New York, as Mr. Johnson probably knew, to confer with their client, Mr. Frank Cowperwood, whom Mr. Johnson knew, of course.

Mr. Johnson admitted that he had heard of him. And what could he do for these gentlemen?

It was one of London's best spring mornings. Sunshine poured down on the cobbled Roman pavement below. Johnson, when they entered, had been stirring in a basket of briefs relating to a certain damage suit against the City and South London. And he was in a cheerful mood because the day was warm and bright; there had been a slight rise in the shares of the District; and a very earnest speech which he had delivered the day before to the International Epworth League had been favorably mentioned by not less than two of the morning papers.

"I'll be as brief as possible," began Jarkins, who, arrayed in a gray suit, a gray silk shirt, a brilliant blue and white tie, a derby and a cane in his hand, was surveying Johnson with an inquiring eye, and deciding that his task would not be easy. Johnson was plainly a canny individual.

"You must understand, of course, Mr. Johnson," went on Jarkins, smiling his best smile, "this visit of ours is unauthorized as far as Mr. Cowperwood is concerned. But I believe you will grant the importance of it, just the same. As you know, Greaves and Henshaw have been dealing with Traffic Electrical, for which I believe you act as solicitor."

"One of the solicitors," said Mr. Johnson, cautiously. "But it has been some time since I've been consulted by them."

"Quite so, quite so," returned Jarkins, "but I think you will be interested, nevertheless. You see, ours was the firm that brought Greaves and Henshaw and Mr. Cowperwood together. As you know, Mr. Cowperwood is an extremely wealthy man. He has been active in all kinds of traction matters in America. And he is rumored to be closing out his Chicago holdings for not less than twenty millions."

At the mention of this sum, Mr. Johnson pricked up his ears. Traffic was traffic—Chicago, London, or elsewhere—and a man who knew enough about it to have extracted twenty million dollars out of it must have some definite knowledge of what he was about. His interest was immediately apparent to Jarkins.

"That may be true," bluffed Mr. Johnson, a little testily, and seemingly unimpressed, "but just what has that to do with me? You must remember that I am merely one of the solicitors for Traffic Electrical, and have nothing whatsoever to do with either Mr. Greaves or Mr. Henshaw."

"But you are interested in the London underground situation in general, or so Mr. Kloorfain tells me," persisted Jarkins. "That is," he added diplomatically, "you represent people who are interested in the development of the underground system."

"I ventured to mention the fact, Mr. Johnson," interpolated Kloorfain here, "that you are referred to from time to time in the newspapers as representing the Metropolitan and the District, as well as the City and South London and the Central of London."

"That is true," returned Johnson, seemingly calm and reassured. "I do represent those companies in a legal way. But I'm still not clear as to what you wish. If it relates to the purchase or sale of anything in connection with the Charing Cross and Hampstead line, I am certainly not the person to see."

"If you will bear with me for just a minute," persisted Jarkins, leaning closer to Johnson. "The point is just this: that Mr. Cowperwood is divesting himself of all his Chicago street railway holdings, and without those to employ him, he will have nothing to do. He is not the kind of man who would want to quit. He has been working in Chicago, you know, for over twenty-five years. I don't mean he is running after an investment of any kind. Mr. Greaves and Mr. Henshaw found that out. They were brought to him by our firm: Jarkins, Kloorfain & Randolph. Mr. Kloorfain here is in charge of our London branch."

Johnson nodded and now listened attentively.

"Of course," continued Jarkins, "neither Mr. Kloorfain nor myself has the least authority from Mr. Cowperwood to speak for him. But we feel there is something in this London situation which, if put before him by the right person in the right way, might bring about something of great value to whomsoever was connected with it. For I know it to be a fact that Mr. Cowperwood rejected this Charing Cross line, not because he thought it might not pay, but because he was not offered a 51 per cent control, which he always insists on. And then, too, it appeared to him to be just a short branch line which had no important connection with the underground system as a whole, and so could only be operated as a small separate property. He is interested only in the traffic problems of an entire city."

Jarkins' voice now took on a note of flattery.

"I asked Mr. Kloorfain," he said, smoothly, "to take me to the one man who would know most about the London underground situation and grasp the importance of interesting Mr. Cowperwood. For if we understand things correctly," and here he eyed Mr. Johnson almost ominously, "we feel that the time has come to unify and modernize the entire system, and it is pretty well known that Mr. Cowperwood is a genius in the traction field. He is to be in London shortly, and we feel he should be met and talked to by someone who could make him see the need here for a man like him.

"If you do not care to go into the matter, Mr. Johnson," and here Jarkins was thinking of Stane and his rumored connections, "you may know someone who would, and perhaps advise us in regard to that person. Of course, we are brokers, and we would like to see Mr. Cowperwood interested, in order that we might come in for our share of the brokerage, which is naturally part of an undertaking like this."

Johnson sat at his desk and stared, not at either Jarkins or Kloorfain, but at the floor.

"Ahem!" he began. "Mr. Cowperwood is an American multimillionaire. He has had enormous experience in running street railways and elevated roads, I believe, in Chicago and elsewhere. I am supposed to interest him in solving the London underground problem. And if I do, I am supposed to pay you—or at least see that you are paid—for getting Mr. Cowperwood to help some other Londoners interested in the traction field to make money." He looked up, eyebrows lifted, while Jarkins stared knowingly but without deigning to comment.

"Very practical, I must say," continued Johnson, "and I don't doubt there are quite a few who might be benefited, and, again, who might not be. London underground problems are very great. Too many lines already planned, too many different companies to be harmonized, too many acts already acquired by speculators and promoters without a shilling between them." He stared depressingly at the two men. "A great deal of money would be required, millions of pounds, not less than twenty-five millions, I should say." He pressed his hands together almost sadly, so great was the financial weight of all this. "Of course, we are not unaware of Mr. Cowperwood over here. If I am not mistaken, there have been charges of various kinds made against him in Chicago—charges, I will admit, that should not stand in the way of the prosecution of a great public enterprise such as you two gentlemen are suggesting—but still, considering the conservatism of the English public . . ."

"Oh, you mean those political charges against his financial methods in Chicago," interjected Jarkins defiantly at this point. "Merely politics, the work of financial rivals, jealous because of his success."

"I know, I know," interrupted Mr. Johnson, still depressively. "Financial men everywhere naturally understand and discount that sort of opposition. At the same time, he would meet with opposition here. For this is a very conservative and tight little island. And we do not like outsiders to come in and manage our affairs for us. However, as you say, Mr. Cowperwood is plainly a very able and resourceful man. Whether there are people here who might care to join with him, I cannot say. Certainly I know that there are few, if any, who would be willing to grant him the sole financial control of such a system as you speak of," and here he got up and brushed from his trousers and waistcoat some flecks of imaginary dust. "He has, you say, rejected the Greaves and Henshaw offer?" he added.

"He has," echoed both Jarkins and Kloorfain.

"But what were their exact terms?"

Jarkins explained.

"I see, I see. So they wished to retain their contract and 50 per cent. Well, until I have had time to think about this and consult with one or two of my associates, I shall be unable to offer an opinion one way or the other. However," he added, "it may be worth while for some of the leading investors to talk with him when he gets here."

Actually, by now, Johnson was of the opinion that Cowperwood was sending these two men about to spy out the situation. In addition, however, he was doubtful as to whether Cowperwood, being an American, and however great his wealth, would ever be able to wrest from the present management even so much as a 50 per cent division. It would be extremely difficult for him to enter this field. At the same time, considering his own and Stane's investments, and the Charing Cross still likely to be thrown back on Traffic Electrical, and so bring about the loss of more money for its investors, well . . .

He addressed the two men now in a tone of finality.

"I shall have to think the matter over, gentlemen. Call me again, say next Tuesday or Wednesday, and I will tell you finally whether I can be of help to you."

And with that he led the way to the door and pulled a bell in order that an office boy might show his visitors to the street door. After they had gone, he walked to one of the windows that looked down into the ancient court, where the April sun was still brightly shining. He had a habit, when thinking, of placing his tongue in his cheek and clasping his hands in a prayerful position, fingers down. In this instance he stood so for some time, staring out the window.

And outside in Storey Street, Kloorfain and Jarkins were saying, one to the other: "Excellent! Very shrewd fellow, that . . . but really interested . . . it's a way out for them, if only they have the sense to see it . . ."

"But that Chicago business! I knew it would come up!" exclaimed Jarkins. "It always does: that prison record of his, or his interest in women . . . as though that made any difference in this case."

"Stupid! Unbelievably stupid!" echoed Kloorfain.

"Just the same, something will have to be done about it. We'll have to fix the press some way," said Jarkins.

"Let me tell you one thing," concluded Kloorfain. "If any of these wealthy people over here should go into this with Cowperwood, they'd soon close down on all unfavorable publicity. Our laws are different from yours, you know. Here, the truer the scandal, the more libelous it is. And it becomes very dangerous to say anything unless the biggest people want it said. In your country, apparently, it's just the other way. But I know most of the financial editors on the papers here, and if it should become necessary to hush things up, I think it could be arranged."

Chapter 20

THE sum total of what Jarkins and Kloorfain achieved in their approach to Johnson was well set forth in a conversation which took place that same afternoon between Johnson and Lord Stane in Stane's office on the ground floor of the Storey Street building.

It should be said, in this connection, that it was Johnson's commercial honesty and his utterly practical ideas that caused Stane to prize him. For Johnson, as Stane always told himself, was the embodiment of a self-conscious religious and moral rectitude which would not allow him to err too far on the side of cunning and sheer legal trickery, however much he might be tempted to gain success for himself. A stickler for the law, he could still search for all the loopholes with the intention of using them, either to his own advantage or the discomfiture of his adversaries. "His honor compels him to keep books, but it allows him to send out large due bills," someone had once said of him. And Stane accepted that as a fair picture. At the same time, he liked him for his very eccentricities and quite frequently laughed over his seemingly honest interest in the International Epworth League, its Sunday-school conventions, and his rigid adherence to a total abstinence from liquor in any form. In money matters, he was not petty. He gave quite liberally for the size of his income to churches, Sunday schools, hospitals, and a Southwark institute for the blind, of which he was one of the board of managers and also its unpaid counsel.

For Stane personally, and for a very modest charge, Johnson looked after his investments, insurance rates, and whatsoever legal problems might beset him. They also discussed together politics and the world's international problems, and usually, as Stane noted, Johnson remained quite close to reality in all matters. Of art, architecture, poetry, letters, women, and the non-acquisitive and purely social pleasures, however, he knew nothing. He once confessed to Stane years before, when both were much younger, that he had no head for such things. "I was brought up under circumstances which did not permit my knowing anything about them," he said. "It pleases me, of course, to see my boys at Eton and my girl at Bedford, and personally I would not deny them any social tastes they may develop. But as for myself, well, I am a solicitor, and very glad to be as well placed as I am."

Young Stane had smiled, for he liked the rugged realism of this statement. At the same time, he was content that they should travel different social levels, with only now and then an invitation on the part of Stane to Johnson to visit his family estate in Tregasal or his handsome old house in Berkeley Square, but nearly always on business.

On this particular occasion Johnson found Stane reclining in a round-armed, high-backed, comfortable Chippendale chair, his long legs stretched out and his feet on the heavy mahogany desk before him. He was wearing well-cut tweeds, sand-colored, a light coffee-colored shirt and a dark orange tie, and from time to time he nonchalantly flicked the ashes from a cigarette he was smoking. He was studying a De Beers South African Diamond Mine report, in which company he was personally interested. Some twenty shares he held, as he reflected, were yielding him approximately two hundred pounds annually. He had a long, sallow face, with a large and slightly beaked nose, low forehead, sharp dark eyes, and a large and decidedly genial mouth and slightly defiant chin.

"So there you are!" he called out as Johnson entered after knocking at the door. "Well, what's up with you now, you honest old Methodist. I read something, this morning, about that address of yours, in Stickney, I believe."

"Oh, that," retorted Johnson, not a little pleased that Stane should have heard of it, and rather nervously buttoning his crinkled black alpaca office coat. "There's some dispute between the ministers of our different churches of that district, and I went down to arbitrate between them. They called for a little address afterward, and I took the occasion to lecture them on their conduct." He drew himself up, quite dictatorially and proudly, as he recalled it. Stane noted the mood.

"The trouble with you, Johnson," he went on lightly, "is that you should either be in Parliament, or on the bench. But if you'll take my advice, you'll make it Parliament first and the bench afterward. We need you too much around here to let you go on the bench yet." He smiled cordially and really quite affectionately on Johnson, who in turn, flattered and warmed by the remark, beamed appreciatively.

"Well, as you know, I've been thinking of Parliament for a long time. There are so many things that come up in connection with our work here that might be helped by my presence there. Rider and Bullock are constantly talking of it. In fact, Rider insists on my standing in the by-election in his district in September. He seems to think I can win if I make a few addresses."

"And why not? Who else better? And Rider has great influence there, as you know. I advise you to do it. And if I can be of any service to you, I or any of my friends, all you need to do is to call on me. I'll be delighted."

"That's certainly kind of you and I appreciate it," replied Johnson. "Besides," and here his tone grew at once more confidential, "there's something that came up in my office this morning which may have some bearing on this." He paused, took out his handkerchief and cleared his nose, while Stane contemplated him interestedly.

"Well, what's the secret?"

"I've just had two men in my office: Willard Jarkins, an American, and Willem Kloorfain, a Dutchman. They are agents and brokers, Kloorfain in London and Jarkins in New York. They've been telling me something interesting. You know that £30,000 option we gave to Greaves and Henshaw?"

Stane, half-curious and slightly amused by Johnson's manner, withdrew his legs from his desk, put down the report he was examining, and looking hard at Johnson said: "That damn Traffic Electrical! What about it?"

"It appears," went on Johnson, "that they went to New York quite recently to interview this multimillionaire Cowperwood. It also appears that they only offered him a half-interest in that £30,000 option for his services in raising the money with which to build the road." Johnson chortled dryly. "And later, of course, he was to pay them a £100,000 for their services as engineers." Both men were unable to repress an additional chuckle at this. "Of course," continued Johnson, "he refused it. At the same time, it appears that what he really wants is to secure complete control; that or nothing. It seems, or so these people say, he expressed an interest in some such combination of lines as you and I have been thinking of here for the past ten years. As you know, he's being driven out of Chicago."

"Yes, I know," said Stane.

"Well, in addition to that, I've just been reading an account of him which these fellows left with me. Here it is," and he extracted from his pocket a full page from the New York *Sun,* the center of which carried a large and quite accurate pen-and-ink drawing of Cowperwood.

Stane unfolded the page and studied the picture, after which he looked up at Johnson. "Not a bad-looking fellow, what? Lots of go!" He then studied a printed chart of some of Cowperwood's holdings. "Two hundred and fifty miles . . . and all in twenty years." Then he concentrated on a paragraph relating to Cowperwood's New York house, after which he added: "Seems to be a bit of a connoisseur, too."

"There's a paragraph there," interjected Johnson, "that tells about the cause of his troubles in Chicago; mostly political and social, I take it." He waited while Stane read that.

"My word, what a fight!" commented Stane after reading for a moment or two. "I see they estimate his holdings at twenty millions."

"All of that, according to these two brokers. But the most interesting thing they had to report was that he is to be here within a week or two. And what they want is for me to meet with him, in order to discuss not only this Charing Cross line, which they somehow feel we are going to have to take back, but some such general system as we had in mind."

"But these fellows Jarkins and Kloorfain," queried Stane, "who are they, anyway? Friends of Cowperwood?"

"Not at all, not at all," explained Johnson quickly. "On the contrary, as they confess, they are mere bankers' agents out for a commission, either from Greaves and Henshaw, or Cowperwood, or us, or anyone they can interest; maybe all of us together. They do not represent the man in any way."

Stane shrugged his shoulders ironically.

"It seems," went on Johnson, "they've heard from some source that we are interested in a plan of unification, and they'd like me to get together a lot of investors and interest them in Mr. Cowperwood as a leader and then present this unification idea in such a way as to interest him. For that they want a commission, of course."

Stane stared amusedly. "How frightfully jolly for everybody!"

"Of course, I declined that part of it," continued Johnson, warily. "But I've been thinking that there might be something more there than appears on the surface. There might be some real inquiry on the part of Cowperwood that you and I might want to consider. For there's still that Charing Cross millstone around our necks. Of course, I know very well no American millionaire is going to be allowed to come in here and take charge of our undergrounds. Still, it is possible that he might be joined up with a group here—yourself, Lord Ettinge, and Haddonfield—and possibly a joint form of control worked out." He paused to observe the effect of this on Stane.

"Quite so, Elverson, quite so," commented Stane. "If some of the investors are still as much interested as they were a few years ago, we might get them to come back into the fight. Cowperwood couldn't very well edge in here without them."

He got up and walked to one of the windows and looked out, while Johnson proceeded to explain that Jarkins and Kloorfain were to call back in a few days for his decision, and might it not be a good idea to caution them that if they expected to deal with himself or anyone he might be able to influence, they would have to maintain the strictest secrecy and leave everything to him.

"Righto!" said Stane.

This plan, as Johnson now added, would necessarily include not only the Charing Cross line but the Traffic Electrical as the sole owner, or at least as agent for it. Then once Stane and he had sounded out Haddonfield and Ettinge and others, they could say finally whether even a tentative agreement might be made. After that, it was entirely possible that Cowperwood would prefer to deal with Stane and himself and these other investors rather than with Jarkins and Kloorfain or Greaves and Henshaw, who, of themselves, could do nothing and hence should be dismissed as mere peddlers.

And with this Stane fully agreed. But before they had finished talking, it was already dark. A London fog was on. Stane recalled a tea, Johnson a legal conference. And so they parted, with a new elation in the hearts of both.

Accordingly, three days later—the length of time he considered necessary to impress them with his own importance—Johnson sent for Jarkins and Kloorfain and announced that he had laid the matter before some of his friends, and finding them not averse to further knowledge of what was in Cowperwood's mind, he would, on invitation from Mr. Cowperwood, but not otherwise, see and confer with him. But only on condition that no prior contacts or arrangements of any kind were made by him. For the men he would try to interest were investors who would, under no circumstances, allow themselves to be trifled with.

With this statement Mr. Johnson rested, while Jarkins and Kloorfain hurried to the nearest cable office to inform Cowperwood of the significant result they had achieved and urge him by all means to come to London; meanwhile, would he be so kind as to suspend consideration of any other proposal, since the coming conference, if it could be brought about, would be all-inclusive in its nature.

The cablegram caused Cowperwood to smile, remembering, as he did, his severe castigation of Jarkins. However, he cabled back that he was very busy at the moment but planned to sail around April fifteenth, and upon his arrival would be glad to see them and hear further as to the nature of their suggestion. He also cabled Sippens in code that he was coming to London, and informed him of his rejection of the Greaves and Henshaw offer; however, perhaps Sippens could arrange it so that they might hear of his pending arrival, since, apart from them, a large and inclusive proposition, entirely unrelated to their Charing Cross line, was to be presented to him. This information might bring them to their senses and cause them to make an offer which could be accepted before any other plan could be presented to him. In that case, he would have a weapon in his possession which might serve to hold his new counsellors in bounds.

And all this time he was also arranging with Berenice, Aileen, and Tollifer for their respective parts in his future plans.

Chapter 21 MEANWHILE, though still darkly dubious within the depths of her emotional self, Aileen, throughout all this, could not fail to be impressed by Cowperwood's sudden change of attitude. For, somewhat ebullient because of the London idea, Berenice, the prospective change of scene, and all, Cowperwood found himself confiding in Aileen. He was taking her with him to England. His will, the stewardship of his house, the guardianship of his contemplated bequests, all arranged themselves in her mind as the rather obvious consequences of his Chicago defeat. Life, as she now saw it, had chosen to deal him a somewhat sobering blow, and at a time in his career when it would naturally be most effective. He had returned to her, or was by way of returning. And this one fact was almost sufficient to restore her faith in love and the validity of other human emotions.

And so she threw herself into extravagant preparations for the journey. She shopped. She visited the dressmaker, the milliner, and the lingerie shops, and luggage of the latest design was purchased. Once more she was demonstrating to her own satisfaction, and to Cowperwood's by this time accustomed dismay, her exaggerated faith in the effect of lavish display. Informed that they were to occupy the finest suite on the *Kaiser Wilhelm der Grosse,* sailing on the following Friday, she indulged in lingerie befitting a bride, although well she knew that all intimate relations between herself and her husband were a closed book.

At about the same time, Tollifer, whose plans for meeting Aileen had thus far failed, was greatly relieved to find in his mail a registered envelope containing the deck plans of this same liner, his ticket, and, to his even greater delight and satisfaction, $3000 in cash—the effect of which was instantly reflected in Tollifer's increased enthusiasm and interest for his new assignment. For now he was determined to make a favorable impression on Cowperwood, a man who, as he could see, was well grounded in the business of getting what he wanted from life. And on looking hurriedly through the newspapers he soon verified what he already suspected, which was that the Cowperwoods would also be aboard the *Kaiser Wilhem der Grosse* when it sailed on Friday.

Berenice, having learned from Cowperwood all of his movements thus far, announced her intention of sailing, with her mother, on the *Saxonia,* a Cunard liner, which left two days ahead of the *Kaiser Wilhelm.* They would be in London awaiting him at Claridge's, a hotel with which they were already familiar.

Plagued by the press as to his plans, Cowperwood informed reporters that he and his wife were sailing for the Continent for a long summer vacation; that he was no longer interested in Chicago, and was not, in fact, contemplating any immediate business ventures.

This announcement drew much editorial comment regarding his career, his genius, the folly of his retirement in view of his wealth, skill, and strength. He welcomed the publicity, because in addition to coming as an unexpected tribute, at the same time it darkened his movements and gave him ample time to decide on his course.

And thereafter, the day of sailing. And Aileen walking the deck with the air of one to whom supremacy in all things was a mere commonplace.

As for Tollifer, now that he was aboard and faced with his real task, he was both physically and mentally tense. Cowperwood, observing him here and there, paid no least attention to him nor gave any sign of knowing him. Conscious of this, Tollifer paraded the decks, observing Aileen without appearing to, and noting that she observed him, and with interest. She was too showy, too lacking in taste and restraint, to his way of thinking. He occupied a minor stateroom on B deck, but dined at the captain's table, while Aileen and Cowperwood dined together in their own suite. But the captain, very much aware of the presence of the Cowperwoods and anxious to make capital of the fact for himself as well as the ship, and quickly discovering that Tollifer was a most engaging person, impressed upon him the significance of these distinguished passengers and offered to arrange an introduction to them.

Therefore, on the second day out, Captain Heinrich Schreiber sent his compliments to Mr. and Mrs. Cowperwood, asking if he could be of any service. Perhaps Mr. Cowperwood might like to be escorted over the ship. There were several admirers whom he would like to present, along with himself—at the convenience of Mr. Cowperwood, of course.

Whereupon Cowperwood, sensing the possible machinations of Tollifer, agreed with Aileen that it might be pleasant to receive the interested passengers, and welcomed the arrival of the captain, along with Mr. Wilson Styles, playwright; C. B. Courtright, Governor of Arkansas; Mr. Bruce Tollifer, New York society man; and Alassandra Givens, of the same city, sailing to join her sister in London. Recalling her father as a man of some social importance, and noting that Alassandra was exceedingly attractive, Tollifer had introduced himself to her as a friend of some of her friends, and Alassandra, captivated, was pleased to allow the lie.

The impromptu reception delighted Aileen. As they entered the suite, she rose from a chair in which she had been sitting reading a magazine, and stood beside her husband to greet the party. Cowperwood's eyes immediately noted Tollifer, also his companion, Miss Givens, whose smart appearance and unmistakable air of breeding impressed him. Aileen quickly singled out Tollifer, who took his introduction to the Cowperwoods as if to total strangers.

"It's such a pleasure to meet the wife of so remarkable a man as Mr. Cowperwood," he told Aileen. "I suppose you are off for the Continent."

"We're going to London first," replied Aileen, "and later to Paris and the Continent. My husband always has a lot of financial affairs to look after wherever he goes."

"Quite likely, from all I have read." He smiled captivatingly. "Living with so versatile a man must be a great experience, Mrs. Cowperwood. By George, almost a business!"

"You are certainly right there," said Aileen. "It *is* almost a business." And flattered by her seeming importance, she evoked a confiding smile in return.

"Will you be spending a few days in Paris?" he queried.

"Oh, yes, indeed! I don't know just what my husband's plans will be after he gets to London, but I intend to run over for a few days."

"I am going to Paris for the races, myself. Maybe I'll see you there. Perhaps if you are there at the same time and free, we could spend an afternoon together."

"Oh, that would be delightful!" Aileen's eyes were alight because of his interest. The attention of such an attractive man as this must certainly tend to raise her in the esteem of Cowperwood. "But you haven't talked to my husband. Shall we go over?" And with Tollifer beside her she walked across the room to where Cowperwood was standing talking with the captain and Mr. Courtright.

"Listen, Frank," she said, lightly, "here's another of your admirers." And to Tollifer: "I find it's impossible to keep the spotlight from him, Mr. Tollifer."

Cowperwood bent on him the blandest of glances, saying: "Well, one can't have too many admirers. Are you a part of the spring flight to the Continent, Mr. Tollifer?" There was no least suggestion of acting. And suiting his method to Cowperwood's, Tollifer smiled and replied easily:

"Yes, I suppose I am. I have friends in London and Paris, and I've been thinking of doing some of the watering places later on. A friend of mine has a place in Brittany." And turning to Aileen, he added: "By the way, you should really see that, Mrs. Cowperwood. It's very lovely."

"Well, I'd certainly like to," said Aileen, looking at Cowperwood. "Do you suppose our plans could be made to include Brittany this summer, Frank?"

"Possibly. Hardly for me, though, with all I have to do. Still, we might arrange for a short visit," he added, encouragingly. "How long are you to be in London, Mr. Tollifer?"

"Just at the moment my plans are a little uncertain," Tollifer answered, calmly. "It may be a week, or a little longer."

At this point, Alassandra, bored by Mr. Styles, who was trying to make an impression, came forward, determined to end this visit. She walked up to Tollifer, and said:

"Aren't you forgetting our engagement, Bruce?"

"Oh, yes. Will you excuse us? We really must leave." And turning to Aileen, he added: "I hope we shall see more of each other, Mrs. Cowperwood."

To which Aileen, venomously irritated by the aloofness and presumptuous manner of this much too attractive young lady, exclaimed: "Oh, yes, indeed, Mr. Tollifer, it will be a pleasure!" And then noting a supercilious smile on the face of Miss Givens, she added: "Sorry you have to leave, Miss . . . ah . . . Miss . . ." whereupon Tollifer instantly interjected: "Miss Givens."

"Oh, yes," continued Aileen, "I didn't get the name."

But Alassandra, dismissing the snub with a lift of her eyebrows, took Tollifer's arm and, smiling a farewell to Cowperwood, left the room.

Once they were alone, Aileen began at once to unburden her feelings. "I hate these little social upstarts, without a thing except their family connections, so ready to upstage everybody else, or try to, at least!" she exclaimed.

"But, Aileen," soothed Cowperwood, "how often have I told you, everyone makes the most of what he has. In her case, she attaches great significance to her social position, and that's why she's so vicious about it. She's not really important, just silly. Why let her irritate you? Please don't."

At the moment he was mentally contrasting Aileen with Berenice. How completely Berenice would have disposed of Alassandra!

"Well, anyhow," concluded Aileen, defiantly, "Mr. Tollifer is gracious and charming enough. And his position is quite as good as hers, I should judge. Don't you think so?"

"I certainly haven't any reason to think otherwise," replied Cowperwood, inwardly smiling, and yet not so much ironically as sadly, because of Aileen's simplicity and innocence in regard to all this. "At least Miss Givens appears to admire Mr. Tollifer. So if you accept her as socially somebody, I suppose you will have to accept him in the same way," he said.

"Well, he has sense enough to be polite, and that's more than she has, or almost any woman when it comes to another woman!"

"The trouble with women, Aileen, is that they are all in the same line of business. Men, or rather, their interests, are more diversified."

"Just the same, I like Mr. Tollifer, and I certainly don't like that girl at all!"

"Well, you don't have to know her. And as for him, there's no reason why we shouldn't be agreeable to him, if you wish. Remember, I want you to be happy on this trip." And here he smiled on her engagingly.

Slyly he contemplated her an hour later as she was changing her dress for an afternoon walk on the upper deck. She was now so plainly interested in herself and in life. It was really wonderful, he thought, how much one could accomplish with another by taking due thought and consideration of the other's weaknesses, tastes, and dreams.

But was it not possible that Berenice was working on him in exactly the same way? She was entirely capable of it. And he would admire her for it as now, in a light way, he was admiring himself.

Chapter 22 THE few remaining days on the boat were spent by Tollifer in planning and executing such moves as might insinuate himself into Aileen's good graces. Among other things, he arranged two card parties, being careful to exclude Miss Givens. He did include, however, a rather well-known actress, a young western banker who was by no means averse to meeting Cowperwood's wife, and a young widow from Buffalo who was sure that she was improving her social connections by associating with anyone of Tollifer's looks and manners, and in consequence anyone whom he considered worth while.

To say that Aileen was heartened by this pleasant and most unexpected social development, and in particular the obvious interest of Tollifer, is rather less than the truth. And all the more so because Cowperwood, while not participating, appeared to consider the connection satisfactory enough. In fact, he suggested that perhaps after they arrived in London and were settled at the Cecil, she might like to invite Tollifer and some of his friends for tea or dinner. He would not mind stopping in for a moment, if he had the time. And Aileen, grateful for the opportunity, seized upon it, not so much in the manner or mood of one seeking to develop a liaison, but rather as if she were eager to prove that she was still capable of such contacts and associations as might be pleasing to him.

Plainly, thought Cowperwood, Tollifer might well be left to his own devices. For obviously he was very clever, diplomatic, and versed in all necessary social graces. Supposing he did go so far as to make love to Aileen with the idea of estranging her and capturing some portion of her personal wealth by marriage? He did not believe he would be successful; Aileen would never fall seriously in love with anyone else.

As for Tollifer, plagued at times by the underhandedness of the intrigue, he felt it to be one of the luckiest breaks that had thus far come into his frustrated life. For if he could share the wages of actresses, as he so recently had done, most surely he could take money for playing social mentor, guide, and companion to this woman. To be sure, she was gauche, likely to do the wrong thing at times, too anxious to please, and might certainly be more tastefully dressed and coached in certain airs and pretensions which would stand her in good stead. But at least she was friendly and grateful, and it was entirely possible that he might do much for her.

Before starting on this trip he had inquired around and discovered that in Cowperwood's absence Aileen was accustomed to indulge in decidedly commonplace philanderings, which, regardless of her neutral social position, could only tend to degrade both Cowperwood and herself. How was it, he asked himself, that Cowperwood should be willing to allow this? Yet after meeting her, and thinking over the history of her husband, he was inclined to feel that after all Cowperwood was taking the wisest course. For she was certainly a woman of force and determination, and in any struggle for freedom which her husband might undertake, she would probably leave no stone unturned to defeat if not intentionally injure him.

On the other hand, of course, there was the possibility that Cowperwood might one day turn on him and, for real or trumped-up reasons, accuse him of relations with her which would furnish him the means of getting rid of her. And yet, if he could prove that Cowperwood had suborned him to this scheme, the revelation would certainly not be any more pleasant for Cowperwood than it would be for him. So what, personally, had he to lose? Most certainly he could arrange his conduct and Aileen's in such a way as to avoid charges on the part of her husband.

And, he could do much for her. He had noticed on this trip that she liked to drink rather freely. He would have to guard her against such a weakness. Next, there was the matter of her clothes. There were dressmakers in Paris who would be grateful to him for the privilege of dressing her properly. Lastly, and, of course, with her money, it would not be difficult to arrange amusing adventures for her—Aix-les-Bains, Biarritz, Dieppe, Cannes, Nice, Monte Carlo—assuming that she came to have faith in him. He could invite old friends, pay old debts, make new contacts!

Lying in his stateroom, smoking a cigarette and sipping a highball, he speculated as to all this. This cabin! This $200-a-week job! And the $3,000!

Chapter 23

THE *Kaiser Wilhelm der Grosse* landed the passengers for Southampton on a hazy April morning, the sun dimly piercing an English fog. From an upper deck, Cowperwood, wearing a smart gray business suit, surveyed the quiet harbor and the placid houses on the shore beyond. Aileen stood beside him, dressed in her best spring finery. Hovering about were her maid, Williams; Cowperwood's valet; and his personal secretary, Jamieson. On the dock below stood Jarkins and Kloorfain, also a group of reporters anxious to question Cowperwood concerning a rumor—concocted by Jarkins—that he was com-

ing to England to buy a distinguished art collection, the property
of a peer of whom Cowperwood had never heard.

At the last moment Tollifer had announced—a very tactful move
on his part, as Cowperwood felt—that he was not leaving the boat
with them but was going on to Cherbourg and then to Paris.
However, as he also explained in his most casual manner, and for
Aileen's benefit, he would come to London the following Monday
or Tuesday, when he hoped to have the pleasure of seeing the
Cowperwoods before they left for the Continent. At this Aileen
looked at Cowperwood for a glance of approval, and, receiving it,
said they would be glad to have him call on them at the Cecil.

At this moment Cowperwood was enjoying to the fullest extent
the sense of importance and well-being surrounding him. Once he
had landed and disposed of Aileen, there would be Berenice, with
her mother, at Claridge's awaiting him. He actually felt young:
Ulysses upon a new and truly mysterious voyage! His feelings were
heightened also by the fact that in the midst of all this there arrived
a messenger with a telegram in Spanish: "The sun shines on the
England you step upon. It is a silver door that opens upon your
greatest achievement and your greatest fame. The sea has been
grey without you. Oro del Oro." It was from Berenice, of course,
and he smiled to himself at the thought of seeing her.

And now the reporters. "Where was he bound for?" "Had he
divested himself of all of his Chicago holdings?" "Was it true that
he had come to England to buy a famous private art collection, as
had been rumored?" To all of which questions, he vouchsafed
guarded but smiling replies. To be exact, he was seeking a holiday
of some duration, since it had been so long since he had had one,
he explained. No, he had not gotten rid of his Chicago holdings;
he was merely rearranging them. No, he had not come to buy the
Fairbanks collection. He had once seen it and admired it enormously.
But he had not even heard that it was for sale.

Throughout all this Aileen posed near at hand, pleased at the
revival of her former grandeur. The *Illustrated News* had sent a
man to make a sketch of her.

At the first lull in the buzz of talk, however, Jarkins, with Kloorfain at his elbow, rushed forward to pay his respects and to ask
Cowperwood not to make any statements until he had an opportu-

nity to talk to him. To which Cowperwood replied, "Very well, if you wish."

After that, at the hotel, Jamieson reporting on various telegrams which had been received. Also, there was Mr. Sippens in Room 741, waiting to be called. Then there was a message from Lord Haddonfield, whom Cowperwood had met years before in Chicago —he would like to have the pleasure of entertaining the Cowperwoods over the week end. Also, a certain distinguished South African banker—a Jewish gentleman—then in London, asked him to luncheon in order to talk of important matters relating to South Africa. The German Ambassador sent his compliments and would be happy if Mr. Cowperwood would have dinner with him at the Embassy at his convenience. From Paris a message from Mr. Dolan, of Philadelphia: "If you go through this burg without doing the town with me, I'll have you stopped at the border. Remember, I know as much about you as you know about me."

The wings of fortune could be heard whirring over his head.

Later, having seen Aileen comfortably established in her suite, he sent for Sippens and learned from him all that he had to report. There was no doubt, Sippens said, eager and birdlike in a new spring suit, that Greaves and Henshaw were at their wits' end. And yet there was no better opening wedge for Cowperwood than the act for the line which they controlled. He would go over the proposed route with him the next day. Far more important, though, was the ultimate control of this central loop, since on that depended any general system. The Charing Cross could most profitably be joined with the loop, and if he owned or controlled that, he would be in a far better position to move in connection with the loop and some other lines. Besides, there were many acts floating about, which had been secured by speculators with the hope of finding operators and investors afterward, and these might all be investigated.

"It's a question, yes, of how to go about all this," said Cowperwood, thoughtfully. "You say Greaves and Henshaw are in a mess, but they haven't approached me yet. In the meantime, Jarkins has apparently talked to this fellow Johnson, of Traffic Electrical, and Johnson agreed with him that if I did nothing until he had a chance to bring together a group that appears to be interested in this central loop—your man, Stane, I assume, is one of them—he would arrange for me to meet them all and talk this over, the entire loop scheme, I suppose. But that would mean, I assume, that I would have to ignore Greaves and Henshaw and let this Charing Cross line drop back into Traffic Electrical by default, which is just what I don't want to do. It would give them an extra club to swing over me."

But at that Sippens was on his feet in an instant.

"Don't you do that, Chief!" he fairly squeaked. "Don't you do that! You'll be sorry if you do. These people over here stick together like glue! They'll fight each other singly, but when it comes to a foreigner, they'll combine and you'll be made to pay dearly unless you have something to fight them with. Better wait until tomorrow or the next day and see whether you hear from Greaves and Henshaw. They're sure to read of your arrival in today's papers, and, unless I miss my guess, they'll get in touch with you, for they haven't a thing to gain by waiting, not a thing. Tell Jarkins to stay away from Johnson, and you do whatever you have to do, but first come with me to look over this Charing Cross route."

But at that moment Jamieson, who was occupying a room next door, entered with a letter brought by hand. Noting the name on the outside of the envelope, Cowperwood smiled, and then, after reading the letter, turned it over to Sippens.

"There you are, De Sota! Now, what about that?" he queried, genially.

The letter was from Greaves and Henshaw, and read:

DEAR MR. COWPERWOOD:

We note in today's paper your arrival in London. If convenient and of interest to you, we would like to arrange an appointment, preferably for Monday or Tuesday of next week. Our purpose is, of course, to discuss the matter laid before you in New York about March 15th last.

Felicitating you upon your safe arrival, and wishing you a very pleasant stay, we are

Cordially yours,
Greaves and Henshaw
per Montague Greaves

Sippens snapped his fingers triumphantly. "There! What did I tell you?" he fairly cackled. "Bringing it to you on your own terms. And the finest route in all London. With that in your bag, Chief, you can afford to sit back and wait, particularly if you start picking up some of these other options that are floating around, for they'll hear of it and have to come to you. This fellow Johnson! He's got a nerve, asking you to do nothing until after you see him," he added, a little sourly, for already he had heard that Johnson was an assured and dictatorial person, and he was prepared not to like him. "Of course, he has some good connections," he continued, "he and this fellow Stane. But without your money and ability and experience, what can they do? They couldn't even swing this Charing Cross line, let alone these others! And they won't, without you!"

"You're probably right, De Sota," said Cowperwood, smiling genially on his loyal associate. "I'll see Greaves and Henshaw, probably on Tuesday, and you may be sure that I won't let anything slip through my fingers. How about tomorrow afternoon for that ride over the Charing Cross? I suppose I ought to see that and these loop lines at one and the same time."

"Great, Chief! How about one o'clock? I can show you everything and have you back here by five."

"Good! Only, just a moment. Do you remember Haddonfield, Lord Haddonfield, who came out to Chicago a few years ago and created such a stir out there? The Palmers, the Fields, the Lesters, were all running after him, remember? I entertained him out at my place, too. Sporty, jaunty type."

"Sure, sure! I remember," returned Sippens. "Wanted to go into the packing business, I believe."

"And into my business, too. I guess I never told you that."

"No, you never did," said Sippens, interestedly.

"Well, anyhow, I had a telegram from him this morning. Wants me to come to his country place—Shropshire, I believe—over this coming week end." He picked up a telegram from his desk. "Beriton Manor, Shropshire."

"That's interesting. He's one of the people connected with the City and South London. Stockholder, or director, or something. I'll know all about him tomorrow. Maybe he's in on this underground development and wants to see you about that. If so, and he's friendly, he's certainly a good man for you. Stranger in a strange land, you know."

"Yes, I know," said Cowperwood. "It may not be a bad idea. I think I'll go. You see what you can find out, and we'll meet here at one."

As Sippens bustled out, Jamieson entered with more notes, but Cowperwood waved him away. "Nothing more until Monday, Jamieson. Write Greaves and Henshaw and say I'll be pleased to meet them here on Tuesday at eleven. Get hold of Jarkins and tell him to do nothing until he hears from me. Wire this Lord Haddonfield that Mr. and Mrs. Cowperwood will be pleased to accept his invitation, and get the directions and the tickets. If anything more comes up, just put it on my desk and I'll see it tomorrow."

He strode out the door, and into the elevator, and once outside, hailed a hansom. Although he announced Oxford Street as his destination, he had not ridden two blocks before he pushed up the lid at the top and hailed the driver, calling: "Oxford and Yewberry Streets, left-hand corner."

And once there, stepped out and walked in a roundabout way to Claridge's.

Chapter 24 COWPERWOOD'S ATTITUDE toward Berenice at this time was a mixture of father and lover. His greater age and unchanging admiration for her mentality and beauty caused him to wish to protect and develop her aesthetically. At the same time, and that decidedly, he shared her sensual emotions, although sensing at times an oddness about the relation, since he could not publicly harmonize his sixty years with her extreme youth. On the other hand, privately, her practical prevision, which so often seemed to match his own, gave him a sense of added strength as well as pride. For her independence and force united not so much with his thoughts of material self-aggrandizement as with that portion of its possible fruits which might by her be utilized to achieve temperamental and social perfection. It explained his presence here in London and gave it real weight. Now, finding her buoyant and enthusiastic as ever, as he took her in his arms he actually absorbed not a little of her gaiety and confidence.

"Welcome to London!" were her first words. "So Caesar has crossed the Rubicon!"

"Thanks, Bevy," he said, releasing her. "I got your message, too, and treasure it. But let me look at you. Walk across the room!"

He surveyed her with intense satisfaction as, smiling an ironic smile, she stepped away and walked, posing in the manner of a fashion model, finally curtseying, and saying: "Direct from Madame Sari! The price is a mere—secret!" and she pouted her lips.

She was wearing a deep-blue velvet frock, cut princess style, with tiny pearls outlining the neck and girdle.

Cowperwood took her hand and led her to a small sofa, just large enough for the two of them. "Exquisite!" he said. "I can't tell you how glad I am to be with you again." He then inquired after her mother, and continued: "This is a new sensation for me, Bevy. I never really cared much for London before, but this time, knowing you were to be here, I found myself delighting in the sight of it."

"And what else?" she asked.

"And seeing you, of course," he beamed, and kissed her, touching her eyes, hair, mouth with his lips and fingers until at last she cautioned him that there was to be no love-making until later. Forced to accept this for the moment, he began giving a brisk account of his passage and all that had occurred.

"Aileen is with me at the Cecil," he went on. "She has just been sketched for the papers. And your friend Tollifer did a great deal, I must say, to make things agreeable for her."

"*My* friend! I don't know him!"

"Of course, you don't, but, anyway, he turns out to be a very clever fellow. You should have seen him when he came to me in New York and again on the boat. Aladdin and the wonderful lamp called money! By the way, he went on to Paris, partially to cover his tracks, I take it. I have seen to it, of course, that he is amply supplied with cash for the present."

"You met him on the boat?" queried Berenice.

"Yes, he was introduced by the captain. But then, he is just the sort of person who could arrange that sort of thing for himself. And he appears to have a positive genius for ingratiating himself with the ladies. He practically monopolized all of the attractive ones."

"With you there? Do you expect me to believe that?"

"A miracle, I admit, but the man is uncanny. He seemed to sense exactly what was needed. I personally saw very little of him, but he managed to impress Aileen—so much so that she wants to have him dine with us."

He looked solemnly at Berenice, and she in turn gazed congratu-latingly upon him, adding, after a moment: "I'm glad; I really am. She needs just such a change as this. She should have had it long ago."

"I agree," said Cowperwood. "Since I can't be to her what she would like me to be, why not someone else? Anyway, I hope he keeps his head, and I'm rather inclined to think he will. Aileen is already planning to go to Paris to shop. So things are going well enough, I think."

"Very well," said Berenice, smiling. "It looks as though our plans might work out. So who is to blame?"

"Well, not you, and not me. It's one of those things that have to be—like your coming to me last Christmas when I least expected you."

He began caressing her again, but, interested in her own plans, she resisted him, saying: "Now, now, I want to hear about London, and then I have something to tell you."

"London? Everything looks most promising so far. I told you in New York about those two men, Greaves and Henshaw, and how I turned them down. Well, just now at the hotel, before I left, there was a letter from them. They want to see me, and I have an appointment with them. As for the larger plan, there is a group here with whom I am planning to talk. As soon as there is anything definite, I'll let you know. But meanwhile, I want to steal away with you somewhere. We should be able to take a vacation for a little while before I go into all this. Of course, there's Aileen. And until she is out of the way . . ." he paused, "my plan, of course, is to urge her to go to Paris, and then we might sail up toward the North Cape or down to the Mediterranean. One of my agents tells me of a yacht he knows of that can be leased for the summer."

"Yacht! Yacht!" exclaimed Berenice, excitedly, and at the same time laying a finger on his lips. "Oh, no, no! Now you're treading on my plans. Fixing things I want to fix. You see——"

But before she could finish he seized her and silenced her with a kiss.

"You *are* impatient!" she said, softly, "but wait . . ." and she led him to a table set by an open window in the adjoining room. "You see, my lord, a feast is laid for two. It is your slave who invites you. If you will be seated, and have a drink with me, and behave yourself, I shall tell you about myself. Believe it or not, I have solved everything!"

"Everything!" commented Cowperwood, banteringly. "And so soon? If only I knew how to do that!"

"Well, nearly everything," she went on, picking up a decanter containing his favorite wine and pouring a drink for each of them. "You see, strange as it may seem, I have been thinking. And when I think . . ." she stopped and looked upward at the ceiling. He seized the glass she was holding, and kissed her, as she knew he would.

"Back, Caesar!" she teased. "We are not to drink yet. You are to sit down there; I will sit here. And then I will tell you all. I'll confess."

"Imp! Be serious, Bevy."

"Never more so," she said. "Now listen, Frank! It was this way. On board our steamer were a half-dozen Englishmen, old and young, and all of them handsome; at least, those with whom I flirted were handsome."

"I'm sure of that," said Cowperwood, tolerantly, and still a little dubiously. "And so?"

"Well, if you're going to be as generous as all that, I'll have to tell you that it was all flirtation in your behalf, and innocent, too, although you needn't believe that. For instance, I found out about a little suburban place called Boveney on the Thames, not more than thirty miles from London. The most attractive young bachelor, Arthur Tavistock, told me about it. He lives there with his mother, Lady Tavistock. He's sure I'd like her. And my mother likes him very much. So you see . . ."

"Well, I see we live at Boveney, Mother and I," said Cowperwood, almost sarcastically.

"Precisely!" mocked Berenice. "And that's another important point —you and Mother, I mean. From now on you're going to have to pay a good deal of attention to her. And very little to me. Except as my guardian, of course," and she tweaked his ear.

"In other words, Cowperwood, the guardian and family friend." He smiled dryly.

"Exactly!" persisted Berenice. "And what's more, I'm to go punting with Arthur very soon. And, better still," and here she chuckled, "he knows of a lovely houseboat which will be ideal for Mother and me. And so, moonlight nights, or sunny afternoons around tea-time, while my mother and his mother sit and crochet or walk in the garden, and you smoke and read, Arthur and I . . ."

"Yes, I know, a charming life together: houseboat, lover, spring, guardian, mother. Quite an ideal summer, in fact."

"It couldn't be better," insisted Berenice vehemently. "He even described the awnings, red and green. And all of his friends."

"Red and green, too, I suppose," commented Cowperwood.

"Well, practically; flannels and blazers, you know. And all perfectly proper. He told Mother so. A host of friends to whom Mother and I are to be introduced."

"And the wedding invitations?"

"By June, at the latest, I promise you."

"May I give the bride away?"

"You could, of course," replied Berenice, without a smile.

"By George!" and Cowperwood laughed loudly. "Quite a successful voyage, I must say!"

"You haven't heard a fraction of it," she went on blatantly, and almost contentiously. "Not a fraction! There's Maidenhead—I blush to mention it——"

"You do? I'll make a note of that."

"I haven't told you yet about Colonel Hawkesberry, of the Royal something-or-other," she said, mock-foolishly. "One of those regiment things; knows a fellow officer who has a cousin who has a cottage in some park or other on the Thames."

"Two cottages and two houseboats! Or are you seeing double?"

"At any rate, this one is rarely let. Vacant for almost the first time, this spring. And a perfect dream. Usually loaned to friends. But as for Mother and myself . . ."

"We now become the daughter of the regiment!"

"Well, so much for the colonel. Then there's Wilton Braithwaite Wriothesley, pronounced Rotisly, with the most perfect little mustache, and six feet tall, and . . ."

"Now, Bevy! These intimacies! I'm getting suspicious!"

"Not of Wilton! Never, I swear! The colonel, maybe, but not Wilton!" She giggled. "Anyway, to make a long story five times as long, I already know of not only four houseboats along the Thames, but four perfectly appointed houses in or near the most exclusive residential squares of London, and all of them to be had for the season, or the year, or forever, if we should decide to stay here forever."

"If you say so, darling," interpolated Cowperwood. "But what a little actress you are!"

"And all of them," continued Berenice, ignoring his admiring comment, "if I should trouble to give my London address—which I haven't as yet—will be shown to me by one or all of my admirers."

"Bravo! My word!" exclaimed Cowperwood.

"But no commitments as yet, and no entanglements, either," she added. "But Mother and I have agreed to look at one in Grosvenor Square and one in Berkeley Square, after which, well, we shall see what we shall see."

"But don't you think you'd better consult your aged guardian as to the contract and all that sort of thing?"

"Well, as to the contract, yes, but as to all else . . ."

"As to all else, I resign, and gladly. I've done enough directing for one lifetime, and it will amuse me to see you try it."

"Well, anyway," she went on, quite impishly, "suppose you let me sit here," and she seated herself in his lap, and reaching over to the table picked up the goblet of wine and proceeded to kiss the rim. "See, I am wishing into it." She then drank half. "And now you wish," she said, handing him the glass and watching him drink the remainder. "And now you must throw it over my right shoulder against the wall, so that no one will ever drink out of it again. It's the way the Danes and the Normans did. Now . . ."

And Cowperwood threw the glass.

"Now, kiss me, and it will all come true," she said. "For I am a witch, you know, and I make things come true."

"I am prepared to believe that," said Cowperwood affectionately, as he solemnly kissed her.

After dinner they discussed the matter of their immediate movements. He found Berenice strongly against any plans for leaving England at this time. It was spring, and she had always wanted to make a tour of the cathedral towns—Canterbury, York, Wells; visit the Roman baths at Bath; Oxford and Cambridge; and some of the old castles. They could make the trip together, but only, of course, after he had looked into the possibilities which were confronting him in connection with this London project. Incidentally, she would also like to inspect the cottages she had mentioned. And then, once placed, they could immediately begin their holiday together.

And now he must go in to see her mother, who was a little upset and brooding these days, fearing she scarcely knew what for all of them. And after that he was to come back to her, and then . . . and then . . .

Cowperwood gathered her up in his arms.

"Well, well, Minerva!" he said, "it may be possible to arrange things the way you want them. I don't know. But one thing is sure: if there is too much of a hitch here, we'll make a tour of the world. I will arrange with Aileen somehow. And if she won't agree, well, then, we'll go in spite of her. The publicity she's always threatening can probably be overcome in some fashion. I'm sure of it. It has so far, anyway."

He kissed her gently, and with great comfort to himself, and then went in to speak to Mrs. Carter, whom he found sitting near an open window, reading a novel by Marie Corelli. She was obviously dressed and coiffed for his coming, and bent on him a most optimistic smile. Nevertheless, he sensed a nervous speculation on her part as to the practicability and danger of all that he and Berenice were doing. In fact, he thought he saw strain and depression in her eyes. So after making a few remarks on the prospects for a pleasant spring in England for all of them, he quite casually, and yet most directly, added:

"And I wouldn't worry about anything, Hattie, if I were you. Bevy and I understand each other perfectly. And I think she understands herself. She is brilliant and beautiful, and I love her. If any trouble comes, I think we can manage it. Try and have a good time. I'm likely to be very busy and so not able to see as much of you as I would like, but I'll be on guard. And so will she. Don't worry."

"Oh, I haven't been worrying, Frank," she said, almost apologetically. "Of course, I know how resourceful and determined Bevy is, and how much you have her interests at heart. And I do hope things go the way you want them. She's just the person for you, Frank; so gifted and charming. I wish you could have seen her on the boat, how cleverly she managed to meet and entertain people. And yet, how she made them keep their places, too. Are you staying a while now? I'm glad. I'm slightly indisposed myself, but I'll see you later, I hope."

She walked to the door with him, her manner that of a hostess entertaining a distinguished guest, as indeed she felt him to be. Once he had gone, and the door was closed, she went over to her mirror, and after gazing into in quite mournfully and dabbing her cheeks with a little rouge—in case Berenice should come in—she took out a brandy bottle which she kept in a locked traveling bag, and poured herself a small drink.

Chapter 25

THE following week end found both of the Cowperwoods in the midst of an interesting group as Lord Haddonfield's guests at Beriton Manor. This was, in truth, a distinguished pile of sixteenth century English architecture, at the southeast corner of Hardown Heath, and the center of a well-preserved patrimony. Approaching it from the northwest was the bleak, almost sea-like heath itself, with its rolling green expanses which remained, after hundreds of years, historically defiant of the plow, the sower, and the builder. Its chief value, to the rich as well as the poor, was the free range it provided for the hare, the deer, and other game, and the hunting parties, with their mounts and hounds and red-coated riders. To the southwest, in which direction the manor faced, were wooded slopes and fields, in the center of which lay Little Beriton, a small thatched market town, giving the impression of a hospitable countryside.

Haddonfield, who met the Cowperwoods at Beriton Station, was the same sophisticated, cheerful individual of five years before. Because of pleasant memories, he was delighted to see them, and while showing the really impressive lawns and courtyards, he remarked to Aileen: "I've been thinking, Mrs. Cowperwood, the heath is likely to prove a sober outlook for you and your husband. So I'm giving you rooms overlooking the garden. There's tea now in the drawing room, if you're tired after the journey."

In spite of her splendid mansion and many servants in New York, and the really much inferior wealth of this man, Aileen, for the moment, at least, was convinced that this was much more desirable. Oh, to have such a place as this, with the social security and connections of this man! Not to have to struggle any more. Forever to be at peace. On the other hand, while Cowperwood's mood welcomed a scene such as this, he was not overawed or even impressed by either title or unearned increment. He had created wealth and fame for himself.

The guests of Lord Haddonfield for this week end were varied, but distinguished. From London, the day before, had come Sir Charles Stoneledge, an actor of position and fame in the London theatrical world, but a stagey and affected individual who seized every opportunity to visit aristocratic friends or acquaintances. He had brought with him Miss Constance Hathaway, an actress then playing in the popular success, *Sentiment*.

By way of contrast, there were Lord and Lady Ettinge, he rather prominent in railway and shipping interests—a large, florid, dictatorial man, inclined to drink heavily and, when sufficiently in his cups, genial in a limited way. When cold sober, he was given to sharp *obiter dicta* rather than to facile argument. Lady Ettinge, on the other hand, was extremely diplomatic, and on this occasion had been invited by Lord Haddonfield to act as hostess. Well aware of her husband's moods and habits, and bearing with them tolerantly, she in no way submerged her own personality. She was tall and heavily built, blue veined, red cheeked, and having rather hard blue eyes. Once she had been as fair and engaging as any lovely maid of sixteen, and remembered it well, as did Ettinge. He had courted her earnestly. She had a better sense of proportion than her husband. He, being one of a long line and inheriting wealth, was inclined to give weight and precedence to primogeniture rather than to immediate achievement, even though he himself was active enough commercially. His wife, however, though as wellborn as himself, was more interested and aware of the changing forces of the day, and inclined to admire such untitled giants as Cowperwood.

Also present were Lord and Lady Bosvike, both young and smart and very popular. They were clever at all sports, enjoyed gambling and the races, and were valuable in any gathering because of their enthusiasm and gaiety. Secretly they laughed at Ettinge and his wife, though at the same time they valued their position and deliberately set themselves out to be agreeable to them.

A really important guest—decidedly so in the eyes of Haddonfield and Ettinge—was Abington Scarr. A man of rather dubious origin —no title, no family—nevertheless he was making quite a financial stir at this time. For one thing, in the past four years, he had been successful in organizing a cattle-raising company in Brazil. The profits from this were already yielding his investors a handsome return. He was now interested in sheep-raising in Africa, where, by reason of almost unheard-of concessions from the government and the methods he had devised for reducing costs and finding markets, he was looked upon as one who might shortly come to be a millionaire. The shrewdest criticisms of his ventures on the part of those who were inclined to doubt had not yet developed anything seriously inimical to his claims. Haddonfield, as well as Ettinge, was impressed by his success, but at the same time both were wary of following him. They did speculate in some of his shares but jumped in and out quickly. One thing that Scarr was seeking to promote at this time—but with less success than in the case of most of his earlier ventures—was the Baker Street & Waterloo Line, a new London underground, for which he had secured a franchise from Parliament. And it was in connection with this that the unexpected appearance of Cowperwood interested him.

Because of Aileen's determination to make an elaborate toilet, the Cowperwoods were late in coming down to dinner. When they entered the drawing room, most of the other guests had assembled and were somewhat annoyed at having to wait. Ettinge, in particular, had decided to pay no great attention to the Cowperwoods. But when they appeared, and Haddonfield called out a hearty welcome, the others turned at once, resumed their amiability and took an unaffected interest in the Americans. Ettinge, slouching to a standing position and bowing stiffly as he was introduced, nevertheless studied Cowperwood intently. And Lady Ettinge, who had been following the recent English comments on his affairs, decided at once that, her husband excepted, Cowperwood was the leading personality at this gathering. Instinctively, she forgave him for Aileen, judging that he had married young and later philosophically decided to make the best of an unfortunate union. As for Scarr, he was intelligent enough to realize that he was in the presence of a master in his own world.

A little ill at ease after her long period of neglect in New York, Aileen did her best to appear natural, yet succeeded only in being overcordial and almost eager, as she smiled at everyone. She made remarks which established in the minds of all that she was quite uncertain of herself. Cowperwood noted it, but decided that, after all, he could manage for her. And, with his usual diplomacy, he addressed himself to Lady Ettinge as the oldest and, plainly, the most significant woman guest.

"I am rather new to English country life," he said, quite simply, "but I must say, even the little glimpse I've had of it this afternoon quite justifies the admiration which is bestowed upon it."

"Indeed!" said Lady Ettinge, a little curious as to his tastes and temperament. "You find it as engaging as all that?"

"Yes, and I think I can explain why. It is the source of what at present is best in my own country." He emphasized the words "at present," as she noted. "The culture of Italy," he went on, "we can appreciate as that of a people entirely different from us; and the same, I think, is true of France and Germany. But here we recognize naturally, and with sympathy, the sources of our own culture and development, even those of us who are not wholly of English extraction."

"You sound almost too kind to England," said Lady Ettinge. "Are you of English descent?"

"Yes, my parents were Quakers. I was brought up in full knowledge of the simplicity of the English Quakers."

"Not all Americans, I fear, are so cordial."

"Mr. Cowperwood can speak with knowledge of any country," said Lord Haddonfield, drawing near, "for he has spent a fortune and a great many years in assembling the art of all of them."

"My collection is very modest," said Cowperwood. "I look upon it merely as a beginning."

"And this art collection is housed in one of the most beautiful museums I have ever visited," continued Lord Haddonfield, addressing Lady Ettinge. "It is in Mr. Cowperwood's home in New York."

"I had the pleasure of hearing a discussion of your collection when I was last in New York, Mr. Cowperwood," interjected Stoneledge. "Is it true that you are over here to add to it? I believe I read something of the sort the other day."

"Unfounded rumor," replied Cowperwood. "I am not collecting anything at the moment but impressions. I'm merely on my way to the Continent."

Pleased beyond words at the triumph which he appeared to be achieving, Aileen was extremely gay throughout dinner, so much so that Cowperwood, from time to time, cast a questioning glance in her direction, as he was especially eager to make a favorable impression. He knew, of course, about the financial interests of Haddonfield and Ettinge, and now here was Scarr, who, he had heard, was seeking to promote an underground. Concerning Lord Ettinge, he was interested to find out what he could about his influence and connections, and in that direction he was not unsuccessful, for Lady Ettinge spoke to him frankly of her husband's political interests. He was a Tory, and in close touch with the leaders of the Tory party, and was being considered at the present time for an important Indian appointment. It all depended on certain political eventualities bound up in the Boer War, then shaking England. So far, the losses had been almost continuous. But the tendency of the present company was to minimize that unfortunate fact, and Cowperwood, for diplomatic reasons, took the same attitude.

Throughout the dinner, chatting lightly enough with the other guests, he was asking himself who, of all these, could be of use to himself as well as Berenice. Lady Bosvike invited him to her lodge in Scotland. Scarr, after the ladies left the table, was the first to draw near and ask him if he were to be long in England. If so, he would like him to visit his place in Wales. Even Ettinge had, by this time, unbent sufficiently to discuss matters American and international.

And this relation was strengthened on Monday, when there was a shooting party, and Cowperwood was seen to be not without skill. In fact, by the time the Cowperwoods prepared to leave, he had won the admiration of all of Haddonfield's guests, if the same could not wholly be said of Aileen.

Chapter 26

CALLING at Berenice's apartment on his return from Beriton Manor, Cowperwood found her preparing for an inspection trip to one of the cottages suggested by Colonel Hawkesberry as a desirable summer residence for her and her mother. It was, she said, situated on the Thames, between Maidenhead and Marlow.

"And who do you think is the owner?" she asked him, with a suggestion of mystery and surprise.

"Not the slightest idea, unless I try to read your mind."

"Then try."

"Not me! Too difficult. Who is it?"

"None other than that English lord your Mr. Sippens wrote you about, unless there are two lords of the same name. Lord Stane."

"Not really?" said Cowperwood, surprised by the coincidence. "Tell me about it. Have you met him?"

"No. But Colonel Hawkesberry is most enthusiastic about the place, says it's just near enough to London. And then, too, he and his sistah ah theyah!" She mimicked the absent Hawkesberry.

"Such being the case, I think we might very well look at it," concluded Cowperwood, at the same time noting with admiration her attractive costume: long skirt and tight jacket of Lincoln green, the jacket trimmed with gold braid and a gold belt. A small green hat, flaunting a single red feather, was perched on the side of her head.

"I'd like to meet Stane," continued Cowperwood, "and this may be a way to do it. But caution is the word here, Bevy. I understand he is wealthy, and very influential. If we could interest him on our own terms . . ." He paused.

"Just what I've been thinking," she said. "So why not come along with me now to see it? Mother is tired today and is staying home."

Her manner, as usual, was light, evasive, bantering, the way which most pleased Cowperwood, since it so wholly reflected her natural strength, resourcefulness, and optimism under any and all circumstances.

"The pleasure of chaperoning this costume, apart from anything else, is enough!" said Cowperwood.

"Of course," continued Berenice, "I've explained to everyone that it is only with the consent of my guardian that I can make any decisions. Are you prepared to assume your duties?" she queried, with the sauciest of glances.

He walked over to her and took her in his arms.

"It's all new to me, of course, but I'll try."

"Well, anyway," said Berenice, "I'm making it easy for you. I've consulted a renting agent, and he will meet us at Windsor. After that I thought we might find a nice little old inn for tea."

"Righto! as we say over here. But first, a word with your mother." And he hurried into Mrs. Carter's room.

"Well, Hattie," he greeted her. "How's everything? How are you making out in dear old England?"

In contrast with Berenice's gaiety, her mother looked not only depressed but a little worn. It had all been so swift, this brilliant and colorful descent from her fool's paradise of social security to this wealth of adventure, which, however lavish its accouterments, was nevertheless frightening because of lurking danger ahead. This perplexing business of living! True, she had bred a gifted and self-sufficient daughter, but one as headstrong and lawless as herself. And one whose fate, for that reason, could not accurately be predicted. And although Cowperwood had always been and was now content to fortify them with the enormous resources of his mind and his wealth, yet she was fearful. The fact that he had brought them to England at a time when he was so openly courting public favor, and with Aileen in the immediate foreground, puzzled her. According to Berenice, this course was necessary, even if not entirely acceptable.

But this explanation did not entirely convince her. She had lived and lost, and the ghost that was tracking her was the fear that Berenice would also lose. For there was Aileen, and the fickleness of Cowperwood, and the relentless world, sparing no one, forgiving no one. It was something of all this that was in her mood, her eyes, and her relaxed figure. Unknown to Berenice, she had returned to drinking, and, but a moment or two before Cowperwood entered, had drained a large glass of brandy in order to brace herself for this certain encounter.

In answer to his greeting, she said: "Oh, I like England very much. Bevy is fascinated by everything here. I suppose you're going out to look at those cottages. It's just a question of the number of people you expect to entertain, or, rather, whom not to entertain, with you two together."

"I think you're speaking for Bevy, not me. She seems to be the magnet. But you look a little down, Hattie. What's the matter?" He eyed her questioningly, but not unsympathetically. "Come, come, don't let these first days get on your nerves! I know it's all a little difficult. You've had a trying trip, and you're tired." He crossed over to her and laid a friendly hand on her shoulder, but in doing so caught the odor of brandy. "Listen, Hattie," he said, "you and I have known each other for a long time. You know that although I've always been infatuated with Bevy, I never indulged in so much as a single gesture that could compromise her in any way, before she came to me in Chicago. Is that true, or isn't it?"

"Yes, Frank, it's true."

"You know, my one desire, since I felt I could not have her, was to place her socially, get her married and off your hands before anything could go wrong."

"Yes, I know."

"Of course, what happened in Chicago is to be charged to me, but even that not entirely, for she came to me at a time when I was very much in need of her. Otherwise, I think I might have resisted her even then. Anyway, we're all in this boat together now, to sink or swim. You look on this adventure over here as hopeless. I can see that. I don't. Remember, Bevy is a very brilliant and resourceful girl. And this is England, not the United States. People over here make way for intelligence and beauty in a way that has never yet been dreamed of at home. If you will only brace up and play your part, everything will be all right."

Once more he patted her shoulder, looking down into her eyes to note the effect of his words.

"You know I'll do my best, Frank," she said.

"Well, there's one thing you must not do, Hattie, and that's to take up drinking. You know your weakness. And if Bevy finds it out, it might discourage her and undo everything we are trying to do."

"Oh, I'll do anything, Frank, anything, if only I can make up to her for other things I have done!"

"That's the attitude!" And he smiled an encouraging smile, and left her to join Berenice.

Chapter 27   IN THE railway carriage Cowperwood discussed with Berenice the fears of her mother. She assured him that they meant nothing, it was merely the sudden change. With a little success here, she would feel better.

"If trouble comes from anywhere, it's likely to come from visiting Americans, not the English people," she added, thoughtfully, as they passed one charming scene after another, almost unnoted by them for the moment. "And I certainly do not intend to accept introductions to Americans, or invitations from them here in London, or entertain them either, if I can avoid it."

"You're right as to that, Bevy. It's the wisest thing to do."

"They are the people who terrify Mother. You know, Americans somehow haven't the manners or courtesy or tolerance of these people over here. I feel at home here."

"It's their older culture and diplomacy that you like," said Cowperwood. "They are less outspoken, slower to jump at conclusions. We Americans have taken an undeveloped continent, and are developing it, or trying to, in a very few years, whereas these people have been working on this little island for a thousand years."

At Windsor they were met by Mr. Warburton, the renting agent, who had much to say about the property he was going to show. It was really one of the most charming places on the river. Lord Stane had occupied it for years until a few summers ago.

"Since his father's death," the agent explained, confidentially, "he has gone mostly to Tregasal, where his main property lies. Last year he let this place to the actress, Miss Constance Hathaway, but this year she is going to Brittany, and it was only a month or two ago that Lord Stane told me I might let it if I found a suitable tenant."

"Has he much of an estate in Tregasal?" asked Cowperwood.

"One of the largest, sir," answered the agent. "About five thousand acres. A really beautiful place, although he seldom uses it."

At that moment a troublesome thought entered Cowperwood's mind. Insisting to himself that he would never again allow himself to be aroused by jealousy, still the truth was that since Berenice had come into his life, he was beginning to feel the pangs. She was so much of all that he desired. Might she not, under such circumstances as these, prefer a younger, if equally brilliant and resourceful, man? Could he expect to hold her if she were to meet and come to know such a personality as Stane? The thought injected into his relationship with Berenice a tinge of something which previously had not been there.

Pryor's Cove proved to be a dream of architecture and landscape gardening. It was over a hundred years old, though most modernly equipped, and trailed along for nearly a hundred feet in a straight line. Under great trees rather grandly overtopping its eighteen feet of height, it was surrounded by a veritable tangle of paths, hedges, flower gardens, and kitchen gardens. At the rear, to the south of the house where it faced the river, was a double ell of picturesque Leicestershire stables, with quaint fences, gates, rockeries, and birdhouses, and, as Mr. Warburton pointed out, there were riding and driving horses for the use of the tenant, black Minorca chickens, sheep dogs, and a flock of sheep, all looked after by a gardener, a hostler, and a farmer, the tenant acquiring their labor along with the house.

Cowperwood, like Berenice, was charmed by the bucolic atmosphere: the glasslike smoothness of the Thames, which crept slowly and silently toward London; the wide expanse of lawn which led down to the river; and the brightly awninged houseboat, with its fluttering curtains and wicker chairs and tables, moored to a landing. He mused over a sundial which stood in the center of a path leading down to the houseboat. How time was passing! He was really an elderly man. And Berenice was about to meet this younger man, who might interest her. On coming to him in Chicago a few months before, Berenice had said she was her own mistress, and came to him only because she desired to do so. And when she no longer desired him, she would leave him. Of course, he need not take this place, and he need not deal with Stane financially. There were other men and other ways. Abington Scarr and Lord Ettinge were possibilities. Why entertain the fear of defeat? He had lived a full life and would continue to do so whatever happened.

He noted Berenice exultingly admiring the beauties of this place. Unconscious of his thoughts, she was already wondering to herself about Lord Stane. He could not be very old, as she had heard that he had only recently come into these great properties of his father's. However, she was chiefly arrested by the social character of the neighborhood, as described by Mr. Warburton. For in the immediate vicinity dwelt Mr. Arthur Garfield Wriothesley Gole, of the Queen's bench; Sir Heberman Kipes, of the Consolidated British Tiles & Patterns Company; the Honorable Runciman Maynes, of the Secretariat for the Colonies; together with various other Sir Bigwigs and Sir Littlewigs and hostesses of title and achievement. Cowperwood was likewise interested by all this, and wondered what Berenice and her mother were likely to make of it. During the spring and summer here, she now pointed out, there would be house parties, garden parties, and country reunions of London city groups in politics, government, the arts, and society, so that with proper introductions one's days and nights might be filled.

"In fact," commented Cowperwood at this point, "altogether an atmosphere in which one could rise or sink, and that most swiftly and fatefully either way."

"Quite!" said Berenice. "But one in which I should try to rise."

He was once more captivated by her optimism and courage.

And then the agent, who had gone over to examine the hedges, returned, and Cowperwood now addressed him.

"I have just advised Miss Fleming," he said, without a previous word to Berenice, "that she and her mother have my permission to lease this place, if they choose. You may send the necessary papers to my solicitor. A mere formality, but a part of my legal duty as Miss Fleming's guardian, you know."

"Certainly, I understand, Mr. Cowperwood," said the agent. "But it will be a few days before the papers are ready, possibly not before next Monday or Tuesday, as Lord Stane's agent, Mr. Bailey, will not be back before then."

Cowperwood was somewhat gratified to learn that Stane did not trouble with his own renting details. That would keep his name out of it for the present, anyway. As for the future, he could not help wondering a little. . . .

Chapter 28

COWPERWOOD'S TOUR of the undergrounds, with Sippens as his guide, having confirmed his opinion as to the importance of securing the Charing Cross franchise as his initial move, he was looking forward with interest to the interview with Greaves and Henshaw in his office this morning. It was Greaves who took the lead in the opening conversation.

"We want to know, Mr. Cowperwood," he began, "if you are willing to take a 51 per cent interest in the Charing Cross line, provided we undertake to raise proportionately the amount necessary to build the line."

"Proportionately?" queried Cowperwood. "It depends on what you mean by that. If the line should cost £1,000,000, do you guarantee to furnish approximately £450,000?"

"Well," said Greaves, somewhat hesitantly, "not directly out of our own pockets. We have some connections which might join us in furnishing it."

"You didn't appear to have any such connections when I saw you in New York," said Cowperwood, "and since then I have decided that £30,000 for a 51-per-cent interest in a company which has only a franchise and some debts, is my limit. There are too many companies with rights, and nothing else, going begging here, as it is. I have had time to find that out. If you are coming to me with a positive guarantee of the £450,000 which the building of 49 per cent of this line is likely to cost, I might be interested. But since you are merely waiting to have me agree to take 51 per cent so that on the strength of that you may be able to raise your 49 per cent, I can't see it. You have really only your rights to offer. Under the circumstances, I must ask for a full control or nothing. For it is only with full control that I will be able to raise the very large amount of money it is going to take to do this. And no one should know that better than you two gentlemen. Therefore, unless you can see your way clear to take my final offer—which is £30,000 for your option, together with a continuance of your contract to build —I cannot give the matter any further thought."

Whereupon he took out his watch, a gesture which confirmed a suspicion in the minds of both Greaves and Henshaw that unless they decided here and now, this was the end. They looked at each other questioningly, and then Henshaw spoke:

"Assuming that we sell you this complete control, Mr. Cowperwood, what guarantee have we that you would immediately proceed with the building of this line? For if we do not get the construction work out of it within a reasonable time, I cannot see that we are getting anything."

"I feel the same way as my partner does," said Greaves.

"As to that," said Cowperwood, "you need have no fear. I would be perfectly willing to write into any contract we may draw that unless the money for the construction of the first division line is furnished within six months after signing, the agreement is not only canceled, but I agree to pay you £10,000 by way of damages. Is that satisfactory?"

The two contractors stared at each other again. They had heard that Cowperwood was shrewd and cold where money was concerned, but they also had heard that he held to his signed contracts.

"Well and good! That sounds reasonable enough. But what about the other divisions?" This from Greaves.

Cowperwood laughed. "Well, gentlemen, I am just disposing of two-thirds of the entire street railway system of Chicago. In the last twenty years in that city I have built thirty-five miles of elevated roads, forty-six miles of electric slot traction lines, and I have built and am now profitably operating seventy-five miles of suburban trolley lines, in all of which I am the majority owner. In connection with these, no investor has ever lost a dime. They have paid, and are paying to this day, more than 6 per cent, and they still belong to me. It is not because they are not profitable that I am disposing of them—and at a profit—but because of political and social jealousies which are irritating to me.

"And, furthermore, it isn't because I need the money that I am bothering with this London situation. You mustn't forget that it was you who came to me, not I to you. But never mind that. I am not boasting, and don't wish to. As to these additional sections, the time and the money for each one can be written into the contract, only, as you must know from experience, all must be subject to the natural delays and contingencies which are always likely to affect such things. The principal point is that I am willing *now* to put up the cash for your option and to do all of the things subsequently that the contract requires."

"What do you say?" asked Greaves, turning to Henshaw. "I am satisfied that we will do as well with Mr. Cowperwood as with anyone."

"Very well," said Henshaw, "I'm ready."

"How do you propose to go about the matter of this transfer?" asked Cowperwood. "As I understand it, you must take up your option with the Traffic Electrical Company before you can transfer it to me."

"That's true," replied Henshaw, who had already been speculating as to this. If now they were first to deal directly with the Traffic Electrical Company and subsequently with Cowperwood, it would mean that they not only would have to secure from somewhere the £30,000 with which to take up their option, but, in addition, temporarily, at least, would have to borrow £60,000 to effect the transfer of the consols which the Traffic Electrical Company had deposited with the government for performance of their obligation. Since a total of £90,000 was not an easy sum to raise, Henshaw bethought himself as to how much better it would be to go to John-

son and the office of the Traffic Electrical Company and explain
what was under way. He would then ask the directors to meet with
Cowperwood, Greaves, and himself, in order that the entire transaction could be met and disposed of with Cowperwood's money.
And this idea so pleased him that he now said:

"I think it would be best if we made one transaction of the whole
thing," and he explained how, if not why. But Cowperwood understood why, well enough.

"Very well," he said. "If you will arrange with the directors, I
am ready. We can complete everything in a few minutes. You can
tender your option for my check for £30,000, together with the
£60,000 national deposit, or a voucher for it, and I will hand you
my check, or checks, for both. All we have to do now, I take it, is
to draw up a temporary agreement as to the details of this, and you
can sign it."

And he rang for his secretary and dictated the substance of the
understanding.

"Now, gentlemen," he said, when it was signed, "I want to feel
that we are no longer bargainers, but associates in an important
enterprise that should lead to agreeable results for all of us. I pledge
you my word that in return for your wholehearted co-operation
from now on, you will have mine." And he gave a most cordial
handclasp to both.

"Well," observed Greaves, "I must say, this has been done very
quickly."

Cowperwood smiled.

"I suppose that is what you would call, in your country, 'fast
work,'" added Henshaw.

"Nothing more than the exercise of good sense on the part of
everybody concerned," said Cowperwood. "If that's American, fine!
If it's English, just as fine! But don't forget that it took one American and two Englishmen to do it!"

As soon as they had left, Cowperwood sent for Sippens.

"I don't know if I can make you believe it or not, De Sota," he
said, when Sippens arrived, "but I have just bought that Charing
Cross line for you."

"You did!" exclaimed Sippens. "Well, that's great!" Already he
saw himself as the organizing general manager of this new line.
And actually at this time Cowperwood was thinking of using

him in that way; long enough, at least, to get things started, only not so much longer, since he looked on Sippens as perhaps too irritatingly American to be able to deal successfully with men of the world of high finance in London.

"Take a look at that!" he went on, picking up a sheet of paper from his desk, the tentative but nonetheless binding understanding between Greaves and Henshaw and himself.

Sippens selected from a box that Cowperwood held out to him a long gold-foil wrapped cigar, and started to read.

"Great!" he snapped, as he concluded his reading, cigar held out at arm's length. "And if that won't make a sensation when they read it in Chicago and New York, and here, too! Jehoshaphat! It'll go all over the world, once you allow it to be announced here."

"But that's one of the things I want to talk to you about, De Sota. An announcement of this kind, and so soon after my coming here . . . well, I'm a little afraid of the effect of it . . . not back home . . . I don't mind their being surprised or shocked . . . but the effect on the prices of underground rights over here bothers me. They may go up, and most likely will, if this gets out." He paused. "And particularly when they read of how much money is going to pass over the table at one sitting, and for one little line: relatively £100,000 . . . for, of course, I have to build that line or lose about £70,000."

"Right, Chief," agreed Sippens.

"There's a lot of nonsense to all this, you know," continued Cowperwood, ruminatively. "Here we are, you and I, both of us getting along in years, and now running around on this new job, which, whether we do it or not, can't mean so much to either of us. For we're not going to be here so much longer, De Sota, and neither of us needs the money."

"Just the same, you're wanting to build it, Chief!"

"I know," said Cowperwood, "and yet neither of us can do much more than eat a little, drink a little, play about a little while longer, that's all. What astonishes me is that we can get so excited over it. Aren't you a little astonished at yourself?"

"Well, Chief, I'm not going to pretend to speak for you, because you're a great man, and anything you do or don't do is important. As for me, I look on it all as some sort of a game that I'm here to play. I used to feel that everything was more important than I feel it is now. Maybe I was right then, for if I hadn't gotten busy and done a lot for myself, life would have slipped by me and I wouldn't have been able to do a lot of things I have done. And I guess that's the answer: to be doing something all the time. There's a game on, and whether we like it or not, we have to play our parts."

"Well," said Cowperwood, "you'll have plenty to play with pretty soon, if this line is to be built on time."

And he gave his small and vigorous friend a hearty smack on the back.

To Berenice, his annnouncement of this Charing Cross control was an occasion for celebration. For was it not she who had originally suggested this London adventure? And now here she was at last, finding herself a part of a great world of affairs such as in the past she had only dimly envisioned. Sensing Cowperwood's exultant mood, she brought out a bottle of wine with which they might toast the occasion, and each other.

At one point in their conversation, she could not resist asking, rather impishly: "Have you, by any chance, met your, our, Lord Stane?"

" 'Our'?" He laughed. "Don't you really mean *your* Lord Stane?"

"Mine and yours," countered Berenice. "For he can help us both, can he not?"

What a creature! thought Cowperwood. The daring and bravado of this chit of a girl!

"To be sure," he said, resignedly. "No, I haven't met him, but I admit he is important. In fact, I am hoping he may mean a great deal. However, Stane or no Stane, I shall go ahead with this project."

"And Stane or no Stane, you will achieve just what you want," said Berenice. "You know that, and so do I. You don't need anyone, not even me," and she came over and took his hand in hers.

Chapter 29 PLEASED with the thought of the probable effect of this purchase on his further activities in London, Cowperwood decided to pay a propitiatory call upon Aileen. He had not heard from Tollifer and was seriously wondering what further steps he could take in that direction without committing himself.

Approaching Aileen's suite, which adjoined his own, he heard her laugh, and, entering, found her standing before a long mirror, surrounded by a group of saleswomen and fitters from one of the London shops. She was surveying her reflection while her maid adjusted the gown. The room was littered with paper, boxes, tags, and dresses, and he noted that the gown she wore was quite magnificent and in better taste than was customary with her. Two fitters, pins in their mouths, were on their knees making rapid adjustments, while a most attractive and smartly dressed woman was giving them instructions.

"Well, well," remarked Cowperwood as he entered, "this makes me feel a little superfluous, although I wouldn't mind playing audience if there's no objection."

"Come in, Frank!" called Aileen. "I'm just trying on an evening gown. We won't be much longer. This is my husband," she added, addressing the assembled group, who bowed respectfully.

"Well, I must say that pale gray is most becoming," said Cowperwood. "It emphasizes your hair. Few women could wear it as well as you do, my dear. But what I really stopped in for was to say that it looks as though we would be in London for some time."

"Really?" asked Aileen, turning her head slightly to look at him.

"I've just completed some of that business I was telling you about. It's all settled except for some minor details. I thought you'd like to know."

"Oh, Frank, isn't that wonderful!" She was delighted.

"Well, I won't take up any more of your time. I have so many things to do."

"By the way," said Aileen, who sensed his desire to escape and wished to put him at ease in regard to herself. "Mr. Tollifer just phoned. He's back, and is coming to dinner. I explained to him that your business might prevent you from dining with us. I'm sure he'll understand."

"It's a little difficult," said Cowperwood, "but I'll do my best to get there"—which remark Aileen took for exactly what it was worth: nothing at all.

"All right, Frank," she said, as he waved good-by and left the room.

She knew that she would not see him again before the morrow, if then, but one thing caused her to feel this routine indifference of his less keenly. In his telephone conversation with her, Tollifer had apologized for his seeming neglect and had inquired anxiously if she were not coming to France. Aileen was puzzled as to the basis of her attraction for so cavalier a personality. For what reason, exactly, was he so much interested in her? Money, no doubt. Yet how attractive he was! Regardless of motive, his attention was most gratifying.

Yet the main reason why Tollifer wished Aileen to come to France—though it happened to coincide with Cowperwood's desire to have her out of London—was the fact that he, himself, was one of the most hopeless victims of the charms of Paris. At that time, before the automobile had come into general use, Paris, even more than at a later time, was the holiday center for wealthy Americans, English, Brazilians, Russians, Greeks, and Italians—people from every country in the world—who came to enjoy themselves, and who made possible the brilliant shops, the charming flower stands, the numerous cafés with their summery outdoor chairs and tables, the gaudy cabarets, the glittering parade in the Bois, the races at Auteil, the gambling, the opera, the theaters, and the underworld.

The international hotel, in the form of the Ritz, had arrived. Also the restaurants of the gourmet: the Café de la Paix, Voisin's, Marguery's, Giroux's, and a half-dozen others. And for the poet or artist or romancer without a dime, there was the Quartier Latin. Rains, snows, spring days, autumn days, brilliant sunshine, or gray skies were alike in achieving effects dear to every responsive and creative temperament. Paris sang. And with it sang youth, reminiscent age, ambition, wealth, even defeat and despair.

It must not be forgotten that, for the first time in his life, Mr. Tollifer was in funds, and with a glittering playboy program before him. It was so delightful to be able to dress well, have the proper address—which for the moment was the Ritz—to hurry to the smartest places, glancing over the lobbies, pausing at the bars, greeting friends and acquaintances.

And in the Bois one Sunday afternoon Tollifer had run into a former flame of his: the onetime Marigold Shoemaker, of Philadelphia, now Mrs. Sidney Brainerd, of the Bar Harbor and Long Island Brainerds. At one time she had been infatuated with him, but because of his poverty had cast him aside for Brainerd, whose money seemed to be inexhaustible. She had a yacht lying off Nice.

The sight of Tollifer, dressed immaculately and with the mood of adventure dominating him, was sufficient to recall her exciting and romantic debutante days. She hailed him cordially, introduced him to her escort, and gave him her Paris address. Through her, as through others, he saw visions of the opening of at least some of the doors which for so long had been closed against him.

There was, however, this business of Aileen. And that was something else again. It was going to require the utmost skill to entertain her while promoting his own interests. He must look about for lesser fry who might be made to appear part and parcel of a better stratum. At once he consulted the various hotel registers for names of actresses, musicians, singers, dancers, whom he knew. Offering assurances of entertainment, he was met with acceptances, and, being thus certain of some immediate diversion for Aileen if she came to Paris, he wound up his labors with a personal canvass of the leading dressmakers, as he considered her present manner of dress far from satisfactory, and believed that with diplomatic advice this could be remedied and at the same time lighten his burden in the matter of presenting her to his friends.

One of his most promising Paris contacts came about when a Chicago acquaintance of his introduced him to an Argentinian named Victor Leon Sabinal. This young man, of distinguished lineage and wealth in his own country, had arrived in Paris some years before, with money, letters, and connections that had given him immediate entry into the varied social circles of that cosmopolitan city. Nevertheless, owing to a temperament that pushed him in the direction of extravagance and dissipation, he had exhausted the patience of his South American parents, who suddenly refused to furnish more money for his escapades. And hence, as in the case of Tollifer, he had been reduced to borrowings and tricks that finally closed the doors of his earlier and more conservative friends.

But it was not forgotten by any of them that his parents were exceedingly wealthy and entirely likely at some future time to change their minds in regard to the punishment of their son. In other words, he might still come into a fortune, and if so, his friends might not be forgotten. This retained for him a circle of light-hearted and variously gifted satellites: artists, soldiers, roués of all nationalities, attractive men and women of the fortune-hunting and pleasure-seeking class. In fact, at this very time, by arrangement with the police and politicians of France, he was being permitted to conduct an establishment, attractive, diverting, and convenient, for his many friends, who were actually patrons as well as intimates.

Sabinal was tall, slender, dark, almost sinister in his general bearing, partly due to his long, narrow, sallow face and arrestingly high forehead. One of his dark lustrous eyes appeared to be exceedingly round and open, as though it were made of glass, while the other was smaller and narrow, partially concealed by a drooping eyelid. He had a thin upper lip and a curiously protruding, and yet attractive, lower one. His teeth were even, strong, and gleaming white. His long, thin hands and feet were like his long, thin body: sinuous and taut. But the ensemble was one of cunning, grace, and not too disarming fascination. Altogether he seemed to suggest that anyone crossing his path must be prepared to look out for himself.

His place in the Rue Pigalle was never closed. One came to tea and as likely as not remained for breakfast. A part of the extensive third floor, reached by a small elevator, was set off for gambling. A chamber on the second floor contained a small bar, with a most efficient barkeeper from Sabinal's native land, who, at times, as the necessities compelled, had two, or even three, assistants. The ground floor, in addition to a cloak room, a lounging room, and a kitchen, had a gallery of fine paintings and an interesting library. There was also a well-stocked wine cellar. The chef, who provided luncheons, teas, formal and informal dinners, and even breakfasts—and for no apparent consideration other than minor tips—was another Argentinian.

On meeting Sabinal, Tollifer at once realized that he was in the presence of a personality of his own persuasion, but of far greater powers, and he gladly accepted an invitation to visit his place. There he encountered an assortment of personalities who interested him very much: bankers and legislators of France, Russian grand dukes, South American millionaires, Greek gamblers, and many others. He sensed immediately that here he could contrive for Aileen such contacts as would not fail to impress her with the thought that she was meeting people of worldly importance.

It was this knowledge that made him so gay on his arrival in London. After telephoning to Aileen, he spent the greater part of the day in Bond Street, properly outfitting himself for the summer on the Continent, after which he made his way to Aileen's hotel.

He decided that he would make no pretense of affection at this time. His was to play the role of uncalculating friend, one who liked her for herself and wished to proffer her, without reward, such social opportunities as she could not otherwise achieve.

Following the usual preliminaries of greeting, she began at once with an account of her visit to the estate of Lord Haddonfield.

"Haddonfield . . . oh, yes. I remember him," said Tollifer. "He was in the United States some years ago. I believe it was either at Newport or Southampton that I ran into him. Quite a gay fellow. Likes clever people."

The truth was that Tollifer had never met Haddonfield, but knew something of him from hearsay. And immediately he launched into an account of his stay in Paris, and added that here in London he had this day lunched with a certain Lady Lessing, of whose social doings Aileen had read that morning in the newspaper.

Delighted by all of this, Tollifer's interest in her still seemed unaccountable to Aileen. Plainly, it could not be that he expected any social advantage from her. It must be something he might hope to get from Frank. She was puzzled, but also certain that little enough would come from Cowperwood as a reward for dancing attendance upon her. He was not like that. In consequence, and in spite of her natural suspicions, she was compelled, even though she hesitated, to entertain the thought that Tollifer was really attracted to her as a person.

They dined together at Prince's that evening, and he entertained her with an intriguing account of the gaieties that might be hers for the asking. He raved about Paris.

"Why can't you—as long as your husband is so busy—run over?" he suggested. "There are so many interesting things to do, to see, to buy. I've never seen Paris more gay."

"I would like very much to go," confessed Aileen, "because I really have some shopping to do. But I don't know whether my husband will be able to go with me or not."

Tollifer was a little amused at this last remark, but not cruelly so.

"I should think any busy husband might spare his wife a fortnight for shopping in Paris," he said.

Aileen, now eager to test the resources of this new-found friend, exclaimed: "I'll tell you what I'll do! I'll ask Frank tomorrow, and let you know."

Dinner was followed by a visit to an informal and regular "Tuesday evening" at the flat of Cecilia Grant, an actress playing in a popular revue, and, incidentally, the mistress of Count Etienne le Bar, a Frenchman of great personal charm and popularity in London. Tollifer knew that a knock at Cecilia's door would produce a welcome for Aileen and himself. And the group they encountered there—including a bizarre countess, the wife of one of the peers of England—seemed to Aileen indubitably important and convinced her that whatever Tollifer's motives, his connections were far more important than hers, or even Cowperwood's. And at once, although she did not then say so, she decided to go to Paris.

Chapter 30 NATURALLY, Greaves and Henshaw lost no time in acquainting Johnson with the details of their negotiations with Cowperwood, for Johnson and Stane, and most of the men connected with the Traffic Electrical Company, were also interested in other London underground lines, and their favor was valuable to Greaves and Henshaw as engineers. They were satisfied that technically as well as ethically they were well within their rights, since, in the first instance, the option was theirs to do with as they chose, and, next, they had not actually agreed to Johnson's direct request that they give him so many days in which to present a repurchase proposition, but had said they would think it over and let him know. They did not know of Jarkins' visit to Johnson, who was now a bit curious as to what was bringing them to see him.

For the first few minutes of their narrative, he was inclined to feel that the best part of the possibilities indicated by a proposed meeting with Cowperwood had evaporated. But gradually he was brought to think more favorably of the plan of contact which they suggested. In short, the fact that at one meeting this American was not only ready to pay over £30,000 and assume the interest on £60,000 in consols, but also to agree to deposit £10,000, no portion of which would ever be returned to him unless he began building within a year, was enough to fascinate him. Probably this matter of the Charing Cross was only a detail, and it was true, as Jarkins had insisted, that Cowperwood was interested mainly in the larger phases of underground unification. If so, why not some general scheme which would include himself and Stane before others were taken in? Plainly, it was still important that he and Stane meet Cowperwood. Well, that could probably be arranged at the meeting in Cowperwood's office which he would attend in connection with the final negotiations concerning the transfer of the Charing Cross line.

Eleven-thirty of the day of the meeting found Cowperwood and Sippens together in Cowperwood's office, Sippens pacing up and down, making such remarks as he could induce his Chief to give ear to. But Cowperwood himself was curiously thoughtful. He had acted so swiftly, he now reflected, more so than was usual with him. And this was an alien land, its ways and moods almost entirely unfamiliar to him. True, it did not follow that because he was buying the rights, he could not sell again. On the other hand, reason as he would, a kind of fatality appeared to be running through the whole affair. For if now, after buying this option, he allowed it to lapse, it would look like a tentative adventure on his part for which he had neither the courage nor the means.

But now Jarkins and Kloorfain arrived, fully conscious of their part in this, and having been assured by Cowperwood that his own obligation to them would not be overlooked. And immediately following them came Mr. Denton, Sippens' secretary, and Mr. Ostade, one of Sippens' investigating committee. Later came Mr. Kitteredge, Sippens' successor to the presidency of Cowperwood's Chicago Union Traction lines, who was there in order to discuss with Cowperwood some of his Chicago affairs. Lastly, there was Oliver Bristol, a youthful but exceedingly alert member of Cowperwood's legal department, who had been sent over to inform himself as to current English procedure. He was now ready for his first task. Cowperwood's principal use for his own people, however, at this time— apart from witnessing the transaction—was to have them serve as color and background for himself, in order to impress these English gentlemen.

At last, and promptly at twelve o'clock, came Messrs. Greaves and Henshaw, accompanied by Johnson, Rider, Calthorpe, and Delafield, of the Traffic Electrical Company; Mr. Calthorpe being its chairman, Mr. Rider its vice-chairman, and Mr. Johnson its solicitor. And all were not a little impressed as, coming at last into the presence of the great man himself, they found him, sitting behind his desk, attended right and left by his lawyer and all of his assistants.

Cowperwood rose and greeted both Greaves and Henshaw very cordially, and they, in turn, with the assistance of Jarkins and Sippens, introduced the members of each group. But it was Johnson who held the attention of both Cowperwood and Sippens, Cowperwood because of his connections and Sippens because on sight he sensed a rival. The authoritativeness of the man, the almost august manner in which he cleared his throat and looked around inquiringly, as if he were a scientist examining insects, infuriated Sippens. And it was Johnson who opened the discussion.

"Well, Mr. Cowperwood and gentlemen," he began, "I believe we all fully understand the nature of what is to take place here. Therefore, the sooner we begin, the sooner we will be through."

("You don't say!" commented Sippens to himself.)

"Yes, I believe that's a good idea," said Cowperwood. And pushing a button, he ordered Jamieson to bring in his official checkbook as well as the temporary agreements.

Johnson now took from a square leather bag—which was carried by an office boy who walked at his heels—the several books of the Traffic Electrical Company, its official seal, together with the act, and placed all upon Cowperwood's desk. And Cowperwood, flanked by Bristol and Kitteredge, proceeded to examine them.

After checking over various commitments, decisions, expenditures, Greaves produced their option to buy, and the company, through its officers, attested to its validity. Mr. Delafield, as secretary and treasurer of Traffic Electrical Company, produced a copy of the act establishing their right to construct the line. Whereupon, a Mr. Blandish, of the London and County Bank, arrived with a certificate of deposit in favor of Frank Algernon Cowperwood for £60,000 in British consols then and there in that bank. These the bank would surrender to him in exchange for his check for that amount.

Cowperwood then signed and handed to Messrs. Greaves and Henshaw his check for £30,000, which by then was endorsed to Traffic Electrical Company. The company, through its officers, endorsed to Greaves and Henshaw their charter, and they duly re-endorsed it to Cowperwood. Whereupon he wrote his check for £60,000, and for that took over from the London and County Bank its legal acknowledgement of his ownership of the consols. After this, he handed Greaves a duly attested and guaranteed one-year's non-negotiable agreement. The meeting then closed, with an atmosphere of enthusiasm which was hardly to be explained by the business of the moment.

The explanation of this was the personality of Cowperwood and its effect on all those present. Calthorpe, the chairman of Traffic Electrical, for instance, a blond and stocky man of fifty, had come stuffed with prejudice against any American attempting to manage a London railway property. Nevertheless, it was plainly evident that he was impressed by Cowperwood's dynamic alertness. Rider studied Cowperwood's clothes, taking note of his beautifully set jade cuff links, his dark tan shoes, and his well-tailored sand-colored suit. Obviously, America was producing a new and distinct type. Here was a man who could, if he wished, become a great force in London's affairs.

Johnson thought Cowperwood had handled the situation with shrewdness and even an agreeable cunning. The man was ruthless, but in a way which the jumbled interests and oppositions of life required. He was about to leave when Cowperwood came over to him.

"From what I hear, Mr. Johnson, you are personally interested in this underground situation," he said, smiling a cordial smile.

"Yes, to some extent," replied Johnson, civilly, and yet with caution.

"My lawyers have informed me," continued Cowperwood, "that you are more or less of an expert in the traction franchise field here. You see, I have been trained on the other side, and this is all new ground to me. If you have no objection, I would like to talk with you further. Perhaps we could have lunch or dinner together, either at my hotel or some place where we would not be likely to be interrupted."

They agreed upon Brown's Hotel for Tuesday evening of the following week.

Alone with Sippens after they had all left, Cowperwood turned to him and said:

"Well, there you are, De Sota! We've just bought a lot more trouble. What do you think of these Englishmen, anyway?"

"Oh, they're all well enough when they're dealing with each other," said Sippens, still irritated by Johnson's manner, "but you'll never see the day when you won't have to look out for them, Chief. Your surest support will be the men you yourself have trained."

"I guess you're right, De Sota," said Cowperwood, sensing what was in Sippens' mind. "But I'm not sure that I won't have to include some of these fellows over here, to make everything smooth and right. They can't be expected to stand for too many of us all at once. You know that."

"True enough, Chief, but you want enough Americans to keep them from catching you napping!"

But there was revolving in Cowperwood's mind the thought that what perhaps was needed was a loyal and enthusiastic English group, men like this Johnson and Greaves and Henshaw, and even that quiet fellow, Rider, who had studied him so carefully but said nothing. In this rapid series of developments, some of these long-time American connections might lose value. He knew only too well that out of sentiment came nothing that was sufficient in any crisis to warrant its preservation. If life had taught him anything, it had taught him that. And he was not one to turn from his most relentlessly cruel and yet constructive teacher.

Chapter 31   ALTHOUGH it had been agreed that no information of any kind in connection with the transfer of the Charing Cross line was at present to be furnished to the press, the news somehow leaked out, possibly due to gossip emanating from Rider, Calthorpe, and Delafield. Having been shareholders as well as officers of Traffic Electrical Company before its property was thus transferred, they feared for their future and were inclined to discuss the matter. So that it was not long before financial as well as news reporters appeared, asking Cowperwood for confirmation of the fact.

Cowperwood informed them frankly that such a transfer was now in process, and that, in due time, a certificate of registration would be filed. Also, that originally he had not come to London to buy anything, seeing that his American interests still required so much of his time, but that certain representatives of London underground ventures had called upon him to urge his managerial as well as financial consideration of routes in which they were interested. The purchase of the Charing Cross had been the result of these overtures, and there were other ventures to which he had promised to give his attention. Whether this would result in a unified system which he would care to build depended on what his coming investigations would reveal.

In Chicago, the editorial comments following this announcement were little more than snarls of rage. That such a ruthless trickster, so recently ejected from that city, should proceed to London, and there, by reason of his wealth, cunning, and general effrontery, be able to cajole the powers of that great city into looking to him for the possible solution of their transit needs, was too much! Plainly, the British had not troubled to inquire into his highly sinister record. But once that was uncovered, as it presently would be, he would be as unwelcome there as he was to this hour and for years past had been in Chicago! There were equally unfavorable comments in the newspapers of a number of other American cities, the editors and publishers of which had taken their mood from that of Chicago.

On the other hand, in the London press, and not strange to relate —since its social, financial, and political opinions were highly realistic and never likely to be based on popular complaint—the reaction toward Cowperwood was most favorable. The *Daily Mail* ventured the opinion that such ability as his might not disadvantageously be centered upon the laggard London underground field, which for years had toddled far behind public necessity. The *Chronicle* deplored the inactivity of English capital and expressed the pious hope that if an American, in so distant a place as Chicago, could discern what London needed, perhaps the traction leaders of London would now awaken and go forward themselves. There were similar comments in the *Times, Express,* and other journals.

These comments were, from a financial point of view, as Cowperwood saw it, unfortunate. They were likely to concentrate not only English but American financial ambition on his own purpose and awaken obstructive activity, and in this he was certainly not wrong. For no sooner were the notices of the sale of the line confirmed, and his admission as to other offers and his possible future interest in the London transit problem made public, than the chief stockholders of both the District and the Metropolitan, the two lines most impugned, were in a fury of indignation, and in so far as the future was concerned, most certain to oppose him.

"Cowperwood! Cowperwood!" sniffed Lord Colvay, shareholder

and one of the twelve directors of the Metropolitan, as well as of the new City and South London. He was having his breakfast, with the *Times* to the right of him, for reasons of mental dignity principally, but at the moment was reading the *Daily Mail,* his favorite paper. "And who the devil is this Cowperwood? One of those mushroom Americans, gadding round the world, telling people what to do! I wonder who his so-called advisers are—Scarr, maybe, with that Baker Street and Waterloo scheme of his, and Wyndham Willets, with his Deptford and Bromley route. And, of course, Greaves and Henshaw, looking for contracts. And the Traffic Electrical anxious to clear out."

Equally annoyed was Sir Hudspeth Dighton, director of the District and a shareholder in the Metropolitan. He was already seventy-five years of age, ultraconservative and not at all interested to enter upon radical railway changes, particularly when they represented large expenditures, the profit outcome of which could not definitely be foretold. He had arisen at five-thirty, and after having his tea and reading his paper, was walking among the flowers on his estate at Brentford, pondering the problem of these Americans, with their newfangled notions about everything. To be sure, the undergrounds were not doing so well as they might, and the equipment might be modernized to advantage. But why should the *Times* and the *Mail* be pointing out the fact, and particularly in connection with the arrival of an American who certainly could do no better than any of a score of Englishmen when put to it? It was no more and no less than belittling British ability, which was nonsense. England ruled, and would continue to rule, the world. It certainly needed no outside help. And from that moment on, he was prepared to argue against any foreign interference in connection with the development of London underground transit.

So, too, with Sir Wilmington Jeems, whose residence was in the region of Wimbley Park. He was also a director of the District. He was willing to admit that modernization and extension were desirable. But why an American? When the proper time came, that could be arranged by Englishmen.

And something related to the opinions of these three men constituted the majority reaction of the directors and largest shareholders of both the Metropolitan and the District, as well as those of the other underground railways of London.

But it was Colvay, the most aggressive and dynamic of the three, who was finally roused to defensive action. That same day he proceeded to consult the other directors, Stane first of all, as to what action should be taken in the matter. But by then Stane had been sufficiently impressed by Johnson's account of Cowperwood, and what he had read in the papers, to answer Colvay very cautiously. He stated that this proposal of Cowperwood's was a natural development. It was something which anyone apart from the older directors of both companies could see as necessary. Certainly, the obvious thing, now that a rival system was proposed, was to call a meeting of the directors of the Metropolitan and the District, and both groups should confer as to a proper course.

Colvay next called on Sir Wilmington Jeems, and found him in a perturbed frame of mind. "It's a hundred to one, Colvay," he said, "if we and the Metropolitan don't join up, this fellow is likely enough to pick off enough shareholders in both companies to do us all in. Count on me for unity against Cowperwood, as long as our individual interests are fully protected."

With this encouragement, Colvay proceeded to call up as many of the directors as he could reach. Out of twelve, he found seven who were alive to the import of what he had to say. Accordingly, special directors' meetings in both companies were scheduled for the following Friday, and at these meetings a request for a joint conference between the directors of the two companies was voted for the following Thursday, when there would be consideration of this new issue.

Stane and Johnson went into conference on this sudden development. It was very interesting, and most opportune, in view of the forthcoming dinner engagement between Johnson and Cowperwood.

"Depend on it!" said Johnson, "he knows everything about us through that fellow Jarkins, and he wants to sound us out."

"Well, two pins to a steam engine," said Stane, "neither the District nor the Metropolitan will do anything unless Cowperwood does something first. Just now, they are considerably stirred up, but our people are not likely to agree on any radical changes. They cannot bring themselves, even now, to unite the two loop lines, let alone electrify them and operate them as a unit. Unless Cowperwood goes ahead with his program, they will do nothing. My feeling is that we

should play with him up to the point where we see just how comprehensive his plan is, and whether he is certain to go through with it.
Then we can decide what it is going to mean to us. Unless it is perfectly clear that the Metropolitan–District people are willing and
ready to do as well or better, I feel we should join with Cowperwood
and compromise with our old friends later."

"Quite sound, quite sound!" interjected Johnson at this point. "I'm
with you entirely as to that. At least, in theory. But don't forget, my
position in this matter is a little different from yours. As a shareholder in both lines, I feel with you that very little is to be expected
from those who are in charge of things now. But as a solicitor for
both lines, I have to consider how my activities in this dual capacity
are likely to turn out. As you can see for yourself, I cannot operate
on both sides at once. My duty, as well as my sincere desire, is to
study the matter thoroughly without taking sides, and to see if the
English and American interests cannot be harmonized. As solicitor, it
seems to me there could be no harm in my confessing that I have been
approached by Mr. Cowperwood as to their general attitude. And as
a shareholder in these companies, I should be able to decide for
myself which is the best program, and, privately, at least, act accordingly. You don't see any moral objection to that, do you?"

"None whatever," said Stane. "It seems to me a very fair and frank
position for both of us to take. If they object, all right. That shouldn't
bother us. And, of course, Mr. Cowperwood will take care of himself."

"Well, I certainly am glad to hear you say that," commented Johnson. "I was beginning to be a little troubled, but now I think it may
work out. At least, there will be no harm in my having this consultation with Cowperwood. And then, if it looks satisfactory to you,
perhaps we can go further. That is, the three of us," he added cautiously.

"Certainly, the three of us," replied Stane. "Whenever you have
anything definite to report, let me know. At least, we can say one
thing," he added, getting up and stretching his long legs, "we have
stirred up the animals a bit. Or, at any rate, Cowperwood has done
it for us. And all we have to do is to sit tight and see which way they
are going to jump."

"Quite so," said Johnson. "I'll get in touch with you immediately
after I see Cowperwood on Tuesday."

Chapter 32   THE dinner at Brown's Hotel was fateful not only for Johnson and all he represented, but for Cowperwood and all that he desired to achieve, although neither of them fully realized this at the time.

As Cowperwood soon learned, Johnson had been deeply impressed by what had just occurred in connection with the directors and investors of the underground interests, and was, for all his previous enthusiasm, seeking to tread a middle course until he should learn exactly what Cowperwood was going to propose. Nevertheless, he was satisfied that Johnson, because of the great stake of future profits in connection with the development of the London transit field, was anxious to side with him if possible. And because of his own desire for social as well as financial rehabilitation, he was determined to make this possible. He began by asking Johnson to tell him quite frankly the difficulties which would confront any foreigner who approached this situation with the end he had in view.

Relieved by this decidedly frank inquiry, Johnson outlined the situation just as frankly. In fact, he talked to Cowperwood as he had talked to Stane about his personal position, making it perfectly clear that he believed his employers to be stubborn, and even obtuse, in failing to take account of the great social and economic changes which were slowly but surely developing here. Until this hour, he admitted, there had been no common sense realization of what must be done. And the present interest was due to jealousy of a foreigner rather than to any intelligent desire to solve the problem on its merits. He was sorry to say so, but it was the truth. And however much he might agree with Cowperwood in his desire to do the wise things, if he personally, as solicitor for the Metropolitan and District lines, were suspected of furthering any outside plan of interference, and regardless of his interest as a shareholder, he would be turned on and divested of his present important connections, shorn of his power to do anything at all, which made his position very difficult.

Nevertheless, Johnson insisted, the invasion was legitimate, and, from a purely practical point of view, should be carried through. And for that reason he was anxious to help, if possible. But he must know the exact details of Cowperwood's program, in order that they might see how far they could go together.

Cowperwood's private plan was, in reality, much more subtle and ruthless than Johnson was ready at the moment to suspect. For one thing, having contemplated the prestige and advantage which this single purchase of the Charing Cross rights had brought him, and considering the various other rights which had already been sanctioned by Parliament—but quite all of which appeared to lack the money with which to proceed—he was thinking of buying as many as possible of these for himself, and without a word to anyone. And later, if he were fought too stubbornly, he would combine them and offer London a rival system—a move which he felt would bring his enemies to terms. At the same time, in connection with the Charing Cross line, which was nothing more than a continuation of the old Traffic Electrical Company, he was prepared, if necessary, to share a fair percentage of its founder's shares with such English investors as could help him get control of the District line.

While Cowperwood had indicated to Berenice that it was his intention to place this London venture on a higher plane than any other·he had ever engaged in, nevertheless, experience had taught him the necessity of keeping the major profits in his own hands until such time as he was sure that he would not to be overreached in such a way as to make absolute honesty on his part ridiculous and destructive. It had been a principle with him to own and control not only at least 51 per cent of every company of which he was the head, but also at least 51 per cent of the various minor companies which he invariably organized and operated through dummies.

Thus, in regard to the electrical equipment required by the new line, he was already planning the organization of the Railway Equipment & Construction Company to take over the contract for electrifying the Charing Cross line. Other subsidiary companies would be organized to supply cars, rails, steel girders, station equipment, and the like. Naturally, the profits would be enormous. Although in Chicago, these had gone to himself alone, here in London, in order to win a battle which threatened to be difficult, he was now planning to divide a percentage of these profits with those who would be most useful to him.

For instance, it was his intention, if necessary, to acquaint Stane and Johnson with this equipment company plan, and if they were truly harmonious, to show them how, in case he, or he and they jointly, should come into possession of the Metropolitan and the

District, their earliest and surest profits would come from this business of construction and equipment. Furthermore, he intended to emphasize that with the building and equipment of each additional extension of this general system, the profits from this equipment and construction company would go on and on, constituting a lever which, from experience, he knew to be immense.

Cowperwood's bearing before Johnson in this friendly conference was that of one who had nothing whatever to conceal. At the same time, he was thinking it would not be easy to outwit such a man. In fact, he was the sort of person who might be a good replacement for Sippens, if it were ever possible to arrange it. In consequence, after sounding out Johnson as to his various potentialities and finding him receptive, though reserved, he asked him whether he would be willing to act as chief counsel and fiscal agent in connection with the very necessary series of overtures which would precede the uniting of all of the lines and rights necessary for a complete London tube system. As he now assured Johnson, his purchase of the Charing Cross line was not really significant or important save as it could be used as an entering wedge for other lines.

"The truth is, Mr. Johnson," he went on, in his most effective manner, "some time before coming here I had this entire situation investigated. And I know as well as you do that this central loop system is the key to the entire business. I also know that you and Lord Stane are among the largest minority stockholders of the District. Now I want to know if there is not some way through you that I can effect a combination with the Metropolitan and the District as well as the other lines."

"It's not going to be easy," said Johnson, solemnly. "We are confronted by tradition, and England stands by her own. However, if I understand you, you are aiming to bring about a combination between yourself and these lines, particularly the loop system, with yourself in charge, of course."

"Precisely," said Cowperwood, "and I can make it worth your while, I assure you."

"You do not need to tell me that," said Johnson. "But I shall have to take some time to think about this, Mr. Cowperwood, do a little underground work of my own. And when I have thought it all out, we can go over the whole matter again."

"Of course," said Cowperwood. "I understand that. Besides, I want to leave London for a little while. Suppose you call me within the next ten or twelve days."

They then shook hands warmly, Johnson thrilled by a dream of activity and possession. It was a little late for him to be triumphing in this field, to which his entire life had been devoted. Yet it now seemed possible.

As for Cowperwood, he was left to meditate upon the practical financial course which he must pursue. In the last analysis, the open sesame to the solution of this problem was simple: to offer enough in pounds sterling. Dangle enough cash before the eyes of the quarreling investors, and, whatever their objections, it was more than likely that they would take the cash and let the quarrel go. Supposing he did have to pay these recalcitrant directors and investors two or three or four pounds for every pound they now controlled? The profit that would flow from his construction corporation plan and the growth of traffic itself in a great and growing city like London would actually cover not only the extraordinary price which he was now prepared to offer, but eventually would yield more in interest than these people had the wit to envision. The thing to do was to secure control, and then later unite these lines, at whatever seemingly fabulous cost. Time, and the current financial growth of the world, would take care of it all.

Of course, since he did not wish to reach down into his own hoardings for the preliminary cost of all this, he would probably have to return to the United States in the near future, and, by cannily outlining the possibilities of the situation, secure from certain banks, trust companies, and individual financiers with whose methods and cupidity he was thoroughly acquainted, subscriptions to an underlying holding company. And this in turn would take over these London properties and then later prorate these acquired holdings to the various subscribers on a basis of two or three dollars for every dollar invested.

But the thing to do now was to refresh himself by a vacation with Berenice. When that was over, he would consult with Johnson and arrange for a meeting with Lord Stane, for upon the attitude of these two, much depended.

Chapter 33

THROUGHOUT this turmoil of business affairs—which had been punctuated by the departure of Aileen for Paris and Berenice's activities in connection with Pryor's Cove—Cowperwood had had to content himself with mere glimpses of his loved one. She was so busy, apparently, shopping and arranging things. The graceful trivialities with which she amused herself, however, only served to make her more of an intriguing personality in his eyes. She is so alive, he often said to himself. She desires things and enjoys them intensely, and makes me do so. She appears to be interested in everything, and therefore people are naturally interested in her.

And now, on his first visit to Pryor's Cove, he found the place completely equipped: cook, maids, housekeeper, butler, to say nothing of the outdoor staff maintained by Stane. And Berenice herself affecting an interest—or pose, he could not say which—in regard to the charms of this rustic life. So often her love of nature appeared to be genuine, and even affecting: a bird, a tree, a flower, a butterfly—she was ecstatic. Marie Antoinette could have played the part no better. When he arrived, she was out with the shepherd, who had assembled the sheep and lambs for her inspection. As his carriage rolled into the drive, she gathered into her arms one of the smallest and wooliest of the new lambs. She made a picture which delighted but in no way deceived him. Acting, and for my benefit, was his thought.

"The shepherdess and her sheep!" he exclaimed, stepping forward and touching the head of the lamb in her arms. "These charming creatures! They come and go like the spring flowers."

His glance acknowledged the artistry of her dress, although he said nothing. He understood clearly that for her to effect an unusual costume was natural. She would pretend to be unconscious of the significance of her poses, considering them natural to herself, a privilege as well as an obligation that was a part of her physical gifts.

"You should have come a little earlier," she said. "You might have met our neighbor, Arthur Tavistock. He's been helping me arrange things. He had to go to London, but he's coming tomorrow to do some more work."

"Really! What a practical chatelaine! Employing her guests! Is this a place where work is to be the chief form of entertainment? What am I to do?"

"Run errands. And lots of them, too."

"But I began life that way."

"Be careful that you don't end it that way." She took his arm. "Come along with me, dear. Here, Dobson!" she called to the shepherd, who came forward and took the lamb from her arms.

They walked across the smooth green lawn to the houseboat. There, on the awninged veranda, a table was spread. Inside, at one of the boat's open windows, Mrs. Carter was reading. After Cowperwood had greeted her cordially, Berenice led him over to the table.

"Now, you're to sit here and contemplate nature," she ordered. "Just relax and forget all about London." Then she put before him his favorite drink, a mint julep. "There! Now let me tell you some of the things I have in mind that we could do, if you're going to have any time. Are you?"

"All the time in the world, sweet," he said. "I've arranged things. We are free. Aileen has gone to Paris," he added confidentially, "and from what she said, I don't expect her back under ten days. Now, what's on your mind?"

"A tour of some of the English cathedrals for mother, daughter, and guardian!" she replied, promptly. "I have always wanted to see Canterbury and York and Wells. Don't you think we might take the time to do that, since we can't very well go to the Continent?"

"I think it would be ideal. I have never seen much of England, and it will be a treat for me. We can be alone." He took her hand in his, while she touched his hair with her lips.

"Don't think I'm not keeping up with all this noise about you in the papers," she said. "Already, the fact that the great Cowperwood is my guardian has gotten around. My furniture mover wanted to know if my guardian and the American millionaire talked of in the *Chronicle* were the same person. I had to admit it. But Arthur Tavistock seems to think it natural enough for me to have so distinguished a mentor."

Cowperwood smiled.

"I suppose you've considered the servants and what they are likely to think."

"I certainly have, dearest! Troublesome, but necessary. That is the reason I want us to take the trip. Now, if you're rested I want to show you something interesting." And she smiled as she signaled Cowperwood to follow her.

She led the way to a bedroom which was beyond the central hall, opened a bureau drawer and extracted from it a pair of hairbrushes, with the coat of arms of the Earl of Stane engraved on the silver backs; also a stray collar button, and several hairpins.

"If hairpins could be identified as easily as hairbrushes, these things might prove a romance," she said, mischievously. "But the noble lord's secret is going to be kept by me."

At that moment, from under the trees surrounding the cottage, came the sound of a sheep bell.

"There!" she exclaimed, as it ceased. "When you hear that, wherever you are, you're to come to dinner. It's going to take the place of a bowing butler."

The trip, as Berenice planned it, was to start south from London, with perhaps a stop at Rochester, and then on to Canterbury. After paying homage to that exquisite poem in stone, they were to motor to some modest streamside inn on the river Stour—no great hotel or resort to break the aesthetic simplicity of this tour—where they would enjoy a room with a fire and the simplest of English fare. For Berenice had been reading Chaucer and books on these English cathedrals, and she hoped to recapture the spirit in which they were conceived. From Canterbury they would go to Winchester, and from there to Salisbury, and from Salisbury to Stonehenge; from thence to Wells, Glastonbury, Bath, Oxford, Peterborough, York, Cambridge, and then home again. But always, as she insisted, the purely conventional was to be avoided. They were to seek the smallest of inns and the simplest of villages.

"It will be good for us," she insisted. "We pamper ourselves too much. If you study all these lovely things, you may build better subways."

"And you ought to be content with simple cotton dresses!" said Cowperwood.

For Cowperwood, the real charm of their vacation trip was not the cathedrals or the village cottages and inns. It was the changeful vividness of Berenice's temperament and tastes that held him. There was not a single woman of his acquaintance who, given a choice of

Paris and the Continent in early May, would have selected the cathedral towns of England. But Berenice was apart from others in that she seemed to find within herself the pleasures and fulfillments which she most craved.

At Rochester, they listened to a guide who talked of King John, William Rufus, Simon de Montfort, and Watt Tyler, all of whom Cowperwood dismissed as mere shadows, men or creatures who had once had their day and selfish notions of one kind or another and had moved on to pass into nothing, as would all who were here. He liked better the sunlight on the river and the sense of spring in the air. Even Berenice seemed a little disappointed at the somewhat commonplace view.

But at Canterbury the mood of all changed greatly, even that of Mrs. Carter, who was by no means interested in religious architecture. "Well, now, I like this place," she commented, as they entered one of its winding streets.

"I want to find out by which road the pilgrims came," said Berenice. "I wonder if it was this one. Oh, look, there's the cathedral!" and she pointed to a tower and spandril visible above the low roof of a stone cottage.

"Lovely!" commented Cowperwood. "And a delightful afternoon for it, too. Do we have lunch first, or feast on the cathedral instead?"

"The cathedral first!" replied Berenice.

"And eat a cold lunch afterwards, I suppose," put in her mother, sarcastically.

"Mother!" chided Berenice. "And at Canterbury, of all places!"

"Well, I happen to know something of these English inns, and I know how important it is not to be last if we can't be the first," said Mrs. Carter.

"And there you have the power of religion in 1900!" remarked Cowperwood. "It must wait on a country inn."

"I haven't a word to say against religion," persisted Mrs. Carter, "but churches are different. They haven't a thing to do with it."

Canterbury. The tenth-century close, with its rabble of winding streets, and within its walls, silence and the stately, time-blackened spires, pinnacles, and buttresses of the cathedral itself. Jackdaws fluttering and quarreling over the vantage points. Within, a welter of tombs, altars, tablets, shrines: Henry IV, Thomas à Becket, Archbishop Laud, the Huguenots, and Edward, the Black Prince. Berenice could scarcely be drawn away. Guides and flocks of sightseers were slowly parading from memory to memory. In the crypt where the Huguenots lived and found shelter, worshiped and wove their clothes, she stayed to meditate, guidebook in hand. And so, too, at the spot where Thomas à Becket was killed.

Cowperwood, who saw things in the large, could scarcely endure this minutae. He was but little interested in the affairs of bygone men and women, being so intensely engaged with the living present. And after a time he slipped outside, preferring the wide sweep of gardens, with their flower-lined walks and views of the cathedral. Its arches and towers and stained-glass windows, this whole carefully executed shrine, still held glamor, but all because of the hands and brains, aspirations and dreams of selfish and self-preserving creatures like himself. And so many of these, as he now mused, walking about, had warred over possession of this church. And now they were within its walls, graced and made respectable, the noble dead! Was any man noble? Had there ever been such a thing as an indubitably noble soul? He was scarcely prepared to believe it. Men killed to live—all of them—and wallowed in lust in order to reproduce themselves. In fact, wars, vanities, pretenses, cruelties, greeds, lusts, murder, spelled their true history, with only the weak running to a mythical saviour or god for aid. And the strong using this belief in a god to further the conquest of the weak. And by such temples or shrines as this. He looked, meditated, and was somehow touched with the futility of so much that was still so beautiful.

But occasional glimpses of Berenice, poised attentively over a cross or religious inscription, were sufficient to restore him. There was about her at such moments a seemingly non-material as well as mentally contemplative grace which brushed aside the tang of that pagan modernity which at other times gave her the force and glare of a red flower in a gray rock. Perhaps, as he now reasoned with himself, her reaction to these faded memories and forms, joined, as it was, with her delight in luxury, was not unakin to his own personal delight in paintings and his pleasure in power. Because of this he was moved to respect, and all the more so when, the pilgrimage over, they were finally preparing to leave for dinner, she exclaimed: "We're coming back here this evening after dinner! There will be a new moon."

"Indeed!" said Cowperwood, amusedly.

Mrs. Carter yawned and announced that she would not return. She was going to her room after dinner.

"Very well, Mother," said Berenice, "but Frank must come back for the good of his soul!"

"There you are! I have a soul!" said Cowperwood, indulgently.

So later, after a simple meal at the inn, Berenice led him down the darkening street. As they entered the carved black gate that led into the close, the moon, a new white feather in a roof of blue-black steel, seemed but an ornament of the topmost pinnacle of the long silhouette of the cathedral. At first, engaged by the temperamental whim of Berenice, Cowperwood stared dutifully. But presently, it was the blend of her own response that swayed him. Oh, to be young, to be so thrilled, to be so deeply moved by color, form, the mystery and meaninglessness of human activity!

But Berenice was not thinking only of the faded memories and jumble of hopes and fears that had produced all this, but also of the mystery and immensity of voiceless time and space. Ah, to have understanding, knowledge! To think earnestly and seekingly for some reason or excuse for life! Was her own life merely to be one of clever, calculating, and ruthless determination to fulfill herself socially, or as an individual? What benefit could that be, to her or to anyone? What beauty would that create or inspire? Now . . . here . . . in this place . . . perfumed with memories and moonlight . . . something was at her elbow and in her heart . . . something that whispered of quiet and peace . . . solitude . . . fulfillment . . . a desire to create something utterly beautiful, so that her life would be complete and significant.

But . . . this was wild dreaming . . . the moon had bewitched her. Why should she want anything? She had all that women desired.

"Let's go back, Frank," she said, at last, something within herself failing her, some sense of beauty gone forever. "Let's go back to the inn."

Chapter 34   WHILE Cowperwood and Berenice were touring the cathedral towns, Aileen and Tollifer were visiting the Paris cafés, smart shops, and popular resorts. Having made sure that Aileen was coming, Tollifer had preceded her by twenty-four hours, and used that time to arrange a program which should prove amusing and so detain her in Paris. For he knew that this French world was not a novelty to her. She had been there, and in most of the European resorts, at numerous times in the past, when Cowperwood was most anxious to see her happy. Even now these were precious memories, and occasionally flashed only too vividly before her.

Nonetheless, she was finding Tollifer a most diverting person. On the evening of her arrival he called at the Ritz, where she had installed herself with her maid, half-wondering why she had come. It was true that she had intended to go to Paris, but she had treasured the idea that Cowperwood would go with her. However, his affairs in London, shouted about by the press and glibly enough presented to her by himself, convinced her that his time was very much occupied. In fact, having encountered Sippens in the lobby of the Cecil one morning, he had regaled her with a brisk and colorful account of the tangle of affairs with which Cowperwood was now burdened.

"He'll turn this town upside down, Mrs. Cowperwood," Sippens had said, "if his interest holds out. I just hope he doesn't work too hard"—which was really not at all what he hoped. "He's not as young as he used to be, although he seems shrewder and quicker than ever."

"I know, I know," Aileen had replied at the time. "There isn't anything about Frank that you can tell me. He'll keep on working until he dies, I suppose."

And she had left Sippens, feeling that this was true, yet suspecting that there must be a woman somewhere . . . possibly Berenice Fleming. However, *she* was Mrs. Frank Cowperwood. She had the consolation of knowing that wherever her name was mentioned, people would turn and look: in the shops, hotels, restaurants. And then there was this Bruce Tollifer. Here he was, on her arrival, as handsome as ever, and saying, as he entered her hotel suite:

"Well, you did take my advice! And now that you're here, I'm going to make myself responsible for you. If you're in the mood, you must dress immediately for dinner. I've arranged a little party for you. Some friends of mine from home are here. I don't know whether you know the Sidney Brainerds, of New York?"

"Oh, yes," said Aileen, her brain a whirl of emotion. She knew by hearsay that the Brainerds were wealthy and socially significant.

Mrs. Brainerd, as she remembered, had been Marigold Shoemaker, of Philadelphia.

"Mrs. Brainerd is here in Paris," continued Tollifer. "She and several of her friends are coming on to dinner with us at Maxim's, and afterward we're going to an Argentinian's place. He'll amuse you, I know. Do you think you can be ready in an hour?" He turned toward the door with the air of one who was anticipating a very gay evening.

"Oh, I think so," said Aileen, laughing. "But you'll have to leave now if I'm to start."

"That fits in perfectly for me. Wear white, if you have it, and dark red roses. You'll look stunning!"

Aileen flushed a little at this familiarity. A high-handed caballero, to say the least!

"I'll wear just that," she said, giving him a vivid smile, "if I can find the dress."

"Great! I'll be back for you in an hour. Until then . . ." and he bowed and left.

As she dressed, she found herself more than ever at a loss to understand this sudden, assured invasion of Tollifer's. It was obvious he was not without money. Yet, with these superior connections of his, why should he bother with her? Why should this Mrs. Brainerd join a dinner party of which she was not to be the principal guest? Pursued as she was by contradictory thoughts, this easy friendship of Tollifer, pretense though it might be, was still fascinating. If he were an adventurer, coldly seeking money, like so many, most certainly he was a clever one. And with diversions at his beck and call, such as all those who had approached her in the past few years had lacked. Their methods had all too often been dull, their manners irritating.

"Ready?" exclaimed Tollifer breezily as he came in an hour or so later, eyeing her white dress and the red roses at her waist. "We'll be just in time if we go now. Mrs. Brainerd is bringing a young Greek banker, and her friend, Mrs. Judith Thorne, no acquaintance of mine, is bringing an Arab sheik, Ibrihim Abbas Bey, who is up to God knows what here in Paris! But, anyway, he speaks English, and so does the Greek."

Tollifer was a little flushed and, if anything, even more assured. He paced the room with an easy stride, drunkenly elevated by the knowledge that he was once more in good form. To Aileen's amusement he railed against the furnishings of her suite.

"Look at those hangings! God, what they get away with! As I came up in the elevator just now, it squeaked. Imagine that in New York! And it's just such people as you who let them do it!"

Aileen was flattered. "Is it so bad?" she asked. "I haven't even thought about it. After all, where else can we go here?"

He poked his finger at the tasseled silk shade of a floor lamp. "This has a wine stain on it. And somebody's been burning this fake tapestry with cigarettes. I don't blame them!"

Aileen laughed at him, amused by his swaggering maleness. "Oh, come on," she said, "we could be in worse places than this. Besides, you're keeping your guests waiting."

"That's right. I wonder if that sheik knows anything about American whiskey. Let's go find out!"

Maxim's of 1900. Glossily waxed black floors, reflecting Pompeian red walls, a gilded ceiling, and the lights of three enormous prismed electroliers. Except for front and rear exits, the walls lined with russet-red leather seats, and before them small and intimate supper tables: a Gallic atmosphere calculated to effect that mental as well as emotional release which the world of that day sought in one place, and one place only—Paris! Merely to enter was to lapse into a happy delirium. Types and costumes and varying temperaments of all the nations of the world. And all at the topmost toss of wealth, title, position, fame, and all tethered by the steel cords of convention in conduct and dress, yet all, seeking freedom from convention, drawn to convention's showplace of unconventionality.

Aileen was gloriously thrilled to see and be seen here. As Tollifer rather anticipated, his friends were late.

"The sheik," he explained, "sometimes goes astray."

But a few minutes later came Mrs. Brainerd and her Greek, and Mrs. Thorne with her Arab cavalier. The sheik in particular caused a slight stir and buzz. At once, in his grandest manner, Tollifer took over the business of ordering, delighting in the half-dozen waiters who hovered like flies about the table. The sheik, he was delighted to discover, was instantly attracted to Aileen. Her rounded form, her bright hair and high coloring suggested more delight to him than the slim and less flamboyant charms of either Mrs. Brainerd or Mrs. Thorne. At once he devoted himself to her, bombarding her with polite inquiries. From where did she come? Was her husband, like all these Americans, a millionaire? Might he have one of her roses? He liked their dark color. Had she ever been to Arabia? She would enjoy the life of a roving Bedouin tribe. It was very beautiful in Arabia.

Aileen, fixed by his blazing black eyes above his smartly clipped beard, his long hooked nose and swarthy complexion, was at once thrilled and dubious. What would intimate contact with this man be like? Suppose one went to Arabia—what would become of one in the clutches of such a creature? Although she smiled and gave all the required information, she was pleased to feel that Tollifer and his friends were near at hand, even though their amused attention was not exactly to her liking.

Ibrihim, learning that she was to be in Paris for a few days, asked to be allowed to see more of her. He had entered a horse for the Grand Prix. She must go with him to see the horse. Later, they would dine together. She was at the Ritz? Ah . . . he was occupying an apartment in the Rue Said, near the Bois.

During this scene, Tollifer, in high spirits, was doing his best to ingratiate himself with Marigold, who twitted him as to this latest affair of his, the nature of which she quite well understood.

"Tell me, Bruce," she teased, at one point, "what are you going to do with all the rest of us, now that you are so amply provided for?"

"If you mean yourself, you can tell me that. I haven't so many bothering me."

"No? Is the poor darling as lonely as that?"

"Just as lonely as that, and more so, if you only knew," he said, soberly. "But what about your husband? Isn't he likely to resent interference?"

"Nothing to worry about there!" she said, smilingly and encouragingly. "I just ran into him before I met you. Besides, how many years has it been since I last saw you?"

"Oh, quite a few. But whose fault is that? And what about your yacht?"

"Only my regular skipper, I swear! How would you like to take a cruise?"

Tollifer was nonplussed. Here was one of those opportunities of which he had been dreaming. And obviously now he could not take advantage of it. He must go on with what he had agreed to do, or there would be an end to all this.

"Well," he said, laughingly, "you're not sailing tomorrow?"

"Oh, no!"

"If you're serious, be careful!"

"Never more serious in my life," she replied.

"That remains to be seen. Anyway, will you have luncheon with me one day this week? We'll walk in the Tuileries afterward."

A little later he paid the bill and they left.

Sabinal's. Midnight. The customary swarm of people. Gambling. Dancing. Intimate groups in brisk or lazy conversation. Sabinal himself coming forward to greet Tollifer and his party, and suggesting they adjourn to his apartment until one o'clock, when a popular troupe of Russian singers and dancers would perform.

Sabinal was the possessor of notable jewels, medieval Italian glass and silver, Asiatic fabrics of rare texture and color, but even more impressive than his collection—which he exhibited in the most casual manner—was his own elusive and Mephistophelean self, a shadowy and yet intriguing force which affected all as might an opiate. He knew so many people, and such interesting places. In the fall, he was planning a trip, he said; closing up his place for a while. He was off to the Orient to collect fine objects which later he would sell to private collectors. Indeed, his income from this sort of quest was considerable.

Aileen, as well as the others, was enchanted. She was delighted with the place. All the more so because Tollifer was careful not to explain to any of them the commercial basis on which it was conducted. He intended sending his personal check to Sabinal, but preferred them to take away the impression that Sabinal was a friend of his.

Chapter 35

THE importance of Tollifer's job was impressed on him by the receipt, on the third day after Aileen's arrival, of an additional $2,000 in cash from the Paris fiscal agent of the Central Trust of New York, which, before his leaving, had notified him to keep their London and Paris offices advised of his address.

There was no doubt of Aileen's compliant mood in regard to him.

Telephoning her some five hours after their visit to Sabinal's, and suggesting they have lunch together, he could tell from the tone of her voice that she was glad to hear from him again. It was the feeling of companionship with someone who seemed to take a personal interest in her that made her happy. In some respects, he was so like the Cowperwood of old, energetic, cordial, and not a little managerial.

He left the telephone whistling. His attitude toward her was more kindly than it had been when he first considered the task. For in studying her so far, he was fully able to grasp what the favor and affection of Cowperwood must have meant to her, and what its complete loss must spell to her now. Often moody himself, and for not dissimilar reasons, he could sympathize with her.

The night before, at Sabinal's, when Marigold and Mrs. Thorne had at times so casually and indifferently excluded her from their conversation, he had noticed a neglected and helpless look on her face. It had moved him to take her away from the group for a few minutes' play at the roulette wheel. Unquestionably, she was going to prove a difficult protégée. But that was his job, and on the success of it rested his future.

But, my God, he said to himself: she ought to take off at least twenty pounds! And she needs the right clothes, and a few attractive mannerisms. She's too tame. She needs to be made to respect herself, and then these other people will respect her. If I can't do that for her, she'll do me more harm than good, money or no money!

Always the industrious struggler for what he wanted, he decided upon immediate and intensive action. Conscious that inspiration for Aileen depended upon his own smart appearance, he took the utmost pains to look his best. He smiled as he contrasted himself with the figure he had cut in New York six months before. Rosalie Harrigan, that wretched room, his disappointing efforts to get a job!

His apartment in the Bois was but a few moments' walk from the Ritz, and he stepped forth this morning with the air of a Parisian favorite. He thought of the various dressmakers, hairdressers, milliners, he would enlist in the making-over of Aileen. Around the corner was Claudel Richard. He would take her to Richard, and persuade him to impress upon her that if she would take off twenty pounds he would design costumes for her that would arrest attention and that she should be among the first to wear. Then there was Kraussmeier, in the Boulevard Haussmann. His footwear was rumored to excel that of all other bootmakers. Tollifer had satisfied himself as to that. In the Rue de la Paix, what ornaments, perfumes, jewels! In the Rue Dupont, what *salons de beauté,* with Sarah Schimmel's as the favored establishment in this particular field. Aileen should learn of her.

At Natasha Lubovsky's balcony restaurant overlooking the park across from Notre Dame, lingering over iced coffee and eggs Sudanoff, he lectured Aileen on current modes and tastes. Had she heard that Teresa Bianca, the Spanish dancing sensation, was wearing Kraussmeier slippers? And Francesca, the youngest daughter of the Duke of Toller, was one of his patronesses. And had she heard of the marvels of beautifying accomplished by Sarah Schimmel? He recited a dozen instances.

Followed a visit to Richard's, then to Kraussmeier's, and a certain Luti, newly favored vendor of perfumes, and the afternoon ended with tea at Germay's. And at nine in the evening, at the Café de Paris, there was a dinner, at which appeared Rhoda Thayer, of American light-opera fame, and her summer companion, the Brazilian Mello Barrios, undersecretary of the Brazilian Embassy. Also a guest was a certain Maria Rezstadt, of Czech and Hungarian extraction. On one of his earlier visits to Paris, Tollifer had met her as the wife of one of the Austria's secret military representatives in France. Lunching in Marguery's one day recently, he had met her again, in company with Santos Castro, a baritone of the French opera, who was singing opposite the new American opera star, Mary Garden. He learned her husband had died, and noted she seemed a little bored with Castro. If Tollifer were free, she would be glad to see him again. And since her mood as well as her natural intelligence and suave maturity seemed better suited to Aileen than some of the younger women he knew, Tollifer had immediately planned to introduce her to Aileen.

And, on presentation, Aileen was strongly impressed by her. She was a woman of arresting appearance: tall, with smooth black hair and strange gray eyes, and this evening dressed in what appeared to be a single length of ruby velvet, draped seductively around her. In sharp contrast to Aileen, she wore no jewels, and her hair was drawn back smoothly from her face. Her attitude toward Castro suggested that he meant little to her, except maybe the publicity which contact with him might bring her. Turning to Aileen and Tollifer, she proceeded to relate that only recently she and Castro had made a tour of the Balkans, an admission—and coming so soon after Tollifer's explanation to Aileen that the two were merely good friends—which somewhat startled Aileen, since always, and regardless of her personal and private transgressions, she was a little overawed by convention. Yet this woman was so suave and assured as practically to laugh at the demands of organized society. Aileen was fascinated.

"You see, in the East," said Madame Rezstadt, commenting on her trip, "the women are slaves. Truly, only the gypsies appear to be free, and they, of course, have no position. The wives of most of the officials and men of title are really slaves, living in fear of their husbands."

Aileen smiled wanly at this. "That is probably not true of the East alone," she said.

Madame Rezstadt smiled wisely. "No," she said, "not exactly. We have slaves here, too. In Ahmayreecah, too, yaays?" She showed her even white teeth.

Aileen laughed, thinking of her emotional enslavement to Cowperwood. How was it that a woman like this could be so wholly emancipated, caring apparently for no man, at least not deeply or torturingly, whereas she . . . At once she wished that she might know her better, perhaps by contact gather some of her emotional calm and social indifference.

Curiously enough, Madame Rezstadt appeared to show more than a casual interest in her. She asked Aileen about her life in America. How long was she to be in Paris? Where was she staying? She suggested they have lunch together on the following day, to which Aileen agreed with alacrity.

At the same time, her head was swimming with all of the practical business of the afternoon, and Tollifer's part in it. For most certainly, and by the pleasant indirection of shopping, there had been conveyed to her a sense of her personal lacks, which, at the same time, she had been convinced could be remedied. There was to be a doctor, a masseuse, a diet, and a new method of facial massage. She was to be changed, and by Tollifer. But for what purpose? And to what end? Plainly, he was not attempting familiarities. There was only this platonic relationship. She was puzzled. Yet what difference? Cowperwood was not interested, and she must find some way to go on with her life.

Back in her hotel suite, Aileen felt a sudden and poignant longing for one person, in all the world, to whom she could confide her troubles, one person with whom she could relax and be natural. She would like a friend whose criticism she need not fear, whose confidence she could trust. There was something about Maria Rezstadt, as she had pressed Aileen's hand in parting, that made her feel that in her she might find these things or a semblance of them.

But the original ten days which she had planned for this visit passed swiftly enough. In fact, when they were gone, she was by no means ready to return to London. For, as she suddenly sensed, Tollifer, with his advice and his array of skilled workers, had launched a campaign which meant a physical as well as aesthetic improvement which would require time, and might even result in a change of attitude on the part of Cowperwood. She was not old, she now said to herself, and now that he was involved in this engrossing commercial struggle, he might be willing to accept her on an affectionate, if not a sensual, basis. He would, in England, she fancied, require a stabilization of his social life and might find it advisable as well as agreeable to live with her more constantly, to make a more open and public profession of his interest and satisfaction in so doing.

And so, eagerly, she began to scan herself in the mirror, to take painstaking care to obey the dietary and beautifying instructions given to her daily by Sarah Schimmel. She began to recognize the effectiveness of the unique costumes being chosen for her. And so, rapidly, as she gained in self-confidence, and accordingly in poise, she began to think constantly of Cowperwood, so much so that she was quite gay in her anticipation of what must be his surprise and, she hoped, pleasure, when he saw her again. For that reason she decided to remain in Paris until she had lost at least twenty pounds in weight, and so could wear the creations which Monsieur Richard so enthusiastically planned for her. And she wished also to test the new coiffures that were being suggested by her hairdresser. Ah, if only this might not be all in vain!

In consequence, she wrote Cowperwood that her Paris visit was proving so interesting—thanks to Mr. Tollifer—that she was staying on three or four weeks longer. "For once in my life," she added, with a trace of gaiety, "I'm getting along very well without you, and am well looked after."

When Cowperwood read this, it had a strangely saddening effect on him. For he had so slyly arranged it all. At the same time there flashed into his mind the thought that Berenice had also had a part in it. Primarily, it had been her suggestion. He had seized upon it as the only way to happiness with her, and so it was. Still, what of a mind that could think so shrewdly and ruthlessly? Might it not one day be turned on him? And then, what, since he cared so much? The idea was irritating. To dismiss it, he reasoned that as he had met all things, so, when the time came, he would meet that.

Chapter 36

As a result of his talk with Cowperwood in Brown's Hotel, Johnson decided that a meeting between Cowperwood and Lord Stane was the next logical step in arriving at a decision as to the part they might play in future negotiations.

"You wouldn't risk anything by talking to him," was the way he put it to Stane. "Of course, we'll make it plain that if we go in with him, our services in helping him get control of the loop will cost him 50 per cent of whatever that control is. Then we might arrange with some of the shareholders of the Metropolitan and the District to come in and help make up the 51 per cent and so keep control."

Lord Stane nodded. "Go on," he said.

"That would fix it, you see," continued Johnson, "so that whatever else happened, we, with some others—Colvay, Jeems, and maybe Dighton—would be in control, and he would have to deal with us as joint owners of this central service."

"That certainly sounds all right to me," said Stane, surveying him calmly. "Anyway, I should like to meet the fellow. You may ask him to my home whenever you wish. Just let me know when it is to be. I can tell more about it after I meet him."

Accordingly, on a certain warm June day, Cowperwood climbed into a carriage with Johnson and together they drove through pleasant London streets to the home of Lord Stane.

Cowperwood was doubtful as to how much of his intricate and secret plan he should reveal in this forthcoming interview. In fact, he had been playing with the thought that however successful he might be with Stane and Johnson, it would be well to sound out Abington Scarr. He might let him in on his Baker Street & Waterloo act. Possessing that, and such other acts as he could pick up through Haddonfield and possibly Lord Ettinge, he would be in a position to dictate even to this loop organization.

As they drew up to Stane's house in Berkeley Square, he was impressed by its square, dignified solidity. It seemed to breathe a security which certainly had nothing to do with trade. Inside, the liveried footman, the silence of the large salon on the first floor, created an atmosphere pleasing to him and yet not sufficient to disturb his personal sense of values. It was quite right for this man to be as secure as he could be. It was quite right for himself, if he could, to involve him and make him richer, or use him, and skill failing him, sweep all away.

But now Johnson suggested that it might interest him to look at some of Lord Stane's paintings, since the butler had just informed him that Stane had telephoned to say that he would be a few minutes late. The attitude of the solicitor in his role of temporary host was anxious. Cowperwood said he would indeed enjoy passing the time in that way, and Johnson led him to an extensive gallery in the main entrance.

As they walked through the gallery, pausing to examine several rare portraits by Romney and Gainsborough, Johnson launched upon a brief history of the House of Stane. The late Earl had been a cautious and studious person, interested principally in Hittite excavations and translations, and had expended a great deal of money, for which historians, so it was said, were duly grateful. Young Stane, rather more than less alienated by his father's antiquarian interests, had turned to society and finance for diversion and development. He was very popular, a distinguished fashion figure as well as financier. And in season this house was the scene of many social functions. His country seat in Tregasal was one of the show places of England. There was also a charming summer cottage at Pryor's Cove, near Marlowe on the Thames, and a wine farm in France.

At the mention of Berenice's present abode, Cowperwood repressed a smile, but was prevented from making any comment by the arrival of Stane himself, who greeted them both in an easy, casual manner.

"Oh, there you are, Johnson! And, of course, this is Mr. Cowperwood." He extended his hand, and Cowperwood, measuring him swiftly and favorably, took it and pressed it heartily.

"This is a pleasure and a privilege, I assure you," he said.

"Not at all, not at all," replied Stane. "Elverson has told me all about you. I think, though, we might be a little more comfortable in the library. Shall we go?"

He pulled a bell rope, telling the man to bring drinks, and led the way into a charming room with french windows looking out on a walled garden. While he moved about, acting the part of host, Cowperwood continued to study him. He found his own mood decidedly friendly toward this man. There was an easy, genial courtesy and awareness about him that bespoke value to the person who could win his confidence. But this confidence could not be won easily. He would have to be fairly and advantageously treated.

Just the same, Cowperwood now decided definitely against revealing at this time the inside workings of his proposition. At the same time, he found himself thinking of Berenice, for he and she had tacitly agreed that she might be called on to play a social role in connection with just such people as Stane. But now that he proved to be so attractive, he was not sure that he was willing to have her do this. He composed himself, however, while Johnson began outlining his ideas on the underground situation.

When Johnson had finished, Cowperwood began, softly and smoothly, expounding his plan of unification. He dwelt especially on electrification, lighting, the new method of separate motor power for each car, air brakes, and automatic signals. And at only one point did Stane interrupt to ask:

"Do you contemplate a personal or directorial control of this entire system?"

"Directorial, of course," replied Cowperwood, who was really contemplating no such thing. "You see," he went on, as both observed him silently, "it is my plan, if I could bring about a unified system, to form a new company and include this Charing Cross which I now own. And in order to get the present shareholders of the loop companies to come in, I would offer them three shares in this larger company for each one they now hold in these smaller ones. And since the Charing Cross is going to cost at least £2,000,000 to build, you can see that there would be a considerable increase in the value of their holdings." He paused to note how this affected his listeners, and saw that it did so favorably. He then proceeded.

"Would you say that the plan should be profitable, particularly when it is agreed beforehand that all of the lines of this new company are to be modernized and operated as one system, and at no additional cost to the shareholders but rather by selling shares to the public?"

"I should certainly say so," commented Stane, to which Johnson nodded in agreement.

"Well, there you have my plan in a general way," said Cowperwood. "Of course, there might be additional ramifications, but that would be something for the directors of the new larger system to decide on." He was thinking of Scarr, Haddonfield, and others whose acts, if he secured control of them, would have to be bought from him.

But at this point Stane scratched his ear meditatively.

"As I see it," he said, "this three-for-one arrangement merely covers the matter of luring such shareholders as might be interested into joining with you on that basis. But you are forgetting, I think, the matter of sentiment, which is certain to be against you. And that being true, you may be sure that offering three shares for one will not bring in enough of the present owners to permit you to do as you wish on your terms, which, as I assume, would mean general control for you. For, you see, they are set on a purely English control. Both Johnson and I, since the announcement of your purchase of the Charing Cross act, have discovered that. Besides, there has already developed quite a little opposition in both the Metropolitan and the District, even a tendency to combine against you. And heaven knows the directors of those two lines have never been too affectionate towards each other up to this time!"

Here Johnson chuckled dryly.

"So unless you move with the greatest caution and tact at every point," continued Stane, "have the right people approached in the right way, and preferably by English rather than American factors, you are likely to find yourself blocked."

"Quite so," said Cowperwood, who saw very clearly what Stane had in mind. If they were to be won over to the task of helping him pull this English chestnut out of the fire, they were going to require, not additional compensation—they could scarcely ask for more than he had already offered—but more likely some form of joint control with him. Or, if that could not be effected, then they would demand security in regard to their investments and, very likely, pro rata opportunities along with himself in connection with the progressive development of this proposed system. And how was that to be arranged?

For the moment he was not a little puzzled, and to clarify his own as well as their thoughts, he now added:

"It was in connection with that that I was thinking how I might interest both of you, for I realize that you understand this situation, and assuming that you are willing to co-operate with me, can do a great deal toward furthering more favorable sentiment. Just how do you think, apart from the three shares to one arrangement, you should be compensated? What particular arrangement between the three of us would be agreeable to you?" He paused.

But the conversation as to this was much too extended and intricate to relate here. In the main, it dealt with preliminary work which would have to be done by Stane and Johnson. And this preliminary work, as they now explained to Cowperwood, related more to social introductions than to anything else, for without those his purely financial affairs were not likely to make much headway.

"In England, you see," went on Stane, "one progresses more through favor and the friendship of financial as well as social groups than through particular individuals, however gifted they may be. And if you are not well and favorably known to certain groups and accepted by them, it may be difficult to proceed. You follow me?"

"Perfectly," replied Cowperwood.

"And, of course, this is never at any point a mere matter of cold and practical bargaining. There must be mutual understanding and respect. And that is not achieved in a moment. It depends not only on introductions but personal endorsements in a casual as well as definite social way. You follow me?"

"Perfectly," replied Cowperwood.

"But before that, there would have to be a very clear understanding as to what, apart from the exchange of shares, would be the reward of those who made possible such an advantageous social entree for you and your undertaking."

As Stane talked, Cowperwood sat relaxed in his chair, and although he seemed to be listening sympathetically enough, a close observer would have noticed a certain hardening of the eyes and tightening of the lips. He realized very clearly that in so instructing him Stane was condescending. For, of course, he had heard of the various scandals connected with his career and was aware of the fact that he was not admitted to the social worlds of Chicago and New York. And although he was extremely diplomatic and courteous, Cowperwood took his explanations for just what they were worth: the explanations of a man who stood well in the *haut monde* to one who had been rejected by it. And yet he was not in the least annoyed or dismayed. In fact, he was rather ironically amused. For he had the upper hand. He was going to make possible for Stane and his friends what no one else had been able to make possible.

When Stane finally paused, Cowperwood questioned him about the details of this understanding, but Stane said very courteously that he thought it would be best to leave that to Johnson. However, he already had in mind not only a guarantee of three for one of his present holdings in the District and Metropolitan but also some secret and inviolable agreement with Cowperwood whereby he and Johnson would be retained, protected, and financially enhanced as part of this great development.

And so, while Stane calmly drew up his monocle and adjusted it in his right eye the better wherewith to contemplate him, Cowperwood now emphasized how really grateful he was for Stane's personal interest and kindness in clarifying the significance of the situation. He was certain it could all be arranged to their mutual satisfaction. However, there was the task of financing, for which he himself would have to arrange. It would probably be necessary for him to return to America shortly to raise this money, before talking with the various English shareholders—a point of view with which Stane agreed.

However, already Cowperwood had in his mind a 49–51 per cent control of a loaning company which might be made to loan enough to this English company to assure its capture and control in the event of disaster. He would see.

As for Berenice and Stane, ah, well, he would wait and see as to that also. He was sixty years old, and except for fame and public acclaim, it might, in a very few years, make no particular difference. Actually, because of the relentless whirl of duties now threatening to engulf him, he was beginning to feel a little weary. Sometimes, at the close of a busy day, he felt this whole London venture to be such a senseless thing for him to be undertaking at this time. Why, only a year or two before, in Chicago, he had been saying to himself that if he could but achieve the extension of his franchises there, he would be willing to disassociate himself from the direction, and retire and travel. He had even thought at the time that if Berenice finally refused his offer, and he were left to himself again, he might patch up some form of peace with Aileen and return to his New York house and such amusements and activities as would not over-tax what he looked upon as a deserved leisure.

But now, here he was. And what was it all about? What was he to get out of it, other than the pleasure with Berenice, which, had she willed it otherwise, he might have found in a more peaceful way. At the same time, there was the point made by her, and even by himself, that he owed it to himself, to his life, his reputation as representing an immense creative force, a financial figure of the first rank, to go forward and round out his career in some such climactic fashion as this. But could it be effected without impairing his reputation as well as his fortune? Would it be possible, in view of the present state of opinion of him at home, to go back and, in a reasonably brief time, assemble the required money?

In short, his position in almost all of its aspects was care-full and trying. He was fagged, and disconcerted. Perhaps the first premonitory breath of the oncoming winter of age.

That evening, after dinner, he talked to Berenice about his plans. It would be best, he thought, to have Aileen accompany him to New York. He would need to entertain a number of people, and it would look better if his wife were there. Besides, at this point, they would have to be especially careful to keep her in a good mood, just when everything was hanging in the balance.

Chapter 37

MEANWHILE, Aileen, in Paris, at the end of a month, was, as all her new friends declared, "a different person!" Twenty pounds lighter; her color, her eyes, as well as her mood brighter; her hair arranged *"à la chanti-cleer,"* as Sarah Schimmel described it; her gowns designed by M. Richard, her shoes by M. Kraussmeier, all as Tollifer had planned.

She had achieved a real friendship with Madame Rezstadt, and the sheik, though his attentions were a little bothersome, was an amusing individual. He seemed to like her for herself alone; in fact, seemed bent on developing an affair with her. But that costume! White, and of the finest silk and wool, with a white silk cord binding it at his waist. And his oily, savage-looking black hair! And the small silver rings in his ears! And long, thin, pointed and upward-curling red leather slippers on his feet, which were certainly not small. And that hawklike nose and dark piercing eyes! When with him, one became part of a show, gazed at by all. And if she entertained him alone, she spent most of the time trying to avoid his caresses.

"Now, please, Ibrihim," she would say. "Don't forget, I'm married, and in love with my husband. I like you, I really do. But you mustn't be begging me to do what I don't want to do, because I won't, and if you keep on, I won't see you at all."

"But, you see," he insisted, in quite good English, "we have so mooch in common. You like to play, and so do I. We like to talk, ride, gamble, play ze races a little. But still, you are like me, sober, not so . . . so. . . ."

"Flighty?" interjected Aileen.

"What you mean, 'flighty'?" he inquired.

"Oh, I don't know." She felt as though she were talking to a child. "Fussy, jumpy." She waved her hands to indicate instability, mental as well as emotional.

"So? So? Ha, ha! Flighty! It is so! I understan'. You are not flighty! Gudd! So I like you, mooch. Ha, ha! Very mooch. And me? You like me—the Sheik Ibrihim?"

Aileen laughed. "Yes, I do," she said. "Of course, I think you drink too much. And I think you are anything but a good man—cruel and selfish and a lot of things. But I like you just the same, and . . ."

"Tchk, tchk," clucked the sheik. "That is not mooch for a man like me. If I do not love, I do not sleep."

"Oh, stop being silly!" exclaimed Aileen. "Do go over there and fix yourself a drink. And then go away and come back tonight and take me to dinner. I'd like to go to that Mr. Sabinal's place again."

And so Aileen's days were passing agreeably enough. Her former tendency toward melancholia was dispelled, and she began to feel that her state was not as hopeless as it had been. Cowperwood had written her that he would be coming to Paris, and in anticipation of his arrival she was prepared to surprise him with the most impressive of M. Richard's creations. And Tollifer had suggested that they take him to Orsignat's for dinner, an interesting little place recently discovered by him. It was charming, located right in the shadow of Notre Dame. Sabinal was to furnish Orsignat, for the occasion, with the wines, brandies, liqueurs, apéritifs, and cigars. And Orsignat, under the direction of Tollifer, was to furnish a repast of which no gourmet could complain. For this time it was Tollifer who was seeking to make an impression. Among the guests were to be Madame Rezstadt, the devoted sheik, and Marigold, who because of her interest in Tollifer was still in Paris and, by his orders, reconciled to Aileen.

"You and your husband," he said to Aileen, "are so familiar with all the well-known places. I think it would be more original if we got up something quite simple for a change." And he explained his plan to her.

To make sure of Cowperwood's presence, Tollifer had her cable him a pressing invitation to the dinner which they had arranged in his honor. And Cowperwood, on receipt of this, smiled, and wired his acceptance. To his genuine surprise, on his arrival, he found Aileen more attractive physically than he had thought she could be at this time in her life, and particularly after all she had endured. Her hair was a study in swirls that emphasized the good points of her face. And her dress was designed to show the lines of her much reduced figure.

"Aileen!" he exclaimed, on seeing her, "I've never seen you looking better! What in the world have you been doing? That dress is most effective. And I like your hair. What have you been living on, birdseed?"

"Well, just about that," returned Aileen, smiling. "I haven't had a single meal that I would call a meal in thirty days. But you may be sure of one thing! Now that I've gotten it off, it's going to stay off! But did you have an easy trip over?" As she talked she was supervising the services of Williams, who was arranging glasses and liqueurs on a table in preparation for guests.

"The Channel was smooth as a pond," he said, "except for about fifteen minutes, when it looked as though everybody would go under. But we were all fine when we landed."

"Oh, that dreadful Channel!" said Aileen, conscious all the while of his eyes upon her, and, in spite of herself, nervously excited by his complimentary remarks.

"But what about this banquet tonight?"

"Well, Mr. Tollifer and I have arranged a little party. You know, that man Tollifer is a perfect jewel. I like him ever so much. And I think you'll be interested in some of the people who are coming, especially my friend, Madame Rezstadt. She and I have been going around together a great deal. She is charming, and different from any woman I have ever known."

Now that she had lived for a month in the company of Tollifer and his colorful group, she felt at ease in pointing out to Cowperwood a woman of Madame Rezstadt's charm, where previously she would have jealously intrigued to prevent his noticing any woman as attractive as her new friend. He noted her new air of confidence, her assurance, good nature, and revived interest in life. If things were going to go as well as this, decidedly there might be no further cause for bitterness between them. At the same time ran the thought that this development was his doing, not hers. And she so unconscious of it. But no sooner had that thought been indulged in than he realized that it was really because of Berenice that this had happened. For he could feel that Aileen was inspired, not so much by his presence as by that of the man whom he had employed.

But where was he? Cowperwood felt he had no right to inquire. He was in the position of a man who contrives a show, a masquerade, but is not permitted to announce himself as showman. But there was Aileen saying: "Frank, you'll want to dress. And I have some things to do before the others arrive."

"That's right," he said. "But I have a piece of news for you. Do you think you could leave Paris just now and run back to New York with me?"

"What do you mean?" Her voice was full of surprise. For she had been hoping that they might visit at least a few of the principal resorts of Europe this summer, and now here he was talking of returning to New York. Perhaps he was giving up his London plans entirely in order to return to America for good. She was a little disturbed, for somehow this seemed to shadow and even threaten all that she had so recently achieved.

"Oh, nothing at all serious," said Cowperwood, smiling. "Nothing has gone wrong in London. I haven't been thrown out. In fact, it looks as though they might like me to stay. But only on condition that I go back home and return with a lot of money." He smiled ironically, and Aileen, relieved, smiled with him. Knowing so much of his past experiences, she could not help sharing his cynicism.

"Well, that doesn't surprise me," she said. "But let's talk about it tomorrow. Suppose you dress now."

"Right! I'll be ready in a half-hour."

Aileen covered him with her eyes as he passed into another room. As usual, he was certainly looking the picture of success. He was cheerful, adroit, aggressive. Plainly, he was interested by her present appearance and manner. She was sure of that, even though still conscious of the fact that he did not love her and that she feared him. What a blessing that the gay, handsome Tollifer had blown into her life! If she were to return to New York now, what was to become of this quite inexplicable and now quite soundly established friendship between herself and this handsome young loafer?

Chapter 38

BEFORE Cowperwood reappeared, Tollifer breezed in. Handing his top hat and stick to Williams, he marched briskly over to Aileen's bedroom door and knocked.

"Hello!" she called out to him. "Mr. Cowperwood is here; he's dressing. I'll be with you in a second."

"Righto! The others should be here any moment now."

As he spoke, he heard a slight noise and turned just in time to note Cowperwood's entrance into the reception room by another door. The two gave each other a swift glance of recognition. Tollifer, conscious of his obligation, stepped quickly and cordially forward. But Cowperwood anticipated his address by saying: "Well, we meet again. How are you enjoying Paris?"

"Oh, very much," said Tollifer. "This season is particularly gay. I've been running into all sorts of people. And the weather has been perfect. You know Paris in the spring. I find it the gayest and most refreshing time."

"I hear we are to be the guests of my wife this evening."

"Yes, along with some others. I'm afraid I'm a little early."

"Suppose we have something to drink!"

They were off on a casual conversation regarding London and Paris, both doing their best to ignore the relationship between them, and both succeeding. Aileen entered and greeted Tollifer. And then Ibrihim arriving, and ignoring Cowperwood as he would a sheep-herder of his own land, proceeded to pay his compliments to Aileen.

Cowperwood was at first a little astonished, then amused. The gleaming eyes of the Arab intrigued him. "Interesting," he said to himself. "This fellow Tollifer is actually creating something here. And this robed Bedouin covets my wife. This should be a fine evening!"

Next entered Marigold Brainerd. Her personality pleased him, and the appreciation appeared to be mutual. But this *rapproachement* was soon interrupted by the arrival of the serene and exotic Rezstadt, swathed in a cream white shawl, the long silken fringe trailing over one arm and about her feet. Cowperwood looked with approval on her olive-tinted face, framed so attractively by sleek black hair and a pair of heavy jet earrings which hung almost to her shoulders.

Observing him, and impressed, as were most women, Madame Rezstadt readily comprehended Aileen's plight. This was not a man for any one woman. One must sip only and be content with that. Aileen should be brought to comprehend that truth.

But Tollifer was impatiently urging that it was time to leave, and obeying his insistence they departed for Orsignat's.

A private dining room that was half-balcony commanded, through open french windows, a full view of Notre Dame and the green square before it. But all, as they entered, commented on the seeming lack of preparation for their dinner party, for there was only a plain wooden table completely bare. Tollifer, entering last, exclaimed:

"Why, what the devil does this mean? I don't understand. There's something wrong here. They're surely expecting us. Wait, I'll go and see," and turning swiftly, he disappeared.

"I really can't understand this," said Aileen. "I thought we had everything arranged." And she frowned and pouted and looked her irritated best.

"We've probably been shown to the wrong room," said Cowperwood.

"They do not expect, what?" the sheik was saying to Marigold, when the door of an adjoining serving room suddenly opened, and in dashed Harlequin, enormously concerned. This was Pantaloon himself, tall and gawky, his garb the usual star-and-moon sewn slip, cornucopia atop his head, his ears yellowed with grease paint, his eyesockets green, his cheeks cerise, ruffs and bangles about his wrists and neck, tufts of hair protruding from under his horn hat, immense white gloves on his hands, long, flail-like shoes on his feet. Looking about with a kind of lunatic anguish and despair, he exclaimed:

"Ah, *Mon Dieu! Sacré-bleu!* Ah, ladies and gentlemen! This is . . . indeed, this is . . . ah, no linen! No silver! No chairs! *Pardon! Pardon!* Something must be done about this! *Pardon,* mesdames and messieurs, something must have gone wrong. Something must be done! Ah!" and clapping his long hands and gazing toward the door, as though troops of servants must immediately respond to his bidding, he waited, without response. Then once more clapping, he waited, one ear cocked toward the door. After which, no sound ensuing, he turned to his audience, who, now comprehending, retreated to the walls to give Harlequin his stage.

Finger to his lips, he tiptoed to the door and listened. Still no sound. After stooping down and peering through the keyhole, his head cocked now this way, now that, he looked back at them, and, with an amazing grimace, again put his finger to his lips and glued one eye to the keyhole. Finally he jumped back, falling flat as he did so, then jumped up and backed away, while the door flew open for a half-dozen waiters bearing linen, dishes, silver, glasses, trays—an orderly and businesslike procession—who proceeded to spread the table, ignoring him completely while he leaped and clattered about, exclaiming:

"So! So! You come, do you? You pigs! You loafers! Put down the plates! Put down the plates, I say!" This to the man who was already swiftly and dexterously laying the plates. And to the waiter who was placing the silver: "Lay the silver, I tell you! And see that you make no noise! Swine!" After which he picked up a knife and re-laid it in exactly the same position. To the waiter who was arranging the glasses, he exclaimed: "No, no, no! Dunce! Will you never learn? See!" and taking up the glasses, replaced them precisely as they had been. Then stepping aside to survey them, he knelt down and squinted, then moved one small liqueur glass a thousandth of an inch.

Of course, during all this folderol, everyone, with the exception of Ibrihim—who simply stared queerly at all this—smiled or laughed by turns, especially when Harlequin proceeded to follow closely upon the heels of the headwaiter, actually stepping on them at times, while the waiter pretended not to see him. As he went out, Harlequin followed him, looking back as he shouted: "Bah! Conspiracy! Bah!"

"A good show!" remarked Cowperwood to Madame Rezstadt.

"That is Grelizan, of the Trocadero, the cleverest clown in Europe," she said.

"No!" exclaimed Marigold, whose estimate of his humor was rapidly heightened by the news of his fame.

At first fearful, but now elated by the success of this adventure, Aileen beamed with pleasure. Since Cowperwood chose to praise her ingenuity, and that of Tollifer, there was nothing Grelizan could do now that did not seem amusing to her, though he did produce a momentary chill when he stumbled and fell while bearing a large silver tureen filled with what appeared to be bright red tomato soup. The brilliant orange confetti was deftly hurled into the air and fell all over the guests, to the accompaniment of gasps, screams and laughter.

Again he hurried back to the pantry, this time to bring no more than a single crouton held in a pair of sugar tongs, and again and again to follow the incoming waiters with exaggerated supervision, while they scrupulously served the courses.

Imitation ices were served last. Beneath the surface of each was a frail inflated balloon, which, when pierced with a fork, revealed, in Cowperwood's case, the key to the city of London; in Aileen's, a bowing and smiling figure of Monsieur Richard, scissors in hand; for Madame Rezstadt, a small world globe, with a dotted line touching all of the places she had traveled to; for Ibrihim, a tiny horse with a sheik astride; for Tollifer, a small roulette wheel, with the indicator at zero; for Marigold, a handful of toy figures of men: a soldier, a king, a dandy, an artist, a musician. There was much laughter over these, and after the coffee, Grelizan bowed himself out, to the applause of all, Cowperwood and Madame Rezstadt calling: "Bravo! Bravo!"

"Delightful!" she exclaimed. "I shall write him a note."

Afterward, at Le Grand Guignol, which began at midnight, they saw the celebrated Laloute impersonate the celebrities of the day. Later Tollifer suggested Sabinal's. And by dawn they were all fully satisfied that this night in Paris had been wonderful.

Chapter 39

COWPERWOOD concluded from all this that in Tollifer he had picked someone even more resourceful than he had hoped for. The man was gifted, decidedly. With the least encouragement, and, of course, financial aid, he could certainly make a world for Aileen with which, in the event of their separation, she might reasonably be satisfied. This was a situation requiring some thought. For, of course, if she were to find out about Berenice, she would probably turn to Tollifer for advice. And then it would be a matter of having to buy them off. A pretty kettle of fish! Also, with Aileen in a social limelight of her own, and with her husband rarely present, there would be increased speculation as to where he was, speculation which could lead but in one direction: Berenice. Best to persuade Aileen to go back to New York with him and leave Tollifer behind. It would, for the time being, modify the ascendancy which obviously he had already achieved, and prevent it from being too obvious to others.

It developed that Aileen, on her part, was entirely willing. There were various reasons. She feared that otherwise Cowperwood might take another woman along with him, or that he might meet one in New York. And there was the effect on Tollifer and his friends. For just now Cowperwood was more of a public figure than ever, and it was among the highest of distinctions to be his acknowledged wife. Her chief curiosity was whether Tollifer would follow her or not. For this was a visit that was likely to last for six months, maybe longer.

Immediately, therefore, she informed him of her forthcoming departure. His reactions were rather complicated, for in the background there was Marigold, who wanted him to cruise with her to the North Cape. By now, he had seen enough of her to feel that if he continued his suit, she might actually arrange a divorce and marry him, and she possessed considerable money of her own.

He did not really love her; he was still dreaming of a romance with a younger girl. Then, there was the matter of immediate and continued income. Any interruption of that would at once end his butterfly existence. He felt that Cowperwood, though having given no hint, would prefer him to return to New York. But whether he went or stayed, it had come to the point, he felt, when continued pursuit of Aileen, without some declaration of affection, would not seem to her reasonable. He was satisfied that she would yield nothing, but it would flatter her. And this, in itself, was excuse enough for the approach.

"Pshaw!" he exclaimed, on hearing the news from her. "This throws me all out!" He paced nervously back and forth, having dropped in to see her after a luncheon with Marigold at Madame Gemy's bar. His face simulated grave concern and disappointment.

"What's the matter?" inquired Aileen, seriously. "What has gone wrong?" She noticed that he had been drinking, not enough to unbalance him in any way but sufficient to darken his mood.

"This is too bad," he said, "and just when I was thinking that something might come out of it all for both of us."

Aileen stared at him, not a little puzzled. To be sure, this more or less anomalous relationship had been growing on her. In an unformulated way, she was attracted to him more than she had acknowledged to herself. Yet having observed him with Marigold and others, she was convinced, as she had said more than once, that a woman could not trust him from one end of the room to the other.

"I don't know whether you feel it or not," he went on, calculatingly, "but there's a lot more than just a social acquaintance between you and me. I'll admit that when I first met you, I didn't think there would be. I was interested by the fact that you were Mrs. Cowperwood, part of a life that I had heard a great deal about. But after we'd had a few talks together, I began to feel something else. I've seen a lot of trouble in my life. I've had my ups and downs, and I suppose I always will. But there was something about you those first few days on the boat that made me think maybe you had, too. That's why I wanted to be with you, although, as you saw for yourself, there were lots of other women whose company I might have had."

He lied with the air of one who had never told anything but

the truth. And this bit of acting impressed her. She had suspected him of fortune-hunting, and possibly that was true. Yet if he did not really like her, why all this effort on his part to improve her appearance and reorganize her onetime power to charm? She experienced a sudden emotional glow, perhaps half motherhood and half youth and desire. For one could not help liking this waster; he was so genial, cheering, and, in a subtle way, affectionate.

"But what difference does it make about my going back to New York?" she asked, wonderingly. "Can't we be friends just the same?"

Tollifer considered. Having established this matter of his affection, now what? Always the thought of Cowperwood dominated him. What would he desire him to do?

"Just think," he said, "you're running off in the ideal time over here, June and July. And just when we were getting into the swing of things!" He lit a cigarette and fixed himself a drink. Why hadn't Cowperwood given him a sign as to whether he wanted him to keep Aileen in Paris or not? Perhaps he would yet, but if so, he'd better be quick about it.

"Frank has asked me to go, and I can't do anything else," she said, calmly. "As for you, I don't imagine you'll be lonely."

"You don't understand," he said. "You've made a kind of center for me over here. I feel happier now and more contented than I have for years. And if you go back now, it may be broken up."

"Nonsense! Please don't be foolish. I'd like to stay here, I admit. Only I don't know how it could be managed. When I get back to New York and see how things are, I'll let you know. But it's my belief we'll be coming back soon. If not, and you still feel this way, you can come home, and I'll be seeing you just the same way in New York."

"Aileen!" exclaimed Tollifer, affectionately, seeing his opportunity. He crossed over and took her arm. "That's wonderful! That's what I've been wanting you to say. Is that how you feel?" he asked, looking coaxingly into her eyes, and, before she could prevent it, slipping his arms around her waist and kissing her, not passionately but with seemingly genuine affection. But Aileen, conscious of her dominant desire to retain him and yet give Cowperwood no real cause for complaint, definitely though good-naturedly resisted.

'No, no, no," she said, "remember what you were just saying. This is to be a real friendship, if you want it that way. But nothing more than that. Besides, why don't we go out somewhere. I haven't been out today, and I have a new gown I want to wear."

Satisfied to let the situation rest for the time being, he suggested a new place out near Fontainebleau, and they were off.

Chapter 40

NEW YORK, and Cowperwood and Aileen stepping off the liner *Saxonia*. The usual interviewers. The newspapers, aware of his expressed intention of invading the London underground field, now wanting to know who were to be his directors, investors, managers, also whether the sudden reported heavy buying of both the common and preferred stock of the District and the Metropolitan was not really being done by his own men. This disclaimed by him in an adroit statement, which, when published, caused many Londoners, as well as Americans, to smile.

Pictures of Aileen, her new clothes, and references to her appearance in what was hinted to be near-society on the Continent.

And, simultaneously, sailing with Marigold for the North Cape, Bruce Tollifer. But no mention of this in any paper.

And at Pryor's Cove, Berenice was an outstanding local success. Since she so carefully concealed her shrewdness behind a veil of simplicity, innocence, and conventionality, everyone convinced that there would follow in due time, for her, a distinguished and correct marriage. For, obviously, she had the instinct for avoiding the dull, the commonplace, and the lecherous, regarding favorably only those who were conventionally minded, men as well as women. Even a more promising trait, as her new friends saw it, was her penchant for that type of unattractive woman—neglected wife, spinster, maiden aunt—who, socially wellborn, was still hard put to it for pleasurable attention of any kind. For, having no need to fear the younger and more attractive hostesses and matrons, she knew that if she won the more lonely women to her, she would be able to make her way into the most important functions.

Just as fortunate was her tendency to admire the wholly innocuous and socially correct stripling or young master of title and social honor. In fact, the young curates and rectors for miles about Pryor's

Cove were already jubilant because of the spiritual discernment of this young newcomer. Her demure appearance of a Sabbath morn in any of the neighborhood chapels of the English High Church, invariably in company with her mother or one of the more conservative of the elder women, was sufficient to verify every good thing that was rumored of her.

Coincidentally, Cowperwood on flying visits to Chicago, Baltimore, Boston, Philadelphia, in connection with his London plans, and within the innermost sanctums of those most religious of all American institutions, the banks and trust companies, conferring with such individuals as would be at once the most useful, the most influential, and the least difficult to manage. And the blandness of his expression as he explained the certainty of larger and more permanent profits than had ever as yet been taken from any underground project. And, despite the so recent denunciations of him, being listened to with awe and even genuine respect. True, in Chicago, there were mumblings of contempt and hatred, but at the same time, envy. For the man was a force, attracting, as always, a veritable glare of publicity.

In so short a time as a month he saw his primary problems solved. In many places, tentative agreements were made to purchase shares of his holding company which was presently to be organized in order to take over all the lines. For each share of the lines taken over, three shares in his own major company were to be paid. Indeed, except for some minor conferences on his Chicago holdings, he was really free to return to England, and would have done so had it not been for a new encounter of an old and familiar type. It had happened so often, in times past, when his name was being paraded before public eyes: he had been approached by ambitious and attractive women to whom his wealth, fame, and personal charm were irresistible. And now, because of a necessary visit to Baltimore, a vivid meeting of this sort.

It occurred in the hotel where he was staying. And to his mind at the time it seemed in no way to shadow the affection he had for Berenice. Nonetheless, at midnight, just returned from the home of the president of the Maryland Trust Company, and while sitting at his desk making notes upon their recent conversation, there was a tap at his door. Answering, he was informed by a feminine voice that a relative wished to speak to him. He smiled, for in all his experience he did not recall exactly that form of approach. He opened the door and saw a girl who, at a glance, he decided was not to be ignored and concerning whom he was instantly curious. She was young, slender, of medium height, assured, forceful, and magnetic. Her features were beautiful, and her dress.

"A relative?" he said, smiling and allowing her to enter.

"Yes," she replied with the utmost calm. "I am a relative of yours, although you may not believe it right away. I am the grand-daughter of a brother of your father's. Only my name is Maris. My mother's name was Cowperwood."

He asked her to be seated and placed himself opposite her. Her eyes, which were large and round and of a silvery blue, contemplated him unwaveringly.

"What part of the country do you come from?" he inquired.

"Cincinnati," she returned, "although my mother was born in North Carolina. It was her father who came from Pennsylvania, and not so far from where you were born, Mr. Cowperwood. Doyles-town."

"That's true," he said. "My father did have a brother who once lived in Doylestown. Besides, I may add, you have the Cowperwood eye."

"Thanks," she returned, and continued looking at him as fixedly as he looked at her. Then she added, unembarrassed by his gaze: "You may think it strange, my coming here at this hour, but I am stopping at this hotel, too, you see. I am a dancer, and the company I am with is playing here this week."

"Is it possible? We Quakers seem to wander into strange fields!"

"Yes," she replied, and smiled warmly, a smile reserved and yet rich, suggesting imagination, romance, mental strength, and sensuality. He felt its force as fully as he observed its character. "I've just come from the theater," she went on. "But I've been reading about you, and seeing your picture in the papers here, and since I've always wanted to know you, I decided I'd better come now."

"Are you a good dancer?" he inquired.

"I wish you'd come and see and judge for yourself."

"I was returning to New York in the morning, but if you will have breakfast with me, I think I might stay over."

"Oh, yes, of course I will," she said. "But do you know, I've been imagining myself talking to you like this for years. Once, two years ago, when I was unable to get a job of any kind, I wrote you a letter, but then I tore it up. You see, we are the poor Cowperwoods."

"Too bad you didn't send it," he commented. "What was it you wanted to tell me?"

"Oh, how talented I was, and that I was your grandniece. And if I were given a chance, how sure I was that I would be a great dancer. And now I'm glad I didn't write you, because I'm here with you now and you can see me dance. By the way," she went on, still fixing him with her magnetic blue eyes, "our company opens in New York for the summer, and I hope you'll see me there, too."

"Well, if you are as lovely a dancer as you are to look at, you should be a sensation."

"I'll let you tell me tomorrow night about that." She stirred as if to move, but then hesitated.

"What is your first name, did you say?" he finally asked.

"Lorna."

"Lorna Maris," he repeated. "Is that your stage name, too?"

"Yes. I did think once of changing it to Cowperwood, so you might hear of me. But I decided that name wasn't as good for a dancer as it was for a financier."

They continued to gaze at each other.

"How old are you, Lorna?"

"Twenty," she said, simply, "or I will be in November."

The silence that followed became full of meaning. Eyes said all that eyes could say. A few seconds more, and he merely signaled with his finger. She rose and went to him quickly, almost dancing as she did so, and threw herself into his arms.

"Beautiful!" he said. "And to have you come just this way . . . charming . . ."

Chapter 41   It was with puzzled thoughts that Cowperwood parted with Lorna the next day at noon. Throughout this fever which had seized upon him, and, for the time being, commanded his every fiber and impulse, he was actually not unmindful of Berenice. One might as well say that a fire, unrestrained by outward forces, would not burn down a house. And there were no outward forces restraining, or even capable of restraining, either Cowperwood or Lorna under the circumstances. But when she left him to go to the theater his mind resumed its normal trend and occupied itself with the anomaly which Lorna and Berenice presented. Throughout all of eight years he had been swayed by the desirability as well as the unobtainability of Berenice, and more recently by her physical and aesthetic perfection. And yet he had allowed this coarser though still beautiful force to becloud and even temporarily efface all that.

Alone in his room, he asked himself whether he was to blame. He had not sought out this latest temptation; it had come upon him, and suddenly. Besides, in his nature there was room, and even necessity, for many phases of experience, many sources and streams of nourishment. True, he had told Berenice in the fever of his zest for her, and almost continuously since, that she was the supreme aspect of his existence. And in the major sense this was still true. Nevertheless, here and now was this consuming and overwhelming force, as represented by Lorna, which might be differentiated as the mysterious, compelling charm of the new and unexplored, especially where youth and beauty and sex are involved.

Its betraying power, he said to himself, could best be explained by the fact that it was more powerful than the individual or his intentions. It came, created its own fever, and worked its results. It had done so with Berenice and himself, and now again with Lorna Maris. But one thing he clearly recognized even now, and that was that it would never supersede his affection for Berenice. There was a difference; he could see it and feel it clearly. And this difference lay in the temperamental as well as mental objectives of the two girls. Although of the same age, Lorna, with a considerably more rugged and extended life experience, was still content with what could be achieved through the glorification of her own physical and purely sensual charm, the fame, rewards, and applause due an enticing and exciting dancer.

Berenice's temperamental response and her resulting program were entirely different: broader, richer, a product of social and aesthetic sense involving peoples and countries. She, like himself, had an abiding faith in the dominance of mind and taste. Hence the ease and grace with which she had blended herself into the atmosphere and social forms and precedents of England. Obviously, and for all the vivid and exciting sensual power of Lorna, the deeper and more enduring power and charm lay within Berenice. In other words, her ambitions and reactions were in every way more significant. And when Lorna had gone, although he did not at the moment care to contemplate that thought, Berenice would still be present.

Yet how, in the ultimate accounting, would he adjust all this? Would he able to conceal this adventure, which he had no intention of immediately terminating? And if Berenice discovered it, how would he satisfy her? He could not solve that before a shaving mirror, or in any bath or dressing room.

That night, after the performance, Cowperwood decided that Lorna Maris was not so much a great as a sensational dancer, one who would shine brilliantly for a few years and eventually perhaps marry a wealthy man. But now, as he saw her dance, he found her enticing, in her silken clown costume, with loose pantaloons and long-fingered gloves. To the accompaniment of lights which cast exaggerated shadows, and ghostly music, she sang and danced the bogey man who might catch you if you didn't watch out! Another dance was corybantic. In a short sleeveless slip of white chiffon, her exquisite arms and legs bare, her hair a whirling mass of powdered gold, she suggested to the utmost the abandon of a bacchante. Still another dance presented her as a pursued and terrified innocent seeking to escape from the lurking figures of would-be ravishers. She was so often recalled that the management had to limit her encores, and later in New York she colored, for that season, the entire summer love mood of the city.

In fact, to Cowperwood's surprise and gratification, Lorna was quite as much talked of as himself. Orchestras everywhere were playing her songs; in the popular vaudeville houses there were imitations of her. Merely to be seen with her was to inspire comment, and therein lay his greatest problem, for the very papers which regularly presented Lorna's fame also presented his own. And this evoked in him the greatest caution, as well as a very real mental distress regarding Berenice. She might read or hear or be whispered to by someone if they were seen publicly together. At the same time, he and Lorna were infatuated and wished to be together as much as possible. In the case of Aileen, at least, he decided on a frank confession to her that in Baltimore he had met the grand-daughter of his brother, a very gifted girl, who was in a theatrical production playing in New York. Would Aileen care to invite her to the house?

Having already read notices of Lorna and seen pictures of her in the papers, Aileen was, of course, curious, and for that reason willing to extend the invitation. At the same time, the beauty, poise, and self-assurance of the girl, as well as the mere fact that she had met and introduced herself to Cowperwood, were sufficient to embitter Aileen against her and to renew her old suspicion as to Cowperwood's real motives. Youth—the irrecoverable. Beauty—that wraith of perfection that came and went as a shadow. Yet were both fire and storm. It gave Aileen no real satisfaction to escort Lorna through the galleries and gardens of the Cowperwood palace. For, as she could see, with what Lorna had she did not need those things, and because of what Aileen lacked, they were of no avail to her. Life went with beauty and desire; where they were not was nothing . . . And Cowperwood desired beauty and achieved it for himself—life, color, fame, romance. Whereas, she . . .

Now enmeshed in the necessity of pretending engagements and business which did not exist, in order to make secure his newest paradise, Cowperwood decided that it would be better if Tollifer were present, and arranged to have him recalled by the Central Trust Company. He might keep Aileen from thinking about Lorna.

So Tollifer, gayly afloat off the North Cape with Marigold and a party of her friends, and greatly disappointed by his recall, was obliged to state that financial affairs required his immediate return to New York. And soon after his return, and doing his best to amuse himself as well as Aileen, he heard rumors of Lorna and Cowperwood, and was, of course, interested. Yet, although envying Cowperwood his luck, he was careful at every point to belittle and deny all gossip that he heard, and in particular to shield him from any suspicion on the part of Aileen.

Unfortunately, he arrived too late to forestall an inevitable article in *Town Topics*, which presently fell into Aileen's hands. It produced in her the usual effect, the old bitter contemplation of her husband's besetting vice. No matter how great his standing before the world, how marvelous his power of achievement, he must allow these petty vagrants, infinitely beneath him, to tarnish and becloud what would otherwise have been a tremendous and untarnished public position.

There was one consolation. If she were once again to be humiliated in this way, there was Berenice Fleming to be humiliated also. For Aileen had long been consciously irritated by the unseen presence of Berenice ever in the background. And observing Berenice's New York house to be closed, she assumed that Cowperwood must be neglecting her also. For most certainly he was showing no desire to leave the city.

One of the excuses which he gave for remaining in New York related to the nomination and possible election of William Jennings Bryan, a political firebrand, who, with economic and social theories somewhat at variance with the current capitalistic views of how money should be managed and divided, was seeking to bridge the then unbridgeable gulf between the rich and the poor. And, in consequence, in the United States there was at that time a genuine commercial fear, bordering almost on panic, lest this man actually win the presidency. This permitted Cowperwood to say to Aileen that it would be dangerous for him to leave the country at this time, since on Bryan's stabilizing defeat depended his own financial success. And he wrote Berenice to the same effect. That ultimately she was not permitted to believe him was due to the fact that Aileen had mailed a copy of *Town Topics* to her New York address, and, in due time, it arrived at Pryor's Cove.

Chapter 42

AMONG all the men Berenice had met thus far, Cowperwood alone, with his strength and achievements, supplied the most glamor. But, apart from men, even Cowperwood and the elements of satisfaction and fulfillment which he offered, there was the color of life itself at Pryor's Cove. Here, for the first time in her life, her social problems, if not settled, were at least temporarily disposed of and she was free to indulge her extreme egoism and yield to her narcissistic impulse to pose and play.

Life at Pryor's Cove was a pleasurably solitary and idle process. In the morning, after hours in her bath and before her mirror, she loved to pick and choose costumes suitable to her mood: this hat did this, this ribbon did that, these earrings, this belt, these slippers; so it went. Sometimes, chin in hand, her elbow resting on the gold-stained marble of her dressing-table, she would gaze into the mirror studying her hair, her lips, her eyes, her breasts, her arms. And it was with the greatest care that she selected the silver, the china, the linen, the flowers, for the table, always with a view to the resulting effect. And although usually only her mother; Mrs. Evans, the housekeeper; and Rose, the maid, were there to see, it was herself who was the chief spectator. And, in the lovely walled garden off her bedroom, when the moon was up, she strolled and dreamed, thinking of Cowperwood, and frequently wishing for him intensely. Yet with the compensating thought that a brief absence would bring an exquisitely satisfying reunion.

Mrs. Carter frequently marveled at her daughter's self-absorption, wondering why she so often sought to be alone when there was a social world steadily unfolding before her. Yet in due course, into the midst of this, came Lord Stane. It was some three weeks after Cowperwood's departure, and he was motoring from Tregasal to London, dropping in ostensibly to look after his horses and bid his new tenants welcome. He was especially curious because he had been informed that the girl was the ward of Frank Cowperwood.

After all that had passed between herself and Cowperwood concerning this man, Berenice was at once interested and not a little amused, remembering the hairpins and brushes and the unknown Miss Hathaway. Nevertheless, she appeared smiling and confident as she greeted him. The effect of her white dress, blue slippers, blue ribbon around her waist and blue velvet band encircling her foaming red hair, was not lost on Stane. As he bowed over her slim hand, he said to himself that here was one to whom every moment of life was an occasion, and certainly a fitting ward for the ambitious and powerful Cowperwood. His eyes concealed inquiry but not admiration.

"I hope you will pardon the intrusion of your landlord," he began. "I have several horses here that I am about to send to France, and I find it necessary to look them over."

"Ever since we have been living here," said Berenice, "Mother and I have been hoping to meet the owner of this adorable place. It is too lovely for words. And my guardian, Mr. Cowperwood, has spoken of you."

"Decidedly, I am obligated to him for that," said Stane, fascinated by her poise. "As for Pryor's Cove, that I can't claim credit for. It's really an heirloom, one of the family treasures."

Invited to stay for tea, he accepted. He asked whether they were to be long in England. Berenice, determined at once to be cautious in regard to him, replied that she could not say; it depended on how much she and her mother liked England. Meanwhile, his gaze returned again and again to meet her still blue eyes, and because of his manner she now ventured upon innocent liberties which otherwise she would not have taken. Since he was going to look at his horses, might she not look at them, too?

Stane was delighted, and together they proceeded to the paddock beyond the stables. He asked whether everything was being looked after to her satisfaction. Would she and her mother accept the use of the horses for riding or driving? Would she prefer that the gardener or farmer make any changes or rearrangements? There were, perhaps, too many sheep. He had been thinking of selling some of them. Berenice protested that she adored the sheep, that she wanted nothing changed. Well, in two or three weeks he would be returning from France and going to Tregasal, and if they were still here, he might stop in again to see them. Perhaps Mr. Cowperwood would be here. If so, it would be a pleasure to meet him again.

Plainly, here was a proffer of friendship, and she decided that she would make the most of it. Here was the possible beginning of a flirtation which somehow had been a possibility in the back of her mind ever since she had learned that Stane was her landlord and possibly Cowperwood's future partner. After he had gone, she recalled to her mind, dreamily, his long, lean figure, his perfect country tweeds, his handsome face, his hands, his eyes. He had an air, a walk, a manner, in which charm was implicit.

But there was Cowperwood's business with him, as well as the anomaly of her own and her mother's position. Would he not guess? He was no Colonel Hawkesberry or Arthur Tavistock to be deceived, along with all these country curates and spinsters. She knew better, just as she knew that neither she nor Cowperwood would have been deceived. And if now she made any least move in the way of a flirtation, would he not immediately proceed upon the basis that she was no better than she should be, one whom he could add to his list of experiences without thought of permanency? Considering her affection for Cowperwood as well as her great interest in his future, she was not willing to even approximate a betrayal of this sort. It would mean too much to him. And it was possible that there would be an angry reprisal on his part. She even debated the wisdom of consenting to see Stane again.

However, early one morning in August, while she was posing Narcissus-like before her mirror, she did receive a message from Stane. He was leaving Paris, preceded by a groom with two of his horses en route to Pryor's Cove, and would like, with her permission, to accompany them. She wrote him a note, saying that she and her mother would be delighted to receive him. And she was thereupon so thrilled that she began to question herself, thinking also of Cowperwood—who, at the moment, was delighting in the charms of Lorna Maris.

Stane, though less keen than Cowperwood in the realm of finance, was a worthy rival in that of affection. When greatly interested, he was aggressive and resourceful. He loved beautiful women, and whatever his other labors, was forever pursuing some new quest. On sight of Berenice he had conceived an emotional passion for her. He thought of her in that lovely setting, alone with her mother, as a fair target for his affections, but, because of Cowperwood, realized that he would have to step carefully. However, considering that Cowperwood had not even mentioned his ward, and she was his tenant, why should he not continue to call on her, at least until he knew more? And so, when the time came, he packed with real gusto, determined to make as much of the occasion as possible.

And on her part, Berenice was ready also. She was wearing her favorite gown of pale green and was less formal and more playful than before. Had he had a good time in France? Which horse had won, the bay with the white circle around his eye, or the tall black one with the white stockings? It was the tall black one, and he had won a 12,000 franc prize as well as some side bets, as much as 35,000 francs all told.

"Enough to turn some poor French family into aristocrats, I suppose," commented Berenice, lightly.

"Well, the French are rather thrifty, you know," said Stane. "It would certainly make an aristocrat of some of their villagers, and, of ours, too, for that matter. Up in Scotland, where some of my father's ancestors come from, it seems to have laid the foundation for an earldom." He smiled reflectively. "The first earl of my family," he added, "began with less than that."

"And the present one ends with winning as much in a single race!"

"Well, this time, yes, but not always. My last venture at the Derby cost me almost twice that."

They were sitting on the deck of the houseboat, waiting for tea to be served. A punt, filled with idlers, went by, and he asked Berenice if she had made use of either the canoes or punts in the boathouse.

"Oh, yes," she said. "Mr. Tavistock and I, and also Colonel Hawkesberry, who lives over near Wimbledon, have explored the river to Windsor in that direction and far beyond Marlow in this. We've talked of going as far as Oxford."

"In a punt?" queried Stane.

"Well, two or three of them. Colonel Hawkesberry has been talking of arranging a party."

"The dear old colonel! So you know him? We knew each other as boys. But I haven't seen him in a year. He's been in India, I believe."

"Yes, so he told me."

"But there's far more interesting country around Tregasal," said Stane, ignoring Hawkesberry and Tavistock. "We have the sea on all sides, and the rockiest coast in England, quite impressive; besides moors and fens and tin and copper mines and old churches, if you care for them. And the climate is delightful, particularly now. I do wish you and your mother would come to Tregasal. There's quite a good small harbor there, where I keep my yacht. We could sail over to the Scilly Isles; they're only about thirty miles away."

"Why, how delightful! And how kind of you," said Berenice, yet thinking of Cowperwood and what he might say, if he knew. "Mother, how would you like a yachting trip to the Scilly Isles?" she called through the open window. "Lord Stane has a yacht and a harbor of his own at Tregasal, and he thinks we would enjoy it."

She rattled it off with an air of good humor, yet touched at the same time with the slightest trace of condescension. Stane was amused by her airy insouciance, the casual regard for an invitation which, in so many other quarters, would actually be prayed for.

Mrs. Carter appeared at the window. "You'll have to excuse my daughter, Lord Stane," she said. "She's a very wilful girl. I have never had any control over her, nor has anyone else that I know of. Just the same, if I may speak for myself"—and here she looked at Berenice as if asking permission—"it sounds delightful. And I'm sure Bevy thinks so, too."

"So now, tea," ran on Berenice. "And then you can come and pole me on the river, although I believe I like the canoe better. Or perhaps we could walk, or we could play a game of squash before dinner. I've been practicing, and I might be good at it."

"I say, it's too warm for squash now, isn't it?" protested Stane.

"Lazy! I thought all Englishmen preferred hard work on a tennis court to quite anything else. The Empire must be decaying!"

But there was no squash that evening; instead, a canoe trip on the Thames, and afterward a leisurely dinner by candlelight, Stane dwelling on the charms of Tregasal, which, as he insisted, while not so modern or so handsome as many another good house in England, commanded a view of the sea and the rocky coast that was strangely, almost eerily, impressive.

But Berenice was still afraid to accept the invitation just then, although she was fascinated by his description of the place.

Chapter 43

BETWEEN Berenice and Stane there was almost a similarity of temperament. Like her, he was less rugged than Cowperwood and, to a degree, less practical. On the other hand, Stane being proportionately excluded from the practical realm in which Cowperwood shone, was more effectively radiant in that atmosphere which Berenice most enjoyed, that of an aesthetically controlled luxury. His taste and philosophy she absorbed in a few moments on their evening walk, during which Stane talked to her freely of himself. Like Cowperwood, he was inclined to accept and even rejoice in his lot as he found it. He was wealthy. He was, after a fashion, gifted. He was titled.

"But I have done nothing to earn or deserve anything that I have," he admitted at one point.

"I can believe that," said Berenice, laughing.

"But here I am," he went on, pretending to ignore her interruption. "The world is like that, unfair, full of gifts for some and nothing for others."

"I do agree with you there," said Berenice, suddenly serious. "Life seems to be shot through with crazy predestinations, some beautiful and some terrible or shameful or brutal."

Stane had then gone on to discuss his life. His father, he said, had wanted him to marry the daughter of a friend of his, also an earl. But, as Stane expressed it, there was not enough attraction between them. And later, at Cambridge, he had decided to delay marriage on any terms until he had seen more of the world.

"But the trouble is," he said, "I seem to have fallen into the habit of travel. And, in between, there's London, Paris, Tregasal, and Pryor's Cove, when it is unoccupied."

"But what troubles me," said Berenice, "is what a lone bachelor can do with all those places."

"They cater to my principal diversion, which is partying," he answered. "There's a great deal of that here, as you must have seen for yourself. You can hardly escape it. But also I work, you know, sometimes very strenuously."

"For the pleasure of it?"

"Yes, I think so. At least, it keeps me in countenance with myself, establishes a balance that I find to be healthy."

And he went on to develop his pet theory that the significance of a title unaccompanied by personal achievement was little. Besides, the world's interest was turning to men who worked in the realm of science and economics, and it was economics which most interested him.

"But that's not what I want to talk about," he concluded, "but rather of Tregasal. It's a little too distant and too bare for ordinary partying, thank goodness, so when I want a real crowd I have to do a little planning. Contrasted with all that goes around London, it's very different, and I frequently use it as an escape."

Immediately Berenice sensed that he was pressing for a better understanding between them. It might be best, she thought, to end the matter at once, to make sure here and now that there would be no further development. Yet she resented the necessity for such action in the case of someone whose view of life seemed as broad as her own. She even speculated, looking at Stane as they walked, as to whether, in case she told him of her true relation to Cowperwood, he might not be inclined to let his natural interest dominate and sustain his social courtesies. For, after all, he was now associated with Cowperwood financially and might respect him sufficiently to respect her also.

At the same time, there was this very real attraction toward him. She decided to postpone the conversation for that evening. But the following morning, and shortly after sunrise, it began again when they met for an early breakfast and horseback ride. For he insisted that he was running off to Tregasal not only to get a few days' rest but also to be able to think clearly concerning some important financial matters which were requiring his attention.

"You see, I have let myself in for a lot of work in connection with your guardian's underground plans," he confided. "Perhaps you may know that he has a very complicated program, for which he seems to think he needs my help. And I am trying to decide whether I can be of any real use to him." He paused as if waiting to see whether she had anything to say.

But Berenice, jogging close beside him, was strongly determined not to express herself in any way. And so now she said:

"Mr. Cowperwood happens to be my guardian, but his financial goings-on are a mystery to me. I am more interested in the lovely things money can accomplish than I am in how it is made." She gave him a wavering smile.

Stane checked his horse for a moment, and turning to look at her, exclaimed: "My word, you think precisely as I do! I often wonder, loving beauty as I do, why I bother with practical matters in any form. I am often at war with myself over this point."

And now once more Berenice began contrasting Stane with her aggressive and ruthless lover. Cowperwood's financial genius and lust for power were tempered, to a degree, by his love of art and beauty. But Stane's strongly developed aesthetic sense was dominant, and, besides, he likewise possessed wealth and personality, plus something Cowperwood could never achieve: the world's acceptance of the significance of a distinguished title. The contrast was intriguing, since so obviously she was making a marked impression on Stane. English nobility as opposed to Frank Cowperwood, American financier and street railway magnate!

Riding under the trees on a dappled gray mare, she tried to think of herself as Lady Stane. They might even have a son, heir to the earldom of Stane. But then, alas, she thought of her mother, the notorious Hattie Starr of Louisville, and her own left-handed relationship with Cowperwood which might appear as a scandal at any moment. For there was Aileen, and possibly Cowperwood's anger and subsequent antagonism, which, considering his genius for intrigue and revenge, could take any form. Her previous thrill vanished, mistlike, before the heat of reality. For a moment she fairly froze because of the complications of her dilemma, but a second later she was partly soothed by Stane saying:

"Will you let me say that you are as brilliant and understanding as you are beautiful?"

And despite her saddened mood, Berenice waved a hand gayly in response.

"Why not? Would you expect me to reject anything I do not deserve?"

Stane was still more intrigued, and so moved to think that the relationship between her and Cowperwood might be quite normal. For the man must be all of fifty-five or sixty! And Berenice looked to be no more than eighteen or nineteen. Perhaps she was an illegitimate daughter. On the other hand, was it not possible that actually, considering her youth and beauty, Cowperwood was hoping to intrigue her by gifts and attentions showered on her mother and herself? For in studying Mrs. Carter, Stane had sensed something he could not easily explain. Obviously, she was the girl's mother, since Berenice resembled her so closely. He was puzzled. But now he wanted to take her to Tregasal, and meditating on how to do this, he said:

"One thing I must congratulate you on, Miss Fleming, and that is your possession of such a brilliant guardian. I find him an exceedingly gifted person."

"Yes, he is," she said. "And it's interesting to know that you are co-operating with him, or thinking of doing so."

"By the way," he said, "do you know when he will be returning from America?"

"The last we heard was that he was in Boston," she replied. "And he had a lot of work to do in Chicago and other places. Really, I don't know when he's likely to return."

"When he does, perhaps I shall have the pleasure of entertaining you all together," said Stane. "But there's still Tregasal, you know. Will that need to wait on Mr. Cowperwood's return?"

"Oh, I think so; at least, for three or four more weeks. Mother isn't feeling well, and her principal desire at the moment is to stay here and rest."

She smiled reassuringly at him while feeling at the same time that once Cowperwood returned, or she had time to write or cable him, the thing might be arranged. Personally, she would like nothing better than to accept this invitation. And a friendship here, with Cowperwood's approval if not his presence, might further his affairs in connection with Stane. She would write Cowperwood at once.

"But after three or four weeks, do you think it will be possible?" asked Stane.

"I'm quite sure of it. And nothing would give us all greater pleasure, I assure you."

And Stane accepted the mixed offer with the best grace in the world. For, plainly, this young American beauty did not need him or Tregasal or his titled connections. She was a person in her own right, and was to be accepted only on her own terms.

Chapter 44

UNCERTAIN as Berenice was about the wisdom of developing this relationship, it was partially furthered by Cowperwood's delay in returning. For already he had written, and this on account of Lorna, that until the approaching presidential election was over, he could not return to London. Also, he shrewdly added, if he could not very soon return, he would send for her to meet him in New York or Chicago.

While this letter provoked speculation, it did not arouse any suspicions. And nothing would have come of it except for the clipping, mailed by Aileen, which arrived the week following Berenice's conversation with Stane. Trifling over her mail in the east bedroom of the cottage one morning, she picked up a commonplace envelope addressed to her New York home and forwarded to her here. It contained pictures as well as descriptions of Lorna Maris, and an article clipped from *Town Topics,* which read:

A tidbit of gossip now going the rounds relates to an internationally famous multimillionaire and his latest protégée, one of the dancing favorites of the hour. The item, as retailed, is romantic in the extreme. It sets forth how this gentleman, famed for his financial triumphs in a certain midwestern city as well as his penchant for young and beautiful maidens, came across, in one of our outlying cities, the most beautiful and now the most famous terpsichorean star of the season, and appears to have made an instantaneous conquest. As great as is the wealth of this Maecenas and his fame for extravagant expenditures or endowments on those who chance to attract his interest, she was not asked to retire from the stage and accompany him to Europe—from where he has recently returned in search of capital for his latest venture—but rather, because of his infatuation, he seems to have been persuaded to remain here. Europe calls, but the supreme financial adventure of his life has been halted, in order that he may bask in the glow of this latest luminary. Silk-hatted stage door Johnnies wait vainly while a private car whisks her away to such joys as we can only infer. The clubs, the restaurants, the bars are agog with talk of the romance. For its conclusion is dubious, and assuredly Europe cannot be made to wait indefinitely. *Veni, vidi, vici!*

Berenice was at first more surprised than shocked. Cowperwood's enthusiasm for her, as well as his seeming extreme contentment in her companionship and his work, had lulled her into the notion that for the present, at least, she was safe. At the same time, as she studied the picture of Lorna, she was quick to perceive the sensual fire that markedly vivified this latest favorite. Was this true? Had he, and so soon, found another? For the moment, she could scarcely forgive the substitution. It had not been more than two months since he had avowed her the sum of the exquisite in womanhood, and that she, of all women, need not fear variability or competition. And yet, here he was in New York, with no honest reason other than Lorna to keep him there. And writing her this nonsense about the presidential election!

By degrees, she grew very, very angry. Her slate-blue eyes turned cold. But finally, reason came to her rescue. For was she not in possession of drastic weapons of her own? There was Tavistock, who, if a fop, was socially so secure that he and his mother were frequently included in Court receptions. And there were others: the glances and appreciative eyes of a score of signally important as well as attractive individuals in this, to her, newer world which plainly said: "Consider me!" And, finally, there was Stane.

But as hostile to Cowperwood as these first thoughts of Berenice might appear, there was in them no desperation. For after all, she cared for him. They both had seen how much of real value had already come to them through each other. She was nonplussed, hurt, startled, not a little angry but not defiantly so. Had she herself not often wondered whether it would be possible for an affection and temperament such as hers to withdraw him entirely from his old moods and ways? She had admitted to herself, or half-believed, that she could not. At best her hope had been that this combination of their qualities and interests would be sufficient to hold both in a relationship that would be enticing, at least profitable. And now, was she going to have to say to herself, and so soon, that all had already failed? Thinking of her own future as well as his, she was not willing to admit this. What had already been was far too wonderful.

Already she had written Cowperwood in regard to Stane's invitation and had been intending to await his reply. But now that this particular evidence was before her, and whatever her ultimate decision in regard to Cowperwood might be, she decided to accept his lordship's invitation, encourage his enthusiasm for her. And thereafter she would decide what she would do about Cowperwood. She was especially interested to see what effect Stane's manifested interest in her was likely to have on him.

And so she now wrote Stane that since her mother had considerably improved and was in a state where a change would be good for her, she would be glad to accept his second invitation which had arrived a few days before.

As for Cowperwood, she decided to stop writing him. And since she did not wish to compromise herself with Stane in any way, she would do nothing there that would bring about a rupture with Cowperwood. It would be better to wait and note the effect of her silence on him.

Chapter 45

MEANWHILE, in New York, Cowperwood was seemingly still in full enjoyment of his latest passion, but in the background, and the very immediate background, at that, were thoughts of Berenice. As was almost always the case with him, his purely sensual enthusiasms were limited in duration. There was something in his very blood stream which, in due course, invariably brought about a sudden and, even to himself, almost inexplicable cessation of interest. After Berenice, however, he found himself troubled by a conviction that at last, and for the first time in his life, he was courting a loss which was not purely sensual and which, therefore, could prove not only aesthetically but mentally devitalizing. Alone among women, she had brought something besides passion and cleverness into his life, something sensitively involved with beauty and creative thought.

And now, there were two other things which gave him pause. The first, and most important, was the receipt of Berenice's letter telling him of Stane's visit to Pryor's Cove and the invitation he had extended to her and her mother to visit Tregasal. This disturbed him very much, for Stane's physical and mental charms were clear to him. And he had sensed that these would appeal to Berenice. Should he be done with Lorna at once and return to England to forefend against any inroads on the part of Stane? Or should he linger a little longer in order to enjoy to the full his relationship with Lorna, and by so doing indicate to Berenice that he was not really jealous, could calmly brook so distinguished and competent a rival, and thereby persuade her to the thought that he was the more secure of the two?

But in addition there was another matter which complicated his mood. This was the sudden and most unexpected illness of Caroline Hand. Of all the personalities preceding Berenice, Caroline had been the most helpful. And her intelligent letters had continued to assure him of her unchanging devotion and to wish him success in his London project. But now came word from her that she would shortly have to be operated on because of appendicitis. She desired to see him, if only for an hour or two. There were many things she wanted to say to him. And since he was back in this country, he might be able to come. Feeling it to be a duty, he decided to go to Chicago to see her.

Now, in all of his life, Cowperwood had never been called upon to attend even so much as a slight illness in connection with one of his mistresses. They had all been such gay, youthful, passing affairs. And now, on his arrival in Chicago, to find Carrie, as he called her, suffering great pain and about to be removed to a hospital, was quite sufficient to cause him to meditate seriously on the tenuousness of human existence. One of Caroline's objects in asking him to come to her was to seek his advice. For assuming that things did not turn out right, as she said gayly enough, she would like him to see that certain wishes of hers were carried out. There was a sister in Colorado, with two children, to whom she was devoted, and to whom she wished certain bonds to be transferred. These Cowperwood had advised her to buy, and they were now in trust for her at his New York bank.

He was quick to belittle Caroline's precautions against death at her age—he was twenty-five years her senior—while at the same time thinking it was possible. She might die, of course, as they all might die, Lorna, Berenice, anyone. And how really futile this brief struggle which at sixty he was entering upon with almost youthful enthusiasm, while Caroline, at thirty-five, was fearing that she would be compelled to relinquish it. Strange. Sad.

Yet true enough, balancing her caution exactly, she did die within forty-eight hours after her entrance into the hospital. On hearing of her death, he felt it advisable to leave Chicago immediately, since locally she had been known to have been his mistress. However, before his departure, he sent for one of his Chicago lawyers and gave him instructions as to what was to be done.

Just the same, her death preyed on his mind. She had been so gallant, so vivid, so witty, even, as she left for the hospital. The last thing she said before leaving the house, and after he had expressed his regret that he could not accompany her, was: "You know me, Frank, I'm a darn good accompanist myself. Only don't go away till I come back. There are still a few duets left in me."

And then she had not returned. And with her had gone one of the gayest of his Chicago memories, the time when he was in the midst of his great fight and had been able to snatch only moments with her. And now Caroline was gone. Aileen, too, was really gone, however much she might seem to be near him. Haguenin was gone, as was Stephanie Platow, and others. He was getting along. How much more was there for him? He had a sudden overwhelming desire to return to Berenice.

Chapter 46

HOWEVER, getting rid of Lorna was not easy. For, like Berenice, or Arlette Wayne, or Caroline Hand, or any of a score of charmers of the past, she was not without her subtleties. And to have the great Cowperwood as her attendant was something too flattering to be relinquished without a struggle.

"Are you going to be in London long? Will you write me regularly? Won't you come back for Christmas? Or at least by February? You know it's settled we're to remain in New York all winter. They're even talking of going to London after that. Would you like it if I came over there?"

She was curled up in his lap and talking into his ear. She added that if she came to London, because of Aileen and his affairs there, she would be as unobtrusive as she had been in New York.

But Cowperwood, thinking of Berenice and Stane, was of no such mind. It was true that sensually Lorna was able to evoke a true delirium of the flesh, but socially, aesthetically and diplomatically, she was no match for Berenice, and he had begun to feel the difference. There must be an end, and a sharp one.

In spite of his various letters and cablegrams subsequent to her letter regarding Stane's visit and her half-indicated desire to go to Tregasal, he had not heard from Berenice. And so by degrees he was beginning to associate the item in *Town Topics* with her silence. His ever-telepathic mind had now decided not to write any more but to leave, and that instantly.

Accordingly, one morning after a night with Lorna, and as she was dressing for a luncheon engagement, he began paving the way for his exit.

"Lorna, you and I have to have a talk. It's about this matter of our separating and my returning to England."

And without heeding such questions and objections as from time to time she chose to interpolate, he proceeded to present his case as exactly as he could, but without mentioning Berenice by name. Yes, there was another woman. And his happy association with her was quite the most necessary and important thing in his life at this time. Besides, there was Aileen, and the nature of his affairs in London. There must be no thought on Lorna's part that this relationship of theirs could go on indefinitely. It had been very beautiful. It still was. But . . .

Despite Lorna's comments and, at certain points, welling tears, it was as though a king were talking to his favorite but about to be discarded mistress. She sat chilled, wounded, and not a little overawed and outfaced. That such a swift end should be made of this was unbelievable. And yet, looking at him, she knew it was so. For never, in all their hours together, had he once said that he deeply cared for her or that it would not end. He was not one to say such things. And yet, because of her beauty and talent, she had not believed it possible that any man, even Cowperwood, once he had entered into this rich intimacy, could find it within his strength to leave her. How could he propose it? Frank Cowperwood, her granduncle, really her own flesh and blood, and her lover!

But Cowperwood, dynamic, thoughtful, cold, the executioner as well as the lover, standing before her and saying that of course there was this blood tie, and because of that and his real affection for her there could be no final mental separation. But there would have to be a physical one.

And so it was, except that during the several days in which he was preparing to sail, there were more long conversations, in which she argued that he should continue to see her as a relative; she would not in any way interfere with him. To which he replied that he would see. At the same time, however, his mind was continually on Berenice. His knowledge of her told him that in spite of Lorna she probably would not leave him, but she might feel less obligated and so withdraw her intellectual and emotional support. And now there was Stane in the background. He must not delay, for unquestionably she was not dependent on him. He would have to make his peace with her as quickly as possible.

After making all the necessary arrangements, and not before, he decided to tell Aileen that they were returning to London. And one evening, as he was entering his home preparatory to speaking to her, he met Tollifer just leaving. Cowperwood greeted him cordially and announced casually, after an inquiry or two relative to his doings in New York, that Aileen and he were returning to London in a day or two. This bit of information Tollifer clearly understood meant that he also would be sailing, and he was delighted. For now he could return to Paris, and probably Marigold Brainerd.

But how easily and skilfully this man arranged things! For at one and the same time he could have Lorna in New York and the Lord only knew whom abroad, and also order Aileen and himself to London or the Continent! And all the while maintaining the same untroubled look that he had noted the first time he saw him. Whereas he, Tollifer, at news of this announced change, must proceed to disturb all his present arrangements in order to accommo-

date and make possible and pleasant this other man's brisk and
dauntless progress through life!

Chapter 47

MEANWHILE, during four days in late
September, Berenice was being enter-
tained by the picturesque and historic phases of Tregasal. Stane had
arranged that his guests should include a jolly and interesting couple
who lived on an adjoining estate, a Mr. and Mrs. Robert Waler;
also Warren Sharpless, the prosperous master of one of the very
considerable fishing industries of the region, who had long since
passed from the tradesman to the gentleman class. These three were
to help entertain Mrs. Carter.

And true to his explanation of himself, Stane impressed Berenice
as being markedly inclined to place diversion on an equal footing
with his considerable financial interests. In other words, he knew
how to play. At Tregasal, an immense plateau of moorland which
at different points led to woods or the slaty promontories and beaches
of this westerly coast, Stane was full of enthusiasm for what his
estate and county had to show. To Berenice, with whom he sought
to be alone as much as possible, he pointed out the circles and lines
of stone, possibly of Druidic or other early religious origin, which
at certain spots lent a mysterious and plainly prehistoric atmosphere
to his property. Also he talked to her of the copper and tin mines
of pre-Roman days, and the great fishing fleets plying out of Mounts
Bay, St. Ives, and Penzance; and of the aged and primitive folk of
some of the inland villages, some of whom, on his own estate, spoke
a now almost forgotten language. In Mounts Bay lay his yacht,
roomy enough, as she discovered, for the entertainment of a dozen
guests. And from the topmost mount of Tregasal plateau could be
seen both the English and St. George's channels.

Berenice noted, in due course, that Stane was proud of this strange
country, almost as much so as of his possessions in it. Here he felt
himself the lord that he was, recognized and respected by all. She
wondered if presently a sobering process would not set in, which
would bring him back to this region permanently. For her, however, it was not so enticing. A little too bleak and primitive, although
she admired it as a spectacle. Tregasal Hall, long and gray and

somber, was only saved in her esteem by its highly decorative interior. There were bright curtains and rugs, old French furniture, French and English paintings, and modern lighting and plumbing. Also she was impressed and even a little overawed by the library, collected by previous earls over a period of a hundred and fifty years and constituting an imposing bibliophilic treasure.

Throughout this visit, which included a day of yachting and one of bathing and picnicking under the cliffs, Berenice was still further impressed by a certain rugged simplicity which contrasted oddly with Stane's love of comfort and material perfection. He was strong, as he demonstrated by chinning himself more than half a dozen times on the limb of a tree. Also an excellent swimmer. He ventured far into the waves and breakers which Berenice could only contemplate with doubt and wonder. He questioned her constantly as to her reactions in regard to all that pleased him, and enthusiastically welcomed every suggestion of concordance, and was forever busying himself throughout her visit with suggestions of things they might possibly do at some future time.

Yet charming as he was, and interesting at this time as a foil to Cowperwood and his unfaithfulness, still, as she decided, and after not a little meditation, he lacked the blazing force of Cowperwood. There was not about him that nimbus of great affairs and powers. He was more the quiet aspirant for position without the fascinating fanfare and uproar that seemed ever to accompany the great in the rush and flare of creation. And in this sense it was that Berenice was still, and always would be, dominated by Cowperwood. Although he was absent and interested in another woman, and his personality dimmed by distance, still he filled her thoughts even at the very time that she found herself moved by the charm of the less strident and more soothing personality of Stane. For was it not possible that after all she might have to forego the fascination of Cowperwood and devote herself to the matter of bringing about an ultimate social rectification for herself by capturing Stane, or someone like him? She could not deny her desire for at least some measure of security. She meditated on what Aileen might do to her once she found out she was in England, and with Cowperwood. Perhaps she did know. She was almost certain that Aileen had sent the *Town Topics* article. And her mother's past life, how could that ever be hushed up? And yet, there was no doubt of Stane's affection for her. Perhaps if certain matters could be covered up, he would marry her. Perhaps, even if he knew all, he might still seek to aid her in concealing what was most inimical to their mutual happiness.

Riding back with him early one morning toward Tregasal, after a gallop over his bleak acres, she wondered how stoutly based and centered in the customs of his class he really was, how much he might be brought to sacrifice to retain one for whom he really cared.

Chapter 48 LONDON. The usual fanfare because of Mr. and Mrs. Cowperwood having re-
turned. Berenice, because of previous cables, fully aware of Cowperwood's arrival, and he really interested in but one thing: peace and affection between himself and Berenice.

And Stane very much pleased because in Cowperwood's absence he had not only made some progress with the underground business but also with Cowperwood's ward. In truth, Stane was half in love. He had been at Pryor's Cove several times following Berenice's Tregasal visit. And hope in connection with his affection was giving strength to the thought that he should persist in his quest. He might win. Berenice might fall in love with him and consent to become his wife. Cowperwood should not look too unfavorably on such a development. It should lead to a closer union between all. Of course, he would need to know more about Berenice and her true relation to Cowperwood. He had not troubled to investigate as yet. But even if he found her background not as perfect as it might be, Berenice was still the most fascinating woman he had ever known. She was certainly not attempting to lure him; it was he who was definitely pursuing her.

At the same time Berenice was at once pleased and troubled by two developments: one the fact that Stane seemed to be so very much interested in her, and the other that since her visit to Tregasal he had suggested, among other things, that she and her mother, together with the Cowperwoods, might join him for a cruise on his yacht, the *Iola,* before the end of autumn. The trip could include a stopover at Cowes, where King Edward and Queen Alexandra were likely to be at that time, and he would be glad to present them to their majesties, for both the king and queen were old friends of his father's.

At the mention of Aileen, Berenice experienced a mental chill. For if Aileen went on such a cruise, neither she nor her mother could go. If Aileen did not go, some accidentproof explanation would have to be made to Stane. If Cowperwood and she together were to accept this invitation, it would mean they would have to reach a diplomatic if not exactly harmonious agreement, and this was not exactly desirable to her at the moment. If she did not go with him, or went without him, it might mean the elimination of him from her life. And that again would mean explanations and readjustments probably fatal to all concerned.

In the face of her present resentment toward Cowperwood, she was in no position to decide quickly. For dream as she might about Stane, it was quite obvious that without Cowperwood's good will, she was not likely to extricate herself from the various complications which confronted her. Sufficiently angered, he could destroy her instantly. Sufficiently indifferent, he might allow Aileen and others to do as much. Also, in turning all this over in her mind she was confronted by the fact that her temperament as well as her general viewpoint appeared to crave Cowperwood and not Stane. She was strongest when supplemented by him. And weighing all that was to be weighed in connection with Stane, there remained the outstanding fact that he did not match Cowperwood in vigor, resourcefulness, naturalness, or the humanness of his approach to life. And it was these things more than anything else that caused her to realize that she desired to be with Cowperwood more than with anyone else, to hear his voice, to observe his gestures, sense his dynamic and seemingly unterrified approach to life. It was when he was with her that she felt her own strength magnified and without his brave support what would her personal reactions to all this now be? It caused her, in the face of Stane's suggestions, to indulge in no definite comment other than that her guardian could, at times, be strangely perverse and intractable, and that she would be compelled to leave these invitations in abeyance pending his return to England. At the same time, as she smilingly indicated, she was very much in favor of it. And if he were willing to leave it to her, perhaps it could be arranged.

A cheerful, if slightly formal, greeting from Berenice, which gave no least hint of difficulties, was waiting for Cowperwood when he reached his hotel. However, he was one who could not only sense danger but fairly register the vigorous thoughts of others in regard to himself, and he was already aware of inimical moods in her direction. In fact, long before he reached England, he had been fully convinced that his affair with Lorna was known to Berenice. He could feel it in the region of his solar plexus. It put him on his guard and sharpened his wits for any possible emergency. Already he had decided not to attempt evasion in any form, but, rather, feel his way according to Berenice's mood and manner.

And so, Pryor's Cove, colored by the mood of autumn, the leaves slightly reddened and yellowed. There were wreaths of mist on the river, even at noon, the hour of his arrival. And as he drew near he was most vividly conscious of all the bright summer days he might have spent here with Berenice. But now the thing to do was to face her frankly; let her once more sense him as he really was. That method had proved so propitious and effective in connection with other difficulties that he was satisfied to think it might prove so now. Besides, was there not Stane to balance Lorna? Guilty or not, Berenice might be made to feel dubious in regard to her own position.

As he drove in, Piggott, the gardener, visible behind a hedge he was trimming, bowed a greeting. In the paddock adjoining Stane's stables, the horses were warming themselves in the autumn sun, and about the stable doors two of the grooms were busy with the harness. Mrs. Carter walked across the lawn to greet him, apparently unaware of the problems that were troubling him and her daughter, for she was all smiles. From her cheerful welcome, he guessed that Berenice had probably not confided in her.

"Well, how's everything?" he called out to her, stepping forward and taking her hand.

Berenice, according to her mother, was as well as ever, and now in the music room practicing. Rimski-Korsakov's "Market Scenes" heard through the open window confirmed this.

For a moment Cowperwood had the feeling that, as in the case of Aileen, he might have to seek her out and begin some sort of irritating explanation, but as he was so thinking, the music suddenly ceased and she appeared in the doorway, as poised and smiling as ever. Oh, he was back! How nice! How had he been? Had he had a pleasant voyage? She was so glad to see him. She ran forward, not kissing him, as he noted, but otherwise acting as though no least ill were troubling her. In fact, she appeared quite enthusiastic as she added that now he was in time for the lovely autumn scenery; every day this place seemed lovelier. And, for the moment, Cowperwood entered upon this play-acting the while he wondered how long it would be before the real storm broke. But since Berenice's gaiety continued with an invitation to go over to the houseboat for a cocktail, he interrupted with:

"Let's walk down by the river, do you mind, Bevy?" And taking her by the arm he led her down to the tree-shaded path. "Bevy," he began, "there's something I have to say to you before we do anything else." He fixed her with a hard, cold gaze. And as instantly she modified her manner.

"Will you pardon me just a minute, Frank, while I speak to Mrs. Evans . . ."

"No," he said, decisively, "don't go, Bevy. This is something much more important than Mrs. Evans or anything else. I want to tell you about Lorna Maris. You probably know about her, but I want to tell you, anyway."

As he spoke she remained silent, walking beside him softly and evenly.

"You know of Lorna Maris?" he asked.

"Yes, I know. A clipping and some pictures were sent me from New York. She is very beautiful."

He noted her reserve. No complaint. No request for information. At the same time, all the more urgent was it that he should discover her true mood.

"Quite a sudden turnabout from all I've been saying to you, isn't it, Bevy?"

"Yes, I think it is. But you're not going to tell me you're sorry, I hope." The corners of her mouth suggested the least trace of irony.

"No, Bevy, I'm not going to tell you anything except what happened. Then you can judge for yourself. Do you wish to hear about it?"

"Not so much. But if you really want to talk about it, all right. I think I understand how it happened."

"Bevy!" he exclaimed, pausing and looking at her, admiration and genuine affection in his every line. "We can't—at least, I can't —get anywhere this way. The only reason I want to tell you is because whatever you're thinking, I want you to know that I still care deeply for you. That may sound shallow and false after all that has happened since I last saw you, but I believe you know it's true. You know and I know that there are personality values that are not to be measured by physical beauty or sexual sensations alone. As between one attractive woman and another, and one man and another judging them, there are always other modifying things: character, understanding, extreme congeniality of purpose and ideals, and . . ."

He paused as she interrupted rather icily: "Really? Of sufficient weight to make a difference in one's conduct, loyalty, or constancy?"

The semisubmerged flash in her eyes warned him that tergiversation in her case was of no least value.

"Enough to make a very great difference, Bevy. You see me here, don't you? Ten days ago in New York . . ."

Berenice interrupted him. "Yes, I know. You left her after a delightful summer in her company. You had enough of her for the time being. And so London, your plans to re-establish yourself . . ." Her pretty mouth curled scornfully. "But really, Frank, you need not clarify all this to me. I am very much like yourself, you know. I can explain as cleverly as you can; only being obligated to you for many things, and perhaps willing to sacrifice to a degree if I continue to need them, I must be more careful than you, much more careful. Or . . ." She paused and gazed at him, and he felt as though he had received a body blow.

"But, Berenice, those things are true. I did leave her. I have returned to you. I am willing to explain or not, just as you please. But one thing I do want to do, and that is to make up with you, get your forgiveness, go on and on with you alone. You won't believe it, but I promise you there won't be any more of this. Can't you sense that? Won't you help me get back to some fair and equitable relation with you? Think what we mean to each other! I can help you, want to, will, whether you choose to break with me or not! Won't you believe that, Bevy?"

They were standing on a small green lawn bordering the Thames, under old trees, with the low thatches of a distant hamlet in view and curls of blue smoke rising from cottage chimneys. All was peaceful about them. But he was thinking that for all this sufficiency and the plain intention to make as little as possible of the provocation that had been given her, Berenice's mood was not forgiving. At the same time, he could not help contrasting her with other women under related circumstances, Aileen in particular. Here was no brooding, weeping, quarreling woman. Although, as he now also thought, and for the first time in his life, real love, true love, however destructive to the lover, might truly brood, weep, quarrel, and be forgiven for it, into the bargain!

On the other hand, here was certainly a type of affection which carried with it values which could not be denied or belittled. Plainly, he had dulled them, and on the instant he became the shrewd, watchful, resourceful, and dynamic Cowperwood of the financial meeting room and parley.

"Listen to me, Bevy!" he said, firmly. "About June twentieth I went down to Baltimore on a business matter . . ." And from there on he related exactly what had happened. The midnight return to his room. Lorna's knock. All. He told exactly how fascinated he had been; how and where he had entertained Lorna; the comments of the critics. He persisted in the excuse that, like Berenice, Lorna had cast a spell. He had intended no unfaithfulness. It was something that had come over him, and, to make himself perfectly plain, he advanced the theory which had come to him because of this and other related affairs in the past: that there was something in sensual desire which superseded and therefore must be superior to reason and will. For, in his case, it undermined and washed away any predetermined course.

"If I want to be honest," he added at this point, "I must say that perhaps the only way to avoid lapses of this kind is to avoid any close contact with attractive women. And that is not always possible, of course."

"Of course not," said Berenice.

"As you know," he went on, determined to continue, "once you are close to a person like Lorna Maris, you have to be pretty tame to escape her. And that's a mighty strong admission from me."

"Quite," said Berenice. "But I agree with you. She is very attractive. But how about me in connection with other men? Are you ready to grant me the same privilege?" She gazed at him inquiringly, while he stared at her in return.

"Theoretically, yes," he replied. "Because I care for you, I would have to stand for it emotionally as long as I could, as long as it was necessary for me to do so. After that, I would probably let you go, just as you will let me go if you don't care enough to keep me. But what I want to know now is, knowing what you do, do you care, my dear? And that is very important, because I still care a great deal."

"Well, Frank, you are asking me something which just at the moment I cannot really answer, because I don't know."

"But, as you see," he persisted, "in this case her influence has not lasted, or I wouldn't be here now. And I am not offering this as an excuse, but as a fact."

"In other words," said Berenice, "she did not come on the same boat."

"She is dancing in New York the whole winter. And any American paper will tell you that. I maintain, Bevy, that the attraction you have for me is not only stronger but superior. I need you, Bevy. We are two minds and temperaments that think and work alike. That's why I'm back here now, and want to stay here. This other affair was less valuable. I felt it all the time. When you stopped writing I realized how much less I cared for Lorna. There, that's the sum of it. Now what, Bevy?"

In the growing dusk he had drawn nearer and nearer. Now he seized her, pressed his lips to hers, and held her tightly. As he did so, she felt herself yielding, mentally and emotionally. But at the same time she felt impelled to make plain her position.

"I do care for you, Frank, yes. But this is only a sensual pull in your case. When it is over . . . when it is over . . ."

Both subsided in each other's arms, letting desire, emotion, blot out for the time being that frail little lamp, the human mind, and submerge for the moment that wholly unreasoning force, the human will.

Chapter 49

LATER, in her bedroom, on that first night, Cowperwood continued his argument as to the wisdom of going on together in their roles of ward and guardian.

"You see, Bevy," he said, "the relationship is already established in the minds of Stane and others."

"Are you trying to discover whether I am planning to leave you?" she queried.

"Well, naturally, I thought you might be considering it. This fellow Stane certainly has everything to offer you."

He was sitting on the edge of her bed. The room was only slightly illumined by a moon that was shining against the drawn blinds. Berenice was sitting up in bed, leaning against the pillows, smoking a cigarette.

"Not so much as you have," she said, "if you were ever really interested enough. But if you must know, I am not considering anything except the problem which you yourself have forced on me. We entered into an arrangement and you disarranged it. What do you expect me to do under the circumstances? Give you every liberty and ask nothing for myself?"

"I don't expect anything which is going to prove distasteful or harmful to you." His tone was aggressive. "I'm merely suggesting that if you're going to become interested in Stane, we'll have to figure out some way to continue this guardian-ward relationship until you are settled in your new state. From one point of view," he added, honestly enough, "I'd be glad to see you established as the wife of a man like Stane. On the other hand, there's the program we planned, and without you as a part of it, Bevy, I can tell you frankly that I'm not going to be very much interested. I might go on, and I might not. It will all depend on how I feel. I know you think that because I went with Lorna Maris I could easily make worth-while conditions for myself. But I don't see it that way. She was a mere incident, something involved with the passions and not the mind, as I've told you. If you had gone to New York with me, it never would have happened. Since it has, the one thing I see to do is to make the best working arrangement I can with you. And you will have to say what that is to be." He got up and went to look for a cigar.

Thus directly approached, Berenice found herself intensely troubled by all he had said. For she cared for him intensely; his problems, his career, were almost more important to her than her own. And yet opposed to them was her own life, her own future. For once she reached the age of thirty-five or forty, the chances of his being present were slight. She lay there silently thinking, while Cowperwood waited. And in due course she answered, although not without extreme misgivings. Yes, she would continue; of course she would continue, for the present, anyway. For what could either he or she say in regard to his future movements or decisions?

"There's no one like you, Frank," she observed at this point, "for me, anyway. I like Lord Stane, of course, but I've not really seen enough of him. It's nonsense to even think of it. Just the same, he is interesting—fascinating, really. And if you're going to leave me to a sort of half-life with you, it does seem impractical for me to ignore him, assuming that he would really marry me. At the same time, relying on you is not even to be considered. I can stay with you, of course, and do my best to work out with you all the things we planned. But if so, it will be because I am relying entirely on myself. I will be making you a present of my youth, my ideals, my enthusiasms, and my love, and expecting not one thing in return."

"Bevy!" he exclaimed, startled by the equity of her statement. "That isn't true!"

"Well, then, show me where it's false. Let's say I go on, as I probably shall; then what?"

"Well," said Cowperwood, seating himself in a chair opposite the bed, "I will admit you raise a serious question. I'm not as young as you, and if you continue with me, you certainly run a great risk of exposure and social ostracism. There's no denying that. About all I can leave you is money, and regardless of what we decide on to-night, I can tell you now that I propose to arrange for that at once. You will have enough, if you manage it intelligently, to maintain you in luxury for the rest of your life."

"Oh, I know," said Berenice. "No one can deny that where you care for anyone, you are the soul of generosity. I am not even questioning that. What troubles me is the lack of real love on your part, and the reasonable certainty that I'm to be not only left without love but I am to pay for my own love in other ways later on."

"I see your problem, Bevy, believe me, I do. And I'm in no position to ask you to do more for me than you feel you want to do. You must do what you think is best for yourself. But I promise you, darling, that if you do continue with me, I will try to be faithful to you. And if ever you feel you ought to leave me and marry someone, I promise not to interfere. And that's final. As I said before, I care for you very much, Bevy. You know that. You are not only my sweetheart but the same as my own child to me."

"Frank!" She called him over to her side. "You know I cannot leave you. It's not possible, at least not in spirit."

"Bevy, darling girl!" And he gathered her up in his arms. "How wonderful it is to have you with me again!"

"But one thing we must settle, Frank," she put in at this point, calmly smoothing her ruffled hair, "and that's this yachting invitation. What about that?"

"I don't know yet, dear, but I guess as long as he's so very much interested in you, he's not likely to be particularly antagonistic toward me."

"Scamp!" cried Berenice, laughing. "If ever there was a deep-dyed villain . . ."

"No, just a young, ambitious American businessman trying to find his way through an English financial jungle! We'll talk it over tomorrow. It's you, just you, I want to think about now . . ."

Chapter 50 LIKE a master chess player, Cowperwood proposed to outwit all of the entirely nationalistic and, of course, humanly selfish elements arrayed against him in his underground project. He had evolved a broad and comprehensive plan, which he hoped to work out as follows:

First, there was the existing Charing Cross line, to which must be added the existing central loop consisting of the District and the Metropolitan Railway, with their utterly impractical and warring factions. If all went well, he, Stane, and Johnson, but principally himself, held the key to this situation.

Next, assuming that he gained control of the District and the Metropolitan—with which he would or would not, as circumstances dictated, join his Railway Equipment & Construction Company—he proposed to organize the Union Traction Underground, Limited, which would control all of these.

Incidentally, however, and unknown to any of his present associates, he proposed to buy from Abington Scarr the charter for the Baker Street and Waterloo Line; also the charter of the Brompton and Piccadilly, a line which he had learned was in about the same condition as the Charing Cross; and certain other routes and prospects, charters for which he would pick up through others.

With these in his bag, he would be able, he felt, to organize the London Underground General, which would include all of the property of the Union Traction Underground, Limited, as well as the charters and lines which he would privately acquire, thus providing a complete metropolitan system and at the same time, by reason of his holdings, give him personal control. Incidentally, if he could not ultimately take publicly the chairmanship of this enormous property, at least he would be acknowledged as its subsurface control. Also, if he could not put in his own directors, he would arrange so that those who were placed in control could do nothing to injure the property.

And eventually, if all went well, he would quietly dispose of his holdings at an enormous profit, and thereafter leave the company to get along as best it could. He would have established his title as not only promoter but builder, and would have given London a modern and comprehensive metropolitan system which would bear the imprint of his genius, just as Chicago's downtown loop bore it. And thereafter, with his wealth, he could maintain his art gallery, organize his charities, build the hospital to which he had given much thought in the past, and at the same time leave to all to whom he felt obligated an unquestionably satisfactory reward. The dream enticed him. A few years of swift work, five or six at the most, as he saw it, would serve to accomplish all.

But to follow all of his activities, mental as well as physical, in connection with this plan would be the same as attempting to follow the swift and confusing thoughts, tricks, and motions of a prestidigitator. There were primarily, of course, his negotiations with Johnson and Stane. On communicating with Johnson, immediately following his reconciliation with Berenice, he found a greater willingness to co-operate than had previously existed. Johnson announced that he and Stane had given a great deal of thought to the matter in Cowperwood's absence, but he would prefer to communicate their conclusions in Stane's presence.

This resulted almost immediately in another conference in Berkeley Square, where Cowperwood found something resembling more a friendly than a commercial atmosphere. Johnson had been detained and was not present when he arrived. Immediately he noticed the joviality of Stane's manner. The latter inquired about conditions in the United States: what the elections there forebode;

did he find London pleasing; and how was his ward, Miss Fleming? And her mother? He had been, as Cowperwood perhaps knew, a fairly frequent visitor to Pryor's Cove. How truly charming they were, mother and daughter. He paused shrewdly, watching Cowperwood's face as he said this. But Cowperwood met the challenge.

"No doubt you are wondering about their relationship to me," he said, suavely. "Well, I have known Mrs. Carter for many years. She married a distant relative of mine, who named me as executor and guardian in loco parentis. Naturally, I have become very fond of Berenice. She is a very brilliant girl."

"I must say I find her so," said Stane. "And I am pleased that Pryor's Cove has appealed to Mrs. Carter and her daughter."

"Yes, they certainly seem to have found it an ideal place. It is really beautiful."

Fortunately, to break the personal trend of the conversation, Johnson arrived at this moment. Bustling in and apologizing for having been unavoidably detained, he inquired after Cowperwood's welfare before putting on his most officially expectant and executive manner. And there followed a concise and vigorous presentation by him of all that had been done, together with a review of the situation as it now stood. Decidedly, he announced, Cowperwood's proposed invasion of the London underground field had evoked a furore. With but few exceptions, directors and shareholders of both of the old loop companies were against him.

"They seem to want to take over your ideas, Mr. Cowperwood," he said, "and work them out themselves. The only thing that is delaying them is lack of agreement among themselves, and, of course," he added, with a twinkle in his eye, "they are a little disturbed by the amount of money it is going to take. They don't know how they're going to get it without too much expense to themselves."

"Precisely," commented Cowperwood, "and for that very reason delay will be the most expensive thing that can be indulged in. There is a program here which, if entered upon vigorously, can be held within attractive financial limits. Delay and argument will only attract speculators and prospectors who will pile up options on whatever shares or franchises are floating about and hold them for a rise. For that reason it is essential that we reach an agreement as quickly as possible."

"Now, as I understand it," put in Stane, agreeably enough, "your proposal was for Johnson and myself to pool our interests in the District as well as the Metropolitan, and in addition either buy, or bring together under some working agreement which you are to control, 51 per cent of either the District or the Metropolitan, or both."

"Right!" said Cowperwood.

"And against that, either on a hundred-year lease or in perpetuity, you agree to guarantee interest at 5 per cent."

"Right!"

"And, in addition, give the refusal of at least 10 per cent of the preferred shares of the Charing Cross, together with 10 per cent of the shares of any additional subsidiary which you or the larger company may see fit to organize and join up with the parent company, at 8 per cent of *their* par value."

"Right!"

"The interest on all these shares to be a first lien on the property of the entire company at the time it is fully organized."

"That is my proposal," said Cowperwood.

"I must say I see nothing wrong with that," said Stane, staring at Johnson, who in turn stared back at him.

"In short," said Johnson, turning to Cowperwood, "once we perform our part, you bind yourself to reconstruct and equip in the most modern fashion both of the old lines and such new ones as you can secure, and to mortgage the entire property in such a way as to guarantee the interest on all of the present shares of the District and the Metropolitan, also on whatsoever amount of the 10 per cent of the shares of these new companies or subsidiaries we may elect to subscribe for at eighty."

"Such is my intention," said Cowperwood.

Once more Johnson and Stane stared at each other.

"Well," said Stane, finally, "subject to such difficulties as we are certain to encounter, I pledge myself to perform my part of the undertaking as quickly as possible, and to the best of my ability."

"And I," said Johnson, "shall be glad to work in entire harmony with Lord Stane, and to do whatever is necessary to bring this to a successful conclusion."

"Well, gentlemen," said Cowperwood, rising, "I am not only pleased but honored by this understanding, and to show you the soundness of my intentions, I propose—if both of you are agreeable to the idea, of course—to ask Mr. Johnson to act as my legal advisor, and have him prepare all papers concluding this general agreement between us. And when the time comes," he added, smiling at them, "I would be delighted to have you both serve as directors."

"As to that, time and circumstances will have to decide," said Stane. "It should be helpful, certainly."

"It will be my pleasure to serve both of you to the very best of my ability," added Johnson.

All three were not a little conscious of the grandiose note that had slipped into these mutual felicitations, but it was quickly eased by Stane's proffer of a parting glass of old cognac—a case of which, without any previous mention, he had sent to Cowperwood's rooms at the Cecil.

Chapter 51

ONE OF the painful phases of Cowperwood's further negotiations at this time was the need he faced, or thought he did, of employing Englishmen rather than Americans as his assistants in all departments of his work. De Sota Sippens was the first victim, and he was almost brokenhearted, for he had come to like London. Joined with his ever-successful Chief, as he argued, he expected to shine here. More than that, he was eager to sharpen his wits and energies against those of these assured and almost condescending Englishmen, who, he was perfectly satisfied, knew nothing about the business of traction. However, to soften the blow as much as possible, Cowperwood placed him in charge of his Chicago financial affairs.

One of Cowperwood's methods of raising capital was the use of the holding company, an underlying organization which would bring in sufficient money to buy the companies which he wished to control and at the same time furnish him with the necessary shares for that control. In this instance, his Railway Equipment & Construction Company was formed, with dummy directors and chairmen, and in which all who joined him were eventually to possess founder's shares. Johnson acted as solicitor and counsel at a salary of £3,000 a year. And thereafter, in a private agreement drawn by him—but most carefully gone over by Cowperwood's attorneys

—and signed by Johnson, Stane, and Cowperwood, it was stipulated that from then on their various shares in both the District and the Metropolitan, either then and there owned or subsequently to be acquired, were to be voted as one in any official vote that looked to the reorganization and sale of the District and the Metropolitan to the new company later to be organized. And in this new company they were to receive three shares of its issue for each one of their old shares.

And now, for Johnson, there was the really great task of running about in quest of blocks of scattered shares of both the District and the Metropolitan, which shares, up to £500,000 he had orders from Cowperwood to buy, but under various names. Also to work up, among the old directors, knowledge of as well as enthusiasm for Cowperwood and his proposed plans. As for Stane, he was to buy as many more shares of these old companies as he could obtain, with a view to voting with Cowperwood in his new undertaking, and he, too, where possible, was to bring his personal influence to bear on all such as he knew.

As a result of these activities, a veritable landslide of investors descended upon Cowperwood. And many American as well as English financiers, realizing the importance of the properties which he was gathering in, now also attempted to get franchises for themselves, which franchises by that time were most difficult to obtain. One of those who became interested was no less a person than Stanford Drake, also an American financier, who made applications to Parliament for franchises for lines which, if built, would have paralleled the Cowperwood lines for a very considerable distance, and thus practically split the income for these territories.

This disturbed Cowperwood not a little, for it had to be stopped without arousing English opposition to both men, since the English were opposed to American entrance into this field, whether it be the entrance of Mr. Drake or Mr. Cowperwood. In consequence, the usual legal battles on the part of each ensued. For each pointed out the assumed defects of the other and each minimized the import of what his rival was trying to do.

For his part, Cowperwood pointed out that the Drake line as planned would run, in part, through fairly good residence sections, but it would also be compelled to run through open fields for a distance of ten miles before it would reach paying territory. He also pointed out that the Drake line was to be a single-track line, one track in a tunnel, while his system would be double-track throughout. At the same time, the Drake interests proceeded to counter with the claim that Cowperwood's roads were under the Thames embankment, while their roads were under the Strand and other business streets; that Mr. Cowperwood's roads were away from trade, and theirs would take people to trade. However, Cowperwood added that parallel lines were mutually destructive, did not pay, for he knew if the Drake crowd succeeded in getting franchises for their system, no matter how it was developed, his own line would be affected to a considerable extent. This, of course, he did not admit at the time; instead, he announced that he could not understand why the House of Drake would indulge in any such venture. And to make matters as smooth as possible, he said he believed that Mr. Drake's London branch, rather than Mr. Drake himself, was responsible for the error. He went on to say further that Mr. Drake was a great man, and he believed eventually, when the matter was made clear to him, he would not put any money into it.

Yet in spite of all these sweet words, Mr. Drake's lawyers, going before Parliament, introduced a bill seeking a franchise, and Mr. Cowperwood's lawyers introduced a rival bill for the lines he wanted to build. The result was that Parliament put both bills off until the following November and did not favor either one, which delay was a kind of victory for Cowperwood, he being so much further ahead in the development of his over-all scheme. In fact, he was heard to say that he did not enjoy going into any project unless there was some opposition, and, as everything was fair in love and war, he was prepared to oppose the Drake interests to the last ditch.

But the interest of Stanford Drake was aroused to the necessity for a real battle with Cowperwood. Having vast funds at his disposal, he made Cowperwood an offer of $5,000,000 for the privilege of sharing the Piccadilly Circus Station, which belonged to Cowperwood and which would obviously be needed by Drake in his system. At the same time he also offered Cowperwood $2,500,000 if he would call off his army of lawyers who were then and there preparing to fight Drake's application to Parliament for permission to build his proposed road. Of course, the offers were refused by Cowperwood.

At the same time there was the London United Company which

was planning to build a road from Hyde Park Corner to Shepherd's Bush, the preliminary negotiations for which they had worked out. They went to Drake and offered to unite their line with his, and asked for a franchise from the city. They also asked Drake to operate the line as a whole if and when completed. Drake refused. Then they asked to be permitted to operate their section. Again Drake refused. Whereupon they offered their section to Cowperwood, although they had as yet no franchise for it. Cowperwood notified them to see Speyer & Company, a financing concern that operated not only in England and America but throughout Europe. This firm, after looking into the matter and seeing that they might, by benefiting Cowperwood, eventually benefit themselves, decided to buy all the existing rights which this particular company owned, after which they proceeded to syndicate the entire block of shares. Their counsel, then and there before the Parliament Tubes Committee on other matters, asked to withdraw their request for a franchise. As Drake had been pleading for only one total franchise for a year, this invalidated the whole plea. Drake returned with a request to be allowed a franchise for their section. But as their original request had called for no such thing, and there was no such bill before the committee, Cowperwood's counsel argued that the whole matter must be thrown out. And Mr. Drake's scheme was withdrawn.

The dramatic conclusion of this fight between two such outstanding adversaries was reported in detail by both English and American newspapers, and the London County Council, which favored a system of transit development which would make travel convenient for all London, enthused over the victory of Mr. Cowperwood, citing him as a man of broad and valuable social qualities which deserved a most favorable reception everywhere.

Cowperwood, taking advantage of this sentiment, made much of the social benefits that would result from his vast enterprise. His system, he announced, would ultimately carry as many as 200,000,000 passengers a year, would have one class of coach, a uniform five-cent fare, and be a fully connected system which would enable a traveler to go all the way by subway, thereby providing an object lesson in rapid transit, cheap fares, and frequent service.

Personally, at this time, Cowperwood was prospering so enormously that he was able to attend to matters other than those concerning the gathering of shares and profits. For instance, for mere publicity purposes, he bought Turner's painting, "Rockets and Blue Lights," for $78,000, and hung it in his office.

Chapter 52

For all of his success, however, there was a new and difficult situation arising in connection with Aileen that was about to descend on Cowperwood with full force.

Aileen had returned to Paris and was again being entertained and amused by Tollifer and his friends. The fact was, however, that Marigold Brainerd, noting that Aileen favored Tollifer to such an extent that she might even wish to marry him eventually, decided that it was time for her to check this growing interest. Aware of his connection with Cowperwood, she believed she had a weapon that might easily clear the field for her. For Tollifer had confessed as much to her one night on the yachting cruise, when he had had too much to drink. And accordingly at her first opportunity she acted.

It was at a party that Tollifer gave at the studio of one of his friends, a celebration in honor of their return to Paris, that Marigold, having consumed more than her share of alcohol and noting how gayly Aileen was trifling with Tollifer, suddenly turned on her.

"If you knew as much as I do about your friend, you might not be so eager to have him at your heels all the time," she said, sarcastically.

"Well, if you know anything that is so certain to annoy me," said Aileen, "why don't you come out with it instead of insinuating? Or is it just your jealousy that is getting the best of you?"

"Jealousy! Me jealous of Tollifer and you! I happen to know what's back of all these attentions he's showering on you, that's all!"

Startled and irritated by this sudden assertion, Aileen exclaimed: "Just what are you driving at? Come on, tell me! Otherwise, turn your jealousy on someone else!"

"Jealousy! How silly! I'm sure it never occurred to you that your attentive friend might be pursuing you for reasons other than your personal charm. And besides, where do you suppose he gets all the money that he spends on you? I've known him for years, and he's never had a shilling of his own, you know."

"No, I didn't know. But please come out with what you want to say," said Aileen.

"I suggest that you ask Mr. Tollifer, or, better yet, your husband. I'm sure he could enlighten you," concluded Marigold, as she edged away from Aileen.

Whereupon, intensely wrought up, Aileen left the room, got her wraps, and returned to her apartment, but not to dismiss the subject from her mind. Tollifer! The peculiar energy with which he had thrust himself into her life! Penniless, and yet spending so much money! And why Cowperwood's willingness to encourage this friendship between them, even occasionally crossing over to Paris to attend these parties given by Tollifer? The darkest aspect of Marigold's suggestion suddenly struck her with great force: that he had used this man to clear her out of his life! She must get to the bottom of this; she must know.

Within the hour, Tollifer, having missed her at the party, called her on the telephone, whereupon she demanded that he come to see her at once, there was something she must discuss with him immediately. And, upon his appearance, a stormy scene. Whose idea was it that he should invite her to Paris and pay her so much attention and at the same time spend so much money on her? Her husband's or his own?

What nonsense! Why should he spend money on her if he did not care for her personally? To which Aileen replied that she heard that he had no money of his own, and never had had any. And, come to think of it, what did he really do to earn money, unless it was for service of some personal nature, such as that of dancing attendance on those who were able to spend their time playing but would not trouble to bother with all the tiresome details? This was an insult that cut him to the bone, since it placed him in the servant class.

"That's not true," he said, weakly.

But there was something in the tone of his voice that made Aileen doubt him, and this awakened a fury in her. To think that any man should stoop to such degrading employment! To think that she, Frank Algernon Cowperwood's wife, due to her husband's plotting, should be the victim of it! To be thus publicly displayed as an unwanted wife, one so distasteful to her husband that he had to hire help to get rid of her!

But wait! Here and now, or by tomorrow at the latest, she would show this parasite and trickster, and also her husband, that she was not to be disgraced in this fashion! For here and now, Tollifer's services, as far as she was concerned, were ended. And Cowperwood was to learn by wire that she was aware of his plotting, and that she was through with him forever; that she was returning to New York to stay in her own home, where she belonged, and that if he attempted to follow her, she would take him into court and expose him in the public press; she would relieve herself once and for all time of his lies, infidelities, and his mental cruelties!

After which, turning to Tollifer, she exclaimed:

"You may go now. Your services to me are ended. I'm returning to New York at once, and if you ever cross my path or annoy me in any way, I'll see that you are exposed for what you are. Run to Mr. Cowperwood and see if he won't give you something more respectable to do!"

With which she walked to the door and opened it for him to depart.

Chapter 53   AT THE same time that all of this was happening to Aileen in Paris, Berenice, still at Pryor's Cove, was finding herself the object of a truly surprising series of social invitations, introductions, and successes which were far beyond anything she had anticipated. And while she felt she must credit a good portion of this success to Cowperwood, a greater portion, as she well knew, was due to Lord Stane's infatuation and his desire to introduce her to his circle of very important social connections.

With Aileen in Paris, Cowperwood had decided it would be safe to accept, for Berenice and himself, the invitation to cruise on Stane's yacht, the *Iola*. Among the guests aboard were Lady Clifford, of Chadleigh, whose husband had one of the oldest titles in England; the Duchess of Marlborough, one of Stane's most intimate friends as well as one of the Queen's favorites; and Sir Wyndham Whitley, a diplomat closely associated with Court life.

When the *Iola* eventually anchored at Cowes, Stane informed his guests that he had had word that the Queen was there and would be pleased to receive him and his friends for tea that afternoon: an announcement which aroused intense excitement in all of them, particularly Berenice, who had been nervously sensitive as to the possible publicity that might follow from this. The Queen was exceedingly gracious and appeared herself to enjoy this informal visit. She evinced a particular interest in Berenice and made various inquiries, which, if Berenice had answered them truthfully, might have resulted in great injury to herself, but since she did not, resulted in the wish, expressed by the Queen, that she might see more of her in London; in fact, that she hoped she would be free to attend her next Court reception. This courtesy on the part of the Queen all but startled Berenice, yet gave her still greater assurance as to what she could achieve for herself, if she wished.

As for Stane, it enormously increased his desire for her affection. At the same time, its effect on Cowperwood was to cause him even more misapprehension as to Stane's possible influence on Berenice.

But there was even greater cause for worry on his part awaiting him on his return to his hotel suite in London. There was the letter from Aileen, mailed to him just before she sailed for New York, and which read as follows:

At last I know the truth about my humiliating position in relation to your servant, Tollifer, and yourself; your shameful employment of him in order to be rid of me and leave you free to go your customary libertine way. What a reward for all my years of devotion! However, don't worry, for you are free to go now, to run with your prostitutes where and when you will. For today I am leaving Paris for New York, where I expect to be finally free from your infidelities and indulgences. I warn you not to follow me. If you do, I will take you and your present mistresses into court and expose you in the press of London and New York. AILEEN.

On receiving this, Cowperwood devoted considerable time to the contemplation of the possible angles and results of this savage indictment of himself. It seemed to him to be the better part of wisdom to return immediately to New York and see what, if anything, he could do to avoid a public scandal. However, closely connected with this was the position of Berenice. For if Aileen proceeded to do as she threatened, Berenice's future would be greatly injured. And that he did not wish to have happen, at any cost.

His first move, therefore, was to go at once to see Berenice, whom he found in a cheerful and highly ambitious mood. But once he told her of Aileen's latest attack, and the nature of her threats, he could tell by her sudden change of expression that she looked upon it as a serious matter. She was interested to know what could have persuaded Tollifer to confess his position.

"Surely, he had everything to gain by silence," she said, nervously.

"You don't understand the Lady Aileen, dear," responded Cowperwood, ironically. "She's not a person who thinks problems through to their ultimate conclusion. Instead, she develops a rage that does more harm than good to herself and everyone concerned. In fact, she can become so violent as to sweep anyone into confessions equally disastrous to both. The only thing I can think of doing at this time is to return to New York by the fastest boat, and maybe get there first. In the meantime, I have already wired Tollifer to come to London at once, because by continuing his employment I can easily arrange with him to say nothing. But I'm wondering what suggestions you might have to make, Bevy."

"I agree with you, Frank," she said. "I think you should return to New York as soon as possible, and see what you can do to placate her. After you talk to her, she's very likely to realize how futile an explosion of this kind would be. For, of course, she has known of me before this, and others also," and here she smiled an ironic smile. "And you certainly are the one to tell her that. After all, you haven't done her any harm in this instance. Nor has Tollifer, for that matter. In fact, you've provided her with the best guide to the pleasures of Paris that anybody would want, and, incidentally, you might also make clear to her that your work over here has taken every moment of your time. After all, it seems to me that could hardly fail to have some ameliorating effect. The papers are full of your labors and achievements, as you could point out to her"—a burst of wisdom which was by no means lost on Cowperwood. His one grief, as he now declared, was that it was he, not Stane, who had to go.

"Never mind, dear," she said, consolingly, "you're too great a man to be broken by this. I know positively you will return triumphant, as usual. And you know I will be with you all the way," and she put her arms around him and smiled up into his face with deep affection.

"If that is so, then I know everything will be all right," he said, confidently.

Chapter 54   BEFORE sailing for New York, Cowperwood talked with Tollifer, who demon-
strated to him his personal innocence in connection with this development; also that as far as he was concerned, his lips were sealed and
would open only to say whatever Cowperwood desired him to say.

Five days later, landing in New York, Cowperwood was met by a
brigade of newspapermen with enough inquiries to fill a small catalogue. Was he after more money to buy more London subways, or
was it for the purpose of disposing of his remaining American street
railway holdings? What paintings had he purchased in London?
Was there anything to the story that he had just paid $78,000 for
Turner's "Rockets and Blue Lights"? And, in connection with paintings, had he agreed to pay a certain artist $20,000 for his portrait, and
on its completion sent the artist $30,000 instead? And also, by now,
what did he think of English business methods?

All of this caused him to realize that while there was more interest
in him as a public figure than had ever previously been manifested,
as yet there was no trace of scandal in connection with him. Accordingly, he was more inclined to answer the questions, at least as many
as it was diplomatically possible for him to answer without injury to
himself.

According to him, everything was progressing smoothly in London. In fact, he was justifiably proud, since he expected to have the
London Underground electrified and in operation by January of
1905. Also, it would have an $85,000,000 capital and one hundred and
forty miles of track. And it was also true that he was now building
the largest electrical power plant in the world, and when it was completed London would have the finest underground in the world. As
to the English, he now asserted that he considered their attitude
toward large business projects, such as his, superior to the American
attitude; that is, the English appeared to understand the importance
of a great constructive program, and when they granted a franchise,
it was not for a limited time, but granted in perpetuity, which gave
men with large creative purposes an opportunity to build things
lasting.

As to paintings, yes, he had purchased several since being in New

York last, and those he was bringing back with him, a Watteau, a Sir Joshua Reynolds (portrait of Lady O'Brien), and a Frans Hals. And yes, he had paid the artist in question $30,000 for his portrait when he needed to give him $20,000 only. But the artist had returned the $10,000 to him with the request that he contribute the sum to a charity—which caused a gasp of surprise from the reporters.

The significance of such data as this, blazoned as it was in all of the newspapers, did not fail to impress Aileen, who, under another name, had arrived only two days before. Notwithstanding her anger, she was moved to meditate on the wisdom of her original plan. What was to become of these paintings that he was purchasing? For she recalled that recently he had spoken of the possibility of enlarging the New York mansion with a view to housing additional art objects. If so, her exposure of him and a threatened divorce suit might force him to change his plans in favor of one other than herself: the same dilemma which some years before she had faced and lost.

But, accepting her threat at its face value, Cowperwood thought it best, during his stay in New York, to make his headquarters at the Waldorf-Astoria instead of the Fifth Avenue residence, and having once settled there, he took up the matter of trying to reach Aileen by telephone, with no success. For she had made up her mind not to allow him to come and discuss his, to her, seemingly inexcusable crime, and she had even gone so far as to request a New York lawyer to call on her. Yet reading the papers, which continued to report his doings, evoked in her, from hour to hour, a change of emotions. For, naturally, she was proud of his success, and yet she was jealous, because she was satisfied that somewhere, lurking in the background, was one of his mistresses—Berenice, no doubt—who was undoubtedly sharing this most iridescent period of his life. For Aileen loved show and glitter. At times she was almost childishly arrested by any startling phase of publicity concerning Cowperwood, good, bad, or indifferent. In fact, one newspaper picture of the immense electrical plant he was building in London so fascinated her as to make her almost forget her ills. On the other hand, when he was savagely attacked in one newspaper article, she could not help resenting it, at the same time that she was moved to attack him herself.

After contemplating the immense variety of opinions and applause which greeted his return, Aileen's rage became confused with a certain degree of admiration, at which point in her oscillating moods it was that Cowperwood calmly walked into the living room of her suite to find her lying on a chaise longue, the floor about her littered with newspapers which she had obviously been reading. She jumped to her feet on his entrance, trying to arouse in herself her treasured anger as he stood facing her.

"Well, I see you keep up with the news, don't you, dear?" he commented, smiling a broad, free smile. "It isn't so bad, is it?"

"You!" she almost screamed. "The effrontery! If they only knew you as I do! The hypocrisy of it all! The cruelty!"

"Now, listen, Aileen," he went on, as calmly as he could, "you know, if you stop to think about it, I haven't injured you in any way. If you've read any of these papers, you know I've been working almost twenty-four hours a day on this proposition ever since I went to London. As for this man, Tollifer, what better guide could a person have in a city like Paris? If I remember correctly, in the old days you never passed through that city with me without complaining bitterly because I couldn't spend all my time with you visiting places you considered interesting but which I had no time for. And so, when Tollifer showed up, and was going to Paris anyhow, I thought, since you appeared to like him, that your going there at the same time might give you the opportunity of satisfying your old desire to see Paris without having me about to interfere in any way. And *that's* the only reason for Tollifer, and you know it!"

"Lies, lies, lies!" cried Aileen, savagely. "Always lies! But this time they won't work. At least, I can let the world know what you really are, and how you've treated me. The articles about you will read a little differently then, you can bet!"

"Now, Aileen," he interrupted, "just be reasonable. You know that from a material point of view I have never deprived you of anything you wanted, and all along I have been counting on you to take charge of my affairs after I'm gone. This house here, of which you certainly are proud. As you know, I've been planning to add to it in a way that will make it even more beautiful. For some time now I've wanted to buy the house next door, in order to enlarge the palm room for you and make an additional gallery for pictures and statuary. I was intending to leave it all in your hands, to express yourself as you pleased."

But true to his natural secretiveness, he failed to state that before leaving London he had already purchased the house in question.

"Why not get Pyne and let him submit some plans," he continued, "and we'll look them over."

"Oh, yes," said Aileen, wistfully, "that would be interesting."

But Cowperwood did not hesitate. "As for my life being separate from yours, Aileen, that's a ridiculous idea, really. In the first place, we've been too long together, and although we have had our troubles, here we are. Outside of my work, which makes strenuous demands on me physically, my personal life is nothing. Besides, I am no longer young, and if you care to make friends with me again, once I get this London underground off my hands, I'll really be glad to return to New York and live with you here."

"Do you mean me with six others?" she asked, sarcastically.

"No, I mean just what I said. I should think you could see that I may have to retire some day. If so, it will be for peace and quiet, and not more work."

Aileen was now getting ready to make an additional ironic comment, but looking up at him she caught a particularly weary and almost depressed look on his face, a look such as never she had previously seen, and this caused her mood to alter from one of criticism to one of unexpected sympathy. Perhaps he was tired and needed rest, for he was getting along in years and had so much to do: one of the kindest thoughts she had experienced in connection with him for years.

At this point, however, her maid came in to tell her that Mr. Robertson, her lawyer, was on the telephone, at which she stirred uneasily, and then said, rather defiantly:

"Tell him I've gone out!"

The import of this was not lost on Cowperwood.

"Have you said anything to anybody about all this?" he asked her.

"No, I have not," she replied.

"Good!" said Cowperwood, genially.

And after explaining that various financial matters made it necessary for him to go to Chicago for a few days, he succeeded in extracting from her a promise not to do anything until he returned. For by that time, as he now argued, he thought they could work things out to their mutual satisfaction.

Since she seemed satisfied to let the matter rest for the present, he took out his watch and remarked that he had just enough time to catch the train; he would see her again on his return. And, calmed down considerably by this time, she accompanied him to the door, and then returned to consult the newspapers which previously she had been reading.

Chapter 55 THE visit to Chicago was important enough, involving, as it did, negotiations for a loan or investment of $5,000,000. And then there was Sippens to see for a report as to the gradual disposal of his real estate holdings.

Another matter that required his attention was a recent lawsuit against one of the large traction companies of Chicago, which, several years before, had taken over two of the elevated lines which Cowperwood had originally built and operated. However, once he had withdrawn from Chicago and gone to London, these lines, due to poor management, had not only lost the income that previously had flowed from an excellent public patronage, but had since been confronted by a tremendous deficit that had wiped out all interest on stocks still held by investors. In fact, it was locally asserted that nothing in the history of public service corporations had shown such an utter collapse as this particular traction company. And since this loss was blamed on Cowperwood, it had become necessary for him to make clear to investors that the fault was not his, that it was due to mismanagement by those who had taken over the property: a clarification that later caused him to be called a "financial wizard" instead of a "sharper," because at the time he had operated the lines it was a well-known fact that he paid an 8 to 12 per cent dividend on stocks in his company. So now, in addition to securing the $5,000,000 he had come to borrow, he left with his reputation greatly enhanced.

However, there was one unexpected incident in connection with this Chicago trip, and that was the reappearance of Lorna Maris, who, because of newspaper notices of his presence in the city, sought him out in the hope of reviving his interest in her. But this thought of hers was doomed to disappointment, because his mood had changed for the time being, and he was anxious to get back to New York, and, eventually, to Berenice. Noticing, however, that her clothes reflected a less successful state of affairs than when he had last seen her, he was moved to inquire into her life, and finding that her popular appeal had shrunk and her income also, he did pretend an interest in her welfare, and assured her that he would arrange a stable drawing account for her, and furthermore would see what he could do toward interesting a theatrical producer in her career: a series of favors which effectively rekindled her original courage and gaiety.

But once he was aboard the train and it had begun to move past Lorna as she stood on the platform waving a final and wistful farewell, he could not help thinking on the changeful crisscross pattern woven by all creatures and forces. For here he was, being attacked by these Chicago stockholders and at the same time watched by the daily press, as well as Aileen in New York, and, for that matter, the beautiful Berenice in London, who, reasonably enough, did not trust him any more than did Aileen. And yet, for what reason? Emotions, sensual predilections, reactions to other types of human beings, which were not of his invention or creation.

Clack, clack, clack! went the wheels on the rails. To-hooo! Toohooo! the whistle of the engine. And a level landscape flowing, not unlike time, past the window through which he gazed, reflecting dreamily on life, time, and change.

Chapter 56

WHEN Cowperwood went to see Aileen in New York on his return, he met with a pleasant surprise, for since he had been away she had been thinking about the value of his suggestions in regard to possible enlargement of the house, and his expressed desire to consider her taste in regard to the alterations. This had pleased her beyond anything he could have said. Consequently, she brought forth several drawings, designs, and color arrangements which already she had had prepared by the architect and now wished him to examine.

He was pleased to see that Raymond Pyne, the American architect who had designed this mansion in the first place, had produced a series of sketches of proposed changes which harmonized the old house with the new. Aileen emphasized the fact that she liked this, that, and the other phase of artistic interpretation. And deciding that he would see Pyne and advise him to take his time in the matter, he finally left her with the feeling that she was to be importantly em-

ployed in connection with something that would not only reflect
their joint artistic tastes but might well bring about their social
reunion.

Nevertheless, adjusting himself to New York and America at this
time was not an easy matter for Cowperwood. His social viewpoint,
since going to London, had changed. It was not that the English
were less shrewd or sharp in their efforts to advance their own interests. But, as he had noticed since encountering Stane, Johnson, and
their associates, there was an almost unconscious consideration of the
need of interweaving rest or pleasure with their commerce and trade,
whereas here at home, business was business, as the phrase ran.

Ever since his arrival in New York there had been nothing but
business dealings. There seemed to him nothing else interesting to do
here, and it was because of this that his mind was constantly returning to Berenice and Pryor's Cove, although he still found it necessary
to visit all of the cities he had listed as sources for capital—hurried
trips all over the east that left him feeling more or less exhausted.
For the first time in his life he began to think rather than feel that
he might be getting old. Satisfactorily enough, however, this situation was finally relieved by the arrival of an urgent cable from Johnson, which said that owing to the activity of various pressure groups,
his presence was of paramount import.

He showed the cable to Aileen, and after she had read it she commented on the weariness which showed in his face and warned him
to remember that his health, after all, was of prime importance, and,
if possible, he ought to wind up his European affairs and retire. He
replied that he had already been thinking of that, and in order to
make it easier for her in his absence had appointed Mr. Cuthbert to
take charge of his entire art collection, because he was one in whose
judgment he had confidence.

In the meantime, Berenice was beginning to wonder when he
would return. She was finding herself, as time went on, more and
more lonely without him. Although Lord Stane had taken her to
various receptions and evening parties to meet more of his friends,
and even to a reception at Court, she missed Cowperwood in some
strange, inexplicable way. He was such a dominant force in her life,
a power that dwarfed the social atmosphere surrounding Lord Stane.
For while she found Stane a warm and attractive companion, on returning to the quiet of Pryor's Cove she always joined Cowperwood

again in thought and mood as well as emotion. What was he doing, whom seeing? Would he become interested again in Lorna Maris? Or someone new? Or would he return to her as he had left her: obviously in love with her? And would Aileen return with him, or had he placated her sufficiently to cause her to give him a period of rest?

The jealousy of women! Her own jealousy, where he was concerned!

And after all he had done for her! Not only for her but for her mother! It was he who had paid for her schooling, and after that had given her a beautiful New York house on fashionable Park Avenue.

Mentally and philosophically, Berenice was more of a cold, realistic turn than otherwise, and just before Cowperwood had been compelled by Aileen's threats to return to New York, she had about made up her mind that if no too great ill flowed to herself from this last assault of Aileen's, she might be more gracious to Lord Stane than up to now she had been. For plainly, he was deeply infatuated with her; he had even led her to believe that he was entertaining the thought of marriage.

If I only cared enough, she thought at this time. If only he was less conventional, not so English. She had heard that there was no law in England to prevent him from divorcing a wife who had deceived him by fraud—such as she would be guilty of if she married him— and this possibility, throughout Cowperwood's absence, kept her silent and semidistant, thinking of her social state in case Aileen should choose to act.

However, her anxiety was gradually relieved by the day to day silence on the part of the London press, and also by a letter from Cowperwood in which he outlined his various difficulties, among them his sudden reduction in health and strength, and at the same time expressed his desire to return to England in order that he might rest and see her again. This reference to his health caused her to ponder on the wisdom of a trip they might take to some region of quiet and beauty which should be comparatively free of the hustle and bustle of trade. But where was such a land? It was possible that he had already seen and wearied of it, for he had traveled so much— Italy, Greece, Switzerland, France, Austria-Hungary, Germany, Turkey, the Holy Land.

But what of Norway? As she now recalled, she had never heard him speak of it. And accordingly, so moved was she by the desire to persuade him to take a rest in a strange and different land that she purchased a book about that country in order to inform herself in detail as to its novelty and beauty. Enthusiastically she turned the pages to study photographs of dark, high cliffs; mountains or fjells rising perpendicularly to thousands of feet over gorges cut by Nature in a stern, relentless mood; cataracts and leaping waterfalls, at the base of which lay beautiful, peaceful lakes. And clinging to the sides of tall mountains, like shipwrecked sailors to a life raft, were little farms. She read about their strange gods: Odin, the god of battle; Thor, the god of thunder; and, Valhalla, a heaven of sorts prepared for the souls of those who had perished in battle.

Reading and examining these pictures, the country appeared to be entirely free of industrialism. This land should indeed prove restful for him.

Chapter 57

By the time Cowperwood, looking exceedingly tired, arrived in England, Berenice was able to inoculate him with some of her own enthusiasm for Norway, which, strangely enough, he had not previously visited.

And so it was, not long after, that he set Jamieson to the task of finding and chartering a yacht. But before one was found, a certain Lord Tilton, hearing through Stane of Cowperwood's intention, very generously insisted on loaning him his own yacht, the *Pelican,* for the purpose. And eventually, toward midsummer, he and Berenice were cruising smoothly along the west coast of Norway toward Stavanger Fjord.

The yacht was a handsome craft, and Eric Hansen, the Norwegian skipper, a man of skill. He was powerfully built, although of not more than medium height, with a florid complexion and sandy-colored hair that fountained out over his forehead. His eyes were a steely blue that seemed to challenge any sea or any experience connected with it. His movements seemed to suggest a natural bracing against rough weather, even when he walked on level ground—a kind of rhythmic oneness with the sea at all times. He had been a seafaring man all of his life, and he truly loved these inland waterways that wound through a maze of mysterious mountains soaring straight up thousands of feet from their depths to thousands of feet below the water line. Some said they were the result of faulting or cracking of the crust of the earth's surface; others thought volcanic eruptions had caused them. But Eric knew that they had been cut through by mighty prehistoric Vikings who had the power to carve their way through any barrier in order to make highways to the rest of the world.

But as Berenice viewed these steep hillsides, with the cottages perched so far above the water's edge, she could not imagine how the inhabitants got down to a passing boat or climbed up to their little homes again. Or for what reason they did it. It all seemed so strange. She was not familiar with the art of mountain-climbing, which the Norwegian had probably learned, out of sheer necessity, from watching his goats maneuver themselves from crag to crag.

"What a strange land," Cowperwood said. "I'm glad you brought me up here, Bevy, but it does seem to me, beautiful as it is, this country is one of Nature's climatic mistakes. There's too much daylight in summer and too little in winter. Too many romantic waterways and too many sterile mountains. Although I must confess that it interests me enormously."

Indeed, Berenice had noticed his interest in the country was intense. He frequently rang for his very respectful skipper in order that he might ask questions.

"What do they live on in these towns, outside of fish?" he inquired of Eric.

"Well, Mr. Dickson"—the name assumed by Cowperwood—"they have a number of other things. They have goats and they sell goat's milk. They have chickens, and so, eggs. They have cows. In fact, they often judge a man's wealth by the number of cows he owns. Also they have butter. These are sturdy, hard-working people, and they can make five acres yield more than you would believe. Although I'm not an expert on the subject, and really can't tell you much about it, they get along better than you would think. Another thing," he continued, "most of the young men of this region go in for training in navigation. When they get a little older, they get positions as captains, mates, or cooks, on the hundreds of vessels coming in and out of Norway and touching the cities and shipping centers all over the world."

At this point Berenice spoke up. "It strikes me that what they lack in quantity, they make up in quality," was her comment.

"You're right, madam," said the skipper, "that's what I mean," and, becoming more enthusiastic, he continued: "In fact, they've learned to live comfortably within themselves. But they know the world, not only from the outside of books but inside. We Norwegians are a bookish people, prizing education. Illiterates are almost non-existent here, and you may not believe it, but Norway has more telephones than Spain or Poland. It also has its literary and musical celebrities: Grieg, Hamsun, Ibsen, Bjornson"—names which caused Cowperwood to pause and think how small a part literature had played in his life, and to suggest to Berenice that she give him some of the books she had been reading.

And Berenice, noting his meditative mood, and suspecting that he might be contrasting this wonder world with his own troublesome one, decided to switch the conversation to something a little more cheerful, and turning to Skipper Hansen, she asked:

"Captain Hansen, are we likely to see any Lapps when we get a little farther north?"

"Oh, yes, madam," returned the captain. "We might run into them anywhere north of Trondheim. We're almost to that point now."

From Trondheim the yacht steamed northward toward Hammerfest, the land of the midnight sun. Several stops were made on the way, one of these being a little extension of rock from one of the great cliffs, called Grotto. It was a very small place of perhaps a dozen houses, used principally as a whaling station. The houses were the usual stone huts, roofed over with grass and earth.

It was customary for the whalers at Grotto to buy coal or wood from any boat that was going north or south. And now a small group of fishermen approached the yacht. And though its supply of coal was not more than was actually needed, Cowperwood instructed the skipper to give them several tons, because he felt that these people had so little in their lives.

After breakfast Captain Hansen went ashore, and on his return told Cowperwood that a tribe of Lapps from much farther north had arrived and pitched their camp on the mainland, about a half-mile from Grotto. There were about fifteen hundred reindeer, he said, and over a hundred Lapps, with their children and dogs. On hearing this,

Berenice expressed a desire to see them. Whereupon Captain Hansen and the mate rowed them over to visit the camp.

After disembarking on the shore of the mainland, they walked over toward the reindeer, which were scattered about the tents which spread in all directions. The captain, who knew a few words of their language, talked with the Lapps, and some of them came toward the visitors, making them welcome by shaking hands and inviting them to their tents. In one tent, there was a large pot hanging over a fire, which the mate proceeded to investigate and pronounced to be "dog stew," but which turned out to be a nice, fat, juicy bear, of which all had a serving.

Another tent was packed with fisherfolk and farmers from the surrounding country, for this gathering was in the nature of an annual fair, at which the Lapps disposed of their reindeer products and bought supplies for the winter. At this point a Lapp woman elbowed her way through the crowd. She greeted Captain Larsen as an old acquaintance, and he informed Cowperwood that she was one of the wealthiest members of the tribe. There followed group singing and dancing, in which all attempted to join. And after liquor and food, and much laughter all around, Cowperwood and his party said good-by and returned to the *Pelican*.

By the light of the never-setting sun, the yacht was turned about, heading its way back to the south. By this time a dozen large bow-head whales came along within sight of the yacht, and the skipper ordered all sails set in such a fashion as to cause the boat to maneuver among them with the utmost grace. There was intense excitement among passengers and crew as they stood watching the whales. But Cowperwood was more interested in the skill of the captain than he was in the spectacle before his eyes.

"There you have it!" he said to Berenice. "Every profession, every trade, every form of labor, requires alertness and skill. The skipper, as you see, has complete control of his yacht, and that, in itself, is an achievement."

She smiled at his remark, but made no comment, while he gave himself up to thinking and philosophizing about this arresting world of which, for the time being, he was a part. The thing that impressed him most about this entire northern scene was the fact that it represented such a sharp and socially insignificant phase of a world that really had no need for any such temperament as his. The immense oceans, in a large sense, supported its inhabitants by the process of supplying them with fish, and there was enough of employment to enable them to build and make habitable sufficient spaces of soil when they returned, and thus round out their lives in comparative comfort. And yet he felt that these people had more from life in sheer beauty, simple comfort, and charming social customs than he and thousands of others like him who were so strenuously engaged in accumulating money. As for himself, he was getting old, and the best part of his life was already gone. What, really, lay ahead for him? More subways? More art galleries? More irritations due to public opinion?

True enough, this trip had been restful. But now hourly he was moving into many things that were far from peaceful, and if continued by him could only result in more arguments, more lawyers, more newspaper criticism, more domestic ills. He smiled to himself ironically. He must not think too much. Take things as they come and make the best of them. After all, the world had done more for him than for most, and the least he could do was to be grateful, and he was.

Several days later as they neared Oslo on the return trip, he suggested that in order to avoid danger of publicity, Berenice would better leave the yacht there and return by steamer to Liverpool, which would bring her within a short distance of Pryor's Cove. He was happy to see how practically she accepted this decision, and yet he could sense from her expression how much she resented the forces which invariably controlled and interrupted their relationship.

Chapter 58   COWPERWOOD's vacation in Norway having put him in such excellent physical condition, he was anxious to proceed with his business affairs, in a concentrated effort to reach the goal he had set for himself of $185,000,000 capital and one hundred and forty miles of track and electrification of the entire underground mileage by January of 1905. He was so driven by his renewed ambition and desire to complete this work and prove its import that he could scarcely permit himself to rest, at Pryor's Cove or anywhere else.

And so, for the next few months, there were directors' meetings, discussions with interested and important investors, engineering problems, and private sessions, sometimes in the evenings, with Lord Stane and Elverson Johnson. Finally, there arose the necessity of making a trip to Vienna, in order to examine an electric motor device invented by a man named Ganz, which promised to reduce the cost of underground operation by a very considerable sum. After seeing the motor and observing its operation, he was convinced of its value, and at once wired several of his engineers to come to Vienna to confirm his opinion.

On his way back to London, he stopped off at the Ritz Hotel, in Paris. On his first evening there he met an old colleague in the lobby of the hotel, one Michael Shanley, a one-time employee of his in Chicago, who suggested that they go to hear a concert at the Paris Opera House. There was much talk of the compositions of a Pole by the name of Chopin that were to be played there. The name was only vaguely familiar to Cowperwood, and even less so to Shanley, but they went; and Cowperwood was so entranced by the music that on reading in the program notes that Chopin was buried at Père-Lachaise, he suggested they visit that world-famous burial ground next day.

Accordingly, the following morning he and Shanley went to Père-Lachaise, where they engaged a guide, who, in English, furnished them with much information as they walked along the cypress-bordered avenues of the cemetery. Thus they learned that here, under this shaft, lay Sarah Bernhardt, who, in past days in Chicago, had so moved him with her golden voice. A little farther on was the tomb of Balzac, of whose works he knew only that they were considered great. As he paused and gazed, he once again became sensible of the fact that his own particular labors had barred him from knowledge of the intellectual and artistic significance of genius in many other fields. They passed the tombs of Bizet, De Musset, Molière, and at last they came to Chopin's resting place, which they found to be strewn with ribbon-tied bouquets of roses and lilies.

"Think of that now!" exclaimed Shanley. "To be sure, he's a great musician, but he's been dead for more than half a century, and here are all these flowers! Be gorra, no one will ever do that for me, I know!"

Which thought caused Cowperwood to question the likelihood of flowers being strewn over his own grave, even a year after his death

—an idea which amused more than it irritated him, for he well knew there were few graves anywhere, earnest labors or no earnest labors, strewn with flowers after so many years.

However, before leaving Père-Lachaise, he was destined for one more surprise. For as they turned south toward an exit, they suddenly came upon the lovely double tomb of Abélard and Héloïse, concerning which their guide proceeded to recite the well-known tragic romance of the ill-starred pair. Héloïse and Abélard! The love of a young girl for the spiritually brilliant monk, and the savage brutality of her father, the cruel member of a bishop's council of a cathedral of the eleventh century! Cowperwood, up to this hour, had never heard of these lovers. But now, as he stood listening to the guide, an obviously refined and very attractive woman, carrying a basket filled with flowers, approached the tomb and began to strew the multicolored blossoms upon and around it. Both Cowperwood and Shanley were so moved by this that they removed their hats, and, catching her eye, respectfully bowed. She acknowledged their interest by saying: *"Merci beaucoup, messieurs,"* and walked away.

But this colorful and moving incident set up a train of thought in Cowperwood's mind which related to himself and the Aileen of his earlier days. For, after all, when he, at one point in his career, had been imprisoned in Philadelphia, it was she who, in face of all of his enemies, including her father, had visited him faithfully to declare her unchanging love and ease his lot in any way she could. Like Héloïse with Abélard, she had wanted him and no one else, and still did so, as he knew.

Suddenly there flashed into his mind the idea of a tomb for the two of them, a beautiful and enduring resting place. Yes, he would employ an architect, secure designs, he would build a beautiful tomb which would commemorate the fact that at least at one time he had cared for her as much as she cared for him.

Chapter 59

ON COWPERWOOD'S return to London, Berenice was startled by the change in his appearance. He seemed utterly weary, and had obviously lost weight. She complained to him about his lack of consideration of his own physical welfare and the fact that she saw so little of him.

"Frank, dear," she began, in an affectionate tone, "why do you let these things take so much of your time and energy? You seem so strained and nervous. Don't you think you should see a doctor and have a thorough examination before you go any further?"

"Bevy, dear," he said, putting his arm around her waist, "there's no need for you to be so concerned. I know I'm working too hard, but this will soon be over and I won't have to bother with so many business angles any more, for the present, anyhow."

"But do you really feel all right?"

"Yes, dear, I think I'm all right. Anyhow, this particular phase of development is so important that I feel I must give it my personal attention."

But even as he said this, he stooped forward as if stricken by a sudden pain. She ran to his side, exclaiming: "Frank, what is it? What's the matter? Have you ever had anything like this before?"

"No, dear, I certainly haven't," he said. "But it can't be anything serious, I'm sure." And he partially recovered himself. "Of course," he continued, "there must be something to cause such a sharp pain. Maybe you'd better call Dr. Wayne and ask him to come over and take a look at me . . ." a suggestion that sent Berenice at once to the telephone.

When the doctor arrived, he was surprised to find Cowperwood looking so drawn, and after partially examining him and writing a prescription to be filled at once, he asked him to come to his office next morning for a thorough check-up, which Cowperwood agreed to do. However, within a week, after two of the best specialists in London had been called in by Dr. Wayne and reported to him their conclusions, he was shocked to learn that a severe kidney condition had developed that might end fatally within a comparatively short time. He ordered Cowperwood to rest and take the prescribed drugs that were meant to induce less activity.

However, when Cowperwood came into Dr. Wayne's office a few days later for his physical report, he told the doctor that he was feeling better and his appetite appeared to be normal.

"The trouble with these cases, Mr. Cowperwood," said Dr. Wayne, very quietly, at this point, "is that they are eccentric in their effects, and the pain they produce sometimes stops for a time. However, that doesn't mean that the patient is cured, or even better. The pains may return, and this often causes definite and disturbing predictions on the part of our specialists, who are not always correct by any means. Rather, the patient may grow better and live for years. On the other hand, he may grow worse, and that is one of the conditions which makes this disease so difficult to deal with. So you see, Mr. Cowperwood, that is why I cannot speak to you as definitely as I would like to."

Here Cowperwood interrupted him.

"I feel there's something you'd like to tell me, Dr. Wayne. And I would most certainly like to know exactly what the report of the specialists is. It doesn't matter what it is, I want to know. Are my kidneys so bad? Is there any organic trouble which is fatal?"

Dr. Wayne looked at him with a steady gaze.

"Well, the specialists report that with rest and no hard work, you may live a year or a little more. With extreme care, you may even live longer. Yours is a case of chronic nephritis, or Bright's disease, Mr. Cowperwood. However, as I have explained to you, they are not always right."

This studied reply was received by Cowperwood calmly and thoughtfully, even though now, for the first time in his almost uniformly healthy life, he was faced with news of a probably fatal disease. Death! Probably no more than a year to live! An end to all of his creative labors! And yet, if it was to be, it was to be, and he must brace himself and take it.

After leaving the doctor's office, he felt himself not so much concerned with his own condition as with the effect of his final passing on the several personalities so closely connected with him throughout his life: Aileen, Berenice, Sippens; his son, Frank Cowperwood, Jr.; his first wife, Anna (now Mrs. Wheeler); and their daughter Anna, whom he had not seen for years, still for whom he had made ample provision over a long period. And there were others to whom he felt obligated.

On his way to Pryor's Cove later on in the day, he kept turning over in his mind the necessity of putting all of his affairs in order. The first thing to do now was to make his will, even though these specialists might be wrong. He must provide financially for all those who were closest to him. And then there was his treasured art gallery, which he intended to leave to the public. There was also the hospital which he had always desired so keenly to establish in New York. He must do something about that. After paying the various heirs and such beneficiaries as he proposed to favor, there should still be ample means for a hospital that offered the best services to all who chanced to be without funds and had no place else to turn.

Besides, there was the matter of the tomb which he wished to erect for himself and Aileen. He must consult an architect and have him carry out a design that would be beautiful and appropriate. It might compensate in some way for his seeming neglect of her.

But what about Berenice? As he now saw it, he could not provide for her openly in his will. He did not wish to expose her to the prying inquiries of the press and the inescapable envy of the public in general. But he would arrange the matter now in a different way. Though he had already established an independent trust fund for her, he would now cash an additional block of bonds and shares which he held in various corporations, and transfer the cash to her. This would insure her against danger of lack of funds in the years to come.

But by now his carriage had arrived at Pryor's Cove, and his troublesome train of thought was interrupted by the appearance of Berenice, smiling affectionately and anxious to hear what the doctor had said. But, as usual, in his independent, stoical way, he waved her inquiry aside as not too important.

"It isn't anything of consequence, dear," he said. "A little irritation of the bladder, possibly due to overeating. He gave me a prescription and advised me to ease up on work."

"There! I knew it! That's what I've been saying all along! You should rest more, Frank, and not be doing so much actual physical labor."

But here Cowperwood successfully changed the subject.

"Speaking of hard work," he said, "is anyone around here doing anything about those squabs and that special bottle of wine you were telling me about this morning. . . ?"

"Oh, you incorrigible! Here comes Phenie now to set the table. We're having dinner on the terrace."

He seized her hand, saying: "You see, God protects the honest and the industrious . . ."

And cheerfully, hand in hand, they walked into the house together.

Chapter 60

ALTHOUGH Cowperwood appeared to have enjoyed his dinner with Berenice very much, his mind had been, treadmill fashion, going round and round in a circle which included in one section his various commercial and financial interests and in another the various individuals, men and women, who had labored with him toward the completion of the great traction systems in which he had been so absorbed. The men, in the main so helpful, the women so entertaining; all of whom, collectively, had made him some thirty colorful years. And now, although he did not really believe the doctors' diagnosis to be as fateful as it had sounded, nevertheless, because of their prediction as to the finality of his days, plus this lovely hour with Berenice, here by the Thames, and this pleasant lawn that spread before them, he could not help but feel the fleeting beauty of life and its haunting poignancy. For his life had been so full, so dramatic, and so memorable. Only now to be made to contemplate the possibility of the sudden cessation of all that he could look upon as himself, had a tendency to emphasize the value of all he had been and enjoyed. Berenice—so young, so wise, and so entertaining—who, under favorable conditions, could be with him for so many years to come. And that was what she was so cheerfully and helpfully thinking about, as he could feel. For once he could not contemplate the fatal processes of life with his usual equanimity. Actually he could only consider the poetic value of this hour, and its fleetingness, which involved sorrow and nothing but sorrow.

However his outward manner indicated nothing of his mental depression, for he had already concluded that he must pretend, act. He must go about his affairs as usual until the very hour or moment when this medical prediction should be fulfilled, if it were to be fulfilled. So he left Pryor's Cove in the morning for his office, as usual, where he went through his daily routine with the same calm and precision as he had always displayed in connection with decisions, procedure, etc. Only now he felt called upon to set in motion such varying processes as would lead to the fulfillment of all of his personal wishes in the event of his death.

One of these was the tomb for himself and the disappointed

Aileen. Accordingly he called in Jamieson, his secretary, and asked him to report to him the names and unquestionable skill of any architect, either in England or on the Continent, who had achieved a reputation for the building of mausoleums. He wished the data as soon as possible, as he was getting it for a friend. This done, he turned his attention to his favorite interest: his art gallery, to which he wanted to add such paintings as would make his an outstanding collection. To this end he addressed a number of letters to persons who bought and sold such masterpieces, and eventually secured some very valuable paintings: among them a Bouguereau, "Invading Cupid's Realm"; Corot's "The Path to the Village"; a Frans Hals, "Portrait of a Woman"; Rembrandt's "Resurrection of St. Lazarus." These he shipped to New York.

Alongside of these specific activities, however, were the inevitable details in connection with the underground project. Claims, quarrels, interference from rivals, petty lawsuits! However, after a time, he was able to meet all of the requirements of the situation, and also, by this time, he was beginning to feel so much better that he concluded there was nothing of import to the original pains which had caused him to consult a physician. In fact, his future looked more rosy than at any time since first he had come to London. Even Berenice decided that his old physical stamina had reasserted itself.

In the meantime, Lord Stane, impressed by Cowperwood's creative energy, which was expressing itself in so many new and original ideas, decided that now would be the time to stage a social affair in Cowperwood's honor at his lovely sea place, Tregasal, where at least two hundred guests could be accommodated. And so, after much meditation as to the important persons to be invited, the date was set, and Tregasal, with its beautiful grounds and its huge ballroom, with chandeliers rivaling the glitter of the moonlight, the scene of the ball.

Lord Stane, standing near the main entrance, greeted the inpouring guests. And, as he now saw Berenice entering on Cowperwood's arm, he thought she was especially beautiful tonight, in a trailing white gown of Greek design and simplicity, held at the waist with a golden cord, her red hair crowning this costume as might a wreath of gold. And to climax all for Stane, as she approached she looked and smiled at him in such a way that all he could say was: "Berenice! Beautiful! You are a dream of loveliness!"—a greeting which

Cowperwood, stopping to exchange a few words with one of his most important stockholders, failed to catch.

"I must have the second dance," said Stane, holding her hand for a moment. And she graciously nodded her head.

After greeting Berenice, he welcomed Cowperwood, his honored guest, in a most cordial manner, detaining him long enough for the numerous officials of the Underground and their wives to greet him.

It was not long before supper was announced, and the guests, entering and seating themselves, were indulging in conversation and sipping wines of rare vintage, plus a special brand of champagne which Stane was satisfied would please the most exacting taste. Laughter and the murmur of conversation increased in volume, pleasingly modified by the soft notes of the music floating in from the adjoining chamber.

Berenice found herself seated near the head of the table, with Lord Stane on one side and the Earl of Bracken on the other, the latter a rather attractive young man, who, long before the end of the third course, was urging her to be charitable enough to save for him at the least the third or fourth dance. But while she was both interested and flattered, her eyes were constantly following the motions of Cowperwood, who, at the other end of the table, was indulging in lively conversation with an exceedingly attractive brunette on one side while obviously not neglecting a very engaging beauty on the other. She was pleased to find him relaxed and entertained, since for some time she had not seen him so.

However, the dining being of considerable duration, and the supply of champagne unlimited, she harbored some fear as to Cowperwood. His gestures and conversation, she noted, were becoming more and more enthusiastic, obviously because of the champagne, and this troubled her. And when, finally, Lord Stane made the announcement that all who wished to dance could now adjourn to the ballroom, and Cowperwood came over to claim her for a dance, she was still further troubled by his elated manner. And yet he walked with the air of one who was as sober as anyone present. As they moved together in the rhythmic measures of the waltz, she whispered to him: "Are you happy, darling?"

"Never happier," he answered. "I'm with you, my beautiful!"

"Darling!" whispered Berenice.

"Isn't it wonderful, Bevy? You, this place, these people! This is what I've been seeking all my life!"

She smiled affectionately at him, but just then she felt him sway slightly and then pause and place his hand to his heart, murmuring: "Air, air; I must get outside!"

She took firm hold of his hand and led him toward an open door out onto a balcony facing the sea. She urged and aided him to the nearest bench, on which he sank limply and heavily. By now she was terribly alarmed, and ran toward a servant who was passing with a tray, exclaiming: "Please! I need help! Get someone, and help me get him to a bedroom. He is seriously ill."

The frightened servant immediately called the butler, who had Cowperwood carried into an unoccupied chamber on the same floor, after which Lord Stane was notified. He, upon his arrival, was so shocked by Berenice's distress that he ordered the butler to remove Cowperwood to his own suite on the second floor, and at once called his own physician, Dr. Middleton. Also the butler was instructed to insure silence on the part of all of the servants in regard to this.

In the meantime, Cowperwood was beginning to stir, and as Dr. Middleton came in, was so revived as to be conscious of the need of caution and to say to Stane that the less said about this the better, other than that he had tripped and fallen. He was sure, he said, he would be all right in the morning. Dr. Middleton, however, had a different idea about his illness, and gave him a sedative. After which he advised that the sick man remain where he was for a day or two, at least, in order that he might discover whether there were any complications. For, as he said to Stane, Cowperwood's condition was probably more serious than a fainting spell.

Chapter 61

THE next morning, when Cowperwood awakened in the Stane suite, he found himself, except for the goings and comings of very courteous servants, alone for a time, and it was then that he began to run over in his mind the fairly disturbing phases of all that had so swiftly happened to him. For he was a little startled by the fact that, after having arrived at a sense of relative security in connection with his physical welfare, he should be so suddenly made aware of his illness.

Was it really true that he had fallen victim to this fatal Bright's disease? At the time of Dr. Middleton's call he had not been sufficiently alert to discuss this matter of his collapse. For one thing, as he now recalled, he had had the sensation of extreme shortness of breath, which finally resulted in the physical weakness which caused him to fall. Was that due to a kidney condition, as earlier described by Dr. Wayne, or was it a matter of too much champagne, too much food? The doctor, as he recalled, had impressed upon him that he was not to drink anything but water and eat very lightly.

To make sure that he was following the right course in regard to himself, he decided to have Berenice cable his old-time friend and personal physician, Dr. Jefferson James, in New York, to come to London at once. This trusted friend would be the one to satisfy him as to his true condition.

However, as he slowly and somewhat calmly surveyed the situation, there was a tap at the door, and Lord Stane entered, making of his coming a very cheerful and gracious affair.

"There you are!" he exclaimed. "You and your beautiful girls and your champagne! Think of it! Aren't you really ashamed of yourself?" Cowperwood smiled broadly. "And, incidentally," went on Stane, "I have an order to inflict severe punishment on you for at least twenty-four hours. No champagne! Instead, water! No caviar, not a grain, only a thin sliver of beef, plus more water! Perhaps, when you're about ready to collapse, a bowl of thin gruel and more water!"

Cowperwood sat up. "I call that tops for cruelty," he said. "But perhaps you can be induced to share my water and gruel. In the meantime, and strictly in confidence, you might tell me what Dr. Middleton told you."

"Well," replied Stane, "what he really said was that you were forgetting that your years are creeping up on you, and that champagne and caviar are entirely outside your present powers of digestion. Also dancing until sunrise. Hence your collapse on my overly polished ballroom floor. And hence Dr. Middleton's approaching visit to find out how you're getting along, although he says he cannot find that there is anything seriously wrong with you other than overwork, which is something you can easily remedy. And I must tell you that your lovely ward, who was good enough to accept my offer of lodging for the night, will be down shortly. I need not tell you, of course, that she is as greatly concerned as I am, regardless of Dr. Middleton's conclusions"—a statement which caused Cowperwood to assert rather positively:

"But there's nothing of any consequence the matter with me. I may not be as good as new, but I'm still somewhere near it. And as far as business is concerned, I'll be on hand to cope with any difficulties there. As a matter of fact, you should be able to judge for yourself, by the results so far, whether our affairs are being managed capably or not."

There was just a tinge of reproach in his tone, which Stane noticed.

"The results have been tremendous," he said. "Anyone who could come over here with such a proposition as yours and secure $25,000,-000 from American investors, certainly deserves nothing but compliments from me. And I'm glad to express my gratitude, and that of our investors, for your interest and your services. The only trouble is, Cowperwood, it all rests on your broad American shoulders and your continued health and strength. And that is important."

At this point there was a knock on the door, following which Berenice entered. After greetings and light conversation, Stane urged both to stay as long as they wished, whether it be a week or a month. But Cowperwood, feeling the need of extreme privacy as well as quiet and rest, insisted on their early departure. After Stane had left, he turned to Berenice, and said:

"It isn't that I feel so badly, dearest. I don't, but because of the need of avoiding publicity of any kind, I would like us to leave here as soon as possible, and if I had my choice, I would rather go to Pryor's Cove than to the hotel. Won't you please arrange it with Lord Stane so that we may leave here in the morning?"

"Of course, dear," replied Berenice, "if that's what you want. I would feel better myself if you were over there near me."

"There's one other thing, Bevy," went on Cowperwood. "I want you to get Jamieson to cable to Dr. Jefferson James in New York. He's my old physician and friend. Ask him, if possible, to come to London. Tell Jamieson this is to be confidential and in code. He can reach him at the New York Medical Society."

"Then you do feel that there is something wrong with you?" Her tone indicated her nervousness.

"No! Not as bad as all that by any means, but, as you see for your-self, I'm in a rather uncertain state as to what's really wrong with me. Besides, as far as my public affairs are concerned, it might strike any person, particularly my stockholders and investors, as very peculiar that a man should suddenly collapse for no apparent reason, although I may have overdone my eating and drinking a little bit last night, particularly as to the champagne. But certainly I never felt like that before. And I surely would like to see Jefferson. He'll know, and will tell me the truth."

"Frank," interrupted Berenice at this point, "what did Dr. Wayne tell you the last time you saw him that you did not tell me? What did the specialists' report show?"

"Oh, Dr. Wayne said that the pain I had at that time might be distantly related to Bright's disease, only he was not sure, because, he said, there are two phases of Bright's disease, chronic and acute. Mine, he said, was neither one nor the other. He said I would have to wait and see if anything of a more serious nature developed before any specialist could give a correct diagnosis."

"Well, if that's the case, I think Dr. James should come over. I'll get Jamieson to cable him tomorrow. In the meantime, I certainly think that Pryor's Cove is the place for you until such time as Dr. James feels you are all right."

Whereupon she crossed to the window, drawing the shade, and asked him to try and rest for a period while she went to make all the arrangements necessary for their departure in the morning. But even as she did this, her mind was wrestling with the import of all this to him, and though she was outwardly gracious, she was trembling inwardly.

"You are quite right, my dear," observed Stane, when she informed him of their decision to go to Pryor's Cove. "It is likely to have a soothing effect on him, I'm sure, as it has had on me many times in the past. Besides, your mother is there, and she will be of help to you. If you will permit me, I'll drive you over myself in the morning. Mr. Cowperwood is far too important to me to overlook anything that might contribute to his comfort and speedy recovery."

Chapter 62

THE aftermath of all this was, in the course of the next two weeks, the arrival at Pryor's Cove of Dr. James, who, seeing Cowperwood resting comfortably in a bedroom overlooking the Thames, paused to observe:

"Well, Frank, I see that you're not so ill that you can't enjoy the beautiful view through these windows. I'm half-inclined to suggest that you get up and hurry over to New York and let me stretch out here until I recover from my labors of getting here. I've been dying for a vacation for years."

"Didn't you enjoy your trip over?" asked Cowperwood.

"I never welcomed a change more in my life. It was beautiful. The sea was calm and there was a minstrel troupe aboard that entertained me enormously. They were headed, if you please, for Vienna, and half of them were Negroes."

"Same old Jeff!" commented Cowperwood. "My, what a pleasure it is to see you again! If I have wished once, I have wished a score of times that you were over here and could study some of the oddities of these English!"

"Bad as all that, are they?" said James, amusedly. "But suppose you tell me the story of all this from the beginning. Where were you, and why were you arrested?"

Whereupon Cowperwood slowly and carefully proceeded to recite the incidents of his life and labors since he had returned from Norway, together with the opinions of Dr. Wayne and the specialists.

"And that's why I wanted you to come over, Jeff," he concluded. "I knew you would tell me the truth. The specialists said it might be Bright's disease. In fact, they said I might not live more than a year and a half at the most, although Dr. Wayne did say that the conclusions of specialists are not necessarily always correct."

"Right!" said Dr. James, emphatically.

"Dr. Wayne's opinion, of course," continued Cowperwood, "may have given me a false sense of security, for it wasn't so very long after that I did quite some celebrating, at Lord Stane's place, and that brought on the disturbing incident I have described to you. I found myself suddenly very short of breath and had to be helped from the room. It's made me rather doubtful of Dr. Wayne's diagnosis. But now that you're here, I expect to be told the truth and put on the right track."

At this point Dr. James stepped forward and put both hands on Cowperwood's chest.

"Now show me how deep you can breathe," he said, and after Cowperwood's best effort in that direction, the doctor said: "Ah, I see, a little dilation of the stomach. I shall have to leave you something for that."

"Does it look as though I have a fatal disease, Jeff?"

"Not so fast, Frank. After all, I have to make some examinations. But I can say this: you have already seen two doctors and three specialists, and you've learned that it might cause your death or it might not cause your death. As you know, there's always a wide margin between the possible and the impossible, between the certain and the uncertain, and there's always a wide margin between sickness and health. But looking at you here now, and taking into consideration your general physical tone, I think you are likely to be around here for some months yet, maybe for several years. You must give me time to work on you, to think out what is best for you. In the meantime, tomorrow morning, fairly early, I'll be back here to make a complete physical examination."

"Wait a minute!" exclaimed Cowperwood. "My orders are that you're to stay here with us, with me and my ward, Miss Fleming, and her mother."

"It's very good of you, Frank, to ask me, but I can't stay today. It just so happens that there are one or two drugs I'll have to find in London before I go on with you. But I'll come back about eleven in the morning, and after that, I'll stay with you, if you wish, at least long enough to make you a better, if not a wiser, man. But now, no champagne, in fact no liquor of any kind, for a while at least, and no food with the exception of a cream soup, perhaps, and plenty of buttermilk."

Whereupon Berenice entered the room and was introduced by Cowperwood. Dr. James, after greeting her turned to Cowperwood and exclaimed:

"How can you be ill, with such a cure for all ills right here at your bedside! You may be sure I'll be here bright and early in the morning."

After which, and very professionally, he explained to Berenice that when he returned he would require hot water, towels, and some charcoal from a brightly blazing fireplace which he saw in an adjoining room.

"To think I should have come all the way from New York to treat him, with the cure right here," he observed to her, smilingly. "This world is too ridiculous for any use."

Berenice, noting how wise and gay he was, liked him at once, and thought of the many strong and interesting people Frank invariably drew to himself.

Accordingly, after an added personal talk with Cowperwood, he left for the city, but not before he had caused Cowperwood to feel that his gigantic financial obligations constituted a form of disease in themselves.

"These varying problems prey on your mind, Frank," he told him, seriously. "The brain is a thinking, creative, and directive organ which can cause you as much trouble as any fatal disease, of which worry is one, and I think you have that disease now. My problem is to make you know that that is true, and that your life is worth more to you than any ten underground systems. If you insist on putting work first, any quack doctor can truthfully assure you that at your age you are likely to die. So now my problem is to get your mind off your underground systems, and get you to take a real rest."

"I will do the best I can," said Cowperwood, "but some of these burdens are not so easy to drop as you may imagine. They concern the interests of hundreds of people who have put their complete faith in me, besides millions of Londoners who have never been able to travel beyond the limits of their own neighborhoods. With my plan, they will be able to ride to all parts of London for as little as tuppence, and so get a fairly good idea of what their city is like."

"There you go, Frank! If your life should suddenly end, where would your Londoners be then?"

"My Londoners will be all right, whether I live or die, assuming that I get my underground plan fully launched before I die. Yes, Jeff, I'm afraid I do put my work far above myself. In fact, this thing I've started has already grown so large that no one man is indispensable to it now, not even me, although there are many things I can do if I live long enough to carry out my ideas."

Chapter 63

Dr. JAMES, meanwhile, had much to ponder over concerning Cowperwood's illness and the financial burdens which troubled him. As for the Bright's disease which the London physician had suggested might be so swiftly fatal, he knew of related cases that had endured for many years. Yet there were aspects of Cowperwood's case that were serious. For one, the dilation of the stomach, and for another, the acute pains that attacked him from time to time; certainly these, along with his mental disturbance in regard to his business affairs, might do him great harm. Another disturbing factor was his worry over various problems in connection with his past life, about which James knew a great deal—his first wife, his son; Aileen, and other attachments which had from time to time been commented on in the newspapers.

 What to do, what to do for this man for whom he cared so much! What particular thing, apart from medicine, might tend to restore him, if for no more than a period of time! The mind! The mind! If he could only mentally, as well as medically, influence his mind to come to its own rescue! Suddenly he felt that he had stumbled upon the required idea. This was that Cowperwood must be strengthened to the point where he would be willing to go on a leisurely trip abroad, not only to interest him in a change of scene but to cause the public, both in England and America, to be astonished by the news that he was well enough to be traveling, so that people would say: Why, this man isn't sick! He's so much recovered that he can travel and enjoy himself!" The effect of this would probably not only restore Cowperwood's somewhat depleted nervous energy but cause him to believe that he was well, or at least very much better.

Strangely enough, the place that the good doctor's mind returned to again and again as a possible solution of his problem was the Riviera, Monte Carlo, the great gambling center. How effective it would be if the press were to announce his presence there, at the gambling tables, among grandiose dukes and Asiatic princes! Psychologically, would that not enhance Cowperwood's standing as a financier? A thousand to one it would!

The next day, when he returned to Pryor's Cove and thoroughly examined Cowperwood, the doctor put forth his suggestion.

"Personally, Frank," he began, "I think that in about three weeks you should be well enough to leave here and take a nice leisurely trip. So my prescription now is that temporarily you abandon this life here and go abroad with me."

"Abroad?" queried Cowperwood, his tone expressing his astonishment.

"Yes, and do you want to know why? Because the newspapers would certainly take note of the fact that you were able to travel. That's what you want, isn't it?"

"Quite!" replied Cowperwood. "Where do we go?"

"Well, Paris, maybe, and probably we might go to Carlsbad— a most detestable watering place, I know, but excellent for you physically."

"For God's sake, where do I go from there?"

"Well," said James, "you may have your choice of Prague, Budapest, Vienna, and the Riviera, including Monte Carlo."

"What!" exclaimed Cowperwood. "Me in Monte Carlo!"

"Yes, you in Monte Carlo, as sick as you imagine yourself to be. Appearing in Monte Carlo at this particular time is certain to produce just the reaction you want in connection with yourself. Yet, actually, you need not do anything more than appear in one of the gambling rooms and lose a few thousand dollars, so that the news can be spread abroad. People will comment on your being there, and the fact that it seems to make no difference to you as to the amount of money you toss away."

"Stop, stop!" shouted Cowperwood. "If I have the strength, I'll go, and if it doesn't turn out right, I'll sue you for breach of promise!"

"Do that," returned James.

Consequently, after three weeks of constant observation and medication on the part of Dr. James, who had taken up his residence at Pryor's Cove, Cowperwood himself felt that he was much better, and James, studying him from day to day, decided that his patient had sufficiently revived physically to undertake the travel program suggested.

However, Berenice, delighted as she was to know that Cowperwood was improving in health, was nevertheless troubled by the idea of the trip. She was well aware that rumors concerning a fatal illness would probably disrupt his whole economic plan, but loving him as she did, she could not help conjuring up fears that such a trip might not prove as valuable and effective as Dr. James and Cowperwood thought. But Cowperwood assured her that she had nothing to worry about, since he felt better, and the plan was ideal.

The following week end they departed. And true enough, the London press immediately announced that Frank Cowperwood, recently rumored to be seriously ill, was apparently so completely recovered as to be able to indulge in a pleasure tour of Europe. A little later there were still other newspaper items, from Paris, from Budapest, from Carlsbad, Vienna, and from Monte Carlo, fabulous Monte Carlo. The papers emphasized this last information by saying that "the indestructable Cowperwood, so recently ill, had chosen Monte Carlo as a place of pleasure and rest."

However, on his return to London, the questions put to him by reporters took on a very frank and open character. One reporter asked: "Is there any truth to the rumor, Mr. Cowperwood, that you've been seriously ill?"

"As a matter of fact, my boy," replied Cowperwood, "I had been working too hard and found I needed a rest. A doctor friend of mine did accompany me on this trip, and we've just been puttering around the Continent."

He laughed heartily when the *World* correspondent asked whether or not it was true that he had bequeathed his priceless art treasures to the Metropolitan Museum of Art.

"If people want to know what is in my will," he said, "they'll have to wait until I'm under the turf, and I can only hope that their charity is as strong as their curiosity."

These comments brought smiles to the faces of Berenice and Dr. James as they read them on the spacious lawn of Pryor's Cove. Dr. James, though steadily conscious of the necessity of returning to New York and his practice there, found himself drawn further and further into the affections of Cowperwood, and Berenice as well. For both were grateful to him beyond measure for having brought Cowperwood back to seemingly normal health and strength. And so, when the time came for the doctor to leave, there was an emotional sense of gratitude and mental union among all three.

"There's really nothing I can say to you, Jeff," said Cowperwood, as he and Berenice walked with the doctor to the gangplank of the steamer on which he was about to leave. "Anything I can do for you is yours to command. I ask but one thing: that our friendship continue as it has in the past."

"Don't try to reward me, Frank," interrupted James. "Knowing you all these years has been my reward. Come to see me in New York when you can. I'll be waiting to see you again." Picking up his bag, he added: "Well, friends, boats wait for no man!" and with that he smiled and again shook hands, finally merging with the throng now boarding the boat.

Chapter 64

Now that Dr. James was gone, Cowperwood was faced with the many labors which had accumulated during his absence. These would require months of concentrated energy and attention, the while he found it necessary to turn to certain phases of his personal problems, one of which was a letter from Aileen, in which she stated that while the alterations being made in the new addition were going forward under the supervision of Pyne, the architect, she felt that Cowperwood should return to New York as soon as possible in order to look the whole plan over, so that he could either approve or disapprove before it was too late. She was not sure there would be space enough in the new gallery for the pictures he had recently added to his collection. While she respected Mr. Cuthbert's opinion as an art expert, there were times when she felt that Cowperwood would disagree wholeheartedly with him if he were present.

Cowperwood realized that this was something that deserved his attention. Still, at this particular time he felt he could ill afford a trip to New York. There were too many urgent matters of policy and practical details concerning the underground that demanded his personal supervision. Of course, Lord Stane, who was frequently about, assured him of the now probably smooth future of the entire system, and by his interest and efforts succeeded in lessening the former friction among the varied interests. Stane seemed to be very much relieved and pleased at his recovery.

"Well, Cowperwood," he said to him the first morning after his return, "you look as good as new. How did you do it?"

"I didn't do it," replied Cowperwood. "It was all the work of my old friend, Jeff James. He's pulled me out of a few illnesses in the past, but this time he pulled me out of a financial jam as well."

"You're right there," said Stane. "You certainly fooled the public in a masterly fashion."

"That was Jeff's brilliant idea. He not only took me on the trip to allay suspicion and rumor, but he cured me en route," said Cowperwood.

Another matter that compelled his personal attention at this time was the discussion with Rexford Lynnwood, one of three American sculptors whose names had been suggested by Jamieson regarding the tomb he proposed to have built. Lynnwood's qualifications appealed to Cowperwood because of the fact that in connection with a prize recently offered for a tomb and statue to mark the grave of a lately deceased governor of one of the southern states, his design carried on one of its surfaces a reproduction of the cabin in which the man had been born, and at the foot of a huge, moss-covered oak tree was drawn the outline of a horse which he had ridden in various battles of the Civil War. As Cowperwood looked at it, he was touched by the pathos and simplicity of the whole conception.

Later as he sat opposite Lynnwood on the other side of his massive working desk, he was struck by the man's classic features, his deep-set eyes, and tall angular figure. In fact, he immediately liked the fellow.

As Cowperwood explained to Lynnwood, his idea for the tomb leaned toward the Greco-Roman style of architecture, but not in its purest conception. Rather, he would like it to be a modification, with some originality of design in its details. It was to be large, because he had always liked the idea of space, and was to be made of pebble-gray granite of rich texture. He would like a narrow slit of a window at one end, and a place for two sarcophagi, with two heavy bronze doors opening into the tomb itself. Lynnwood approved and was even delighted with the opportunity of executing this structure. He drew several sketches as Cowperwood talked, and these pleased Cowperwood greatly. A contract was agreed upon and he was instructed to begin work at once. As Lynnwood began gathering his designs and placing them in his portfolio, he paused and looked at Cowperwood.

"Well, Mr. Cowperwood," he said as he was leaving, "judging from the way you look, I'm sure it will be a long time before you will be needing this. At least, I sincerely hope so."

"Well, thank you very much," said Cowperwood. "But don't count on that."

Chapter 65 DURING this time Cowperwood lived principally in the agreeable thought of returning, at the end of the day, to Pryor's Cove and Berenice. For the first time in years he was enjoying the simplicities of a genuine home, a place which, because of the spirit with which Berenice infused it, caused anything and everything from a game of checkers to a short walk along the Thames to seem rich in color and feeling and make him wish that it would go on forever. Even growing old would not be such an ordeal if it could be passed under such circumstances.

Yet one afternoon, about five months after his return to business, as he sat in his office preparing a note for Aileen, he was suddenly seized with the sharpest pain of any thus far experienced in connection with his illness. It was not unlike a sharp knife being pushed and turned in the region of his left kidney, and from there it seemed to leap to his heart. When he attempted to get up from his chair, he was unable to do so. In fact, as at Tregasal, his breath seemed to fail him, and he could not move. But in a few moments the pain lessened and he was able to reach over to a push button to summon Jamieson. As he was about to press the button, however, he drew back his hand and decided that perhaps this was simply one of those acute pains he had been warned to expect, and which he had been assured would not be fatal. And so he sat for a few moments, extremely reduced by the plain evidence that he was not cured, and fearing this might be the way it would eventually end. And what was worse, he had no one to confide in. For word as to this would bring back his public situation exactly where it had been before. And Berenice! Stane! Aileen! The newspapers! And more and more days in bed!

One thing he thought he should do was to return to New York. For there he would be close to Dr. James, and also he could see

Aileen again and go over the problems that were troubling her. If he were going to die, there were things that should be put in order. As for Berenice, he could explain to her his need without telling her all in regard to this latest attack, and have her also return to New York.

After arriving at this decision he very cautiously rose from his chair, and a few hours later was able to return to Pryor's Cove, pretending that there was nothing wrong in any way. However, after dinner, Berenice, who was in a particularly pleasant frame of mind, asked him if everything was going all right.

"Well, no, not exactly," he replied. "I had a letter from Aileen complaining about conditions in New York: the work on the house, and that sort of thing. She thinks there isn't sufficient room being left for the pictures I've added to the collection. And some of the dealers who have looked in on the alterations seem to agree with her, regardless of Pyne's opinion. I'm beginning to feel that I should go over, not only for that reason, but also to look after some of the follow-ups in connection with the loans that were made to me when I was there last."

"Are you sure you are strong enough to undertake the trip?" asked Berenice, a look of anxiety in her eyes.

"Quite," replied Cowperwood. "As a matter of fact, I am feeling better than I have been for months. And I cannot go too long without contact with New York."

"What about me?" she inquired, in a troubled tone.

"Why, you will go with me, and, for convenience sake, you can stay at the Waldorf when you get there, incognito, of course"—a reply that modified the look of distress in her face.

"But on different boats, as usual?"

"Unfortunately, that would be the best way, hard as it is for me to even think of it. You know so well, dear, the danger of publicity."

"Yes, I know. I understand how you feel about it. If you have to go, you must, and I'll be right behind you on the next boat. When do we go?"

"Jamieson tells me the next boat sails Wednesday. Can you get ready by then?"

"I could be ready tomorrow if it were necessary," replied Berenice.

"Darling! You are always so willing, so helpful—I don't know what my life would be without you . . ."

As he said this Berenice walked toward him and put her arms around him, whispering: "I love you, Frank. So why shouldn't I do everything I can to help you . . ."

Chapter 66 ONCE on the boat, Cowperwood felt alone, spiritually alone, at last admitting to himself that neither he nor any man knew anything about life or its Creator. He now felt that for some reason he was facing a change which involved all this great and beautiful mystery as it related itself to him.

He had cabled Dr. James to meet him at the dock, and this immediately brought the following reply: "Welcome to New York. I will be there to meet you. Yours, Monte Carlo Jeff." A message which provided Cowperwood with a laugh and a peaceful night. Only, before he turned to rest, he took paper and ink and penned the following message to Berenice, who was traveling under the name of Kathryn Trent on the *S.S. King Haakan*: "We are only a day apart but to me it is worse than a dozen years. Good night, beautiful spirit, your mere vicinity comforts me and brings me rest."

On Sunday morning Cowperwood awoke feeling less vigorous and less physically secure than he had the night before. And by the time his valet had helped him dress, he felt greatly reduced in strength; in fact, he returned to bed to rest for the entire day. At first, his entourage, which consisted of Jamieson; Mr. Hartley, Jamieson's assistant; Frederickson, the valet, was not alarmed, as it was thought he was merely relaxing. But toward the late afternoon he asked Jamieson to call the ship's physician, for he was feeling quite ill. Dr. Camden, after an examination, decided that he was a very sick man, with a temperature of 105°, and advised that his personal physician be notified to meet the boat in the morning and have an ambulance there.

On hearing this news Jamieson took it upon himself to wire Aileen that her husband was very ill, that it was necessary to remove him from the boat in an ambulance, and what did she have to suggest in regard to further arrangements. Whereupon Aileen answered at once, saying that owing to the fact that Mr. Cowperwood's residence was being altered to house an additional art gallery, there was an undue amount of noise and confusion; she therefore thought it wiser for him to go to the Waldorf-Astoria, where arrangements could be made for his proper care, and where he would be decidedly more comfortable.

After Dr. Camden had eased his patient by a shot of morphine, Jamieson communicated the contents of Aileen's message to Cowperwood.

"Yes, that would be much better," he said weakly. "Make the arrangements."

But this disruption of all of his plans, and such thoughts as he was now able to indulge in, caused him to feel very weary. His house! His art gallery! His planned hospital! The idea of having to return to London and his underground affairs! Suddenly he found himself desiring not to think of anything or anyone, other than Berenice.

And so he remained until morning, when the boat was nearing New York and in process of being docked, and the hustle and bustle and movement all about him caused him to awaken to the fact that they were arriving.

At this point, Dr. James, having chartered a pilot boat, boarded the S.S. *Empress* while it was still in the lower harbor, and after he had consulted Dr. Camden and Jamieson about such plans as had been made, walked into Cowperwood's room.

"Now, Frank, this is Jeff," he announced, "and I want to know exactly how you're feeling. This is something that will pass, I believe, as soon as I can administer the right sort of medicine. But I want you not to worry about anything. Just leave it to me, your old Monte Carlo pal."

"I knew when you came, Jeff," said Cowperwood, weakly, "everything would be all right," and he squeezed the doctor's hand affectionately.

"We've made arrangements to move you to the Waldorf in an ambulance," continued James. "You won't mind that, will you? It's really better that way, much easier on you, you know."

"No," replied Cowperwood, "I have no objection. But I wish you could arrange so that I wouldn't be annoyed by the newspapermen, at least until I am settled at the hotel. I'm not sure that Jamieson will know how to handle them."

"Just leave it to me, Frank. I'll take care of it. The important thing for you to do is to rest and say nothing at all, until I talk to you later. And now I'll have to be going to take charge."

Just then Jamieson entered the room.

"Come on, Jamieson," said Dr. James, "the first thing we have to do is see the captain." Whereupon they left the room together.

Three-quarters of an hour later an ambulance that had been waiting in the street below was allowed to back up to Exit 4, which was as vacant as though there were no passengers still waiting to leave the ship. At the direction of Jamieson, two carriers bearing a canvas stretcher proceeded to Cowperwood's suite, and he was carried to the waiting ambulance. The doors were closed, the driver sounded his gong, and drove away, while an astonished group of reporters standing a short distance away exclaimed, one to another:

"What do you know about that? We've been double-crossed this time! Who was that?"

Frustrated in their attempt to learn who had been so ill that it was necessary to remove him, or her, in an ambulance, it was not long before one of them, boasting a friendship with one of the nurses on the vessel, returned with the information that it was none other than Frank Algernon Cowperwood, the celebrated financier. However, as to what the nature of his illness was, or where he had been taken, these were items that had to be traced down. But when one reporter suggested getting in touch with Mrs. Cowperwood, several of those present immediately hurried to the nearest telephone to inquire from Aileen if her husband had been taken off the S.S. *Empress* in an ambulance, and if so, where was he? It was true, she replied; he was ill, but it was also true that he would have been transferred to the Cowperwood mansion if it were not for the fact that the entire building was in process of alteration in order to make room for an additional art and statuary collection which later was to become the property of the city of New York. Meanwhile, it was also Mr. Cowperwood's wish that he be transferred to the Waldorf-Astoria, where he could have such quiet and attention as at present he could not obtain in his own home.

Accordingly, by one o'clock of this same day, the news of Cowperwood's arrival and illness and present whereabouts was in every afternoon paper in the city, although, due to the precaution of Dr. James, no visitors were allowed without a written consent from the doctor himself, and three nurses were placed in charge.

However, Cowperwood, realizing the possibility of Berenice receiving alarming news concerning his illness, requested Dr. James to send the following telegram to her still on board ship: "Report of my illness greatly exaggerated. Do everything exactly as planned. Dr. James in charge. Will tell you what to do. Affectionately, Frank."

In spite of the fact that this telegram brought such distressing news, Berenice was somehow consoled by the fact that he was able to wire her so reassuringly. And yet she was haunted by uncertainty as to the nature of this illness. At any rate, whatever the result, her place, as she felt, was beside him.

Yet walking through the main salon of the vessel later in the afternoon, she was startled by the news poster tacked on the news board: "Frank Cowperwood, celebrated American financier and London traction magnate, stricken on board S.S. *Empress,* and removed on arrival in New York to Waldorf-Astoria Hotel."

Stunned and grieved by these cold words in black and white, she was still relieved to learn that he was to be at the hotel instead of his home. She had a suite reserved there, so at least she would be near him. Nonetheless, there was the possibility of encountering Aileen, and this would be painful, not only for her but for Cowperwood. And yet he had asked her to come to the hotel, as originally planned, so he must have some procedure worked out. However, this new vulnerable social arrangement was such an extreme contrast to her protected seclusion at Pryor's Cove that she now wondered if she had the necessary courage or stamina to go through with it. But even in the face of these difficulties and dangers she felt that she must be near him, regardless of consequences. For he needed her, and she must answer that need.

Once so decided, the following morning, as soon as the vessel docked and she had declared her luggage, she went to the hotel, where she calmly registered under the name of Kathryn Trent. But once within the privacy of her own suite, she was faced with the numerous angles of her situation. What to do? For, as she knew, Aileen might already be with him. But while she was meditating on the problem, a call came from Dr. James, telling her that Cowperwood would like to see her, and that his suite was number 1020. She thanked him very cordially and said she would go to him at once. Dr. James added that although Cowperwood was in no immediate danger, rest and quiet being his principal needs at present, he had ordered that no one be allowed to see him for a few days, with the exception of herself.

Upon arriving at his suite, she was ushered directly into his presence, where she found him lying propped up on pillows, looking pale and not a little distrait, but brightening as she neared him. She bent over and kissed him.

"Darling! I'm so sorry. I was afraid that this trip might be too much for you. And I was not with you! But Dr. James assures me that it isn't serious. You know you recovered from your first attack, and I'm sure, with care, you'll recover from this one. But, oh, if only I could be with you all of the time. I think I could nurse you back to health!"

"But Bevy, darling," observed Cowperwood, "just to look at you makes me feel better. And this matter of your seeing me shall be arranged. Of course, there's a lot of publicity now, and the less you are involved, the better I would feel. But I have explained the whole matter to Jeff, and he understands and sympathizes. And, better than that, he will keep in touch with you as to times and opportunities for seeing me. There's just one person, you know, that you will have to do your best to avoid. But if you will keep in touch with Dr. James from day to day, I think we can manage until I'm out of this. As a matter of fact, I am sure of it."

"Darling, you are so brave, and you know that I am delighted to be here in any capacity. I'll be as cautious and circumspect as possible. Meanwhile, I'll be loving you and praying for you constantly."

She bent over and kissed him again.

Chapter 67

THE sudden illness and collapse of Cowperwood, flashed first by the local New York papers to their readers, was nothing less than an international sensation. For it affected and included the interests and investments of thousands of persons, to say nothing of their banks and bankers. As a matter of fact, the day after he was stricken, reporters from the principal newspapers of England and France, and Europe in general, through the United and Associated press services, interviewed not only Jamieson and Dr. James but also called upon distinguished financiers in the United States for comments as to what the effect of his death might be.

Indeed, so numerous were the apprehensive comments and misgivings on the part of some investors that most of the remaining managers of the London underground were compelled to express themselves as to the actual import of Cowperwood's illness. For one, Mr. Leeks, acting chairman of the District Railway at the time, and who was said to have been very close to Cowperwood, was quoted as saying that "the necessary arrangements for every possible contingency arising from the possible indisposition of Mr. Cowperwood at any time had long before been made. Complete harmony," added Mr. Leeks, "exists in the entire Underground directorate. As to the future policy of this great system, I wish to say that there is not a trace of confusion or disorder."

Again, one William Edmunds, director of the Railway Equipment & Construction Company of London, stated: "Everything is in perfect working order. The organization is so good that Mr. Cowperwood's illness or temporary absence can make no difference."

Lord Stane made the following comment: "The Underground is in splendid condition, and its affairs have been so administered from the start, by Mr. Cowperwood himself, that his unavoidable absence cannot bring about any serious injury to the system. Mr. Cowperwood is too great an organizer to found any vast enterprise on the indispensability of any one man. Naturally, we are all hoping for his speedy recovery and return, for his is a welcome presence here."

While Dr. James had attempted to keep this publicity away from Cowperwood, there were a few people he could not very well restrain and had to admit. One was Cowperwood's daughter, Anna, and his son, Frank, Jr., neither of whom he had seen for a number of years. From his conversation with them he was able to sense the reaction of the public to his illness, and it was not unflattering, to say the least.

Following these came Aileen, who was extremely disturbed by his physical state, for at this time he looked and felt very weak. Dr. James insisted that she wait for a later time to discuss any pressing problems, and she readily accepted his suggestion and considerately made her first visit a very short one.

After Aileen departed, Cowperwood was mentally constrained to meditate on the various social and financial angles which his sudden illness had brought into being as problems which he must solve if he could. One of these concerned the choice of someone to take on his duties temporarily in the face of his present unavoidable absence. Naturally, he first thought of Lord Stane, but considering his numerous and pressing interests, decided that Stane would not be the man. But there was one Horace Albertson, president of the St. Louis Electric Traction System, who, as he knew from previous financial relations, was one of the ablest railroad men in America. Albertson, he felt, should prove entirely satisfactory in such a crisis as this. And immediately following this thought he instructed Jamieson to see Mr. Albertson in St. Louis and present to him the entire problem, his reward to be whatever sum he felt he deserved.

However, Mr. Albertson declined the offer, saying that he was highly honored, but his own labors were constantly increasing in volume and he could not consider retiring from the American field. This was a disappointment to Cowperwood, but one that he could understand and justify. Although it did, for a time, cause him a degree of worry, he was relieved by a cable from Stane and the directors of the London Underground stating that they had that day appointed Sir Humphrey Babbs, well-known to Cowperwood, to take his place temporarily at the head of the system. Aside from this cable, came several others from his London associates, including Elverson Johnson, emphasizing their unhappiness over his illness and their deep desire for his speedy recovery and return to London.

Nonetheless, in spite of all their praises, Cowperwood's mind was troubled by the somewhat complicated and ominous drift of all of his affairs at this time. For one thing, here was Berenice, his devoted love, risking so much for the rare opportunity of secretly visiting him at night, or in the early dawn, with the aid and connivance of Dr. James. And here again was Aileen—her lack of understanding of life in general, its inexplicable eccentricities and vagaries—also visiting him occasionally, unaware of the presence of Berenice in the hotel. He felt that he must try to live, and yet, in spite of his efforts, felt himself losing ground physically. So much so that one day when Dr. James was alone with him in his room, he began talking to him about it.

"Jeff, I've been ill for about four weeks now, and I have the feeling that I am not getting any better."

"Now, Frank," said James, quickly, "that's not the right attitude to take. You must try to get well, and the chances are you will. Other cases as bad as yours have gotten better."

"I know that," said Cowperwood to his friend, "and naturally you want to encourage me. But I still have the feeling that I am not going to recover. And in connection with this, I would like you to call Aileen and ask her to come here and talk over some estate matters with me. I've been thinking of this for some time, but now I feel I'd better not wait any longer."

"Just as you say, Frank," said James. "But I do wish you would not decide that you are not going to get well. It isn't good, you know. And besides, I think to the contrary. As a favor to me, you might try a little."

"I'll try, Jeff, but please call Aileen, will you?"

"Why, certainly, Frank, but don't talk too long, remember!"

And James retired to his own room, where he called Aileen on the telephone and asked her to come over to see her husband.

"Would you be good enough to come this afternoon, if possible, say around three o'clock?" he asked her.

She hesitated for a moment, and then replied: "Why, yes, of course, Dr. James," and accordingly at about the time agreed upon she came, disturbed and wondering and not a little sad.

Upon seeing her, Cowperwood experienced a sense of weariness, such as for years he had often experienced in regard to her, not so much physical weariness as aesthetic weariness. She was so sadly lacking in that rare inner refinement that characterized a woman like Berenice. And yet, here she was, still his wife, and for that reason he felt that he owed her a reasonable degree of consideration in return for the kindness and affection which she had displayed at a time when he most needed them. And thus thinking, his mood softened somewhat toward her, and he reached out and took her hand as she greeted him.

"How are you, Frank?" she asked.

"Well, Aileen, I've been here four weeks now, and although the doctor thinks I am doing well enough, I realize that I am getting weaker all the time. And since there are a number of things I wanted to talk to you about, I thought I'd send for you. Is there anything you would like to tell me first about the house?"

"Well, yes, a few things," she said hesitantly. "But whatever they are, they can wait until you are better, don't you think?"

"But you see, Aileen, I don't think I'm going to get any better.

And that's the reason I wanted to see you now, today," said Cowperwood, softly.

Aileen hesitated and did not answer.

"You see, Aileen," he continued, "the bulk of my estate is going
to you, although I've taken care of some others in my will, such as
my son and my daughter. But the great responsibility of the care
of this estate is going to fall on you. It's a large amount of money,
and I want to know if you feel equal to the task; and if so, if you
will faithfully carry out the instructions I have written out for you
in my will."

"Oh, yes, Frank, I will do everything you say."

He sighed inwardly, and continued: "Although I have made a
will which gives you full control, nevertheless, that is the very reason
I feel the necessity of warning you of overconfidence in anyone; for
the moment I am gone, I'm sure there will be any number of people
who will come to you with this and that plan, to do something for
this cause or the other, or this or that institution. I have tried to
guard against that by instructing the executors to submit any plan
they may have to you for your approval. You are to be the judge,
and you must decide whether it is worthy or not. Dr. James, you
know, is one of the executors, and he is the one on whose judgment
I can rely. He is a man of not only great medical skill but goodness
of heart and intention. I have told him that you may stand in need
of advice, and he has promised me faithfully to advise you to the
best of his knowledge and ability. I want to tell you that he is so
honest a man that when I told him he was to be left a sum of money
for his services to me, he refused to allow it, although he was willing
to act as your advisor. So if ever you should find yourself troubled
as to what to do, please go to him first and see what he thinks."

"Yes, Frank, I will do exactly as you say. If you believe in him,
I certainly will also."

"Of course," he continued, "there are specific provisions in my
will to be taken care of after the beneficiaries are satisfied. One of
these is the completion and preservation of my art gallery. I want
the mansion kept intact as it now stands; that is, as a museum for
the benefit of the public. And since I have left plenty of money for
its upkeep, it will be your duty to see that it is maintained in the
best possible state.

"In fact, Aileen, I don't know if you ever realized how much that place has meant to me. It has helped me to live through the endless practical problems to which I have had to devote myself. In building it and buying things for it, I have tried to bring into my life and yours the beauty which is entirely outside of cities and business."

And as Cowperwood talked on, Aileen at last realized to a degree, at least, and perhaps for the first time, what all this meant to him, and again she promised to do everything as he directed.

"There's another thing," he went on, "and that is the hospital. You know I have wanted for a long time to build one. It doesn't have to occupy an expensive site. A rather convenient Bronx location has been suggested in my will. Furthermore, it is to be for the poor—not for people with money who can afford to go elsewhere— and neither race, creed, nor color are to have anything to do with the right of admission."

She sat there silently while he paused for a moment.

"There's one more thing, Aileen. I haven't mentioned it to you before, because I wasn't certain how you would feel about it. I am having a tomb erected over in Greenwood Cemetery, and it's very near completion: a beautiful copy of an ancient Greek design. It contains two bronze sarcophagi, one for me and one for you, if you choose to be buried there."

At this she stirred uneasily, for he seemed to be considering his prospective death as practically as he had taken his business affairs.

"You say it is in Greenwood?" she asked.

"Yes," said Cowperwood, solemnly.

"And that it is already completed?"

"So nearly completed that I could be buried there if I died within a short time."

"Certainly, Frank, you are the strangest of men! The idea of building your own tomb—and mine—and you aren't certain at all that you're going to die of this . . ."

"But this tomb, Aileen, will last for a thousand years," he said, with a slight lift in his voice. "And besides, we're all going to die sometime, and you might as well rest there with me; that is, if you care to."

She remained silent.

"Well, there it is," he concluded, "and I feel it should be for the two of us, particularly since it has been built that way. However, if you feel you do not want to be there . . ."

But here she interrupted him. "Oh, Frank, let's not talk about that now. If you want me there, I'll be there. You know that," and a restrained sob manifested itself in her voice.

However, at this point the door opened and Dr. James came in to say that it was unwise for Cowperwood to talk any longer; she might come another day if she would call up beforehand. She got up from where she had been sitting beside his bed, and taking his hand, said: "I'll come in again tomorrow, Frank, just for a little while, and if there is anything I can do, please have Dr. James call me. But you must get well, Frank. You must believe that you will. There is so much that you want to do. Try . . ."

"Well, all right, dear, I will do my best," he said, waving his hand and adding: "See you tomorrow."

She turned and passed out into the hall. Walking toward the elevators, sadly pondering their conversation, she noticed a woman just stepping out of an elevator. She stared, and, to her astonishment, realized that the woman was Berenice. They both stood as if transfixed for a few seconds, after which Berenice crossed the hall and opened a door and disappeared down a stairway leading to the floor below. Aileen, still transfixed, turned, with seeming determination to re-enter Cowperwood's suite, but instead suddenly turned in the opposite direction toward the elevators. But before going many steps, she stopped and stood still. Berenice! So here she was in New York, and obviously at Cowperwood's request. Of course, at his request! And he pretending even now that he was dying! Would the man's perfidy never reach a limit? Imagine him asking her to come tomorrow! And talking of the tomb in which she was to lie with him! With him! Well, this was the end! Never again would she see him in this world, if they called her as many as a thousand times a day! She would instruct her servants to ignore all calls from her husband, or his accomplice, Dr. James, or any other person who pretended to represent them!

As she entered the elevator, her mind was a mental storm center, a cyclone roaring with clashing waves of rage. She would tell the press about this scoundrel: his abuse and humiliation of a wife who had done so much for him! She would repay him yet!

Outside the hotel, she hurried into a taxicab and stormily urged the driver to drive, just drive, the while she repeated to herself, like a rosary of trebled length, all of the ills which she could conjure, that might be and would be, if she could manage, heaped upon Cowperwood. And as she rode, the vibration of her rage traveled directly back to Berenice.

Chapter 68

BERENICE, in the meantime, having reached her room, sat there woodenly, finding herself powerless to think, so filled with fear was she, for Cowperwood as well as herself. Aileen might have returned to his apartment, and how dreadful the effect of that on him at this time! It might actually bring about his death! And how terrible it was that she could not do anything for him! Finally, she thought of going to Dr. James and asking him how to defeat this vicious, merciless mood on the part of Aileen. But she was held back by the fear of again meeting her. Perhaps she was in the hall, or in Dr. James' room! By degrees the situation became so unbearable to her that at last it produced a practical idea. She went to the telephone and called Dr. James, and, much to her relief, he answered.

"Dr. James," she began, shakily, "this is Berenice. I want to know if you won't please be good enough to come to my room at once. Something dreadful has happened, and I am so unstrung and nervous I must talk to you!"

"Why, certainly, Berenice. I will come at once," he replied.

Then she added, in a most unsteady voice: "If you should see Mrs. Cowperwood in the hall, please don't allow her to follow you here."

But here her voice broke off, and James, sensing danger, hung the phone up hurriedly and, seizing his medical kit, went directly to her apartment and knocked at the door. Berenice responded by whispering from behind the door:

"Are you alone, Doctor?"

When he assured her he was alone, she opened the door and he stepped inside.

"What is the matter, Berenice? What is all this?" he asked, almost brusquely, at the same time studying her white face. "Why are you so terrified?"

"Oh, Doctor, I can't tell you." She was actually trembling with fear. "It's Mrs. Cowperwood. I saw her here in the hall as I was coming in, and she saw me. Her expression was so savage that I am afraid for Frank. Do you know whether or not she has seen him since I left? I have the feeling that she might have returned to his apartment."

"Certainly not," said James. "I have just come from there. Frank is all right, quite safe. But here," and taking a few small white pills from his medicine case he handed her one. "Take this, and don't say anything more for a few moments. It will quiet your nerves, and then you can tell me all about it." And going toward a sofa, he motioned her to sit beside him. Gradually she showed signs of becoming more quiet. "Now, listen, Berenice," he added, "I know that your situation here is a very difficult one. I have known it ever since you came here, but why are you so wrought up? Do you expect Mrs. Cowperwood to attack you personally?"

"Oh, no, I am not worried about myself," she replied, more calmly. "It's Frank I'm really worried about. He is so ill and so weak and helpless at this time, and I'm afraid that she may say or do things that might hurt him so terribly he would not want to live. And, oh, he has been so liberal and so well-meaning toward her. And just now when he needs love, not hate, and after all he has done for her, she is ready to do I don't know what—abuse him so violently that he may suffer a relapse. He's told me many times that she always loses control of her emotions when she becomes jealous."

"Yes, I know," said James. "He is a very great man, who has married the wrong woman, and to tell you the truth, I feared something of this kind. I thought it unwise for you to be in the same hotel. However, love is a powerful force, and I saw how deeply you cared for each other when I was in England. But I also knew, as did many people, that his relations with Mrs. Cowperwood were unsatisfactory to him. By the way, did you exchange any words with her?"

"Oh, no," replied Berenice. "I just saw her as I stepped out of the elevator, and her anger and opposition, as she recognized me, were so real that I felt it through my whole body. It came to me that she might do something desperate to both of us, if she could. Besides, I was afraid she might return to his apartment immediately."

At this point Dr. James advised Berenice to stay in her suite until this storm subsided, and to wait until she heard from him. Above all, as he instructed her, she was not to say a word to Cowperwood about this when she saw him again. He was far too ill to endure it. In the meantime, as he patiently explained, he would brave the anger of Mrs. Cowperwood and call her, to determine, if possible, what she might be doing or planning to say publicly. And then he left Berenice to go to his own room to think the matter over.

However, before he had time to reach Aileen on the telephone, one of the nurses came into his room to ask if he would not please step in and look at Mr. Cowperwood; he seemed more restless than usual. When he did so, he found Cowperwood stirring around in his bed as though he were uncomfortable. And when he asked him how his visit with Aileen came out, he answered wearily:

"Oh, everything worked out all right, I think. At least, I went over the most important points with her. But somehow, Jeff, I feel very tired and exhausted from our long conversation."

"Well, I expected that. Next time, don't talk for such a long time. And now here is something for you to take. It will give you a little rest for the present." And with that he handed Cowperwood a powder with a glass of water, which he swallowed as Dr. James added: "Well, that will do for now, and I'll look in on you a little later this afternoon."

Whereupon he returned to his own room and called Aileen, who by that time had returned home. Upon hearing his name announced by her maid, she came directly to the phone. James, in his most courteous tone, told her he was calling to find out how her visit with her husband had worked out, and asked if there was anything he could do to help her.

Her voice was angry and uncontrolled as she spoke.

"Yes, Dr. James, you can help me very much by not calling me any more, if you please, for I've just found out what has been going on all the time—in London and here—between my so-called husband and Miss Fleming. I know she has been living with him there and is now living with him under your eyes, and apparently with your aid and approval. And you want to know whether I had a satisfactory interview with him! And that woman hiding in the same hotel! It's the most outrageous thing I ever heard of, and one which I'm sure the public will be glad to hear about! And it will, depend on that!" And then, her voice almost breaking with rage, she added: "You, a doctor! A man supposed to be concerned with the decencies of life . . ."

Whereupon Dr. James, sensing the fierceness of her rage, managed to interrupt her sufficiently to say, forcefully but calmly:

"Mrs. Cowperwood, I beg to take exception to your accusations. I was called in on this case in a professional capacity, not as a judge of situations which are none of my making. And you have no right to judge the motives of a man about whom you know as little as you do about me. Whether you believe it or not, your husband is a very sick man, very, and if you make the grave error of giving out any story to the press, you will be hurting yourself a thousand times more than you could ever hurt him, or anyone connected with him. For he not only has powerful friends, but admirers, as you know—friends who will deeply resent any such action as you propose, and who will not fail him. If he dies, as he well may . . . well, judge for yourself how any such public attack as you have in mind will be received."

These cutting words reminded Aileen of some of her own indiscretions in the not too distant past, and her voice suddenly lost some of its vibrato as she said:

"I don't want to discuss any of the personal angles of this matter with you or anyone else, Dr. James, so please don't call me again on any matter connected with Mr. Cowperwood, no matter what happens. You have Miss Fleming there to wait on and comfort my husband. Let her take charge, and please don't call me. I'm tired of the whole wretched relationship. And that's final, Dr. James." Here the telephone clicked, for she had hung up.

As Dr. James turned away from the phone, his face wore a faint smile. From his long years of professional experience with hysterical women, he knew that the force of her rage had spent itself in the hours since she had seen Berenice. For, after all, as he also knew, this was not a new story to Aileen. And he felt reasonably sure that her vanity would not allow her to give free reign to public utterances. She had not done so in the past and would not do so now, he felt. And with this much assurance, he went to call on and report to Berenice, whom he found still nervous and impatiently waiting to hear from him.

He still smiled as he proceeded to explain that he felt sure that Aileen's bark was worse than her bite. For although she had threatened him and Cowperwood and Berenice with exposure, still, after his talk with her, he had the definite feeling that her rage had spent itself and that nothing more of a violent nature was likely to occur. Now, he added, since Aileen had declared finally that she proposed never to see her husband again, it looked to him as if he should have to ask Berenice to take charge, and they would, both of them, see if they could not pull him through. She might take the evening nursing shift from four to twelve.

"Oh, how wonderful!" exclaimed Berenice. "I'll be so happy to do all I possibly can to help him—anything within my power! For, oh, Doctor, he must live! He must get well and be free to do the things he has planned. And we must help him."

"I'm very grateful to you for this. I know that he cares for you deeply," said James, "and he will no doubt be much better in your care."

"Oh, Doctor, it is I who am truly grateful to you!" she exclaimed, taking both of his hands in hers.

Chapter 69   COWPERWOOD'S ATTEMPT to clarify for
Aileen the significance of the wealth
that would be hers at his death, and the necessity on her part for a practical understanding of the problems she would be likely to encounter as its custodian, instead of inducing an atmosphere of tender regard, left him with a sense of the probable futility of it all. And this because of his knowledge of her lack of realization of how important these matters were to him, as well as to her. For he knew well she could not read the characters and intentions of men, and were he no longer here, what assurance could he have of the fulfillment of the various ideals which most of his bequests embodied? And this thought, instead of favorably affecting his mood in regard to living, really discouraged him. So much so that he was not only a little weary, but a little bored and spiritually dubious of the import of life itself.

For how strange the almost unbroken irritability of their lives together, covering, as they did, a period of over thirty years! There was, to begin with, his early enthusiasm for her when she was seventeen and he was twenty-seven, and then a little later his discovery that her beauty and physical strength concealed also a lack of understanding that had kept her unaware of his financial and mental stature, at the same time that it caused her to consider that he was an unchanging possession of hers which was not to be modified by so much as a glance in any other direction than that which led to her. And yet, for all the storms that followed his least diversion, here they were, after all these years, with little understanding on her part of the qualities in him which had slowly and yet surely led him to his present wealth.

Even so, he had finally discovered a woman whose temperament made his life supremely worth while. For he had found Berenice, and she had found him. Together they had clarified themselves, each to the other. Her wondrous love shone in her voice, her eyes, her words, her touch. For bending over him from time to time, he could hear her say: "Darling! Beloved! This love of ours is not just for today, it is forever. It will live in you wherever you are, and yours in me. We shall not forget. Darling, rest and be happy."

It was at this point in his meditations that Berenice, clad in the white uniform of a nurse, entered the room. He stirred at the sound of her familiar voice as she greeted him, and gazed as if not fully comprehending what his eyes beheld. Her costume made such an attractive setting for her unusual beauty. With an effort he raised his head, and although obviously very weak, exclaimed:

"You! Aphrodite! Goddess of the sea! Immaculately white!"

She bent down and kissed him.

"A goddess!" he murmured. "The golden red of your hair! The blue of your eyes!" And then, pressing her hand, he drew her closer to him. "And now I have you with me. I see you as you beckoned to me that day in Thessalonika by the blue Aegean!"

"Frank! Frank! If only I were your goddess, forever and ever!" She knew that he had become delirious, and tried to pacify him.

"That smile," went on Cowperwood. "Smile on me again. It is like sunshine. Hold my hands, my Aphrodite of the Sea!"

Berenice sat on the side of the bed and began to cry softly to herself.

"Aphrodite, don't ever leave me! I need you so!" and he clung to her.

At this point Dr. James walked into the room, and noting Cowperwood's condition, went directly to him. Turning and surveying Berenice, he said: "Be proud, my dear! A giant of the world salutes you. But leave us alone for a minute or two. I need to restore him. He is not going to die."

She left the room while the doctor administered a restorative. In a few moments, Cowperwood came out of his delirium, for he said: "Where is Berenice?"

"She will be with you in a moment, Frank, only now rest and quiet will be best for you," said James.

But Berenice heard him call her, and came in and sat on a little chair beside his bed, waiting. In a few moments he opened his eyes, and began talking.

"You know, Berenice," he said, as if they had been discussing the matter, "it is so important to keep the mansion intact as a home for my art objects."

"Yes, I know, Frank," replied Berenice, softly and sympathetically. "You have always loved it so."

"Yes, I have always loved it. To leave the asphalt of Fifth Avenue and in ten seconds, after crossing the threshold, to be within a palm garden, walk through flowers and growing things, sit down among them, hear the plash of water, the tinkle of a rill dropping into the little pool, so that I heard notes of water music, like a brook in the cool greenness of the woods——"

"I know, darling," whispered Berenice. "But now you must rest. I will be right near you even when you sleep. I am your nurse."

And as Berenice went about her duties that night, and on every other night, she was impressed by his unbroken interest in the many affairs which he could no longer possibly manage. One day it was the art gallery, next day the underground, and next, the hospital.

Although she did not actually anticipate it, any more than did Dr. James, Cowperwood had only a very few more days to live. And yet, during such hours as she spent with him, he seemed more cheerful, except that after talking for a moment or two, he now invariably manifested a great weariness and a desire to sleep.

"Let him sleep as much as possible," counseled Dr. James. "He is merely conserving his strength." A statement which discouraged Berenice greatly. So much so that she asked if something more could not be done for him.

"No," replied James. "Sleep is truly the best thing for him, and he may pull through. I am trying the best restoratives I know, but we can only wait. He may take a turn for the better."

Only he did not take a turn for the better. Instead, forty-eight hours before he died he took a definite turn for the worse, which caused Dr. James to send for his son, Frank A. Cowperwood, Jr., and Anna, his daughter, who was now Mrs. Templeton. But not Aileen, as his daughter and son noticed when they arrived. When asked why Mrs. Cowperwood was not present, Dr. James explained to them that for reasons of her own she had refused to come to visit him any more.

However, although they had known of the existing estrangement between Aileen and Cowperwood, his son and daughter still had their own misgivings as to why she refused to come to see Cowperwood at this crucial time, and they felt obligated to inform her as to his condition. Therefore, they hurried to a public telephone and called her. But, much to their surprise, they found she was not in a mood to consider anything in connection with him or them, asserting that Dr. James and Miss Fleming, having arranged Cowperwood's affairs with his consent and with no regard for her wishes, surely could take care of everything. She flatly refused to come.

And so, while they were stunned by this seeming cruelty on Aileen's part, they felt there was nothing they could do but return to watch the outcome of his turn for the worse. For fear controlled all present: Dr. James, Berenice, and Jamieson, all of whom stood by helpless for the want of a single clarifying idea. They waited for hours, the while they listened to his heavy breathing or periods of silence, until suddenly, twenty-four hours later, as if seeking to conclude a great weariness, he stirred sharply, even half-rose on one elbow as though looking about, and then as suddenly fell back and lay still.

Death! Death! There it was—irresistible and bleak in the face of all of them!

"Frank!" cried Berenice, stiffening and staring as if in supreme wonder. She hurried to his side and fell to her knees, seizing his damp hands and covering her face with them. "Oh, Frank, my darling, not you!" she cried out, and then drooped slowly to the floor, half-fainting.

Chapter 70 THE consternation that followed Cowperwood's death involved so many immediate, as well as remote, problems that for several minutes all stood as if stupefied. Of the entire group, the doctor was the calmest and most resourceful in his thoughts and actions, his first direction being that he and Jamieson remove Berenice to one of the couches that were in his room. After doing this, he suggested to Jamieson that he call up Mrs. Cowperwood at once in order to obtain from her instructions as to the burial.

This inquiry, when made by Jamieson, resulted in a most shocking and disturbing reaction on the part of Aileen, a reaction plus an attitude which posed a problem that was seemingly insurmountable without resulting in practically a national scandal.

"Why do you ask me?" she said. "Why don't you ask Dr. James and Miss Fleming? They have been in complete charge of his affairs ever since he has been here, and before."

"But, Mrs. Cowperwood," said Jamieson, astounded. "This is your husband. Do you mean to say that you do not wish to have him removed to your home?" An inquiry which brought from her the sharp and staccato reply:

"I have been personally ignored and lied to by Mr. Cowperwood, and also by his doctor and his mistress. Let them arrange to have his body sent to a funeral parlor and have the funeral from there."

"But, Mrs. Cowperwood," insisted Jamieson, in an agitated voice, "this is a most unheard-of proceeding. All the newspapers will find out. Surely you wouldn't like that in connection with so great a figure as your husband."

But at this point Dr. James, hearing this shocking statement, came forward and took the telephone receiver from Jamieson.

"Mrs. Cowperwood, this is Dr. James," he said, coldly. "I am the physician, as you know, who was called in by Mr. Cowperwood when he came back to this country. Mr. Cowperwood is no relative of mine, and I have served him as I would any other patient, you included. But if you persist in this astounding attitude toward a man who is your husband, and whose property you are to inherit, I assure you that you will never be done with the scandal of it.

It will follow you to the end of your days. Surely you must realize the significance of that."

He waited for a second, but there was silence on her part.

"Now, I am not asking you to do me any favor, Mrs. Cowperwood," he went on. "Only yourself. Certainly his body can be removed to an undertaker's establishment, and buried anywhere, if that is what you wish. But is it? As you know, the press can learn from me or from the undertaker as to what has become of his body. But once more, and finally, for your own sake, I am asking you to think this over, for if you do as you say, I will see that tomorrow's papers print the whole story."

At this point he stopped talking, waiting and hoping for a more humane reply. But hearing the telephone click, he realized that she had hung up the receiver. Whereupon he turned to Jamieson, saying:

"That woman is, for the time being, not wholly sane. We'll simply have to take this matter into our own hands and act for her. Mr. Cowperwood is so well liked by his own servants that I am sure there will be no difficulty in reaching them, so that, without her knowledge, his body can be transferred to the house and remain there until it can be properly removed to his tomb. This is something that we can and must do. We cannot possibly allow this tragedy to occur."

And taking his hat, he went out, but not before looking in on Berenice, who by then had recovered her composure, and asking her to return to her room and wait there until she heard from him.

"Do not despair, Berenice. Believe me, this will all be arranged in the most correct and unobtrusive manner possible. I can promise you that," and he pressed her hand affectionately.

His next move was to have Cowperwood's body taken to an undertaking establishment located near the hotel. Next, he intended to consult with Jamieson as to the character and mentality of the Cowperwood servants. Surely one or two of them could be depended on for assistance. For he was morally convinced that Aileen should not have her way. He might have to overstep his rights, but he saw no other course. Long before this he had sensed the basis of the difference between her and Cowperwood. She was, as he had seen for himself, really deeply in love with her husband, but so jealous of his every action as to make her dream of happiness a vehicle of pain.

Curiously enough, at this very difficult moment, Jamieson was called upon by one Buckner Carr, head butler at the Cowperwood home, a man who had been in Cowperwood's service since his Chicago years. His purpose in calling, as it turned out, was to convey to Jamieson not only his great sorrow and dismay at Mr. Cowperwood's death, but, because of a telephone conversation which he had overheard, and which seemed to indicate that Mrs. Cowperwood was charging her husband with unjust accusations and, most terrible of all, refusing to allow him now to be brought into his own home, he desired to offer his services toward averting such a tragedy.

When Dr. James returned to the hotel, he found Jamieson and Carr together, and he immediately explained to them the plan he had worked out in his own mind. He had instructed the undertaker, he said, to prepare the body for burial, provide a suitable casket, and await further directions. The problem now was to decide when it could be transferred to the mansion, and whether the servants would be there to assist in the arrangement of a secret and silent reception of the body, together with the labor of taking it to the proper room, and in the most noiseless fashion, in order that Mrs. Cowperwood would not be aware of its arrival, at least until the following morning. Did Buckner Carr believe that this could be done without interference? Carr replied that if he were now allowed to return to the Cowperwood home for an hour or two he would call back and state whether the exact conditions outlined by Dr. James could be fulfilled. After which he left, and at the end of two hours called on the telephone to say that the best time would be between ten o'clock in the evening and one o'clock in the morning; all of the servants were anxious to help, and the house would be dark and silent.

And, in consequence, as planned, the transfer of Cowperwood's body in its casket was executed, at one o'clock in the morning, while Carr outside silently patrolled a practically deserted street. The faithful servant followers of their former master had arranged the large living room on the second floor for the reception of the richly ornamented casket in which he lay. As he was being carried in, one of them stood before Aileen's door, listening, in anticipation of any least stir.

Thus the unheralded funeral cortege of Frank Algernon Cowper-

wood, in the silence of the night—he and Aileen once more united
in their own home.

Chapter 71   No TROUBLESOME thoughts or dreams
concerning the entire proceedings of the
night disturbed Aileen before the light of early morning awakened
her. Although usually she felt disposed to linger in her bed for a
period, on this occasion, hearing a noise as though some heavy object
had dropped to the floor of the balcony below, and fearing that it
might have been a valuable Greek marble recently purchased and
more recently temporarily placed, she arose and descended the stair-
case that led to the balcony. Looking around curiously as she walked
past the large double doors leading into the main drawing room,
she went directly to the newly placed art piece, but found it quite
in order.

Yet, as she turned about to retrace her steps, and as she again
approached the doors to the drawing room, she was startled by the
presence and appearance of a large black, heavily draped, oblong
box, standing in the center of the huge room. A shivering cold
swept across her body, and for the time being she could not move.
Then she turned as if to run away, but then, pausing, returned
again to the entrance of the room and stood there, amazed and
staring. A coffin! God! Cowperwood! Her husband! Cold and
dead! And he had come to her, although she had refused to go to
him when he was alive!

With trembling and remorseful steps she walked forward to
gaze on his cold and death-stilled body. The high forehead! The
distinguished, well-shaped head! The smooth brown hair, even at
this time not gray! The impressive features, all of which were so
familiar to her! The whole figure suggesting power, thought, genius,
which the world had so readily recognized in him from the beginning! And she had refused to go to him! She stood stiffly, inwardly
regretting something—his own errors and hers. And the endless,
almost inhuman storms that had come and gone between them.
And yet, here he was, at home at last! At home!

But then suddenly, the strangeness, the mystery, the final defiance
of her will, emphasized by his being here, aroused her to anger.

Who had brought him, and how? At what hour? For only the previous evening, she, by her orders and commands to the servants, had barred all doors. Yet here he was! Obviously, his, not her, friends and servants must have collaborated to have done this for him. And so plainly now, all would be anticipating a change of attitude on her part, and if so, all the customary and formal last rites due to any such distinguished man. In other words, he would have won. It would appear as though she had altered her views and condoned his unfettered self-directing actions. But no, never should they do this to her! Insulted and triumphed over to the very last! Never! And yet, even as she declared her defiance to herself, there he lay, and even as she gazed on him, there was the sound of footsteps behind her, and as she turned her head, Carr, the butler, approached, a letter in his hand, saying:

"Madam, this has just been delivered at the door for you."

And although at first she gestured as if to wave him away, he had no more than turned his back when she exclaimed: "Give it to me!" And then, tearing it open, she read:

Aileen, I am dying. When this reaches you, I will be no more. I know all my sins and all those you charge me with, and I blame only myself. But I cannot forget the Aileen who helped me through my prison days in Philadelphia. Yet it will not help me now, or either of us, to say I am sorry. But somehow, I feel that in the depths of your heart you will forgive me, once I am gone. Also it comforts me to know that you will be taken care of. I have arranged for all that, as you know. So now, good-by, Aileen! No more evil thoughts from your Frank, no more ever!

A conclusion on his part which caused Aileen to go forward to the casket and take his hands and kiss them. And then, after gazing at him for a moment, she turned and hurried away.

However, a few hours later, Carr, having been the recipient, through Jamieson and others, of various requests, was compelled to consult with Aileen concerning procedure in connection with the burial. The requests for permission to attend were so numerous that finally Carr was forced to bring forward a list of names, so long a list that it caused Aileen to say:

"Oh, let them come! What harm can it do now? Let Mr. Jamieson and Mr. Cowperwood's son and daughter arrange everything as they please. I will keep to my room, as I am not well enough to help in any way."

"But, Mrs. Cowperwood, wouldn't you be willing to have a minister present to pronounce the last rites?" asked Carr, a suggestion that had been made by Dr. James, but which fitted Carr's religious nature.

"Oh, yes, let one come. It can do no harm," said Aileen, as her thoughts wandered back to the extreme religiosity of her parents. "But limit the number of those who are to come here to fifty, no more"—a decision which caused Carr to get in immediate touch with Jamieson and Cowperwood's son and daughter, in order to inform them that they were to go ahead with such funeral arrangements as they felt appropriate. This news, reaching Dr. James' ears, caused him to heave a sigh of relief, at the same time that he proceeded to have the many admirers of Cowperwood informed of this fact.

Chapter 72

AMONG the friends of Cowperwood who called at the mansion that same afternoon, and the morning following, those whose names were on Buckner Carr's list were allowed to enter to view the body now lying in state in the spacious drawing room on the second floor. The others were advised to attend the tombside ceremonial at Greenwood Cemetery in Brooklyn the following day at 2 P.M.

In the meantime, Cowperwood's son and daughter had called on Aileen, and it was arranged that they were to ride with her in the first mourner's carriage. By that time, however, every New York newspaper was ablaze with the so-called sudden end of Cowperwood, who only six weeks before had arrived in New York. Because of his great number of friends, the articles stated, the funeral services would be attended by intimate friends of the family only: a statement which, however, did not deter many people from going out to the cemetery.

Accordingly, the next day at noon, the funeral cortege began forming in front of the Cowperwood mansion. Groups of people gathered on the streets outside to observe the spectacle. Following the hearse was the carriage containing Aileen, Frank A. Cowperwood, Jr., and Cowperwood's daughter, Anna Templeton. And then, one by one, the other carriages moved into line, and proceeded along the highway, under an overcast sky, until finally they passed through the gates to Greenwood Cemetery. The gravel drive gradually mounted a long incline, bordered by heavy trees, behind which ranged stones and monuments of all descriptions. About a quarter of mile in, as the drive continued to rise, a roadway branched off to the right, and a few hundred feet farther on, between great trees, the tomb loomed solemnly high and majestic.

It stood alone, no other monument being within thirty feet of it, a gray, austere, and northern version of a Greek temple. Four graceful columns of modified Ionic design formed the "porch" and supported a plain triangular pediment, without decoration or religious symbol of any sort. Above the doors of the tomb, in heavy square-cut letters, was his name: FRANK ALGERNON COWPERWOOD. The three graduated platforms of granite were piled high with flowers, and the massive bronze double doors stood wide open, awaiting the arrival of the distinguished occupant. As all must have felt who viewed it for the first time, this was a severely impressive artistic achievement in the matter of design, for its tall and stately serenity seemed to dominate the entire area.

And as her carriage came into full view of the tomb, Aileen was again and finally impressed by her husband's power of self-presentation. But even as she thought this, she closed her eyes, as if trying to shut out the sight of the tomb, and seeking to revive her last impression of him as he stood vividly alive and self-assertive before her. Her carriage waited until the hearse had reached the door of the tomb, and the heavy bronze casket was carried up and placed among the flowers, before the minister's rostrum. Following that, the occupants of the carriages emerged and crossed over to a large marquee tent set up in front of the tomb, under the shelter of which benches and chairs awaited them.

In one of the carriages Berenice sat silently beside Dr. James, gazing at the tomb that was to seal her beloved away from her forever. Tears she could not cry, and would not. For why seek to oppose an avalanche which had already gone so far as to obliterate the import of life itself, for her? At any rate, such was her mood or reaction to all of this. However, a word that repeated itself over and over in her mind was the word: "Endure! Endure! Endure!"

After all of the friends and relatives had settled themselves, the

Episcopal clergyman, Reverend Hayward Crenshaw, came forward and took his place on the rostrum, and in a few moments, when all had become very quiet, he began to speak, his utterances grave and clear:

"I am the resurrection and the life, saith the Lord; he that believeth in me, though he were dead, yet shall he live; And whosoever liveth and believeth in me shall never die.

"I know that my Redeemer liveth, and that he shall stand at the latter day upon the earth; and though this body be destroyed, yet shall I see God; whom I shall see for myself, and mine eyes shall behold, and not as a stranger.

"We brought nothing into this world, and it is certain we can carry nothing out. The Lord gave and the Lord hath taken away; blessed be the name of the Lord.

"Behold, thou hast made my days as it were a span long; and mine age is even as nothing in respect of thee; and verily every man living is altogether vanity.

"For man walketh in a vain shadow, and disquieteth himself in vain: he heapeth up riches, and cannot tell who shall gather them.

"And now, Lord, what is my hope: truly my hope is even in Thee.

"When thou with rebukes doth chasten man for sin, Thou makest his beauty to consume away, like as it were a moth fretting a garment: every man therefore is but vanity.

"Lord, thou has been our refuge from one generation to another.

"Before the mountains were brought forth, or ever the earth and the world were made; Thou art God from everlasting and world without end.

"Thou turnest man to destruction: again Thou sayest, Come again, ye children of men.

"For a thousand years in Thy sight are but as yesterday; when it is past, and as a watch in the night.

"As soon as thou scatterest them they are even as asleep; and fade away suddenly like the grass.

"In the morning it is green, and groweth up; but in the evening it is cut down, dried up, and withered.

"For we consume away in Thy displeasure, and are afraid of thy wrathful indignation.

"Thou hast set aside our misdeeds before Thee; and our secret sins in the light of Thy countenance.

"For when Thou art angry, all our days are gone; we bring our years to an end, as it were a tale that is told.

"The days of our age are three score years and ten; and though men be so strong that they come to four score years; yet is their strength then but labor and sorrow; so soon passeth it away, and we are gone.

"O teach us to number our days: that we may apply our hearts unto wisdom.

"Glory be to the Father, and to the Son, and to the Holy Ghost.

"As it was in the beginning, is now, and ever shall be: world without end, Amen."

The casket was then lifted by the pallbearers and carried into the tomb and placed in the sarcophagus, while the minister knelt and prayed. Aileen having refused to enter, the other mourners remained with her. And shortly afterward, when the minister came outside, the heavy bronze doors were closed, and the burial services for Frank Algernon Cowperwood were over.

The clergyman went over to Aileen to offer a few words of comfort; the friends and relatives began to leave, and soon the space about the tomb was empty. However, Dr. James and Berenice lingered a while in the shadow of a large birch tree, and then walked slowly down the slope along a winding path, as Berenice did not wish to leave with the others. Walking down the path some hundred feet, Berenice looked back to see the last resting place of her beloved, as it stood high and proud in anonymity, the name not being visible from where she stood. High and proud, and yet small, under the protective elms grown tall around it.

Chapter 73

BECAUSE of the troubled state of her mind following the illness and death of Cowperwood, Berenice decided that it would be best for her to remove to her own home on Park Avenue, which had been closed during her absence in England. Now that she was uncertain as to her future, she would use it as a retreat, temporarily, at least, from prying contacts with the local press. Dr. James agreed with her decision, believing that it would be best for him also if he could truthfully say she had departed and he did not know her present whereabouts: a ruse that subsequently worked very well, for having answered a number of times that he knew nothing more than the newspapers did, the inquiries ceased as far as he was concerned.

Nonetheless, from time to time there began to appear in print, references, not only to her disappearance, but her possible whereabouts. Had she returned to London? And to make sure of that, the London papers queried whether she had returned to her former residence at Pryor's Cove: a series of inquiries that brought the unsatisfactory news that although her mother was there, she stated that she knew nothing of her daughter's plans, and that they would have to wait until she obtained that information herself. This reply was prompted by the receipt of a cable from Berenice requesting her mother to furnish no information until she heard from her.

While Berenice got some satisfaction out of outwitting the reporters, she found she was quite lonely in her own home, and spent most of her evenings reading. However, she was shocked by a special feature article in one of the New York Sunday papers which dealt entirely with herself and her previous relations with Cowperwood. While she was referred to as his ward, the whole tenor of the article tended to single her out as an opportunist who had used her beauty to further her personal comfort and social pleasures in general: an interpretation and presentation of herself which irritated as well as pained her greatly. For as she saw herself, then and before, she was wholly concerned with the beauty of life, and such creative achievements as tended to broaden and expand its experiences. However, as she now felt, this type of article was likely to be repeated and even reproduced in other papers, abroad as well as in her own country, for it was obvious that she had been singled out as a romantic and dramatic personality.

What could she do about it? Where go to live to get away from such publicity?

In her troubled and somewhat confused state of mind, she walked about the library of her home, the shelves of which were crowded with long-neglected volumes, and haphazardly withdrawing one of the books, she opened it casually and her eyes fell on the following words:

> Part of myself is the God within every creature,
> Keeps that nature eternal, yet seems to be separate,
> Putting on mind and senses five, the garment
> Made of Prakriti.

When the Lord puts on a body, or casts it from Him,
He enters or departs, taking the mind and senses
Away with Him, as the wind steals perfume
Out of the flowers.

Watching over the ear and the eye, and presiding
There behind touch, and taste, and smell, He is also
Within the mind: He enjoys and suffers
The things of the senses.
Dwelling in flesh, or departing, or one with the gunas,
Knowing their moods and motions, He is invisible
Always to the ignorant, but his sages see him
With the eye of wisdom.

Yogis who have gained tranquility through the practice of spiritual discipline, behold Him in their own consciousness. But those who lack tranquility and discernment will not find Him, even though they may try hard to do so.

So arresting were these thoughts that she turned the book over to see the name of it. And noting that it was the Bhagavad-Gita, she remembered a certain Lord Severence's brilliant discourse on the subject matter at a dinner given one evening by Lord Stane at his town house. She had been deeply impressed by Severence's vivid account of his sojourn in India, where for a considerable period he had lived the monastic life in a retreat near Bombay and studied with a guru. She recalled how stirred she had been by his impressions, and had wished at the time that she also might one day go to India and do likewise. And now, in the face of her threatened social isolation, she felt even more keenly disposed to seek sanctuary somewhere. Indeed, this might be the solution of her present complicated affairs.

India! Why not? The more she thought about going there, the more the idea appealed to her.

According to another book on India which she found on her shelf, there were many swamis, many gurus, or teachers and interpreters of the mysteries of life or God, who had founded for themselves ashramas or retreats in the mountains or forests to which the troubled seekers after the meaning of the marvels or mysteries of life might turn in their hours of grief or failure or dismay, to learn of spiritual resources within themselves, which, if studied and followed, might readily dispel their own ills. Might not such a teacher of these great truths lead her into a realm of light or spiritual peace sufficiently illuminating to dispel the dark hours of loneliness and shadow which might permanently engulf her?

She would go to India! As she arranged it in her mind, she would sail to Bombay from London after closing Pryor's Cove, taking her mother with her if she wished to go.

The next morning she called Dr. James to get his opinion regarding her decision, and when she told him of her plan to study there, much to her surprise, he said he thought it a very good plan indeed. For he himself had long been intrigued by no less an ambition, only he was not as free as Berenice to avail himself of the opportunity. It would be the kind of retreat and change she most needed, he said. In fact, he had a few patients, with physical and mental condition greatly deranged by social and personal difficulties, whom he had sent to a certain Hindu swami in New York, and they had later returned to him completely restored to health. For, as he had noted, there was something about the limited thought of the self that was lost in the larger thought of the not self that brought about forgetfulness of self in the nervous person, and so health.

And so encouraged was Berenice by his approval of her decision that she made immediate arrangements for the care of her Park Avenue home in her absence, and left New York for London.

Chapter 74 To THE world in general, the main subject of interest in connection with the death of Frank Algernon Cowperwood was his fortune: its size, who would inherit it, how much they would each receive. Before the will had been admitted to probate, gossip and rumor had it that Aileen was being cut off with a minimum, that Cowperwood's two children received the bulk of the estate, also that various London favorites had already received huge gifts.

In less than a week after the death of her husband, Aileen had dismissed his lawyer, and in his place made one Charles Day her sole legal representative.

The will, admitted for probate in the Cook County Superior Court five weeks after the death of Cowperwood, contained gifts ranging

in size from $2,000 left to each of his servants to $50,000 left to Albert
Jamieson, and $100,000 to the Frank A. Cowperwood Observatory,
an institution presented to the University of Chicago ten years
previously. Included among the ten persons or organizations listed
were his two children, and the amount of money involved in these
specific gifts totalled approximately half of a million dollars.

Aileen was provided for from the income of the balance of the
estate. At her death, his art gallery and collection of paintings and
sculpture, valued at $3,000,000, were to be given to the City of New
York for the education and enjoyment of the public. Cowperwood
had heretofore placed in the hands of trustees $750,000 for these gal-
leries. In addition to this, he willed that a plot of land be purchased
in the borough of the Bronx, and a hospital, the buildings to cost
not more than $800,000, be erected thereon. The balance of his
estate—part of the income from which would provide maintenance
of the hospital—was to be placed in the hands of his appointed
executors, among whom were Aileen, Dr. James, and Albert Jamieson. The hospital was to be named the Frank A. Cowperwood
Hospital, and patients were to be admitted regardless of race, color,
or creed. If they lacked financial means with which to pay for treat-
ment, they were to receive it free of charge.

Aileen, once Cowperwood was gone, being extremely sentimental
about his last wishes and desires, focussed her first attention on the
hospital. In fact, she gave out interviews to the newspapers elaborat-
ing her plans, which included a convalescent home which was to
be free of any institutional air. She concluded one of these interviews
by saying:

"All my energies will be directed toward the accomplishment of
my husband's plan, and I shall make the hospital my lifework."

Cowperwood had failed to take into consideration, however, the
workings of the American courts throughout the nation: the administration of justice or the lack of it; the length of time American
lawyers were capable of delaying a settlement in any of these courts.

For instance, the decision of the United States Supreme Court,
killing off Cowperwood's Combination Traction Company of
Chicago, was the first blow to the estate. Four and a half million
dollars of his, invested in his Union Traction Company bonds, had
been guaranteed by the Combination Traction Company. Now they
were faced with years of wrangling in court to decide not only their

value but their ownership. It was too much for Aileen. She promptly
retired as executrix and turned the problem over to Jamieson. And in
consequence, almost two years passed with little or nothing accomplished. In fact, all of this was during the panic of 1907, by reason of
which Jamieson, without knowledge of the court, Aileen, or her attorney, turned the bonds in question over to a reorganizing committee.

"If they were sold out, they would be valueless as they are," Jamieson explained. "The reorganization committee hopes to work out a
plan to save the Combination Traction Company."

Whereupon the reorganization committee deposited the bonds
with the Middle Trust Company, the organization interested in combining all of the Chicago railways into one big company.

"What did Jamieson get out of it?" was the query.

And while the estate had now been in the course of probation for
two years in Chicago, no move had been made to settle affairs in
New York. The Reciprocal Life Insurance Company, holding a
mortgage of $225,000 on the addition to the Fifth Avenue mansion,
along with $17,000 of unpaid interest on this mortgage, started pro-
ceedings to collect. And their lawyers, without the knowledge of
Aileen or her lawyers, worked out a plan with Jamieson and Frank
Cowperwood, Jr., whereby an auction was held and this gallery,
along with the pictures in it, was sold. The proceeds of this sale
barely covered the claims of the insurance company and the City of
New York for unpaid water bills and taxes amounting to around
$30,000. To add to all this, Aileen and her lawyers appealed to the
Probate Court in Chicago to have Jamieson removed as executor.

In sum, as Aileen informed Judge Severing:

"It has been all talk and no money ever since my husband's death.
Mr. Jamieson talked pleasantly about money and was a good one at
making promises, but I was never able to get much real money out
of him. When I demanded it directly, he would say there wasn't any.
I have lost faith in him and have come to mistrust him."

She then related to the court how he had transferred $4,500,000
worth of bonds without her knowledge; how he had arranged for an
auction of the art gallery, which was sold for the sum of $277,000,
whereas it was valued at $400,000; how he had charged her $1500
collection fee when he had already been paid as executor; and how
he had refused her attorney access to the books of the estate.

"When Mr. Jamieson asked me to sell my house and art collection," she concluded, "and pay him 6 per cent on the transaction, I simply told him I wouldn't do it. He threatened to blow me higher than Gilroy's kite if I didn't."

The hearing was adjourned for three weeks.

"It is a case of a woman meddling in things she does not understand," observed Frank A. Cowperwood, Jr.

Thus, while Aileen was attempting to remove Jamieson as executor in the Probate Court in Chicago, Jamieson, after three years of inaction in New York, was applying for ancillary papers there. However, Aileen's move brought up the question of his fitness, which caused Surrogate Monahan to postpone action for fifteen days to show cause why he should or should not be granted ancillary papers. At the same time, in Chicago, Jamieson, replying to Judge Severing on the charges of Aileen, insisted that he had done no wrong and had never received a dime illegally. Rather, he asserted, he had done much to preserve the estate.

However, Judge Severing, refusing to remove Jamieson as executor, remarked:

"On the question of the widow's award, an executor who would charge a percentage for the collection of her award, in addition to his fee from the whole estate, and who would be so forgetful of his duties, ought to be removed, it is true. But it is doubtful if I have the power to remove for that cause alone."

Whereupon Aileen started plans for an appeal to the Supreme Court.

At this point, however, the London Underground Company brought suit in New York in the United States Circuit Court, to collect $800,000 due them. They did not question the solvency of the estate, although authoritative statements did show some $3,000,000 had vanished into thin air in the process of litigation. The Court appointed one William H. Cunningham as receiver in connection with this suit, and this receiver, although Aileen was ill of pneumonia at the time, proceeded to place guards on duty at the Fifth Avenue property, and three days later arranged for a three-day auction of pictures, rugs, and tapestries to meet the claim of the London Underground. The guards were on hand twenty-four hours a day to insure against disappearance of any portion of the property that was to be auctioned. They roamed over the premises, to the great prejudice of orderly management of the household, and in defiance of the right of possession and occupancy.

Charles Day, one of Aileen's lawyers, submitted to the court that the proceeding was one of the worst pieces of judicial tyranny ever attempted in this country; that it was purely a conspiracy to get into the house by illegal means, for the purpose of forcing a sale of the house and pictures and destroying Cowperwood's intention and desire to leave the mansion and its contents as a museum for the public.

However, at the same time that her New York attorneys were trying to prevent the temporary receivership being made permanent, her lawyers in Chicago were attempting to have a receiver appointed there for the entire estate.

A clear title to the additional art gallery, sold as a result of the foreclosure proceedings of the Reciprocal Life Insurance Company, had never been obtained, and after four months the insurance company filed a suit against Receiver Cunningham and against the title company which refused to take title to the art gallery.

In addition, while the reorganization committee of Chicago capitalists were working on a plan with representatives of the House of Brenton Diggs, the bondholders of the three underlying companies demanded that bills of foreclosure be filed. Contending that the Cook County Court had jurisdiction over all of the Cowperwood property, Aileen's lawyers asserted that the Circuit Court had no jurisdiction. The judge of the said Circuit Court admitted as much by announcing that it would withdraw as soon as Jamieson succeeded in taking charge of the New York property.

However, five months following Aileen's appeal to the United States Circuit Court of Appeals, a two-to-one decision was reached, which made permanent the temporary receivership of William H. Cunningham. Nonetheless, a dissenting judge contended that the Federal Court could not meddle in probate matters, which were the business of the State. The agreeing judges, on the other hand, claimed the receiver should remain until a reasonable time had elapsed—as judged by the Circuit Court—for creditors to ask the Surrogate Court to appoint an administrator, at which time they would turn over the property to him. At the same time, a temporary injunction preventing Jamieson from applying for ancillary letters was dissolved.

And now there were endless delays, courts, claims to be satisfied, and decisions to be made. And opposed to these, a legally uninformed widow, whose total supply of money, left her by her dead husband, was being used in defense of her complicated rights. And lying ill, her health completely shattered, and her actual means now dangerously low.

Therefore, Aileen's lawyers, together with Jamieson's lawyers, and the legal representatives of the London Underground, arranged a settlement whereby she would receive $800,000 in lieu of her dower rights, and as a part of her personal estate due her. A petition was filed in the Probate Court in Chicago for confirmation of this unrecorded agreement.

The Inheritance Tax Appraiser pronounced a total value of the estate, four years after the death of Cowperwood, at $11,467,370.65. Hearing on the motion to have the appraiser withhold his report was taken up and argued in Judge Roberts' chambers. Mr. Day, appearing for Aileen, claimed that if Judge Severing confirmed the agreement, nothing remained but to sell the assets of the estate. Day claimed the appraisal was too high, both in value of the art collection at $4,000,000 and of the furniture, which, he said, above the second floor, was not worth more than $1,000.

Then Jamieson applied to Surrogate Henry for ancillary letters in New York. At approximately the same time that Aileen lost her suit to prevent him from obtaining these ancillary letters, Judge Severing confirmed the agreement between her and Jamieson whereby she was to receive $800,000 and the widow's one-third of all personal property after the debts were paid. Under this agreement, Aileen transferred to Receiver Cunningham the house, art gallery, pictures, stable, etc., to be auctioned off, and Jamieson, more than four years after probation proceedings had been begun in Chicago, was appointed ancillary executor in New York. He should have stopped proceedings for the auction of the property in New York, but he did not. Included in the gallery were 300 pictures valued at $1,500,000, among them works of Rembrandt, Hobbema, Teniers, Ruysdael, Holbein, Frans Hals, Rubens, Van Dyck, Reynolds, and Turner.

And yet, out in Chicago, and at the very same time, lawyers for Jamieson were going before Judge Severing, in the Probate Court, claiming that the only way to save the estate from insolvency was to turn over the $4,494,000 in bonds of the Union Traction Company to the reorganization committee for the purpose of forming a new company, and Aileen's lawyers were contending the action had taken place secretly and without the sanction of the court. At this point

Judge Severing announced that he did not believe he could enter an order to that effect unless both sides agreed to it. Hence action was postponed indefinitely to give attorneys for both sides opportunity to reach an agreement.

More delay! Delay! Delay!

Corporations! Corporations! Corporations!

Decisions! Decisions! Decisions!

Courts! Courts! Courts!

Until, in fact, five years had passed, ending in the auction of everything that had belonged to Frank Cowperwood, the proceeds of which, including all the real property, amounted to $3,610,150!

Chapter 75

FIVE years of wandering through the endless wilderness of law, lawyers, corporations, courts, and judges had left Aileen with the painful realization that at the end of whatever steps she took in any direction, there was nothing. In fact, the sum and substance of all those years and efforts was that she lived alone, was visited by no true friend, legally defeated in one honest claim after another, until at last she fully realized that the dream of grandeur which this house represented had vanished into thin air. There remained only, as her part of the estate, the $800,000 and the widow's one-third of all personal property after debts were paid, in return for her transfer and surrender to Receiver Cunningham of the mansion, art gallery, pictures, and everything else. The law and the corporations and the executors, like wolves, were constantly on her trail, and finally they had caught up with her to the place where she now had to move out of her own home in order that it could be auctioned off to strangers.

But even before she could move into the apartment she had chosen on Madison Avenue, the house was overrun with agents of the auctioneers, tagging articles of every description with their appropriate catalogue numbers. Wagons drove up to take away paintings—300 of them—to the Liberty Art Galleries on Twenty-third Street. Collectors came and sauntered about, speculating. She was ill and depressed, having to listen to Receiver Cunningham explain that it was his duty to make a complete inventory of the house and gallery and submit it to the court.

There followed announcements in the newspapers to the effect that beginning Wednesday of the following week and continuing for three days and evenings, the furniture, bronzes, statuary, ceiling and overdoor panels, and art objects of all descriptions, including the large library, were to be disposed of. The place: 864 Fifth Avenue; the auctioneer: J. L. Donahue.

Amid the irritating confusion, Aileen wandered about collecting her personal belongings and having her few faithful servants remove them to her apartment.

The interest and curiosity of the public in the Cowperwood possessions grew steadily from day to day, and the demand for admission tickets to the house was so great that the auctioneers were unable to meet it. The charge of one dollar admission fee, both to the exhibitions and the sales sessions, was apparently no deterrent to those interested.

On the day the sale opened at the Liberty Art Galleries, the auditorium was crowded from pit to gallery. There was tremendous applause when certain masterpieces of art were offered. On the other hand, at the Cowperwood mansion, the difficulties increased. The catalogue of objects to be sold there contained more than thirteen hundred numbers. And when the day of the auction finally arrived, motors, taxicabs, and carriages hugged the curb at Fifth Avenue and Sixty-eighth Street while the sale was going on. There were millionaire collectors, famous artists, and celebrated society women—whose motors had never stopped there in earlier days—all clamoring to get inside to bid on the beautiful personal belongings of Aileen and Frank Cowperwood.

His gold bedstead, once owned by the king of Belgium and bought for $80,000; the pink marble bathtub in Aileen's bathroom, which had cost $50,000; the fabulous silk carpets from the Mosque of Ardebil; the bronzes, red African vases, Louis XIV gilt sofas; candelabras, also Louis XIV, of cut crystal, with amethyst and topaz drops; exquisite porcelain, glass, silver, and smaller objects such as cameos, rings, pins, necklaces, precious stones, and figurines.

From one room to another they followed the booming voice of the auctioneer which reverberated through the great rooms. They saw "Cupid and Psyche" by Rodin sold to a dealer for $51,000. One bidder, who had gone as high as $1600 on a Botticelli, lost it to a $1700 voice. A large, impressive woman in purple, who stood near the auctioneer most of the time, for some reason always bid $390 on an article, never lower, never higher. When the crowd rushed into the palm room on the heels of the auctioneer to view a Rodin statue, he called out to them "Don't lean against the palms!"

Throughout the sale, a brougham drove slowly up and down Fifth Avenue two or three times, its occupant a lone woman. She looked at the motors and carriages rolling up to the entrance to the Cowperwood mansion, and watched the men and women crowding up the steps into the house. It meant much to her, for she was viewing her own last struggle: a final separation from her earlier ambitions. Twenty-three years ago she was one of the most ravishingly beautiful women in America. To a certain degree she retained something of her former spirit and bearing. She had been subdued but not altogether crushed, as yet. But Mrs. Frank Algernon Cowperwood did no go in to attend the sale. Yet she saw her most treasured possessions being carried out by buyers, and occasionally heard the voice of the auctioneer crying: "What am I bid? What am I bid? What am I bid?" Eventually she decided she could endure no more, and told the driver to take her back to her Madison Avenue apartment.

A half-hour later she stood alone in her bedroom, silent and feeling the need of silence. No trace of all that had almost magically on this day disappeared. She would be alone now. Cowperwood would not return, even if he had desired to do so.

And then, one year later, she was suddenly seized with another attack of pneumonia, and passed from this world. Before she died she sent a note to Dr. James:

If you will be so good, I beg of you to see that I am buried in the tomb alongside of my husband, as he wished. Will you please forgive me for my discourtesies to you in the past? They were due to miseries beyond my power to convey.

And James, folding the letter and meditating on the anachronisms of life, said to himself: Yes, Aileen, I will.

Chapter 76 During the period in which the estate of Cowperwood had disintegrated and the death of Aileen had occurred, Berenice had slowly but surely embarked on a course that she felt would adjust her to society and life in any form, provided, as she reasoned from time to time, she could equip herself with the mental and spiritual data that would brush completely out of her consideration the whole Western materialistic viewpoint which made money and luxury its only god. Primarily, the desire for this change in thought had originated in a struggle against the sorrow that had seized upon her after Cowperwood's death, and which had almost embittered her life. Then, quite accidentally, or seemingly so, she had come upon a little volume known as the Bhagavad-Gita, which seemed to condense and epitomize thousands of years of Asiatic religious thought.

> Who knows the Atman
> Knows that happiness
> Born of pure knowledge:
> The joy of sattwa.
> Deep his delight
> After strict self-schooling:
> Sour toil at first,
> But at last what sweetness,
> The end of sorrow.
>
> Who cares to seek
> For that perfect freedom?
> One man, perhaps,
> In many thousands.
> Then tell me how many
> Of those who find freedom
> Shall know the total
> Truth of my being?
> Perhaps one only.

As she found herself singing these songs of God, she began to wonder if she might be the one to find truth and understanding. It was worth striving for, and she had gone in search of it.

But before arriving in India to pursue her studies, she had gone to England to arrange for her mother to accompany her. And it was only a few hours after her arrival at Pryor's Cove that Lord Stane came to see her. When she told him of her decision to go to India to take up the serious study of Hindu philosophy, Stane, while he was interested, was also shocked. For many years he had heard the reports of Englishmen, who, for the government or other interests, had been sent to India, and recalling these he felt that India was no place for a young and beautiful woman.

Stane understood well enough by now that Berenice was more to Cowperwood than a ward, and that there was some sort of shadow over her mother's past; but he was still in love with her, and felt that even with her social handicaps, his own life would be mentally and spiritually happier if she were near him and he could enjoy her companionship and her liberal and intellectual viewpoint. He would, in fact, consider himself fortunate to marry such a charming and distinguished temperament.

But when Berenice explained to him what had been crystallizing in her mind these past few weeks since Cowperwood's death, and how convinced she had become that she would receive mental and spiritual help there, away from the Western world and its crass materialism, he was inclined to defer his personal desires in connection with her until such time as experiences of her own might have clarified all the various conflicting emotions and interests which now for the time being dominated her. And so he made no particular reference to his feeling for her, except to say that he hoped she would be willing to avail herself of the advice of his good friend, Lord Severence. For, as she knew, Severence was richly informed as to prevailing conditions in India, and would be glad to be of service to her. Berenice replied that she would be happy to receive any advice or aid that Lord Severence wished to give her, although she knew she would be led directly to whatever it was she needed. As she said: "Something appears to be drawing me like a magnet, and I feel I shall not be deflected in any way."

"In other words, Berenice, you believe in fate," said Stane. "Well, I believe in it, too, to a degree, but plainly you have the force and the faith that will cause your desires to be realized. And now all I can think of in relation to all this is that you will be willing to call on me for any service whatsoever that I may be able to render. I hope you will write me from time to time and inform me of your progress." And this she promised to do.

After which Lord Stane took it upon himself to make all the arrangements for the departure of Berenice and her mother for India. This included the securing of several letters of introduction from Lord Severence. And Bombay being the city chosen by her to visit,

he obtained the necessary passports and tickets, and subsequently saw
them off.

Chapter 77 Arriving in Bombay, Berenice and her
mother were impressed by the approach
to this beautiful city. From the sea a long wide waterway, studded
with mountainous islands, led to the city. On the left towered a group
of stately buildings, and far to the right the palm-fringed shore of the
mainland, gradually rising to the peaks of the Western Ghats in the
far distance.

In Bombay itself, bearing a letter to the management of the Majestic Hotel from Lord Severence, they were granted a most courteous and gratifying service for the entire period of their stay. So much
so that they were moved to remain for several weeks in order to
explore the city's many contrasting characteristics as opposed to those
of the Western cities. And, to their delight, they were richly rewarded by their many varied impressions. The wide thoroughfares,
dotted with oxcarts hauling merchandise; the crowded bazaars, with
their richness and variety of display and seething with people of
many races and religions, many of them scantily clothed and bare-
footed, peoples of every color, from light brown to black: Afghans,
Sikhs, Tibetans, Singhalese, Baghdad Jews, Japanese, Chinese, and
many others. But, ah, the poorer and more emaciated groups: thin
bodies, sunken chests, many of them running with jinrikishas here
and there about the city, past beautiful buildings, richly ornamented
temples, the university, all bordered with palms: coconut, date,
palmyra, areca catechu, fruit and nut, as well as gum trees. In sum,
new tropic sights and peoples, which held their constant interest
until they finally left Bombay by train for Nagpur, a city lying to the
east of Bombay on the main line to Calcutta.

The reason for this was that they chose to follow the directions
offered them by Lord Severence, who had advised that they search
out one Guru Borodandaj, who was spoken of by him as the Dis-
solver of Matter and the Controller of Energy, and who resided near
the city of Nagpur, where travelers were accepted from time to time
at a simple frame building of ancient design overlooking a square
in the heart of the city.

No sooner were they settled than Berenice, eager to continue her quest of the Guru, started out with her letter of instructions from Lord Severence. As directed, she followed the main north and south highway which ran through Nagpur until it came to an old and somewhat dilapidated structure which looked like an abandoned mill. Then she took a sharp turn to the right and walked along a deserted cottonfield for about half a mile, which brought her to a grove of large blackwood and teakwood trees, so closely planted as to shut out the bright heat of the sun. She knew instinctively that this was the abode of the Guru, for Severence had described it accurately. Hesitating and looking about dubiously, she saw a rough and narrow path winding inward toward the center of the grove. This she followed to the point where it ended. There she saw a large square, semi-decayed wooden structure, which, as she learned later, had once been a government administration building controlling the forests of which this grove formed a part. There were several large openings in the walls which had never been repaired, and these, in turn, gave into other chambers, equally dilapidated. In fact, as she later learned, the abandoned building had been given to Guru Borodandaj for his classes in meditation and his demonstrations of power, through Yogi, to control all internal physical energy.

As she somewhat timidly approached, the silence and shade of the tall, overhanging trees somehow suggested a realm in which solitude and peace prevailed: to her a much needed peace, since the world she had left behind was entirely unacceptable and unsatisfactory to her. As she walked toward one of the inner buildings, a dark and elderly Hindu woman appeared before her and beckoned her toward an arched-over court, which led to a rear building, saying at the same time: "Come right through here. The Master awaits you."

Berenice followed the woman through a shattered segment of wall, past some broken bowls scattered about a few logs which were evidently used for benches. The Hindu woman then pushed open a large, heavy door, and Berenice, after removing her shoes, stepped across the threshold.

Her eyes fell on a dark, lean-faced, lengthy figure, seated, Yogi fashion, on a large white cloth in the center of the room. His hands were folded between his knees as though he might have been praying. However, he neither stirred nor said anything, merely turned on her his deep, almost black, penetrating and searching eyes. And then he spoke:

"Where have you been?" he asked. "It has been all of four months since your husband died, and I have been expecting you."

Startled by this inquiry and his attitude in general, Berenice involuntarily receded several paces as though she were truly fearful.

"Do not be frightened," said the Guru. "Fear has no place in Brahman, the Reality which you are seeking. Instead, daughter, come and be seated." And he waved a long thin arm toward the white cloth on which he was sitting, indicating the corner of it which she was to occupy. As she sat down, he began to speak.

"You have come a long way to find that which will give you peace. You seek your own Samadhi, or your union with God. Is that not true?"

"Oh, yes, Master," replied Berenice, in great wonder and awe. "That is true."

"And you feel that you have suffered greatly from the ills of the world," he continued. "And now you are ready for the change."

"Yes, yes, Master, yes. I am ready for the change. For now I feel that perhaps I have injured the world."

"And now you are ready to repair that injury, if possible?"

"Oh, yes; oh, yes!" she said, softly.

"But are you ready to devote some years to this labor, or is this a passing interest?"

"I am ready to devote years to the study of how I can repair the injuries I have caused. I want to know. I feel that I must learn." Her voice was anxious.

"Yet that, you know, requires patience, labor, self-discipline. You become great by obeying that which Brahma teaches."

"Oh, I will do anything that is necessary," said Berenice. "It is for that purpose I came. I know I must learn to concentrate and meditate in order to be wise enough to repay or even repair."

"Only he who meditates can realize truth," said the Guru, as he continued to study Berenice, until at last he added: "Yes, I will take you as a disciple. Your sincerity is your admission to my class. You can attend tomorrow the class in breath control. We will discuss high breathing, mid-breathing, Yogi complete breathing, nostril breathing. Holding the breath is like holding life in the body. It is the first step. And this is the foundation on which you will build your new world. Through it you will achieve non-attachment. You will lose the suffering that comes from desire."

"Master, for rest of the spirit I would give up many things," said Berenice.

The Guru paused for a few moments of silence, and then he began, almost solemnly:

"The man who gives up living in fine houses, wearing fine clothes, and eating good food, and goes into the desert, may be a most attached person. His only possession, his own body, may become everything to him, and as he lives, he may be simply struggling for the sake of his body. In truth, non-attachment does not mean anything that we may do in relation to our eternal body. It is all in the mind. A man may be on a throne and perfectly non-attached; another may be in rags and very much attached. But when man is endowed with spiritual discrimination and illumined by knowledge of the Atman, all his doubts are dispelled. He does not shrink from doing what is disagreeable to him, nor does he long to do what is agreeable. No human being can give up action altogether, but he who gives up the fruits of action is said to be non-attached."

"Oh, Master, if I could gain but a slight portion of this great knowledge!" said Berenice.

"All knowledge, my daughter," he continued, "is a gift of the spirit; and only to those who are grateful in the spirit will knowledge unfold like the petals of the lotus. From your Western teachers you will learn of art and the sciences, but from your Eastern masters, you will discover the inner mystery of wisdom. You are not educated when merely you are well-schooled. You are truly educated only when you are enlightened by inner truth. For inner truth takes dead facts and makes them live; it inspires the heart to the use of knowledge for the service of others. It is through the heart, not the intellect, that the Lord is seen. Do good for its own sake. Then alone will come perfect non-attachment."

"I will work hard to learn the breathing exercises, Master," said Berenice. "I know enough about Yoga to realize that it is the foundation of all illumination. I know that breath is life."

"Not necessarily," said the Guru. "If you wish to see, I will show you now that there is life where there is no breath."

He picked up a small mirror, which he handed to her, saying: "When I stop breathing, hold this mirror in front of my nose and mouth, to see if you can detect any moisture on it."

He closed his eyes, and then by degrees his body became more erect and statue-like in its steadiness. He seemed to have fallen into a deep stupor. Observing him, Berenice waited, holding her palm near to his nostrils. Minutes passed before she felt his breathing to be lighter on her hand. And then, to her surprise, it stopped. There was no least trace of rhythmic breathing. She waited. And then she took the mirror and held it in front of his nose and mouth for a few seconds. There was no trace of moisture on it. Rather, as she could now see, respiration had ceased, and he seemed like an image cut in stone. At that, she nervously consulted her watch. Ten long minutes passed before she saw a trace of respiration, and then it assumed perfect normalcy. For the Guru, seeming very tired, opened his eyes and looked at her and smiled.

"What a wonderful demonstration!" she exclaimed.

"I can hold my breath thus for hours," said the Guru. "And some Yogins keep the locked breath for months. There have even been cases where Yogins have been locked in airtight vaults for weeks, and yet have emerged in perfect health. Besides this," he continued, "the control of the heart beat is but a similar test. I can stop it completely, for the connection between blood and breath is very close, as you know, perhaps. But that I will show you another day. You will learn that breath is but the expression of a subtler force which hides in the vital organs, though it is unseeable. When it leaves the body, the breathing stops, in obedience, and death is the result. But through the control of breath it is possible to get some control over this unseen current.

"But this, I must tell you, is the study of Raja-yoga, which will come only after you have worked some time on the study of Hatha-yoga. So now, since you look a little tired, you may go, and come tomorrow, at which time you may begin your studies."

And with this Berenice knew that her interview with this most unusual man was at an end for the day. And yet, as she reluctantly left his presence, she felt that she was leaving a great reservoir of untouched knowledge. And as she retraced her steps along the crude road over which she had come, she felt she must walk a little faster, for she knew by now that the Indian night comes quickly on the heels of evening, and there are no lingering sunsets as in Europe or America; rather, a swift, dark approach that suggests lonely envelopment.

As she once more neared the village of Nagpur she was suddenly overcome by the beauty of the sacred Hill of Ramtek, with its gleaming white temples, a landmark which dominated the entire surrounding country. And here she stopped to meditate on the exquisite beauty of the scene, held spellbound by the distant sounds of steady chanting of the Hindu mantrams which slowly rose and floated through the thin air. She knew that these were the voices of the holy men of Ramtek, who gathered at the end of the day to intone the sacred syllables of their faith. At first their voices sounded like a low murmur, soft but sweet, but as she drew nearer, the tempo of the chanting became like the steady beating of a great drum. And then it was as though her heart changed its rate of beating to conform with the pulse of this great God-seeking, spirit-loving land, and she knew that this was the realm in which she would find her soul.

Chapter 78

IN THE course of the next four years, Berenice practiced many different phases of Yoga discipline, the first of which was the Yoga posture, which is used to keep the spine straight and make the body so firm, when one is sitting in meditation, that one does not feel it. For Dhyana—meditation—according to Yoga, is non-attachment. And when the spine is straight, the coiled-up Kundalini (triangular in form at the base of the spine) is aroused and rises through the Susumna, up the spine to the seven plexuses or centers of consciousness, finally ending with the Sahasrara, the highest or thousand-petal lotus of the brain. When this highest state of consciousness is reached, according to Yoga, one has achieved Samadhi, or superconsciousness. But whether or not one's power of Kundalini reaches this last point, one's perception is enlarged and elevated to the degree of its rise.

Berenice studied Pranayana—the control of the vital forces of the body; Pratyahara—or making the mind introspective; Dharana, or concentration; dhyana—meditation; and often compared notes with some of the other students who were attending classes with her: one Englishman and one young and highly intelligent Hindu, as well as two Hindu women. In the course of time she studied Hatha, Raja, Karma, Jnanai, and Bhakti Yoga. She learned that Brahman, the Reality, is the total Godhead. It can never be defined or expressed. The Upanishads say that Brahman is Existence, Knowledge, and

Bliss, but these are not attributes. Brahman cannot be said to exist. Brahman is Existence. Brahman is not wise or happy, but absolute Knowledge, absolute Joy.

"The Infinite cannot be divided into parts, and be contained in the Finite.

"This entire universe is pervaded by me, in that eternal form of mine which is not manifest to the senses. Although I am not within any creature, all creatures exist in me. I do not mean that they exist within me physically. That is my divine mystery. You must try to understand its nature. My Being sustains all creatures and brings them to birth, but has no physical contact with them.

"But if a man will worship me, and meditate upon me with an undistracted mind, devoting every moment to me, I shall supply all his needs, and protect his possessions from loss. Even those who worship other deities and sacrifice to them with faith in their hearts, are really worshiping me, though with a mistaken approach. For I am the only enjoyer and the only God of all sacrifices. Nevertheless, such men must return to life on earth, because they do not recognize me in my true nature.

"Those who sacrifice to the various deities will go to those deities. The ancestor worshipers will go to their ancestors. Those who worship elemental powers and spirits will go to them. So, also, my devotees will come to me."

As her Guru said one day: "The very air we breathe will tell us with each of its pulsations: 'Thou art That.' And the whole universe with its myriads of suns and moons, through everything that speaks, with one voice will cry: 'Thou art That!'"

Berenice was reminded of Emily Brontë's beautiful poem, which had long been one of her favorites:

LAST LINES

No coward soul is mine
No trembler in the world's storm-troubled sphere
I see Heaven's glories shine,
And Faith shines equal, arming me from fear.

Oh, God within my breast,
Almighty, ever-present Deity!
Life that in me hast rest,
As I, undying Life, have power in Thee.

Vain are the thousand creeds
That move men's hearts; unutterably vain,
Worthless as wither'd weeds
Or idlest froth amid the boundless main.

To waken doubt in me
Holding so fast by Thine infinity,
So surely anchor'd on
The steadfast rock of immortality.

With wide embracing love
Thy spirit animates eternal years,
Pervades and broods above,
Changes, sustains, dissolves, creates and rears.

Though earth and man are gone,
And suns and universes cease to be,
And Thou were left alone,
Every existence would exist in Thee.

There is not room for Death
Nor atom that His might could render void;
Thou—Thou art Being and Breath,
And what Thou art may never be destroyed.

At another time, the Guru asked:
"Where is there anyone that is not you? You are the soul of the
Universe. If a man come to your door, go and meet yourself. For all
are one. The idea of separateness is hallucination. You hate. You
love. You fear. All hallucinations; ignorance and delusion."

"Every thought and word that weakens is the only evil that exists."

"If the suns come down, the moons crumble in dust, systems after
systems are hurled into annihilation, what is that to you? Stand as a
rock; you are indestructible."

On Immortality: "The particle of energy which, a few months ago,
was in the sun, may be in the human being now.

"There is nothing new. The same series of manifestations are presenting themselves alternately, like a wheel coming up and down. All
motion in this universe is in the form of successively rising and falling. Systems after systems are coming out of the finer forms, evolving
themselves, taking the grosser forms, again melting down, as it were,

and going back again to the cause. So with all life. Each manifestation of life is coming up and then going back again. What goes down? The form. In one sense, even the body is immortal. In one sense, bodies and forms are eternal. How? Suppose we take a number of dice and throw them. Suppose the dice fall in this ratio: 5-6-3-4. We take the dice up and throw them again, and again. There must come a time when the same number will fall again, the same combinations will come.

"Now, the atoms comprising the universe are like dice being thrown out and combined, again and again. But there must come a time when exactly the same combination comes again, when you will be here, and this form will be here, this subject will be talked, and this pitcher, for instance, will be here. An infinite number of times this has been, and an infinite number of times will be repeated.

"We are never born and we never die. Each atom is a living thing, leading its own independent life. These atoms combine into groups for an end, and the groups manifest a group intelligence, so long as it remains a group, these groups again combining in turn and forming bodies of a more complex nature, which serve as vehicles for higher forms of consciousness. When death comes to the physical body, the cells separate and scatter and that which we call decay sets in. The force which held the cells together is withdrawn, and they become free to go their own way and to form new combinations. Death is but an aspect of life, and the destruction of one material form is but a prelude to the building up of another."

And on involution: "The seed is becoming the plant; a grain of sand never becomes a plant. It is the father that becomes the child. A lump of clay never becomes a child. Out of what does this involution come, is the question. What was the seed? It is the same as the tree. All the possibilities of a future tree are in that seed; all the possibilities of a future man are in the baby; all the possibilities of any life are in the germ. What is this? We find then that every evolution presupposes an involution. Nothing can be evolved which is not already involved. Here again, modern science comes to our help. You know by mathematical reasoning that the sum total of the energy that is displayed in the universe is the same throughout. You cannot take away one atom of matter or one foot-pound of force. As such, evolution did not come out of zero. Then, where does this come from? It came in involution before. The child is the man involved and the man is the child evolved; the seed is the tree involved, and the tree is the seed evolved. All the possibilities of life are in the germ. The question becomes a little clearer. Add to it the first idea of continuation of life. From the lowest protoplasm to the most perfect human being, there is only one life. The design is inheritent in the seed before the form is evolved."

One day Berenice asked: "What about charity?"

The Guru answered: "When you help the poor, feel not the slightest pride. Be thankful for the opportunity to give. To do so is your worship and no cause for pride. Is not the whole universe yourself? Be grateful that the poor man is there so that by making a gift to him you are able to help yourself. It is not the receiver that is blessed, but the giver."

Again she asked about beauty. So many people worshiped beauty in all its forms; in fact, they were slaves to beauty.

The Guru answered: "Even in the lowest kinds of attraction there is the germ of Divine Love. One of the names of the Lord in Sanskrit is Hari, and this means that He attracts all things to Himself. His is, in fact, the only attraction worthy of human hearts. Who can attract a soul, really? Only He. When you see a man being drawn to a beautiful face, do you think that it is a handful of arranged material molecules which really attracts the man? Not at all! Behind those material particles there must be and is the play of divine influence and divine love. The ignorant man does not know it, but yet, consciously or unconsciously, he is attracted by it, and it alone. So even the lowest forms of attraction derive their power from God Himself. 'None, O beloved, ever loved the husband for the husband's sake; it is the Atman, the Lord, who is inside, and for His sake the husband is loved.' The Lord is the great magnet, and we are all like iron filings; all of us are being constantly attracted by Him, and all of us are struggling to reach Him, the face of Brahman reflected through all forms and designs. We think we worship beauty, but we are really worshiping the face of Brahman shining through. The Reality behind the scenes."

Again: "The raja-yogin knows that the whole of nature is intended for the soul to acquire experience, and that the results of all the experiences of the soul are for it to become aware of its eternal separateness from nature. The human soul has to understand and realize that it has been spirit, and not matter, through eternity; and that this conjunction of it with matter is and can be only for a time. The raja-yogin learns the lessons of renunciation through the harshest of all renunciations, as he has to realize from the very first that the whole of this solid-looking nature is all an illusion. He has to understand that all that is any kind of manifestation of power in nature belongs to the soul, and not to nature. He has to know, from the very beginning, that all knowledge and all experiences are in the soul, and not in nature, so he has at once and by the sheer force of rational conviction to tear himself off from all bondage to nature.

"But of all renunciations, the most natural is that of the Bhakti-yogin. Here there is no violence, nothing to tear off, as it were, from ourselves, nothing from which we have to separate ourselves with violence. The bhakti's renunciation is easy, smooth, flowing, and as natural as things around us. A man loves his own city, then he begins to love his country, and the intense love for his little city drops off, smoothly, naturally. Again, a man learns to love the whole world; his love for his country; his intense, fanatical patriotism drops off, without hurting him, without any manifestation of violence. Uncultured man loves the pleasures of the senses intensely; as he becomes cultured, he begins to love intellectual pleasures, and his sense enjoyments become less and less.

"The renunciation necessary for the attainment of bhakti is not obtained by killing anything, but just comes as naturally as, in the presence of a stronger light, the less intense lights become dimmer and dimmer until they vanish completely. So this love of pleasures of the senses and of the intellect is all made dim, and thrown aside and cast into the shade by the love of God Himself. That love of God grows and assumes a form which is called Para-bhakti, or supreme devotion. Forms vanish, rituals fly away, books are superseded, images, temples, churches, religions and sects, countries and nationalities, all these little limitations and bondages fall off by their own nature from him who knows this love of God. Nothing remains to bind him or fetter his freedom. A ship, all of a sudden, comes near a magnetic rock and its iron bolts and bars are all attracted and drawn out, and the planks are loosened and float freely on the water. Divine grace thus loosens the binding bolts and bars of the soul, and it becomes free. So, in this renunciation auxiliary to devotion, there is no harshness, no struggle, no repression or suppression. The Bhakti has not to suppress any single one of his emotions; he only strives to intensify them and direct them to God.

"Set aside this apparent, illusive world, and by seeing God in everything one can find real happiness. Have what you will, but deify all. Possess nothing. Love God in all. Working thus you will find the way which corresponds to the Christian tenet: 'Seek ye first the Kingdom of God.'

"The Lord lives in the heart of every creature. He turns them round and round upon the wheel of his Maya. Take refuge utterly in Him. By His grace you will find supreme peace, and the state which is beyond all change.

"When at the end of a time-cycle, or Kalpa, the universe is dissolved, it passes into a phase of potentiality—a seed-state—and thus awaits its next creation. The phase of expression is called by Sri Krishna 'the day of Brahma' and the phase of potentiality 'the night of Brahma.' The creatures inhabiting the world, subject to these cycles, are perpetually being reborn and redissolved, with each succeeding cosmic day and night. This dissolution should not, however, be thought of as 'going back to God.' The creature merely returns to the power of Brahman which sent it forth, and remains there in an unmanifested state until the time comes for its re-manifestation.

"Hinduism accepts the belief in many divine incarnations, including Krishna, Buddha, and Jesus, and foresees that there will be many more."

> In every age I come back
> To deliver the holy,
> To destroy the sin of the sinner,
> To establish righteousness.

And then, one day, came the last words spoken to Berenice by the Guru. For, as he knew, her call had come, and she was about to leave him.

"Now I have taught you that wisdom which is the secret of secrets," he said. "Ponder it carefully. Then act as you think best. For according to Brahman, he who is free from delusion, and knows me as the supreme Reality, knows all that can be known. Therefore he adores me with his whole heart.

"This is the most sacred of all the truths I have taught you. He who has realized it becomes truly wise. The purpose of his life is fulfilled."

Chapter 79 THE following year was spent by Berenice and her mother traveling over a good part of India, because they were anxious to see and know more of that fascinating country. Although she had devoted four years of her life to the serious study of Hindu philosophy, she had seen enough of the way in which the natives lived to realize that this was a deluded and neglected people, and she wanted to know everything she could learn about them before her return home.

And so, by degrees, they extended their travels to Jaipur, Cawnpore, Peshawar, Lahore, Rawalpindi, Amritsar, Nepal, New Delhi, Calcutta, Madras, as well as to the southern border of Tibet. And the farther they traveled, the more shocked was Berenice by the low mental and social status of the millions of inhabitants of this startling and perplexing land. She was puzzled as to how a country could have evolved such a noble and profoundly religious philosophy of life and yet, at the same time, have evoked and maintained such a low, cruel, and oppressive social system, whereby a few managed to live a princely existence while millions struggled for even less than bread. The stark disillusion of such a sharp contrast was too much for Berenice to comprehend.

For she saw streets and roads lined with dirty, ragged or naked and seemingly despairing beggars, some of them begging for alms for the migratory holy men of whom they were disciples. In some regions the types of mental and physical destitution were without parallel. In one village almost the entire population was stricken with a plague, yet, possessing no source of aid or relief, was allowed to die. Again, in many hamlets, it was common to find as many as thirty persons occupying one small room, the consequences being disease and famine. And yet when windows or openings of any kind were cut in their rooms, they sealed them up.

The worst of the social ills, to Berenice, was the shocking practice of the child-wife custom. In fact, the result of this custom had already reduced the majority of the child wives of India to a physical and mental state that could scarcely be compared to health or sanity, and their ensuing deaths were more of a blessing than an injury.

The deplorable problem of the untouchables caused Berenice to inquire as to the origin of this idea. She was told that when the light-skinned ancestors of the present Hindus first came to India, they found there a darker, thicker-featured native race, the Dravidians, builders of the great temples of the south. And the priests of the new-comers desired that the blood of their people be not mixed with the native stock but be kept of one strain. They therefore declared the Dravidians to be unclean, "untouchable." So, in the beginning, race hatred was the origin of untouchability!

And yet, as Berenice was told, Gandhi had once said:

"Untouchability in India is on its way out, and in spite of all opposition, going fast. It has degraded Indian humanity. The 'untouchables' are treated as if less than beasts. Their very shadow defiles the name of God. I am as strong or stronger in denouncing untouchability as I am in denouncing British methods imposed on India. Untouchability, for me, is more insufferable than British rule. If Hinduism hugs untouchability, then Hinduism is dead and gone."

But Berenice had seen several of the young untouchable mothers with their puny infants, always in the far distance, looking wistfully and sadly at her as she stood talking with a Hindu instructor. And she could not help but observe how sensitive of face and form some of them were. In fact, one or two of them looked to her about as any ordinary but attractive and intelligent American girl might look if she were exposed to the filth, neglect, and isolation of her Indian sister. And yet, as she had heard, there had been five million untouchables freed from the curse through becoming Christians.

Added to this, Berenice was forced to witness the pitiable plight of so many of the children, little starvelings, groping about, weakened and emaciated beyond recovery by malnutrition, neglect, and disease. She was spiritually lacerated, and there sprang into her mind the assurance of the Gurus that God, Brahman, was All Existence, Bliss. If so, where was He? The thought stayed with her until it became all but unbearable, when suddenly there flamed the counterthought that this degradation must be met and overcome. And was not the All in All God speaking and directing her thus to assist, aid, change, until this earthly phase of Himself would be altered or transmuted into the exchange of evil for good? She wished so with all her heart.

The time eventually arrived when Berenice and her mother, shocked and tortured by the impact of these endless scenes of misery, felt that they must return to America where they would have more time and peace to meditate on all they had seen, and the means of aiding, if possible, in the elimination of such mass wretchedness.

And so their return home, one bright, warm October day, on the S.S. *Halliwell* direct from Lisbon, arriving in the lower harbor of New York and steaming up the Hudson to dock at Twenty-third Street. As they cruised slowly along, paralleling the familiar towering skyline of the city, Berenice became lost in thought of the enormous contrast which her years in India was now presenting to her. Here were clean streets, tall, expensive buildings, power, wealth, material comforts of all descriptions, well-fed and well-dressed people. She felt that she had changed, but what that change was comprised of she was not as yet aware. She had seen hunger in its ugliest form, and she could not forget it. Nor could she forget the haunting expressions of some of the faces she had looked into, especially the children's. What, if anything, could be done about it?

And yet, this was her country, her native land, which she loved more than any soil in the world. And for reason of this her heart throbbed a little faster at the most commonplace sights, such as, for instance, the endless advertising signs and their pretense to values which, even when blared in color or type twelve inches high, were still so often non-existent; the loud shrill cries of the newsboys; the raucous horns of the taxis, autos, and trucks; and the vanity and show of the average American traveler, with often so little to substantiate it.

After deciding to take residence at the Plaza Hotel, for a few weeks at least, she and her mother declared their baggage and later climbed into a taxi with a happy sense of being home at last. Berenice's first impulse, after they were settled in their hotel suite, was to call on Dr. James. She longed to talk to him about Cowperwood, herself, India, and everything pertaining to the past, as well as her own future. And when she saw him in his private office in his home on West Eightieth Street, she was overjoyed by his warm and cordial reception and his very great interest in all she had to tell about her travels and experiences.

At the same time, he felt that she was wanting to hear everything relating to Cowperwood's estate. And as much as he disliked reviewing the unsatisfactory handling of the entire affair, he felt it his duty to explain to her exactly what had happened during her absence.

Hence, first he told her of Aileen's death a few months before. This greatly shocked and surprised Berenice, for she had always thought of Aileen as the one to carry out Cowperwood's wishes in connection with his estate. Immediately she thought of the hospital, the founding of which she knew had been one of his sincerest desires.

"What about the hospital he intended to have built in the Bronx?" she earnestly inquired.

"Oh, that," replied Dr. James. "That never materialized. Too many legal vultures descended on the estate right after Frank's death. They came from everywhere, with their claims and counterclaims, foreclosure papers, and even legal disputes over the choice of executors. Four and a half million dollars' worth of bonds were declared worthless. Bills for interest on mortgages, legal expenses of all kinds, always mounting against the estate, until finally it dwindled to a tenth of what it had been originally."

"And the art gallery?" queried Berenice anxiously.

"All dissipated—auctioned off. The mansion itself sold for taxes and other claims against it. Aileen was compelled to move to an apartment. Then she got pneumonia and died. Unquestionably, grief over all of this trouble contributed to her death."

"Oh, how terrible!" exclaimed Berenice. "How sad it would make him feel if he knew! He worked so hard to build it up."

"Yes, he did," commented James, "but they never gave him credit for good intentions. Why, even after Aileen's death, there were articles in the newspapers describing Cowperwood as a social and almost a criminal failure, because, as they said, his millions 'had faded like a dream.' In fact, one article was headed 'What Availeth It?' and painted Frank as a complete failure. Yes, there were many unkind articles, and all based on the fact that after he was gone, his fortune, through the legal connivance of many people, had shrunk to almost nothing."

"Oh, Dr. James, isn't it dreadful to think that the fine things he contemplated doing should have come to nothing?"

"Yes, nothing is left but a tomb, and memories."

Berenice went on to tell him of her philosophical findings: the inward change she felt had come over her. The things that she once had felt were so important had lost their glamor, her anxiety over her own social position in connection with Cowperwood, for instance. More important to her now, she said, was the tragic situation of the

Indian people as a whole, some of which she recited to him: the poverty, starvation, malnutrition, illiteracy, and ignorance, much of which had grown out of religious and social delusions connected with superstitions; in sum, the absolute non-understanding of the world's social, technical, and scientific advance. James listened intently, remarking, in places, "Dreadful!" "Amazing!" until she had finished, after which he observed:

"Actually, Berenice, all that you say of India is true. But it is also true, I fear, that America and England are not without their social defects. In fact, right here in this country, there are certainly many social evils and miseries. If you would care to come with me some day on a little tour of New York, I could show you large districts filled with people just about as miserable as your Hindu beggars, and neglected children, whose chance for physical and mental survival is practically non-existent. They are born to poverty, and, in most cases, end in it, and their intermediate years are nothing that could be called living in the sense that we think of it. And then there are the poor sections in our manufacturing and mill towns, where the living conditions are as deplorable as those to be found in any part of the world."

At this point Berenice expressed the wish that he take her to see some of the sections of New York which would substantiate his statements, for she had seen or heard little of such conditions throughout her life. Dr. James was not surprised to hear her say that, for he knew that her social path from her youth onward had been a sheltered one.

After visiting with him a little longer, Berenice left for her hotel. But on her way home she could not drive from her mind the account by James of the dissipation of Cowperwood's wealth. She was filled with sorrow as she inwardly reviewed the wreckage of all of his plans. How completely they had failed! At the same time, she was thinking of his love for her, his mental and emotional dependency on her, and her affection for him. It was through her influence, as she recalled, that he had decided to go to London and work on his plan for the underground system. And now, here she was, planning on the morrow to visit his tomb again, the last material vestige of all the values that had seemed so vividly real and wonderful to her at the time, but which now, in comparison with all she had experienced in India, were no longer important to her.

The following day was almost a duplicate of the day on which

Cowperwood had been buried. For the sky was again gray and overcast, and, as she approached the tomb, it was as though a lone finger of stone pointed upward to the leaden noonday sky. As she walked down the pebbled path, her arms filled with flowers, she noted the name: AILEEN BUTLER COWPERWOOD, under the name, FRANK ALGERNON COWPERWOOD, and she was grateful that Aileen was now at last alongside of the man for whom she had suffered so intensely and lost. She, Berenice, had seemingly won, but only for a time, for she also had suffered and lost in the end.

As she stood gazing thoughtfully at Cowperwood's last resting place, she felt she could hear again the sonorous tones of the minister as he had spoken at the burial service:

"As soon as Thou scatterest them, they are even as asleep and fade suddenly like the grass. In the morning, it is green, and groweth up; but in the evening it is cut down, dried up and withered."

But now she could not think of death as she had thought of it before going to India. There death was considered but a phase of life, and the destruction of one material form but a prelude to the building up of another. "We are never born and we never die," they said.

And as she walked about arranging the flowers in a bronze urn on the steps of the tomb, she thought that Cowperwood must know, if he had not when he was here in the flesh, that his worship and constant search for beauty in every form, and especially in the form of a woman, was nothing more than a search for the Divine design behind all forms—the face of Brahman shining through. She wished that he might have shared these thoughts with her when they were together, and recalled the words:

> Absorbed in Brahman
> He overcomes the world,
> Even here, alive in the world,
> Brahman is one,
> Changeless, untouched by evil;
> What home have we but Him?

And what was it that the Guru had said of charity? "Be thankful for the opportunity to give to others. Be grateful that by helping a poor man, you are able to help yourself. For, is not the universe yourself? If a man come to your door, go and meet yourself."

But, as she now searched her conscience, what place had charity ever had in her life? What had she ever done to help others? What had she ever done to justify her right to live? True, Cowperwood had not only conceived the idea of founding a hospital for the poor, but he had done everything humanly possible to bring it into existence, even though his plans had failed. But she—had she ever had a desire to help the poor? Not that she could recall. Her entire life, as she realized—with the exception of the past few years—had been spent in the pursuit of pleasure and self-advancement. But now she knew that one must live for something outside of one's self, something that would tend to answer the needs of the many as opposed to the vanities and comforts of the few, of which she herself was one. What could she do to help?

And suddenly at that point in her meditations, the thought of Cowperwood's hospital crossed her mind. Why couldn't she, herself, found a hospital? After all, he had left her a large fortune, a fine home filled with valuable art objects on which she could easily realize a considerable sum of money, which, added to what she already had, might enable her at least to start the project. And perhaps she could induce others to help. Dr. James would surely be one of these.

What a wonderful thought this was!

APPENDIX

The preceding chapter consists of the last lines ever written by Theodore Dreiser on the day before his death, December 28, 1945. He left notes, however, for an additional chapter and a summary of the three books of the trilogy: *The Financier, The Titan* and *The Stoic*. The summary would have been written in the form of a soliloquy which, Mrs. Dreiser points out, would have left no doubt in the mind of the reader as to his conception of life, strength and weakness, wealth and poverty, good and evil.

The following was prepared by Mrs. Theodore Dreiser from the notes of her husband.

As Berenice rode home from Green Wood in her carriage, she contemplated the possibilities of promoting a hospital, realistically facing the complicated practical, as well as technical and medical aspects, which would necessitate the enlistment of people of wealth and a charitable turn of mind and those of the proper technical skill and knowledge that it would take to correctly organize and promote such a large undertaking. She planned to sell her house on Park Avenue with all of its contents, which would bring at least four hundred thousand dollars. She would add to this half of her present fortune, which, altogether, would be a small beginning. Of course, as she thought, Dr. James would be the right man as head physician and director, but could she interest him? Her mind was filled with thoughts and anticipations of the possibilities in connection with the hospital until she again saw Dr. James, who had invited her to accompany him on a tour of one of the worst of New York's East Side tenements.

To Berenice, who, never in her youth, had visited any of the poverty-stricken, beggarly, or neglected sections of New York, this first visit to the East Side streets was a painful revelation. Sheltered as she had always been, by her mother, until the fateful night she was so bitterly embarrassed in a dining room of one of New York's principal hotels, when she publicly learned the truth about her mother,

Hattie Starr of Louisville, and when for the first time the import and horror of social ostracism had flashed upon her!

But Berenice had survived all this. Her values, as she was to learn later, had changed immeasurably. Her social ambitions of the past seemed a thin crust to her now. In India a desire had been born in her to dip deeper into life—to observe and study at closer hand life forces, which, as she now realized, she had never touched on before. Instead of looking for a socially secure position for herself personally, she was now becoming aware of wanting to find a socially worthwhile vocation.

And so when she and Dr. James visited a tenement with which he was familiar, Berenice was so affected by the appalling conditions, the stench and squalor of the place, that she became ill. For, as she saw, there were no beds. Instead, pallets were put down on the floor at night and piled up in a corner in the daytime. In a room twelve by fifteen, adjoining a smaller room nine by twelve, six adults and seven children existed. No windows. But large openings in the walls that revealed from odors and unmistakable markings the presence of rats.

When they finally reached the street and fresh air again, Berenice told Dr. James that her one ambition was to found the Cowperwood Hospital herself in an endeavor to help some of these wretched and neglected children whom they had just seen. She would gladly give, so she said, half of all her possessions to the project.

Dr. James, intensely moved by this turn of mind in Berenice, realized that a change had taken place in her since leaving America a few years before. And Berenice, sensing his approving reaction to her wish, asked him if he would help her raise the money for it, and whether he would personally take over the medical and technical direction of the hospital. And Dr. James, realizing for a long time the pressing need of a hospital in the Bronx vicinity, as well as it being one of his deepest desires, heartily agreed to the idea, and said he would be honored to become the director and head physician.

Six years later the hospital became a reality; Dr. James, director in charge. Berenice had taken a nurse's course, and, to her own astonishment, had discovered that she possessed a deep maternal instinct, hitherto unexplored. She loved the children and was placed in charge of the children's ward. As Dr. James noticed, from time to time she had a strange and powerful attraction for these neglected waifs. They responded to her in a marked way.

Two small blind children had, in some way, gotten into the ward.

They had been blind from birth. One, a small frail blond child named Patricia—five years old—a daughter of a hard-working girl who had had no time for her child, had been allowed to sit for hours and hours in a little rocking chair in a corner, with no least stimuli or interest—a procedure of neglect which had retarded her natural development. The mother also had a guilt complex in relation to her handicapped child. When Berenice found this little isolated mite of humanity, she became fascinated by her and desired to help her, teaching her many little things, among them being how to slide with confidence down a chute in the Children's Court. So much joy had Patricia experienced from this simple stunt that she slid over and over and over again for hours, each time radiating with happiness at her newly found independence.

Then there was David—also about five, blind from birth. He was more fortunate in his parentage, having had an intelligent mother, with love and understanding. As a result, he was more advanced than Patricia in his development. He had been taught by Berenice to climb a tree and sit among the upper branches, where he sang repeatedly "In the Gloaming," waving his head from side to side and lifting his thin, sensitive face to the sun, as blind children are wont to do. One day, as Dr. James passed a large window overlooking the Children's Court, he paused to watch Berenice moving back and forth among the children. He noticed how radiantly happy she was when at work with them. He remarked about it to Miss Slater, the head nurse, as she passed. They both agreed that Berenice had far surpassed anything expected of her and was worthy of unstinted praise. The same evening, as Berenice was leaving the hospital for her home, Miss Slater and Dr. James told her what a success she had made of her work with the children, and how much everyone loved and appreciated her. Berenice graciously thanked them, expressing gratitude at being able to contribute something of worth to these unfortunate children.

However, as she walked home to her modest apartment, she could not help but think what a minute part she was playing in the world panorama of life. A speck of human kindness in the sea of need and despair! She recalled the poor starving children of India—their tortured faces! The cruelty, neglect and torturesome indifference of the rest of the world to their pathetic plight.

"What is the world anyway?" she asked herself. "Why should millions of little things come into it only to be tortured and so denied—to be allowed to die from want, cold, starvation?" Yes, to be sure, she thought, she was now at last trying to do what she could to relieve the sufferings of a few children, who were fortunate enough to be taken into her hospital. But what about all of those thousands who could not be taken in? What of them? A drop in the ocean was her contribution. One drop!

Berenice relived in her mind her entire life. She thought of Cowperwood and the part she had played in his life. How long he had struggled and fought—for what? Wealth, power, luxury, influence, social position? Where were they now, the aspirations and dreams of achievement that so haunted and drove Frank Cowperwood? And how far away from all this she had moved in so short a time! How suddenly she was awakened to the grim realities of life from her own protected, abundant and indulged way of living—a way of living she might never have been able to evaluate to herself if she had not in the first place acted upon the impulse to go to a strange country like India, where she had at every turn contrasts thrust upon her sensibilities—contrasts from which there was no escape.

There, for the first time, she had experienced the dawn of a spiritual awakening, which was even now enabling her to see more clearly. She must go on, she must grow, she thought, and acquire, if possible, a real and deep understanding of the meaning of life and its spiritual import.